OPEN AT ROCK BOTTOM

L.M.REED

MALARE
BOOKS

Trigger Warnings: Includes depictions and/or discussion of rape, self harm, panic attacks, drug and alcohol use.

Dedicated to Michelle and Kathy, whose feedback and encouragement over the years made all the difference.

Junior Year: Thursday, March 21
Escape Hatch

I stare at the wall where some previous occupant of Isolation Cell 4B scratched WELCOME TO HELL into the concrete. Not sure how he managed it. They wouldn't even let me keep the Rubik's cube Charlie sent with Dad last week. "Could be used as a weapon," the inspector concluded. Even meals come through the slot on a styrofoam tray with a flimsy plastic spork, and they always check to make sure the spork gets returned with the tray. I know because I tried to keep it once, just to see. Anything to add variety to the disorienting sameness of day after day in this dank, silent, windowless box.

You deserve this. You deserve to be here. You raped Kendra Daniels. I remind myself whenever self-pity threatens to break me. Then the guilt overwhelms me until I'm shaking and sobbing and feeling sorry for myself again. For myself and Kendra and my dad and sister and brother and everyone else whose life is fucked up now because of what I did. At least Mom escaped my mess, the only upside of dying young. Then I think, as I have countless times since last fall: *At least the cancer took her before she had to be ashamed of me.* And the nagging follow up worry: *If heaven is real and she can see you from up there, then she can* still *be ashamed. You'll just never know.* And the tears just keep coming until eventually exhaustion sets in and I manage to sleep.

"Iso Cells" are bare except for a bed, a toilet, and a tap built into the wall over a drain in the floor. They're supposed to be for short term containment only, used as punishment for rule breaking or, in my case, protection if somebody has a target on their back. It took all of twenty-eight minutes for a teenager built like a pro wrestler with several missing teeth to use my body as a punching bag. The Duke (as he introduced himself) said he was sending a message to my dad--the District Attorney who'd got The Duke's uncle sent away for twenty years on drug trafficking charges. Being a six-foot-two football player, I might have held my own for the half minute it took for the guard to break it up. But The Duke wasn't alone. Five-on-one meant I was lucky to escape with only bruised ribs, a black eye, and a ruptured eardrum.

Dad was livid. He'd warned them I could be a target for retribution, that I should have been in a protected population from the start. The warden countered that they'd checked everyone in my detention cohort to make sure none had immediate family members who Dad had personally prosecuted. No, they had not checked into extended family. It was near impossible to do so with any degree of certainty as that information wasn't in inmates' electronic records. Yes, they would try, but that would take time and manpower, both of which were in short supply. For now it was best if I was kept in isolation for my own protection.

So for two weeks, I've been safe and sound in this little HELL box. The only time I'm out of Cell 4B is the hour of "yard time" each day where I can run laps in a small, sectioned off area while guys in the main yard line up along the dividing fence and taunt that my daddy can't keep me safe forever and how they have plans for dealing with a pampered rich-boy rapist like me. I have my own crime *and* my father's to answer for. Each day they add some new gruesome or humiliating element to their plan. Each day they remind me I'm one day closer to thirty--the State max for keeping a prisoner in isolation. My safety has an expiration date.

But as miserable as these yard time torment sessions are, they're almost preferable to the other twenty-three hours spent in silence, ruminating on what I did to end up here and what's going to happen to me next. Distraction is the name of the game. The library cart comes every three days, and I get to pick one book from the selection of beat-up paperbacks people donated. Two days ago, I picked Stephen King's *The Shining* because it was thick enough to last me awhile, and I thought reading about someone else's horror story life might be comforting.

It wasn't. In fact, it gave me a nightmare where I was trapped in the creepy hotel from the book, haunted by a seven-year-old version of Kendra with her long braids and ruffles and pursued by a manic, ax-wielding version of The Duke. Waking up drenched in cold sweat, I told myself, *Breathe like Dr. Eduway taught you. Take back control of your body.* But I was too far gone to pull myself back from the brink. After vomiting the dregs of dinner into my metal toilet, I shoved the book back through the slot to get it as far from me as possible.

So today I have nothing to read and nothing to do but simmer in the lingering scent of last night's puke and speculate about the etched words that so aptly describe life in isolation. The letters are only scratched about a quarter inch deep. *Fingernails, maybe?* I consider my own--longer than I usually keep them but not jagged enough to cut concrete. *Nah...maybe--*

A *BANG* on my cell door interrupts my speculation.

"Hey, White, you got visitors!" the guard calls.

I jump to my feet. "Visitors *plural*?" Dad's been my only visitor so far. We'd agreed that it's best that sensitive, six-year-old Charlie not see me in here--phone calls only. And Ellen...well, my sister hasn't spoken to me since the night after

Kendra's testimony when I confessed my newly realized guilt to her. She...didn't take it so well. But that was weeks ago, so maybe... "Who are they?" *Please be Ellen, please be Ellen, please be Ellen.*

"Your dad and your lawyer."

"Oh..." Now that *is* a surprise. For Bronston Aster to come all the way from New York City in the middle of the week, something big must be up. My stomach constricts with an unexpected surge of hope. Could they be transferring me to a facility in a different part of the state? Somewhere well outside Dad's jurisdiction? Then again, with the complex network of loyalties, debts, and vendettas between prisoners, could any facility really be safe? Not to mention, any move would take me even further from my family.

I put out my hands to get cuffed and follow the guard, keeping my head down and expectations low.

Dad and Bronston stand when I come into the private visitation room, both of them beaming. I halt in confusion. "What's going on?"

"It's your lucky day, kid." Bronston slides a manila folder across the table and nods at it. "Your ticket out of here."

"What?" I lower myself into the chair and open the folder. It's printed screenshots of text messages between Kendra Daniels and Frankie Gurlance who'd been a star witness for the prosecution. Flipping through, I note the part that Bronston has highlighted and added sender names.

Kendra--I told you it wasn't
like that. It was my fault.
I started it, not him.

> **Frankie**--You told him
> to stop so

that makes it rape

Kendra--No I didn't. It wasn't like you think. Please, I don't want to talkabout this anymore.

Frankie--EJ White is a terrible person
He raped you
You can't let him get away with it

Kendra--He didn't force me. It's wasn't his fault.

Frankie--They why did I find you all huddled up and crying?

Kendra--It just wasn't what I expected and I realized it was a mistake.

Frankie--It wasn't a mistake it was rape and you need to
report it

Kendra--There's nothing to report. Please don't tell anyone. Especially my parents. I'm begging you!! Please please please
Let it go.

When I look up, Dad's expression is all righteous vindication. Bronston just looks smug. He taps the paper with two fingers as he explains, "These are from the same night as the supposed rape. And they directly contradict what she said in court. She outright says it wasn't rape."

I look from Bronston to Dad and back down at the screenshots. What I see is a girl in denial. One who's still processing what happened to her. Who's scared shitless that someone is about to take her private pain to the police, or worse, to her insanely strict parents. I see the girl who's had a crush on me since we were kids still trying to protect me, even after what I did to her. It's no use saying any of that to them though, not when they still label my mid-trial realization as "trauma-induced, misplaced guilt."

Instead, I swallow hard and ask my lawyer, "Where did you get these?"

"Sent to me by an anonymous source. I forwarded the images on to the police who confiscated Kendra and Frankie's phones and verified the messages. Bada bing, bada boom!" Bronston smooths his tie and smiles like he half expected something like this to happen. Divine justice. Or injustice, in this case.

"Well, I don't see how this matters now," I tell them, closing the folder and sliding it back to Bronston. "The trial's over. Jury already said I'm guilty."

"EJ, don't you realize what this new evidence means?" Dad asks, as he leans in, palms down on the table. "It's proof that Kendra and Frankie perjured themselves at trial. If we can get the judge to throw their testimony out--"

"That over-the-top sob story she gave on the stand that convinced the jury--" Bronston throws in.

"--then we can get your conviction overturned," Dad finished, his hazel eyes bright.

"Overturned?" I repeat like a stunned idiot. They're right. The whole case had come down to that testimony. No one on the jury could discount Kendra's raw and obvious pain as she forced the words out, almost like she was reliving it. The confused anguish on her face when she turned to look at me from the stand. Like she still couldn't reconcile the inconsolable me she'd held after his mother's funeral with the one who'd left her to sob alone in the back seat of someone else's car.

And it wasn't just the jury she had convinced. Being face to face again, hearing that night from her perspective, finally got through the tangled mess of self-justifications I'd constructed. Her choked words drowned out Dad's confidence that his son would never knowingly have forced himself on a girl and Bronston's assurances that no one would have called what happened between me and Kendra rape before "all this MeToo bullshit." It forced me to confront the damage I'd done. The trust I'd broken. The human being I'd so callously used and discarded. By the time the jury foreman had read the guilty verdict, it was almost a relief.

Almost.

"This is good news, kid--*the best*." Bronston insists as if my lack of excitement is due to a lack of comprehension. "We'll have you outta here by Easter. And in another year or so you'll be off at college, and it'll be like none of this ever happened."

I blinked at him. *Just forget, pretend like it never happened... Is that what his other clients did when he got them off?* When I try to imagine what that would be like, the mere attempt makes my stomach convulse.

"EJ..." I look at Dad and notice the dark circles under his eyes, the way the skin sags around his jawline, the

7

smattering white hairs in his patchy blonde stubble. *He's not doing okay,* I realize. *He's lost weight. And I bet he hasn't been sleeping.*

Because of me. Because he believes he failed me.

Even though it's the other way around.

"EJ, I know the trial was a terrible experience, that it confused you, made you think you should be in here. But these texts--they prove that isn't true. And now, you'll get to come home." His voice is choked with emotion. He turns his hands over, wanting me to understand, to embrace this gift, this miracle that's been dropped in our laps. "Home and out of danger," he adds, focusing in on the fading purple and yellow ring around my eye.

I look down at my gray inmate jumpsuit. At the light tan institutional walls. Dad doesn't want to believe it, but I know the truth.

You do *deserve to be here. You* did *rape Kendra Daniels. You* belong *in Cell 4B.*

Except I won't be in 4B much longer. In two more weeks, I go back into a cohort with fifty other guys.

In two weeks, I could be bleeding out in some security camera blind spot. I could be fucking dead. I close my eyes and rest my elbows on the table, chains clinking as I drop my face into my hands.

No--the Duke and his crew are just trying to scare you. They won't follow through. The guards will protect you this time.

As I take a deep breath, my still-tender ribs ache as if to ask, *You so sure about that?* A lot of damage could be done in half a minute, especially if someone has something sharp...like whatever gouged those letters in my cell wall. And would every fresh attack mean another thirty days all on my own in Cell 4B, slowly going crazy? Alone or at risk, in and out...for the next eighteen months? It was one thing to reconcile myself to lockup when I had no choice, but now... All I have to do is keep my guilty mouth shut and I'm home free. Literally.

How much do I have to endure before I've paid my debt to Kendra or God or Karma or whatever else? What makes eighteen months so morally important? Considering what a fucking nightmare my Juvie stay has been so far, my one month time served could equal the full sentence for someone who didn't have a target on their back.

Dad must sense my weakening defenses. "Home, son, with your familywho misses you...who *needs* you. Please, it's what your mother would have wanted...all of us together."

Yes, Mom would want me to be there for Charlie and Ellen and Dad.

She'd also want me not to rape Kendra.

It's too late for the one...but not for the other.

"Home," Dad repeats, like it's a magic word. Maybe it is, the way it sets off something in my brain, a wave of childish relief like you get when you're little and lost in a store and finally hear a familiar voice call your name. The sound of rescue.

I lift my head and lower my hands to rest them in my father's. He squeezes, and I squeeze back as a sob rises in my throat.

"Don't worry, kid, we'll have you out of here in no time," Bronston promises.

I nod and let my chin drop so they won't see the tears that come.

9

Junior Year: Wednesday, March 27
Not-So-Very Home Free

The only personal belongings I have to collect are the clothes I wore to the sentencing—a charcoal suit and the steel blue silk tie Dad had selected for the occasion. The guy at the desk behind a thick plastic window hands them out to me in a clear bag labeled—New York State, Monroe County Correctional Facility: Youthful Offender ID# 66438—Eric James White.

I hold up the bag and paste on a smile. "Thanks for the hospitality."

No reaction.

"Heard that one before, huh?"

"You can leave as soon as you change back into your civies. Exit's off the changing room."

"Perfect. And uh, what d'you want me to do with the jumpsuit?"

"Leave it in the changing room." He draws out the words to imply my idiocy and sneers, "What, you wanna keep it as a souvenir?"

"No. No I do not." I keep smiling. I worry that if I stop pretending to be anything but delighted about my release, guilt will bubble to the surface like a RAPIST tattoo across my forehead. Or worse, standing here on the cusp of freedom, my self-protective instinct might fritz and let me blubber out a confession. Either way, they'll know they've made a terrible mistake and throw me back in lockup.

Home, I remind myself. *Keep it together just a little longer and you'll be safe at home with your family.*

...Instead of back in lockup where you belong, my conscience prods.

Shut up, I tell it. Because, what else can I do at this point?

Dad is waiting for me in "The Reunion Room," a small lobby with a few molded plastic chairs and a magazine rack. He pulls me in for a hug, his chest heaving against mine. James Charles White III Esq. is not usually a hugger, but hey, it's not every day a guy gets to take his son home from Juvie. When Dad lets me go, he clears his throat and warns me, "Heads up-- there are some protesters outside."

Like all youthful offender cases, my trial and the hearing that cleared me had taken place in closed proceedings, the documents sealed and the press restricted from reporting names or using pictures. So no one should know about me or Kendra or any of it--technically. But there was no way a story about the D.A.'s son getting arrested, tried, and convicted of rape wasn't going to explode all over social media. And when he gets off shortly after, based on mysterious new evidence, now permanently sealed in a juvenile case file...yeah, people are gonna be skeptical. Not to mention pissed.

"How many is 'some'?" I ask, trying and failing to sound unconcerned.

"Around...fifty or so."

Fuck. I swallow, squeeze my eyes shut, and pray I'm not dizzy when I open them. "People sure found out quick."

"That Survivors for Justice group put the word out online." His frown lines deepen as he adds, "There're also some people from those anti-gender discrimination groups, come to, uh...show their support."

11

Which is his politic way of saying the radical far-right fringe has shown up to make it a confrontation custom fit for social media, with me at the symbolic center. I'm either a martyr or a monster to these people. *Why can't everyone just leave me alone?*

I sway and Dad reaches out to steady me. "EJ, do you feel okay? Have you been taking your, um…"

"My Lexapro?" *God, he can't even say it, the name of his son's head meds.* I open my eyes and am relieved when the world doesn't swim. "They gave it to me every day."

"And you *took* it every day?"

"*Yes,*" I hiss through my teeth. "I'm fine. Let's go." I walk out the security door into the sunshine and pause to let it warm my skin.

Now I can go outside anytime I want.

The moment of relief doesn't last. Calls from outside the fence come in a sharp cacophony.

"Rapist pig!"   "Stay strong, EJ!"
        "Justice for Kendra!"
                "Justice for our boys!"
"Corruption!   "We believe women!"
"--rich entitled prick!"   "Lying bitches ruin lives!"

The fence may keep the energized mix of reporters, protesters, and supporters from swarming us, but it can't keep them from livestreaming my exit. I make sure to keep my expression as neutral as possible, just like they'd trained me for the trial. *Give them nothing. Don't look guilty. Don't look smug.*

We get to Dad's silver BMW X6 without incident, and I grab shotgun out of habit but then wish I'd chosen the back where I could have laid down out of sight. Cold sweat coats my fingertips where they touch my forehead. *Relax, breathe, you're safe. You're going home.*

Dad lets out his own held breath and loosens his tie with one hand. "We made it, son. This whole nightmare is all finally over."

Over? Had we just experienced the same thing? I have a bizarre pang of longing for the relative quiet and safety of my dank isolation cell. *Where I still deserve to be...*

I bark a strained, shaky laugh. "Right, sure, *done.* And all is right with the world. Oh my God, is that a rainbow?"

My snarky humor doesn't elicit a laugh from Dad. It rarely does, especially not since the police showed up at our door back in December. I'd gone from being the personable, athletic, handsome, honor student who stood smiling and waving next to him at the end of every election ad to being a liability. A career ending liability.

But instead of rising to the bait, he reaches over and puts a hand on my knee, following Dr. Eduway's suggestion in one of our joint father-son sessions to "strengthen the parent-child bond through positive physical contact." That kind of touchy-feely stuff had been a natural part of Mom's parenting style but foreign to Dad with his nannies-to-boarding-school upbringing. It's encouraging that he didn't flush all Dr. Eduway's advice after my erstwhile therapist declined to play along with Bronston's plan to portray me as an addled trauma victim who couldn't be held responsible for their actions.

Giving my knee an awkward half-pat-half-squeeze, Dad advises, "Be patient. It will take time to put this behind you for good. But today, if nothing else, your legal record is clear. You're out of that deathtrap and off the Sex Offenders Registry. Soon enough, you'll have your *life* back."

I lean my head against the window and regard him with narrowed eyes. "You really think getting out of Juvie without serving my full sentence gets me my life back?"

"Your conviction was overturned," he says slowly, like I'm a student failing to grasp basic facts. "You'll finish high school, play sports again, go to Cornell, everything like you planned."

"Just because the court cleared me doesn't mean the general public agrees. Or do you think those protesters were just out there for the exercise?"

His lip curls as familiar irritation slips into his voice. "And you think putting yourself through another seventeen months in there would have satisfied them? Those...*people*," he inflects in place of whatever insult he's thinking, "wouldn't be satisfied if you served seventeen years. They may talk about justice, but they don't understand what it means."

"Uh-huh, and these are the same people you think will forget about me as soon as the mayor's son drives drunk and kills a car full of people or something?"

He draws a hand over his thin lips and square jaw before checking the blind spot to change lanes with a fast jerk of the steering wheel. Therapy Dad is definitely MIA. "Fine, you know what? Fine--go ahead and get this cynical, self-pitying bullshit out of your system. But whatever you do, don't show that attitude in public. My political rivals are already implying to the press that some kind of corruption was involved. That I used my position, money, or family connections to make this happen."

Not for the first time, I wonder the same thing. "So...did you?" Could Dad have hired someone or called in a favor from his police contacts to illegally access and search Kendra and

Frankie's phones...or even plant the texts there? Was planting fake texts even possible? It certainly was one explanation for Bronston somehow getting alerted about texts that happened to say exactly what we needed them to in order to get key testimony thrown out.

Dad looks appalled and offended at the very suggestion. "What? Of course not! I would *never* subvert the system."

"Alright, fine, sorry...It's just, don't you think it's a little, I don't know...*convenient*, those texts--"

"We had faith in the justice system, and in the end, justice was done."

Except it wasn't. I look out at the downtown Rochester skyline reflected in my side mirror as we cross the bridge, heading for the suburbs. What had Kendra thought, when she heard I was getting my slate rubbed clean? She hadn't shown up to hear the judge deliver his decision in person... Maybe she'd already guessed which way it would go. Does she think it was all for nothing, everything she had to go through after reporting me? The die-hard sign-wielders aside, how many people who supported her at first will doubt her story now? Kendra's face comes uninvited to my mind--eyes squeezed shut, tears leaking from the corners, lips pressed tight together, chin quivering as I move above her...

The air catches in my throat. I turn the choked gasp into a cough and press my forehead against the cool window, replacing her face with the joyful one my little brother will wear when I walk back in the door.

Dad keeps checking me out of the corner of his eye every few seconds, waiting for...I'm not sure what. After a couple of awkward minutes, I fill the space by turning on the radio to 98PXY and upping the volume until the hip-hop beat

15

makes the speaker vibrate against my leg. But the song isn't even half over before Dad decides he's heard enough and pushes the preset for NPR. I let it go. It isn't worth a fight over the stupid radio. We spend the next fifteen minutes silently listening to reports on such vital topics as "Fresh, Feisty Arugula: More Than a Salad Green" and "Affect or Effect? 'Grammar Girl' is Here to Help."

When Dad passes the turn for our street, I jerk around to face him. "Where are we going?" I cringe internally at the note of childish panic in my voice.

Dad must hear it too because he raises both eyebrows and explains, "We're getting an early dinner at D'Amico's. I thought it'd be nice to celebrate all together. You can get Chicken French--your favorite."

Acid rises in my throat at the idea of family dinner in public, something we haven't done since my arrest. "What if people there give us shit?"

"At D'Amico's?" Dad gives me a sidelong glance meant to communicate how absurd the idea is. "People know us there. We've been going there since you were in diapers, and I'm sure they'll be glad to see us all again."

"Maybe…" Worry snakes through my abdomen. "I'd rather just eat at home though. We can get takeout."

"Well, I already texted Charlie's babysitter to bring him and Ellen there."

So...case closed. *Perfect. Just* perfect. The muscle in my jaw twitches with the effort to keep my mouth shut. I cross my arms and go back to looking out the window.

***

Dad and I are sitting in the back-corner booth, surrounded by framed newspaper articles dating from the late

16

1950s and photos of various low-level celebrities standing with the OG Mr. D'Amico. There used to be one of his grandson (the current Mr. D'Amico) and Dad taken after Dad won his first election for District Attorney six years ago. The whole family had come in to celebrate. I see it's been replaced by one with a local radio DJ stuffing his face with lasagna. If Dad noticed the change when we came in, he hadn't said anything, and I certainly wasn't going to point it out.

It's barely after 5:00 p.m., so the place is half empty. Still, just in case, I hold my menu as a barrier between me and the other diners and pretend to read the list of specials. Dad checks email on his phone and doesn't look up when the waiter brings us waters, setting them down hard enough for the contents to slosh onto the table cloth. "Thank you," I say from behind my laminated shield, but the waiter has already left.

I've had time to leaf through the menu twice before the latest pinch-hit babysitter rushes over to us with my brother in tow, his Avengers backpack bouncing up and down as she pulls him along. "Hi! Sorry, we're late. Charlie couldn't find his left shoe and then...Anyway, sorry."

"Hey there, Charlie!" I grin at him, a genuine grin, and my cheeks ache from disuse.

Charlie smiles back--a brief, unsure smile. He keeps holding the babysitter's hand and drops his gaze to the floor. My own grin falters. *Gone three weeks and I'm already a stranger?* He'd seemed okay when we'd talked on the phone...

Dad is perturbed for a different reason. "Where's Ellen? I told her to be home by 4:00."

"Oh, she was, but then she went to Kelly's house."

"What? Why did you let her do that?" Dad asks in his quiet-scolding-in-public voice.

The sitter hesitates, awkward and unsure what's wrong. "Um...she showed me a text from you that said it was okay...?"

Ah, the old change-your-friend's-name-in-your-contacts trick. I'd taught her that. Back when we were tight, two teens united in parental deception. *So Ellen still doesn't want to see or be seen with me.* I can't blame her. She'd defended me and paid a steep price for her loyalty only to find out I didn't deserve it. Looks like our relationship is yet another thing my vacated conviction won't fix.

Dad pinches the bridge of his nose then takes a deep breath and holds it. I'm ninety percent sure he's counting to ten in his head. Therapy Dad is back. I don't have much sympathy for him though--if he'd only admit he needs to hire a consistent nanny-type, he wouldn't have to deal with these kinds of problems. These random fill-in sitters are too easy to fool. But for him, that would be an admission that he can't handle the whole single parent thing. And James Charles White III will *not* admit failure.

"It's alright," he tells her, calm tone at odds with his tight jaw. "I'll discuss it with Ellen later. Thanks for bringing Charlie."

"Yeah, no problem." She smiles down at the sandy-haired six-year-old who still holds her hand. "Have fun, okay, Charlie?"

He doesn't let go.

I pat the seat next to me. "Here, bud, I saved you the best seat in the house. A bunch of other kids wanted it, but I was like, nah, I got someone special comin' for this spot." He smiles, a little broader this time. The sitter nudges him to sit and gently extracts her hand from his before making a bee-line for the exit.

I ruffle Charlie's hair and pull him in for a side hug. "Missed you, brother."

"You too," he replies with a shyness that confuses me. Dad told me he asked every day to call me, begging to visit, and now...

Dad's cell rings, and he immediately takes the call. "Hi, Harry...Yes, thank you. We appreciated your support...Yes, we're having dinner out together. No, It's okay. I have a minute. Did you read that brief on the Compton case I sent yesterday? Good. Hang on a second." Dad lowers the phone to say, "You boys go ahead and order. I'll have the Bolognese," before getting up to continue the call outside.

"Whataya say, Charlie, should we go with the usual or get adventurous?"

He shrugs, slides out of the chair, and sets up camp under the table where Captain America can battle Hydra operatives in a more cave-like environment. Mouth explosion noises soon follow.

"The usual it is then..." I close the menu and raise a hand to flag down our waiter. I catch his eye as he walks past with a tray of drinks, but he doesn't stop on his way back to the kitchen. He's worked here for years, waited on us a dozen times. Just not since my arrest. I thought again of Dad's picture gone from the wall. No doubt the long-time employees here know all about the downfall of the House of White. But Dad is a creature of habit, a lover of tradition, so here we are.

I scan the room for another waiter or busboy. The host passes nearby, seating a middle-aged couple. The woman has curly brown hair pulled back in a messy bun and a long floral skirt that swirls around her ankles. It's the kind of thing Mom had liked to wear in the spring when the weather finally got

19

warm enough. Lost in the thought, I stare a moment too long. The woman meets my eyes and stops, causing the man behind her to almost run into her. She tips her head to the side and squints. *Look away!* my brain shouts to no effect. I just keep staring, frozen like a deer in the damn headlights, with the horrible realization that I know this woman. And she knows me. It only takes another second for her face to shift from suspicious to certain.

Regaining motor functions, I fumble to reopen my menu to hide my face. *Relax*, I tell myself. *Don't panic, don't panic...So she recognizes you, that doesn't mean she'll--Oh God, no...please don't come over here...Oh shit.*

"Hello, EJ."

I clutched tight to the menu, slouching as low as I can manage without pulling a Charlie and hiding under the table. But I can feel her standing right at the edge of our table, waiting. For a few beats, I considered pretending I'm someone else or just ignoring her. But I suspect that will only make this worse. So I force on my courtroom neutral face again and close the menu.

"So, your father managed to get you out in under a month." Her tone is mild enough, but insinuating that my father is corrupt is throwing down a gauntlet. And I'm sure there'll be no shortage of people who share that view of my speedy release. *Don't engage.*

"You don't recognize me? I'm Mrs. Layton, from church," she reminds me, her jaw hardly moving as she speaks.

"Yes, Mrs. Layton. Of course I remember." She'd been my Sunday School teacher from second through fourth grade...mine and Kendra's. I swallow hard and attempt a smile. She must have some good memories of me, right? I was pretty well behaved back then, though maybe not in comparison to Kendra, who never disobeyed an adult. "It's good to see you again," I lied.

"Is it? I can't say the same." Her chin tilts up, her nostrils flare.

Shit. My heart is pumping fast, but I keep my voice even and reasonable, doing my best impression of Courtroom Dad. "Please...we're just trying to have a family dinner." *Please don't make a scene.*

Her scowl deepens. "Do you have any idea what it's been like for Kendra?"

"I, um…" I look towards the door. *Come on, Dad…*

"No, you don't, and you don't even care, do you? Here you are," she gestures with an outflung arm, "...having your nice 'family dinner,' putting it all behind you." Her soft, middle-aged features have gone rigid, lips pulled tight over teeth.

I feel Charlie's shoulder press against my calf, his skinny frame instinctively angled toward my larger, muscular one. "My brother Charlie is with me, *please*…" At the mention of his name, he appears next to me. His eyes are wide, his favorite Captain America action figure clutched in both hands against his chest.

Mrs. Layton looks at Charlie, alarm registering in her eyes. Her husband reaches out a tentative hand to her elbow. "This isn't the place, Clara," he murmurs with a furtive look around the room.

She glances over her shoulder at him, almost like she'd forgotten he was there. But his gesture seems to have the opposite effect than intended. My small spark of hope fizzles as she shakes him off with a single jerk of her arm.

Mrs. Layton's mouth twists in disdain as she tells me, "I guess I shouldn't be surprised that you'd try to use a child as a shield. The person the poor boy really needs protection from is *you*. You're the reason he's been exposed to all this ugliness."

An angry defense surges up my throat but ebbs as soon as it reaches my tongue. She isn't wrong. Not completely anyway. I put a hand on Charlie's shoulder and gently press until he's back under the table, out of the way of whatever comes next. Because Mrs. Layton has plenty more to say.

"This may be over for you, but it will *never* be over for Kendra. Do you understand that? Do you understand what it's like after someone..." Mrs. Layton's voice chokes off. She looks up at the ceiling and takes in a long, broken breath.

"Clara...please, enough... This won't help," her husband says in a hushed, coaxing voice, this time without touching her.

The sound of his voice seems to galvanize her fury. She snaps her eyes back to mine and leans closer, bracing herself on our tabletop with shaking hands. "You destroyed her life. The courts may have failed her, but God knows what you did, and deep down, you know it too."

Be sure your sin will find you out. The verse floats up from some dusty recess of my brain, lashing my conscience like a jellyfish sting. I want to unburden my soul, blurt out the confession I couldn't bring myself to make on the stand. Tell her I know what a piece of shit I am. That if a literal hell actually exists, I deserve to end up there. But once again, my throat won't let me. Some form of psychosomatic self-protection is still in place even though the threat of incarceration is gone. *Coward.* I drop my eyes.

"You think you're free?" she asks, her voice now a low rasp.

No. I will never be free of what I did. Never. I manage to look at her again, letting her read the answer I can't speak.

I'm not sure what she sees in my eyes, but after a long second, she closes hers. A layer of unshed tears appears as she opens them and swallows. In a choked whisper she adds, "I hope the guilt rots your bones."

"Ma'am?" The manager approaches us at a fast walk, wearing a tight, worried smile. "Can I show you to your table?"

Mrs. Layton looks at the manager, looks at me, looks at her husband, and steps back.

"Ma'am?" The manager motions towards the other side of the large dining room.

"Thank you, but no. I've lost my appetite." She turns in a swift, unsteady motion, her skirt flaring out around her, and heads for the door. Seconds later, Mrs. Layton and her husband are gone, but the stares from the rest of the dining room linger. Now I'm the one shaking. Under the table, I press my fingers hard into my thighs, willing myself to stay calm and in control.

Charlie slowly gets back into his chair and asks in a small voice, "Where's Dad?"

Outside, but hopefully not right outside the exit. I wish he'd given me my phone back so I could text him a warning. "He'll be back in just a minute, buddy."

"I wanna go home."

"Yeah...me too." I breathe deeply through my nostrils and hold the air in my lungs, counting to seven before releasing the stream through my mouth. *Do not have a panic attack,* I self-willed. *Not in front of Charlie. Not in front of all these people armed with cell phones.*

Dad walks in the door, and I feel my body relax a fraction. He's about to pass the hostess stand when the same manager steps into his path and says something I can't hear. Dad glances in our direction, his face calm and professional as he nods to the manager and says something in reply. The manager looks relieved. Dad motions for us with two fingers. I take Charlie by the hand, and we make our way through the dining room, now silent except for Frank Sinatra coming through the speakers. Charlie focuses on the floor while I look straight ahead, ignoring the stares, the looks of disdain, the carefully averted eyes... As we pass a young couple, the guy leans toward me and says, "And don't fucking come back." The girl glares at me in agreement.

I walk faster, my throat doing that thing where it aches so bad it closes up on me. I can feel their hatred burning my back even as the glass exit door closes behind me. When we round the corner, Dad is standing ten feet from the bimmer, red faced and rigid.

"Not again..." Dad closed his eyes to block out the sight of two freshly-smashed headlights. During the trial, someone keyed DA DICK DEFENDER all along the driver's side. And back in November when I was first arrested, it was four slashed tires and a shattered windshield. Yet he'd refused to get rid of the personalized license plate he'd had since he was sixteen: JWHITE3.

Charlie sucked in a shuddering breath, and I could tell he was trying hard not to cry. "Who did that?"

Dad and I exchanged a look. The manager must have explained enough. I think of the waiter who ignored me, and the one who unceremoniously dropped our waters at the table without a word... Too many suspects to be sure.

"I don't know," I tell Charlie, squeezing his hand.

Dad shakes his head, and takes out his cell to call the police.

My stomach tenses itself into a tight ball. "Don't report it."

"What?" Dad pauses, brow furrowed.

"No police. Let's just go."

He hesitates. "We need a report for the insurance."

"Dad...please. I just can't right now. How much can it be to replace headlights?"

"EJ, the restaurant will have security footage. We can—"

"For God's sake, Dad, is that what you want? Another case?" My heart is beating too fast, I feel the dizzying panic lapping at the edges of my brain. "How does that help the media move on, huh?"

Dad looks at the broken headlights, then at us, lingering on Charlie. "Okay, alright, we'll go." He shakes his head, the prosecutor in him hating to let the vandal get away with it.

I get into the back seat with Charlie while Dad uses the snowbrush to clear the glass and plastic shards away from the tires. I try to calm myself down, focusing on different parts of my body and releasing the tensed muscles in turn. Another Dr. Eduway trick. Still dressed in my court clothes, I loosen my tie and undo the top shirt button. Charlie sits very still, looking out the window and picking mindlessly at the ridges on Captain America's shield. This silence is weird from a kid who's usually a million miles a minute, wanting me to play with him, telling a story, peppering me with questions.

I search for something to get his mind off this disaster of a celebration dinner. "So...how's school? That kid Brendan still giving you a hard time?" I wince. *Good one, EJ. Bring up getting bullied. Yet another shitty thing in his life.*

Charlie shrugs, still looking at nothing out the window.

As I search fruitlessly for some happier subject, Charlie comes up with a topic of his own, "Dad said if the judge released you, it would be for good. You wouldn't have to go back to jail or to court ever again... Is that true?"

I blow out a puff of air and pull it back in with a single laugh. "I sure hope so, buddy."

He turns his face toward me, and I realize that it was a mistake to take such a light tone. Charlie's bright blue eyes— our mother's eyes—telegraph anxiety, fear even. I feel like a complete idiot.

"Hey...hey." I unbuckle and slide into the middle so I can put my arm around him. "I'm not going anywhere, okay, Charlie?" When he doesn't respond, I prompt, "Okay? I'm home and all that stuff..." I catch myself before I repeat the same lie Dad had told me on the drive here about getting our normal life back. If this dinner has proven anything, it's that this shitstorm I started is far from over. And I don't want to make him promises I can't keep. But I feel like I have to give him something solid, so I tell him, "Charlie, I promise I will do everything I can to stick with you, okay?"

His eyes search mine and he nods, accepting this less-than-total reassurance. I hug him closer and feel him shake as he starts to cry against my shoulder. Then I'm crying too. My vision blurs, my breath coming in stuttering gasps.

This so-called freedom, going home, moving on with our lives--it's an illusion. This whole mess comes back to me, to what I did that night. My own personal apocalypse, destroying everyone and everything in its path. Including the people I love, who I'm supposed to protect. And if we stay here, it'll never be over, for me or my family. We need a tactical retreat, to get out of this city—all of us. Somewhere no one knows us, who I am or what I've done.

Senior Year: Tuesday, September 3
~~EJ White~~ Eric Madison--Welcome to Ohkwali

Aunt Kari takes away my half-eaten bowl of cereal and dumps the soggy flakes in the garbage disposal.

"Hey! I was still eating that."

"No you weren't." She wipes her hands on the towel draped over her shoulder before picking up a coffee mug twice the size of her fist and downing the dregs. I want a cup myself but know from experience it will only make the nerves worse.

I've been compulsively checking the microwave clock for the last fifteen minutes, watching my time run out. Everything feels off. Ellen hasn't even come down yet. Charlie is in the living room with Kari's six-year-old daughter Maggie, spending his last minutes transfixed by an episode of *Teen Titans*, his current obsession. We Whites have rituals for the first day back to school, one that involves music and making breakfast together and saying a prayer for the year ahead. I wanted this--a new town, new house, new school, new name, new life. I had just hoped we could bring the good stuff with us and leave the bad behind. *Wishful thinking, White.*

At least Charlie hasn't seemed to notice the break with tradition. I stand to look in on him and spy my reflection in the sliding glass door. The mix-n-match wardrobe showcases the worst Salvation Army had to offer. The red CareBears graphic tee is the immediate eye-assaulting item, but the pants are the real prize find--shiny blue, baggie parachute style, no doubt once owned by an MC Hammer wannabe. I touch the top of the sleek black faux hawk, crafted using half the tub of hair glue I bought at CVS yesterday. Then there's the waxy blue lipstick and heavy guyliner--very Green Day's Billie Joe Armstrong circa 2004. But the strangest, most disorienting change is the eyes themselves. My distinctive blue irises--light near the pupil progressing to a darker ocean blue ring around the outer edge-- transformed with contacts to a deep amber brown.

I take in the total effect. It's intense, bizarre, even comical. Most importantly, it's not someone people will recognize as the infamous once-convicted, once-acquitted sex offender, EJ White.

Aunt Kari notices me admiring my ingenious disguise and clears her throat. "It's not too late, y'know. The jeans and t-shirt you had on last night--"

"Would make it too easy for someone to recognize me. We're only three hours from Rochester, and if someone from home is at college here--"

"Honey, I don't think there's much risk of someone coming all this way to attend a community college."

She has a point there, but it's still a possibility. And any risk is too great. "Well, people from all over followed the case on social media, and there were plenty of pictures of me out there...not to mention *the video*... My new look has to be extreme."

"Oh, I'm pretty sure the hair and makeup are extreme enough all on their own. The clothes..." she wrinkles her nose and gestures up and down with her mug at my outfit. "I think that getup will make the other kids *more* curious about you--the opposite of what you want."

"*Or* they'll take one look and write me off as a freak. Then they can avoid and ignore me for the rest of the year, and I can graduate and be done with high school forever."

"EJ—"

"*Eric*, remember, even at home."

"Yes, sorry, *Eric*. I just think alienating everyone on your first day is a bit...unhealthy. You might actually want a friend or two."

I shake my head, not wanting to get into it with her. This year is already going to be complicated enough without tricking people into being my friends. *She doesn't get it because she didn't live the last ten nightmarish months with the rest of us*, I remind myself. "I can't take that chance." I look over at Charlie and Maggie again. "It's not just me they'll go after if they find out. And don't think they'll leave you and Maggie out of it." Aunt Kari doesn't understand how bad it got for our whole family. If anything, it had gotten worse after my release. I need her to take the risks seriously.

Another sigh. "Okay, fine, your call. Senior year, no friends. Sounds fabulous."

That dry, sarcastic tone reminds me of Mom. So does the way she pulls her thick, wavy black hair into a messy bun in the mornings. She looks to the heavens and shakes her head in surrender, and for a moment the resemblance between sisters is so strong I have to look away.

Beyond the physical similarities and shared mannerisms, my brain doesn't usually mistake Aunt Kari for Mom. The two Madison sisters loved each other, but they'd had very different personalities and interests. Kari was the rebellious wild-child to

Mom's more straight-laced bookworm. Mom went to Cornell and became an English Lit professor. Kari went straight from high school to a farming commune out in Northern California and then all the way to an ashram in India for a year before backpacking around Asia and ending up working at a sheep ranch in New Zealand. There were a few more far-flung adventures before moving back after she got pregnant with Maggie. Now the wandering sister is full-on adulting, even (semi)renovating this (semi)dilapidated farmhouse and running her own dog grooming business. And from what I've seen, she's pretty great at the whole mom thing… She's just not *my* mom.

Wanting to get going before I could slip too far into a missing-Mom-funk, I ask, "Where the heck is Ellen?" and check the time again. "She's not gonna have time to eat."

"She took the bus. It came about a half an hour ago."

I look at Aunt Kari in surprise.

She takes another sip of coffee and says, "Your sister needs this fresh start as much as you do. Give her some space."

"Yeah, but she's *had* space," I reason. "She hung out here on her own all summer before Charlie and I got here last week."

"She was working all that time, helping me groom dogs during the busy season. And you don't get to decide how much space she needs or how long she needs it," she says with a new edge to her voice. "Right, Eric?" Unlike Dad, Aunt Kari didn't have much trouble believing me when I admitted my guilt. And while I was grateful for that, it still kinda hurt.

I nod, picking at the raw skin around my thumbnails. "Yes, I know. You're right."

To Ellen, my being here now is yet another betrayal. She'd made it clear during the summer that she wanted me to take the boarding school option. If I wanted to make things right with her, I'd remove myself as far as possible from her life. But Aunt Kari and Dad agreed it would be best for Charlie to live with Kari for a year, until Dad's term as D.A. ends and he gets another job. And wherever Charlie is, I have to be too, just like I promised. I won't leave him again, even if that makes things harder between Ellen and me.

My stomach churns. I shouldn't have eaten breakfast. Too high risk.

"Did you take your pill?" Aunt Kari looks at my ragged fingers, a crease forming between her eyebrows.

I shove my hands in my pockets, hiding the patches of raw pink skin. "Yes."

She glances at my Lexapro bottle sitting next to the spice rack, her brow creased. But she doesn't need to worry. I *did* take my pill. Just like I have every day since I started on them, back before the trial when I spent nearly every day sleeping or freaking out or throwing up.

Whether Aunt Kari believes me or not, she doesn't press the issue. Instead she crosses the room and squeezes my shoulders. "You got this, Eric."

"Yeah…It's gonna be fine." I tell her.

I only wish I could believe it.

Ohkwali High School
~Home of the Bears~
New York State Class C Football Champions!

At least my matte black, 1995 Pontiac Grand Prix with its unibrow headlights isn't the shittiest car in the lot. In fact, age and neglect seem to be the whole campus's architectural theme. The main building's brick façade is a crumbling patchwork surrounded by a bramble of shrubs in desperate need of pruning. But the football stadium is state of the art, complete with digital scoreboards and massive HD screen for graphics and close-up game footage. *Typical.*

Ha! What a *Mom* thing to think. Maybe channeling Mom is a good sign. Swapping out White for Madison--Mom's maiden name--is just the start. I need to get into character. I'm no longer EJ White, starting quarterback, serviceable lacrosse player, and decent basketballer. I'm Eric Madison, scholar-minus-the-athlete. And Eric Madison is the kind of person who hates to see school districts pour inordinate amounts of taxpayer dollars into sports programs while academic facilities fall into disrepair. *Am I? Yes...yes, I am.* That's me now—anti-jock.

I sit for a couple extra minutes, waiting for Nina Simone's "Feeling Good" to finish playing. In the side mirror, I see a crowd of girls empty out of a bright red convertible, all wearing shorts and tank tops that show off their impressive summer tans. One with long blonde hair has an amazing set of legs. I adjust my mirror with the interior control so I can watch her as she approaches. *What are you doing?* The pleasant tingling of attraction fizzles in a snap second. I'm doing it again--the objectification thing. *She is a person, not a body on display for your viewing pleasure,* I remind myself. I don't do that anymore--I'm Eric Madison, anti-ogler.

They pass on my left, and I have a sudden urge to duck my head to make sure they don't see me, followed by an opposite urge to jump out of the car and see what their reaction would be. I do neither, just watch them disappear into the crowds disembarking from the busses. There are so many people. Hundreds. Or what seems like hundreds.

The panic that always lurks in the back of my gut spills through my torso like ice water. "No!" I hiss, gripping the dash. *No, please God, not now.* I close my eyes and begin a Dr. Eduway stress-reducing deep breathing exercise to keep it at bay. I recognize the signs: Dizziness blurs my vision. Tingling starts in my hands and feet and spreads, like all the blood in my body is being sucked into the cold void, leaving behind a layer of chilled sweat all over my body. It's like some alien virus hijacks my brain and takes control of my whole body. I try to hang on to myself, but there are no edges to grab hold of and everything goes dark. I call it The Black Hole. And once it has me, the only way to escape it is to vomit. Purge everything from my gut until it finally releases my mind with the last of the bile.

But there is a brief window when I can fight it, force it back into the tight ball that has taken up permanent residence in my core. I refuse to vomit in the parking lot on the first day of school! "...Dear God...please give me the strength to go through with this. Please let this work out. Let no one recognize me. Let me not throw up or cry or get in a fight...Let me not screw this up." Not exactly eloquent, but I figure that God, in His omniscience, gets the idea.

Time strains and slows. I count--five seconds breathing in through my nose, seven to hold, ten to let air slip out between my lips. I repeat the cycle six times, seven times. It gets easier, my pulse slowing, and by the eighth cycle, I know I've escaped The Black Hole...this time.

Most of the buses are pulling out now, the sidewalk in front of the main entrance is clearing. You wanted this, I remind myself. You could have been at Deerfield Academy, a protected enclave of wealth and privilege, where you wouldn't have had to hide to survive. You chose to stay with Charlie. And Ellen, even if she hates you for it right now. *Just don't screw this up.*

I pull down the sun visor and check myself in the mirror. My face and neck are coated in a sheen of sweat. My eyes are slightly bloodshot. *Shit...I look strung out.* I open the glove box for a napkin, a tissue, anything to soak it up, but the only things in there are the insurance and registration cards. *Shit!* I rifle through my backpack but again find nothing that will do the trick, so I reach inside my t-shirt and use the cloth like a towel. Now there are damp patches around the graphic and a couple of black streaks. From what? *Oh shit—the eyeliner!* How had I forgotten I was wearing it? The mirror reveals that the left is smudged worse than the right. Now my eyes are glazed with a damp of their own.

Stop it! You are not gonna fucking cry!

I do another breathing cycle.

Enough already. Like ripping off a Band-Aid, I grab my bag and yank the door open, slamming it behind me. I repeat the breathing cycle as I walk. I tell myself that I don't care what these people think of me. As long as it's not *rapist.*

"Whoa! Jess, look."

I hear the words and laughter from outside the range of my peripheral vision, so I can't tell if they are talking about me or if I'm just being paranoid.

"Oh God! Who is that?"

Yeah, they're definitely talking about me. More laughter. Good...laughter is good. If I saw a guy dressed like me, I'd be laughing too.

As I weave my way through the halls, there are more giggles, some wide-eyed looks and sidelong glances, and a lot of people pointedly shifting away from my path. But instead of making me feel worse, it's strangely bolstering. I feel calmer than I have all morning, all week for that matter. The protective Freak Bubble I've designed for myself is working beautifully. *Take that, Aunt Kari!*

I find my locker (one so scratched and warped that I wonder if the principal purposely assigned it to me), but it's blocked by a girl with a long, shiny brown ponytail in the middle of decorating her neighboring locker. In no rush, I wait and watch as she uses tiny magnetic clips to attach pictures to her locker door. There's one of her wedged between two parent-looking types. She's wearing a Sweet 16 tiara and all three are grinning. Then there's a bunch of soccer-themed pics with her in uniform, mid kick, mid header, surrounded by teammates, holding up a trophy. And the last is a random shot of her looking about eleven or twelve, arm slung over the neck of a blonde kid about the same age whose grin exposes a serious set of braces. Brother? Boyfriend? *Who cares? None of your business anyway.*

The girl shuts her locker door and spins around so quickly that we're standing face to face and way too close for comfort. She gasps. We both stand there, frozen for a second. My adrenaline spikes with the irrational thought that she's recognized me and is about to scream or hit me or--

"Hi!" She blinks twice, then looks from my face all the way down to my purple Chuck Taylors before stepping back. "Hi," she repeats, smiling like she's on the edge of a laugh.

"Uh, hi, I'm Eric." When she doesn't respond, I say, "I'm new."

"Yeah...no kidding." She does laugh then, but not unkindly. It relaxes me for some reason. "Welcome to Ohkwali, Eric."

"Thanks. Uh, my homeroom is A-127...Is that around here?" It's a normal, safe enough thing to ask.

"Just keep going down the hall and turn left."

"Cool, thanks."

Neither of us move. She points for clarification and waits for me to leave.

"Um...I gotta get to my locker first." I point over her left shoulder.

"Oh my gosh, I didn't realize. I thought...nevermind. Sorry about that!" She rolls her green eyes good naturedly and slides over. "Well, have a good first day!" She shrugs her bag higher up her shoulder and peels away into the stream of people headed to homeroom.

"Thanks!" I call after, which is stupid, because she definitely can't hear me over the general cacophony of a hundred other kids at their lockers. *Doesn't matter. You two won't be getting friendly.*

My homeroom is in one of the art classrooms, and even though artists are supposed to be these funky, free spirit types, the art teacher looks more like the grandma from a Norman Rockwell painting. I give her what I hope is an innocent smile, but that only makes her eyes bulge wide enough that you can see white all the way around. "Yo, teach," I greet her with a casual, two finger salute.

She realizes she's staring and looks down at her laptop screen, clearing her throat. "Ah, you must be...Eric Madison."

"That's me, new senior on campus."

"Yes, well...why don't you...find yourself a seat?" She waves a little too frantically towards the tables near the windows, furthest from her desk. *Does she know?* I dismiss the paranoia. Dad made it very clear to the principal and guidance counselor that if anything connected with my sealed--and now expunged--juvenile record was shared with the staff, he'd ensure they lost their licenses. Not to mention they'd be named personally in the civil suit he'd file against the school.

I pick a table with only two occupants. The one guy's too busy on his phone to look up when I grab the seat across from him. The other is a frizzy-haired girl wearing a Blake Shelton concert tour tee. She does glance up from her phone. It takes two seconds for her to determine I'm no one she either knows or cares to know. She scrunches her nose like I not only look but smell offensive and returns her attention phoneward.

Ouch, I think, but remind myself, *This is good. My Freak Bubble plan is proving effective.*

I am here to hide, to finish school and graduate without anyone figuring out who I am. That is the entirety of my goal. To be ignored is to be safe. To be an object of mild disgust or amusement is infinitely preferable to being hated. Here at Ohkwali, they know nothing but the exterior show I put on for them. I've been on the fringe of society for a while now, but this time, I control the version of me they know. I *choose* to be excluded.

The announcements come with an intro song that sounds like it was recorded in the 80s. Journalism Club members take turns reading the upcoming events and sports scores before the principal gets on to reiterate that dress code--no hats, no undergarments showing, and shorts must pass the "finger-tip" length rule. That gets a good laugh out of the students around me, half of whom are in violation of one or more of these. As bizarre as my outfit is, the principal at least has nothing to object to.

Right before the bell rings, I fish out my schedule and school map and locate my Stats classroom...all the way on the other side of the building. Though since this place is a third the size of my last school building, I guess I shouldn't complain.

As I navigate the hallway traffic, I spot my sister coming towards me. My stomach flips like a leaden pancake. Everything about Ellen is calculated to make the right impression. Her outfit is simple--jeans and a loose, short-sleeved black top--but it's all the right brands with just the right shoes and accessories. Her black hair is flat ironed into a glossy sheet. Natural makeup subtly draws attention to the large hazel eyes she shares with Dad. Pretty but not intimidating, stylish but not showy. It all says, *I'm one of you. Accept me. Invite me in.*

It would seem to be Mission Accomplished. She's flanked by a blond girl on one side and a redhead on the other, smiling and pointing, giving her the guided tour. They look like a stock photo of "Bubbly Teen Girls in Hallway." I can't remember the last time Ellen looked that way--Happy.

And I'm happy for her. Or I should be.

No, I am. Of course I am.

They're ten feet away. I stop walking, and form the White sibling W with three fingers of my right hand and lay it over my heart. I stand still, disrupting the flow, waiting for her to see me. Willing it.

Look at me!

She sees me. How can she not? I'm a six-foot-two punk clown in her direct eyeline.

But she gives no sign, no reaction. I don't exist to her. Not anymore.

Junior Year: Tuesday, September 4
Sibling Solidarity

My sophomore year, Mom was in bad shape at the start of the school year, but she still got up at 5:00 a.m. and mixed the pancake batter and set up an omelet-to-order station and blasted our custom Back-to-School-Special playlist as a wake-up call, singing along and praying a blessing over the new year and waving us off on the bus.

Two weeks later, she was dead.

First day of school the next year, we sat in near silence, eating cereal with half-and-half because we were out of milk.

After five minutes of spoons clicking forlornly against bowls, Dad made an effort to lighten the mood. "So, El, freshman year, huh? You excited to finally be a high schooler?"

Ellen nodded and forced a smile that vanished the moment Dad shifted his focus to me.

"And a junior--only two years left until you head off to Cornell. I can't wait to order a Big Red Player Parent bumper sticker for the bimmer."

I rolled my eyes even though my chest warmed ever-so-slightly at the thought of finally being at school the White men had attended for five generations, the school where my parents met, where we've visited every summer since I was an infant, taking an annual family picture all dressed in Big Red gear.

Except for last summer when Mom was too sick to leave the house. And now she's gone and nothing will ever be like it was. The reminder acted as a boot heel stomping out my brief spark of excitement. "Like you'd ever defile your precious BMW with a bumper sticker," I muttered through a mouthful of Honey Nut Cheerios.

"Well, one of those removable decals for inside the rear window then." Dad amended before walking over to set his half-eaten bowl of cereal by the sink. "Alright, you three. Have a wonderful first day. You have lunches?"

"Yeah, Ellen and I packed them last night." I said, trying not to be annoyed that he never seemed to think about meals until the very last minute.

"Excellent." His phone started to ring. "I'll see you later tonight. I should be in time for dinner," he told us as he walked into his office, shutting the door behind him.

The three of us stood there staring after him for a few seconds before Charlie asked, "Can I watch TV now?"

"Sure." I ruffled his hair and kissed him on the top of his head before he made a dash for the family room couch. "I already set an 8:30 alarm so you won't forget to watch for your bus. When it rings, go stand at the door. Can you do that, buddy?"

"Yes," he called back, already getting sucked into the bright colors and sounds on the TV.

I followed Ellen to the front door. This was the point where Mom would kiss us on the cheek and hand us our backpacks and tell us to "have a good day, progeny! Do me proud!"

I picked up my own bag and handed Ellen hers. "Do her proud?"

"Do her proud." She nodded then sucked in her lips and squeezed her eyes shut. We'd promised each other the night before that we would not cry. Mom always made it such a happy morning. She would want it to stay that way.

I let my own bag drop and pulled my sister in for a hug. "It's okay…" Her tears made a wet spot on my t-shirt. "She's here with us. She's watching." It seemed like the right thing to say, even though half the time I wasn't sure it was true.

Ellen pulled back and nodded, taking in a deep breath. "I know…thanks." She wiped carefully under her eyes. "Does my face look like total shit now?"

I stepped back and assessed the situation. "Yes, it's hideous. Like, Frankenstein's monster bad. I'm gonna pretend like I don't know you when we get to school."

"Shut up." She punched me lightly in the stomach.

I pretended to double over at the force of her blow. "Abuse! Domestic abuse!"

"Shut up, faker!" But she was smiling again.

As we boarded the bus a few minutes later, multiple voices called out greetings.

"EJ, m'man."

"There he is!"

"Hey hey, QB, what up?"

I walked the aisle giving a variety of fist bumps and high-five handshakes as I followed Ellen to a seat in the mid-back of the bus. We always sat together if we were on the same bus, starting from her first day of kindergarten. We didn't care that no one else sat with their siblings by high school, and I had enough clout as the Lions' newly crowned QB1 that I doubted anyone would give us grief about it.

The two of us didn't say much, just sat scrolling through our social media feeds, showing each other funny posts. But the closer we got to school, the more agitated she got, her leg jumping up and down in a nervous rhythm.

While the bus unloaded students at one of the two middle schools that feed into the high school, I told her, "You got this," bumping her shoulder with mine. "Anybody messes with you, they'll have me to deal with." And few fools would try to take me on. I was already bulked up from pre-season weightlifting. Not to mention the full three inches I'd grown over the summer. The only guys significantly bigger than me now were some of my teammates like Jake Kaminski and Gavin Holmes, but they were my friends, so no worries from that quarter.

Since my assurances of popularity-by-proxy and physical protection only produced the ghost of a smile from Ellen, I tried to think of what Mom would say. "Look, El, you're funny and crazy smart and you always know what to say to make people feel good about themselves--"

"Stop it," she glanced around like she was afraid someone would overhear the pep talk.

"Not to mention, you have zero pimples today."

"That's not true. I had two on my chin this morning. I had to use a ton of concealer." Her hand hovered mere centimeters from her chin as if sensing the offending bumps below.

I squinted. "Well, you've done a masterful job hiding them."

"Thank you," she checked her face with her phone camera. "I did, didn't I?" She took a deep breath and sat up straight against the seat.

"You got this," I assured her again. "Relax."

Her leg was still doing microjumps next to mine. I bumped her knee with mine and lowered my voice. "Hey, not for nothing, you're my sister. You'll be popular by association, I promise."

She looked at me out of the corner of her eye, skeptical but hopeful. "I don't think that's how it works."

"Oh, that's definitely how it works. You'll see. As I go, you go, lil' sis."

She still seemed unconvinced. "The high school is so huge, and we'll probably barely see each other. We don't even have the same lunch except on C schedule days.

That was true. Our actual interaction during the school day would likely be minimal.

"Hey," I nudged her, "I have an idea. Whenever we see each other, like in the hallway or wherever, we do this." I pull my right pinkie down with my thumb and spread my three remaining fingers to look like a W. Then I cross my arm over my chest to lay the fingers over my heart. "It'll be our White sibling symbol of..."

"Solidarity," she finished, grinning and returning the gesture. It was cheesy, but Ellen loved sappy and cheesy.

I nodded. "So no matter what's going on, we've got each other's back."

Senior Year: Wednesday, September 4
Leak in the Freak Bubble

Day Two at Ohkwali High starts nausea free, so that's a plus. I do the breathing cycle exercise in the car anyway. Today I have on maroon pajama pants covered with kittens chasing

43

balls of yarn, a Grumpy Cat meme t-shirt, and a black leather spiked collar to match my spiked hair and black lipstick. I leave my leather jacket behind because at 7:45 a.m. it's already pushing seventy degrees.

People are less shocked than amused and perplexed by me today. The new guy's a weirdo, fodder for their entertainment and mockery. From what I overhear of people's "What the hell is that guy's deal?" conversations, current theories include: He does drugs. Maybe he knows where *we* can get drugs. He's in a gang. He's gay. He's a foster kid. He's mentally unstable AKA "totally wacko."

I grit my teeth and tell myself I don't care what these people think as long as they don't suspect the truth. Besides, their interest in me is temporary. A new guy at a small school was always bound to attract attention. As long as I don't *do* anything interesting, their attention will turn elsewhere soon enough. And despite all the hushed speculation, no one actually comes up and talks to me, and I don't talk to them. That is, until last block in AP Chem. The teacher, Mr. Norris, a muscular man in his mid-forties with a close-cropped red beard, notices me standing at the front of the room and calls me over to his desk. "Mr. Madison."

"Yes, sir?"

"Manners, that's a good sign. So tell me, do you like chemistry?"

"Yes, sir?"

"Is that an honest answer?"

"Yes, sir. I mean, it's not my favorite subject, but yeah, I like it."

He grunts and leans back in his chair, crossing thick arms over a barrel chest. "This is a tough class. I've already taught all the rest of these jokers, so I know what they have to offer. I approved their placement in AP."

"I got 98% on the Chem Regents Exam."

He grunts. "So the guidance counselor told me. Well, we'll see how you do. Seating is assigned alphabetically." He directs me to the lab tables where the rest of the students have already started sorting themselves out. "Your table mate is your lab partner for the year. They can catch you up to speed on classroom policies."

I start to wander, scanning the name cards in front of each seat. At first I go too far, still looking for White out of habit. As I backtrack, I realize exactly where I'll be--

Madison right next to Mackenzie.

Oh shit...of all people... My insides dropped like I'd swallowed a lead brick.

Ohkwali's own superstar QB, Theodore "Teddy" Mackenzie, is sitting on his stool, holding my card in his hand and looking pensive, a sweep of blonde hair partially shading his eyes. I knew I'd run into him eventually, but the reality of him sitting three feet away still manages to take me by surprise, sending a spike of adrenaline through my system.

Teddy Mackenzie's the one person in Ohkwali I knew from my previous life--or knew *of*, anyway. The massive size difference between our respective schools meant we'd never been matched up on the field. But I'd seen him play, both on film and in person. Last season he took the Ohkwali Bears to State and absolutely crushed it. "Extraordinary" the commissioner called his performance before handing him the MVP trophy. I'll bet the college scouts practically wet themselves in excitement. *My* performance at State was extraordinary in a different way. If any scouts wet themselves, it was from laughing too hard.

While football is in my rearview, Teddy Mackenzie and I currently have something different in common--being the subject of general interest and speculation. Word is, Teddy's long-time girlfriend, Cassidy Scott, dumped him at the Amtrak station before heading off to the Fashion Institute of Technology in New York City. The girls in yesterday's English class used our small group Social Emotional Learning activity to debate how soon was too soon to make a move and which "opportunistic bitches" were likely to ignore any polite "grieving period."

I clear my throat and the now-single school heartthrob glances up. After only the briefest widening of his brown eyes, he covers with a courteous smile and asks "This'll be you then?" holding up my name card between two fingers.

"Yup," I acknowledge, hating how awkward I feel. *What do I, anti-jock Eric Madison, care what QB1 Teddy Mackenzie thinks? Nothing.* A thought belied by the uptick in my pulse.

The bell rings, and I sit. Mr. Norris wastes no time in getting class started.

"...Since you're in my AP class, I expect that you're all decent chemists to start with. Today, you have the chance to prove that you're ready to start AP work...or show you need some extra practice." He rests a hand on a tall stack of review packets. "Use the next hour and half to complete a range of equations and lab activities. This also gives lab partners a chance to figure out how your team will work best in the coming year. You can work jointly on problems or divide and conquer based on each person's strengths. Don't waste time.

Part of the assessment is how much you can finish before the end of the period. Questions? No? Alright, you may begin."

Without preamble, Teddy snaps up the task sheets from right in front of me and flips through the pages, skimming the problems and instructions. Without looking at me again, he says, "The first two are lab tasks...I know how to do them. You can be the recorder, okay?"

"The recorder?" *What the fuck?* Does he think I have brain damage or something?

"Yeah, I'll set up the experiment and take measurements and tell you what to write down on the sheet." His smile now strikes me as less courteous and more condescending. *Arrogant asshole.*

I put a hand to my chest. "Wow, what an honor. Although, are you sure you trust me to write stuff down when you've never even seen my penmanship?"

He arches his eyebrows. "Um, is it legible?"

"Oh yeah, doctor quality."

"Alright, fine" he replies, smile still in place, ignoring the sarcasm. "If you really wanna do something else, then you can...take the measurements." He points to the digital scale.

I let out a slow, uncertain breath. "I don't know, that seems like a *very* challenging task. First writing, now reading. Are you sure I can handle it?"

His cheek muscle twitches, lips stretching against annoyingly straight, white teeth. "I figured, since you're new, I'd do you a favor and give you the easier stuff."

I feign horror. "But what if I need remediation and you deprive me of it by hiding my incompetence?"

That did it. He drops the smile altogether. "Look, Madison, if we don't do well enough, Norris'll make us *both* stay after school for review until the next assessment. And that could be weeks from now, so..."

I drop the act too. "I don't need you to do me any favors, Mackenzie. I can pull my weight."

"Okay, whatever." He drops the sheets in front of me and lays both his hands flat on the tabletop. "You take the lead. What d'you wanna do?"

I pick up the tasks sheets, praying that I really *can* do them. They seem clear enough, nothing I couldn't handle on my own...But now that oh-so-familiar guilty nausea creeps through my system. Why did I have to be so confrontational, so EJ White? Eric Madison was supposed to be the chill, less competitive version of me. Eric Madison didn't have an anger problem. Nor did he let nasty sarcastic impulses get the upper hand. Eric Madison didn't give a shit about what other people thought about him. Especially not Ohkwali QB1 Teddy Mackenzie.

Maybe Teddy's whole attitude had just caught me off guard. While I expected my disguise would lead people to assume I was any number of undesirable things, *stupid* was not one of them, and neither was *lazy*.

Hoping it isn't too late to salvage the situation, I pull out two pieces of lined scrap paper from my binder and shift one of the worksheets so Teddy can see it too. "You can have odds on the equation problems. I'll do evens. Then we can take turns doing the lab practice measurements."

He nods and we get to work without further comment.

With the joint effort, we finish with almost twenty minutes to spare. The class is small, only sixteen students, and the guys across from us are still working, so neither of us has other people to talk to. Teddy flips back through the papers to check my answers. I choose to ignore this indignity, leaning back on my stool and whistling the first song that comes into my head, which happens to be the theme from cousin Maggie's favorite show, *Sesame Street*. Teddy turns to eye me like he's worried something may have come disconnected in my brain.

"Madison," called Mr. Norris. "If I wanted music, I'd play the radio. We clear?"

"Yes, sir," I cease and desist all noisemaking.

Teddy is still staring, eyebrows raised. I ignore him by fiddling with the scale in front of me. My pencil weighs 6.379 grams.

Eventually Teddy goes back to checking my work, but he keeps looking back over at me every few seconds as if he wants to say something but can't make up his mind to spit it out...probably because of how our first conversation went.

Starting to feel uncomfortable myself, I say, "Stop staring already. You're making me blush."

At that, Teddy's the one who blushes. "Sorry, I'm just...trying to get a read on you."

"And how's that going for you? I'd *love* to get your take."

"Honestly?"

"No, please lie t' me." I roll my eyes. I honestly was curious what a guy like him would think of the person I was posing as.

"Okay then--you seem pleasant and easy to work with."

"Aw, right back at ya, buddy," I shoot back, matching him for sarcastic snark.

Teddy shakes his head like, *why bother?*, and goes quiet again.

I resume my fiddling while trying to figure out why this guy is getting under my skin. Maybe because in my past life, Teddy Mackenzie would have been exactly the kind of guy I'd have gravitated toward. Fellow athlete, top of the social order, chick magnet. EJ White would make sure to get in good with a guy like him, just like I had with guys like D'Marcus and Gavin. So maybe I saw Teddy Mackenzie as a stand in for all those shit "friends" and teammates who deserted me. Worse than deserted me. Who set--*Stop it! You're gonna get yourself all worked up.* I make myself breathe slowly while counting to ten before managing to say, "Hey, I'm sorry. Go ahead. Tell me what you think. I'm curious."

Teddy would be well justified in ignoring me, but he doesn't. Instead, he considers me for another few seconds before shaking his head and admitting defeat. "That's the thing--I can't tell if you're basically a decent guy in a bad mood or if I just managed to hit some kinda sore spot. Or maybe you're one of those dicks who gets confrontational about every little thing. Or maybe you're just a nut job. And I have no freaking clue what the deal is with the cat clothes."

I spread my arms wide. "What can I say? I'm a man of mystery." Sometimes a mystery even to myself. How sad is that? I laugh at the tragic humor of it.

"See—like that, what the hell's so funny?"

I pull a serious face. "I'm not at liberty to say." It comes out sounding so much like Dad that I immediately start laughing again.

Teddy starts to laugh with me (or *at* me, as the case may be). "Dude, are you *high*?"

"Yeah man, huffing catnip gives me mad chem skills."

He laughs even harder, causing Mr. Norris to call over, "Gentlemen," in a low warning tone.

"Sorry, Coach." Teddy schools his face into contrition. When *Coach* Norris refocuses on whatever's on his laptop, Teddy narrows his eyes at me. Clearly he's not used to getting in trouble.

I grin at him with maniacal delight. With today's black lipstick, it must be quite a sight, but it doesn't throw him.

He just sighs and shakes his head at me again. "So Madison, what is your story, anyway?"

"Hmm, where to begin...Once upon a time, in a land not so far away, a boy child was born to a woman of surpassing beauty—"

"Come on, you know what I mean. Where you from? What brings you to this neck of the wood? Any siblings? Hobbies and interests? Favorite color? That kinda stuff."

"You think I'm the kinda gal who gives it all up on a first date?" I flutter my eyelashes at him.

His eyes widen a fraction, and I think he might be about to step away and say NoHomo. At which point I can roll my eyes and tell him not to be such a homophobe (because anti-jock Eric Madison doesn't have to play into that uber-straight alpha male, locker room bullshit anymore).

But Teddy surprises me. He grins and plays along, "Oh come on, sweetheart, I thought first dates were all about getting to know each other."

So, this jock's got a sense of humor. That's promising. I lean over conspiratorially and say, "Okay, I'll give you one factoid. I've never gotten less than 94% on a chemistry test."

He puts his hands up in surrender, "I get it, man. You're good at chemistry. I'll never question your abilities again. I apologize, okay?"

"Oh, very well, I accept."

"Great. Now it's your turn. What's your read on me?"

"Hmm," I tap a rhythm with my pencil on the edge of the lab table and lean back, regarding him from beneath half-closed lids. "Depends. Right now or an hour ago?"

"Can I hear both?"

"Nope, pick one."

"Can you stop with the tapping, please?"

"Nope."

He sighs, plucks the pencil out of my hand, and sets it out on the table. "Fine, first impression."

I pick the pencil back up but only to stick it behind my right ear. "Okay, I might have pegged you as some stuck-up super-jock, who decided to take an AP class taught by his coach, knowing he'd go easy on you, 'cause strong transcripts will bolster your chances of a Division 1 football scholarship."

His whole body tenses, and I can tell that I've stepped in it. "For your information, I've been ranked in the top ten of my class since freshman year. Since the start of junior year, I've been number one. And not because teachers or coaches did me any favors."

I put up a hand. "Relax, Mackenzie. That was my first impression, remember? A prejudiced snap judgment, which I've since amended."

"Sorry," Teddy's spine softens. "Guess we both get offended when people think we're dumb, huh? You were spot on about me playing football though. Good guess."

I give him a sidelong look and admit, "I'd love to take credit for the insight, but I saw the giant poster of you at the SuperCuts." It's true. There was a half-size Teddy Mackenzie, smiling in his blue and white uniform, smackdab in front of me while I sat waiting for Charlie and Maggie to get their back-to-school haircuts. But Teddy doesn't need to know I was aware of his football skills long before that.

"Oh God...I forgot about that. They printed up a whole bunch of those last year." He blushes again and rubs the back of his neck. "It's ridiculous. I wish shops would take 'em down already."

And he really seems to mean it. Which makes him a hell of a lot different than those former teammates I've been comparing him with. Showboats who'd have loved nothing more than having huge posters of themselves in all the local businesses. To be honest, QB1 EJ White would have loved that too. Though by now, any posters with my visage would've been torn down, defaced, or used for target practice.

The bell rings. Day Two down, 178 to go.

Teddy hoists his bag over his shoulder. "Sooo...I guess I'll see you Thursday, Madison."

"See ya then, Mackenzie."

There—that wasn't so bad. Not that Teddy and I would be friends. Even if he was secure enough in his social power to risk being seen with a cat-covered clothes wearing freak like me outside of class, it would only raise eyebrows and questions. Ones neither of us would want to deal with. After this inevitable period of new-guy curiosity, I need people to file me into the category of weirdo loaner and ignore me.

Still...it felt good to have a normal-ish conversation with somebody again, even if that somebody had no idea who they were really talking to. And if I want to keep our bristly-yet-fun banter thing going, I need to make sure he never finds out.

Senior Year: Weekend, September 7 & 8
Parental Visitation

I wake up in a cold sweat, struggling against my blankets. I'd been back in Iso Cell 4B. The stale vomit and urine smell of it still lingers in my nostrils.

I need fresh fucking air. Throwing on sweats and sneakers, I go for a run along the miles of open road, not in circles around a fenced yard. Birds singing from the trees, not fellow inmates shouting taunts and threats.

When I get back, the kitchen smells of bacon and Dad's aftershave. He's at the table talking with Ellen. His face is mock sympathetic as he listens to Ellen complain that her social studies teacher was "extreme" for expecting them to write an essay for his class *every week* with no time in class to work on it!

Charlie, Maggie, and Aunt Kari come in with eggs from the coop.

"Dad!" Charlie runs to him and shows him the collecting basket. "Look how many eggs we got. Aunt Kari's gonna make a...What was it called again?"

"A frittata," she answers, taking the basket from his arms.

I fill a glass with water and sit at the table.

"Morning, EJ," says Dad.

"Eric, remember?" I give him a gentle reminder.

"Right, yes, Eric…" He takes a sip of his coffee and looks absently out the kitchen window.

It's been hard on him--me going just by my full first name and dropping the J that stands for James, *his* name. Not to mention changing his children's last name completely, even if it is to Mom's maiden name. Both Bronston and his firm's PR consultant insisted it was necessary if we wanted to make this move work. They'd assured us it would be possible, when enough time has passed, to change back to White. But that was a future maybe. It didn't keep it from stinging now. Especially for a man like my dad, who'd have named me James Charles White IV if Mom hadn't put a stop to all that "self-aggrandizing, patriarchal WASP legacy bullshit." Okay, "bullshit" wasn't part of the direct quote, but it was definitely there if you translated for tone.

For me, the name change helps me get into the character I've created for life here in Ohkwali. Charlie was sold as soon as I compared it to superheroes having a secret identity to protect themselves and their loved ones. Fortunately, he's still too young to note the irony of the comparison, that we were in hiding because his big brother was the opposite of a superhero. I have no idea how Ellen feels about becoming a Madison, or about much of anything these days, except hating that I'm here at all.

"How'd you sleep?" I ask Dad.

"Pretty well." He arches his back, and a grimace belies his claim.

Aunt Kari's fixer upper, full of 70s and 80s furniture inherited from Grandma and Grandpa Madison and the odd curbside find, is a far cry from the comforts us Whites are used to.

"You can take my bed tonight if you want. I can sleep on the couch," I offer, happy for the chance to be helpful.

"No, no, I'm fine--"

"Dad, really, I don't mind."

"I want to sleep in the living room too. Please?" Charlie hangs on to the back of a chair and bobs up and down on the balls of his feet. "We can stay up and watch movies. It'll be like a sleepover."

"I wanna go to the sleepover too," Maggie insists. "Please, Mommy?"

"Mags, they're just talking about our own living room."

"But I want to sleep there and watch the movies," she whines, wrapping her arms around her mother's legs.

"Honey...I don't think it's actually happening."

"Pleeeeease? This one time?"

"Maybe another night." Aunt Kari narrows her eyes at me as if to say, *Thanks a lot. Now look what you started.*

Sorry, I mouth back. "Hey you guys, if we wait, we can buy a bunch of old blankets at Salvo and make a whole blanket fort to play in before bed. What d'you think?"

Charlie and Maggie make a combination of excited, high-pitched noises.

Dad winces.

"Okay you two, go wash your hands." Aunt Kari points them towards the first-floor bathroom. As soon as they're out of the room, she rounds on me, arms crossed, one hand still in an oven mitt. "You're going to buy a bunch of ratty old blankets?"

"Sure," I shrug. "It'll be a fun outing for me and the littles."

"Hmm...and you'll be paying for these blankets?"

"Yes, I will."

"And washing them."

"Yes, and washing them."

"And you will personally supervise the building of said fort and the playtime that follows?"

"*Yes.*"

"Perfect," she grins, "Let's plan it for next Thursday. I'll be going out after dinner to quiz night at O'Malley's with a few friends."

"What? Wait a minute. You were..." I sputter. "Oh...this is just not right." I try to look pissed but the smile breaks through.

Dad's mouth is slightly ajar as he regards Aunt Kari with new respect. "You've gotta teach me how to do that."

She laughs as she starts rinsing off the eggs. "What? Tricking someone else into taking over your responsibilities? Abigail used to call me Tom Sawyer. I can't count how many times I got her to take over my nights on dish duty."

I blink, still unused to the easy, casual way my aunt mentions Mom, like memories of her don't hurt. Maybe they don't. After all, Mom's death didn't upend Aunt Kari's life like it did ours. The sisters hadn't seen much of each other after Mom went off to Cornell and Aunt Kari started wandering the globe.

I look over to Ellen, curious if she's gotten comfortable with these sudden recollections and references to Mom. But her chair is empty. She must have snuck back up to her room. Even when Dad's here and we're supposed to be having "family time," she can't bring herself to share air with me for more than a few minutes.

"Speaking of Abigail," Aunt Kari continues breezily, "There're bins of her old stuff up in the attic that need sorting."

"What kind of stuff? From when?" Dad asks, eyebrows raised in surprise.

"From after our parents died, when Abigail and I cleaned out the house to get it ready to sell. It's twenty some years' worth of journals, a binder of short stories and poems, notebooks from every class she ever took, papers from high school through grad school, pads filled with sermon notes...she was pretty prolific. She couldn't bear to throw them out but didn't know what to do with them either, so we just packed them all up to go through later."

"Right...I remember her mentioning something at the time. But she said she'd already pulled out anything important. Her birth certificate and such."

Aunt Kari nods. "Anyway, I brought them here a few months ago when I closed out the storage unit. But there's eight full bins taking up quite a bit of space. So if someone wanted to go through and pick out what's worth saving...?"

"Would she even--I mean, do you think Mom would mind us kids reading her stuff? Especially the journals."

"What? You afraid her college journal will have detailed descriptions of your parents' sex lives?" She asks with a wink.

Dad's head rears back, alarmed at the possibility.

Aunt Kari's lips form a teasing smirk. "Don't worry, gentlemen, the journals only go up through high school. And I can attest that the steamiest she got back then was a few makeout sessions with the guy from her junior year mission trip."

Dad relaxes visibly as this, but my face burns as I insist, "There could be *all sorts* of private things in there she wouldn't want her children knowing about."

Aunt Kari gives me a penetrating look over the rim of her coffee cup. "Well, I doubt Abigail would have kept her journals for posterity if she wanted to preserve some kind of posthumous sainthood. But if you'd rather not risk reading something that might change how you remember your mother, then that's fine too."

Is that what I'm afraid of--finding out that teenage Abigail Madison wasn't the same wise, compassionate, and all-around amazing adult who'd raised me? ...Or that she'd always been that good of a person? My stomach churns, but not from hunger.

"I'm gonna go shower," I mumble and make my own escape, bounding up the stairs two at a time. As I pass my room on the way to the bathroom I slide to a stop. On my bed is an old guitar case that has seen better days. The black leather is barely visible through the collection of stickers that document its journey through almost three decades and forty-three states. They overlap each other and surround a big square sticker in the middle, a classic smiley face with the words "Smile—Jesus Loves You!" below it in bubble letters.

It's Mom's guitar.

Dad must have brought it.

This is the instrument she used to play me lullabies on when I had trouble getting to sleep as a little kid, when we sang Christmas carols with Youth Choir at nursing homes, when the Christian folk group she was in during college got to play at a Billy Graham Crusade in Washington D.C. This guitar has a legacy. I'm not sure I'm ready for it. I'm not even sure I should let it stay on my bed getting sullied by the rest of my possessions, polluted by my very presence.

The smiley face stares at me with its big, silent, empty black eyes. I back away and walk down the hall to the bathroom. My reflection in the bathroom mirror looks vaguely sick. I grab the sides of the sink to steady myself as memories of my mother come thick and fast and raw, one after another like blows. Like the way she held the guitar pick between her teeth while she tuned, the OCD way she would adjust messy songbook displays at The House of Guitars, how her mass of dark curls would half cover her face as she bobbed her head along to the beat when she played. My hands start tingling and I know it's no good. The Black Hole is going to suck me in, and I don't even bother to fight it this time.

I've vomited up what little was in my stomach by the time Ellen bangs on the door. "It's time t' eat!"

"I'll be down in ten minutes."

"Dad's making us wait for you, and the food is getting cold."

"You can start without me."

"Fine...*asshole*."

I hear her stomping back down the stairs.

Well, at least she's speaking to me.

Later that night, after the boys' team gets crushed at Pictionary, I go up to my room and stare at Mom's guitar case. Maybe I'll drop dead from laying a finger on it, like those people God struck down for daring to touch the Arc of the Covenant. I slip tentative fingers through the handle. When I'm not struck by lightning, I set the case gently in the corner next to my electric guitar, a cobalt blue Fender that I picked out with Mom for my twelfth birthday. I pick up the Fender, turn the amp volume on low, and sit propped against my headboard as I start to strum.

By Sunday night, I still can't bring myself to touch Mom's guitar. It seems right to leave it encased and preserved. It's a precious artifact. Not something I should use to figure out the chords for "King of the Road."

"I thought you might want it," says Dad. He stands at the threshold of the room. "It wasn't doing anyone any good packed away in the basement."

"Oh...thanks. That's...I really appreciate it."

He looks back at me like he can tell my pleasure in the gift is less than genuine. He stuffs his hands into his pockets and takes an uncharacteristically hesitant step into the room. "She really did want you to have it, you know."

"Thank you, really," I reply, trying to force all the sincerity possible into my face and voice.

"No, it's true...She left it to you in her will." Something I recognized as shame leaks into his features as he glances away again.

I take several beats before responding. "Wait, what? Then why..." This was the first I'd heard that Mom'd left me anything directly besides the one-third share of her life insurance that was strictly allocated to my trust fund to be used for "educational purposes."

He cleared his throat. "Honestly, there was so much to take care of...when she passed. And then there was the pool incident...so I decided to wait, just a couple of weeks."

Ah yes, the pool incident. I nod in understanding.

"Then it slipped my mind. And by the time I remembered, you weren't really playing much anymore, so..."

I wait for him to say it, to admit that a son who'd been arrested for rape, who'd muddied the family name and torpedoed his father's political career, did not deserve to inherit treasured possessions.

But instead he says, "I'm sorry, Eric, I know it's overdue."

It should make me feel better that he remembered to use the right name, but it doesn't really register. My gaze is fixed on the smiley's black oval eye holes. "She could have told me herself...before..."

"I think she wanted it to be a surprise."

"Why though?"

Dad shrugs and sighs. "I don't know."

No way to ask her, no way to know. Mom is gone, along with all her answers, explanations, and advice.

"...I'll pay for lessons again, if you're interested," Dad offers.

"Yeah...maybe," I shrug.

He runs a hand through his hair. "Let your aunt know if you do...She can set things up."

"Right...I'll think about it."

He turns to leave then pauses, his hand on the doorframe. I'm still not looking at him, just standing there staring vacuously at the case. Whatever it was he wanted to add, he loses the nerve, and simply says, "Sleep well, son."

I wish he'd said "I love you" so my responding silence would be a tiny stab of punishment for withholding my rightful inheritance for all this time. Then in the next breath I'm sorry for the wish, because I do love my dad, and I would never want him to believe, even for a minute, that I don't. I've already put him through so much worse than he deserves.

Sophomore Year: Friday, October 5
The Pool Incident

"Dude, that was fucked up!"

"Shut up, idiot. I think he's really hurt."

"No shit, he's hurt—He just jumped off a diving board into an empty pool."

"EJ? You okay, man? Yo, EJ!"

"He's out cold."

"Should we call an ambulance or something?"

"Nah, man, look, he's getting up—Awe, *hell*!"

"Oh shit, he's bleeding like crazy. I think he hurt his head."

"Yeah...Oh fuck."

"I'm calling an ambulance."

"Dude, not from here—from the car."

"I don't think we should leave 'im."

"You wanna be here when the cops show up? Look, a light just came on upstairs. I bet it's the little sister."

"He's layin' down again...You think he passed out?"

"I dunno. Maybe. Come on, man, the sister'll deal with it."

"What if she doesn't come down?"

"Whatever, man, call 911 then."

"But then they'll have my number!"

"Shit...We'll use a payphone."

"Where the hell do they still have payphones?"

"Hey, you see the way he, like, flailed just before he hit? Like he was tryin' to swim in the air? Too bad we didn't get video."

***

"You're very lucky, EJ. This could have been a lot worse if you'd hit head first. The cuts on your hand and arm are superficial, but you needed ten stitches for the head wound. It'll leave a small scar, but since it's under the hairline, it shouldn't be too big an issue, aesthetically speaking…until you have androgenic alopecia."

"Huh?"

"Premature balding." The doctor grinned and smoothed a hand over the hairless, shiny top of his own head. I was too exhausted and nauseous to pretend to be entertained. Dad though, ever the diplomat, smiled back and gave me a wink. Yes, we were all friends here, friends who had agreed to see the situation as "Grieving Son Gets Tipsy and Has a Little Accident" rather than "Delinquent Teen Downs a Six-Pack of Beer, Chases It With Vodka, and Nearly Gets Himself Killed."

"…should be taking it easy with the concussion, though. So no sports."

That got my attention. "I have a game next Sunday—"

"Which you will not be playing in." Dad didn't look at me when he said it.

"But, I *need*—"

"You need to rest and recover."

"But if I'm not—"

"You're only the backup quarterback, son. The team will be fine. Besides, the decision's not up to you or me or even the coach. There are rules about head injuries these days, right Doctor?"

"Absolutely. Concussions are no joke," the doctor agreed, showing his professional concerned face. "There's a whole list of restrictions I'll give you for the school nurse. A two-week minimum--no games, no practice, no P.E. Then your

64

family doctor will re-examine you and have to sign off before you're allowed back on the field."

So this was my punishment, missing two games and any chance at regular season play time as QB. My throat felt tight. I looked at the far wall with its mounted sharps container and Purell dispenser and imagined how satisfying it would be to rip them off the drywall. I didn't dare object further though. There was always the risk that Dad would use this incident to bar me from contact sports altogether, force me into some elitist "country club sport" like rowing or squash.

Taking my silence for agreement, the doctor nodded, pleased with our cooperation.

Dad waited to unload on me until we were safely alone in the car. "I still can't believe you would do something so reckless and dangerous and just...monumentally stupid, EJ." Stopped at a red light, Dad pinched the bridge of his nose and squeezed his eyes closed like he was fighting off a headache of his own.

I stared at the windshield wipers as they cleared the fine spray of droplets. "'Grief makes people do foolish things.' Wasn't that what you told the doctor?"

"Do *not* be flip right now."

"But you--"

"I used that line to buy sympathy and silence. And now you expect me to swallow my own bullshit? Huh?"

"I'm not...I'm just saying, maybe it's not just a line, okay? Mom's only been dead for, like, six weeks now. So maybe..."

"Okay then, if missing your mother has got you so messed up that you jumped into a pool you knew damn well was empty--" He stopped short, his knuckles going white. "You could have died. Do you get that? If you'd landed head first, if the angle had been different, if…" The light changed and the car behind us beeped. "E.J., did you...did you mean to…"

"What?! No, Dad, I wasn't trying to *kill* myself. I didn't jump on purpose. I don't even remember jumping at all."

My answer didn't seem to reassure him. The car behind us beeped again, and Dad waved an apology before hitting the gas. "Well...regardless of intent, I think you'd better go see the therapist again."

I gave a single, derisive laugh. "So she can tell me 'It's okay to be sad' a few more times? I'm pretty sure she's an android programmed with like, twelve basic responses. But hey, you wanna blow a hundred bucks a session for me to sit in a room with a chatbot--"

Tires squealed as Dad cranked the steering wheel to the right and parked the car on an angle, half on the pavement, half on the edge of someone's lawn. "Enough, EJ, *enough*! You aren't the only one who misses your mother. You think I'm not *devastated*? You think I wouldn't rather dull the pain with liquor and lock myself away? But I don't have that luxury, do I? And guess what--you don't either. You were supposed to be in charge last night. You were responsible for your sibling's safety. Did that even give you pause? You've completely broken my trust. Do you understand that?"

He was red in the face now, breathing heavily against my silence. I'd never seen him so angry, or at least not at such close quarters. Clearly, pleading bereavement to Dad had been the wrong call, but I had no other explanation for what I'd done. How I hadn't meant to drink so much, but once I started, the better I felt. The *less* I felt.

Speaking of feelings...the good painkillers were already wearing off and the stitched gash across my skull throbbed with increasing insistence. The rest of me was just one big ache.

"Did you know it was your sister who found you down there, unconscious, and called 911? Huh? Did you?"

*Oh God...*I hadn't known that.

"We're going to sit here until you answer me. I need to know you understand the gravity of your actions."

I closed my eyes and worked to come up with a response, something that would put an end to this and get me home to my own bed. Best to go with simple, tried and true.

"I know I messed up, Dad. I'm sorry."

"You could have *died*!" he repeats. "Doesn't that scare you? Because it terrifies me."

"I know. I'm so sorry, Dad. I am."

"And EJ?" He waited a few beats to be sure I was listening. "The drinking...you can never let yourself lose control like that again. *Never again*. It is not a healthy way to cope."

"I know."

"In a fair world, you'd have more space and privacy to deal with all of this. But you can't forget that you're the son of a public figure. You're a White. You're almost a man. I need you to act like one, not like some...self-indulgent child."

Anger surged a hot trail up the back of my throat. I'd said I was sorry. I knew I'd fucked up. If he didn't want me acting like a child, why did he still talk to me like one? I swallowed hard, forcing the anger back down into my gut, and responded as I knew I must. "I promise it'll never happen again."

"Alright then. And you're going to that therapist your mother wanted you to start seeing. Dr. Eduway, the one she met at some U of R faculty mixer. He specializes in adolescent behavior or trauma or something."

This decree, more anything that came before it, told me how completely freaked out Dad was. He *hated* shrinks, or as he once called them, "pseudoscience bullshitters who make a living convincing perfectly normal people they're not." And he hated when the defense called them as witnesses, "as if a crummy childhood excused criminal behavior." Hopefully this long-standing antipathy would mean I'd only have to do a few sessions.

But somehow reading my mind, he added, "And you'll meet with this Dr. Eduway every week until he assures me you won't be taking any more stupid risks. Clear?"

What the hell? So now I'm expected to pass as the one teenage boy in the universe who'll never take a stupid risk? But it wasn't the moment to point out how ridiculous that expectation was, so I just said, "Yes, sir." I'd just have to figure out what this doctor guy wanted to hear and play along, make it clear I was normal-level sad about my dead mom, not some suicidal headcase.

Dad nodded, satisfied with my agreement, and there was the Zip-lock again. Lecture over. His face was the picture of control, but the way he jerked the wheel to put us back on the road and blew past a stop sign belied the mask. I noticed his hand shake as he reached to jab the radio icon. NPR reported that over 1,800 people were believed dead following yesterday's earthquake in Indonesia. Nothing like a little global reporting to put an adolescent screw up in perspective.

Senior Year: Thursday, Sept. 19
Not-So-Solitary Lunch

Teddy Mackenzie asks altogether too many questions. It's like he's on a mission to solve the mystery of me. And our assigned proximity every-other-day during chem gives him the opportunity to mine my appearance for context clues. Like when I wore one of those shirts that looks like animal fur with a huge St. Bernard's face on the chest, he asked if I wore clothes featuring animals because my family was pet-deprived? I made the mistake of joking that in fact we had at least five new dogs a day to play with if we wanted, and he guessed I was related to "the Madison dog groomer lady who bought that big ol' farmhouse a few years back."

Or when I was holding up the pipette and he noted "Nice calluses. What kind of guitar do you have?" And when I tried to play it off with "How do you know I don't play, um, cello?", he smirked and shot back with "Because, *um*, I play clarinet, and you're not in Orchestra with me." I was so thrown by the fact that A--this little backwoods school has an orchestra and B-- QB1 Teddy Makenzie plays the clarinet, that I went ahead and told him about my Fender and how I was learning to play Blackbird, which lead to a whole discussion/argument about the best Beatles songs until the bell rang I was like, *Shit, what am I doing? Damn his sneaky, insidious chumminess!*

It means I constantly have to keep my guard up with him, and it's exhausting.

The only place I can really relax away from curious gazes around here is outdoors. Thursday the weather is perfect—80 degrees, low humidity, slight breeze, blue sky with just the right amount of cumulus puffs for texture. So when lunch rolls around, I take my bag lunch and head to the benches in the shady area near the soccer fields. Perching on the top of a bench, I pull out a tuna sandwich, an orange, and a blue Gatorade. Before I can take a bite, I see Teddy walking towards me.

He smiles and raises a hand in greeting. "Hey, Madison."

"Mackenzie," I nod. "You lost?"

"Nah. I saw you come out here, thought some fresh air might do me some good too. Can I join you?"

And there goes my relaxing solitude. I sigh in resignation and motion to the empty half of the bench with my free hand. "Sure, I guess."

He perches next to me.

"Is that what you call a nutritionally complete meal?" I ask, nodding at his bag of potato chips.

"All I could afford. Some tough guys beat me up and stole my lunch money," he smirks.

"Ah...you should really report that. You can't let bullies make you live in fear—Or worse, live hungry." I hand him my partially-drunk Gatorade.

"Thanks." He takes a swig.

"So...what are you doing here?"

"Hm? I said--"

"Yeah, yeah, fresh air. Why aren't you getting it with your football friends in the courtyard? I saw them out there hogging the best tables."

He picks at the label and shrugs. "Didn't feel like listening to Booth go on about all the schools scouting him. He visited Clemson over the summer, and...anyway, I'm just sick of hearing him talk about it."

70

I raise an eyebrow. "He got scouted by *Clemson*?"

"He *visited* Clemson," Teddy scoffs, "but he makes it out like they want him bad."

"I'll bet he does. God, what a tool." I shake my head and take a bite of sandwich. "But you're *actually* getting scouted, right?"

"Yeah, sure," Teddy shrugs.

Last year, I'd been jealous of the praise and attention Teddy Mackenzie was getting. His name paired with descriptions like "exceptional," "intuitive," "one to watch," "star in the making," and "the complete package." Occasionally, I'd wished his school was big enough that we could get matched up on the field, where I'd prove myself the superior QB and take all that buzz for myself. But now that I was well out of the high school quarterback stakes, I could take noncompetitive interest in his prospects. "So you got your heart set on a specific school? Or like, any school in the Power Five conferences will do?"

He shrugs again and makes noise between a grunt and a snort.

"Dude, no need for this Mr. Humble schtick. I mean, I know Ohkwali is a Class C team, so you've only gotten to play against other small schools, but with your skill and stats, you've gotta have caught the attention of--"

"Can we talk about something else?" Teddy leans back, rolls his shoulders, and opens the Gatorade bottle.

"Okay." Clearly I've hit a nerve. But hey, whatever his issues are, they were none of my business. "Let's see then…" I hurry to think of a topic that he can't twist into a personal information mining expedition. "Did you know that capuchin monkeys pee on their hands to wash their feet?"

Teddy chokes mid-gulp. "What the hell?"

"It's true."

"Where'd you hear that?"

"My brother. It was in his *Discovery Kids* magazine." Teddy's eyes go a fraction wider, and I realize what I've just done--dropped another personal nibblet. *Damn it.* I tense, waiting for him to jump on the opening.

Instead he says, "I love that magazine! When I was little, my mom would bring me to the library every Wednesday after school, and I'd read *Discovery Kids* and *Sports Illustrated for Kids* cover to cover."

"Seriously?"

"Yes! They were in those giant plastic covers with the metal bar down the middle so you couldn't steal them. I'd sit in the beanbag in the corner by the spinner racks."

"That's adorable."

He laughs. "Did you know that the force of a grizzly bear's bite can crush a bowling ball?"

"I did not."

"And did you know that in 1924 a Labrador was sentenced to life in prison for killing the governor's cat?"

I take a bite of my sandwich and shake my head in awe. "Dude, how--and why--do you remember random shit like that?"

He taps his temple with two fingers. "Steel trap. That's how I beat out Booth for QB back in eighth grade. We were pretty equal skill-wise, but I was the one who could remember all the plays." He demonstrates his stellar memory by listing another ten useless factoids.

I finish my sandwich half and wipe my hands on my shorts.

"I have to admit, Mackenzie, if this is the kind of lunchtime conversation you were looking for, you did well to avoid your teammates. Jocks have a really low tolerance for weirdness."

"True," he agrees and looks out over the field toward the school. The easy, cheerful energy drains from his features, leaving Teddy looking...sad. I'm seeing a glimpse of something, but I'm not sure what.

After a few seconds lost in thought, he adds, "They'd overlook a lot for me though. They need me too much."

"No kidding," I snort. "They'd be stuck with Tim Ruckle as backup quarterback. I mean, sure, he can get some distance on the ball, but his accuracy's a joke. It's no wonder Coach Norris only plays him when you've got at least a twenty-five-point lead."

"Aw, he's not *that* bad."

"*Pft.* Last season he completed, what, four passes? Five if you count the interception."

"Yeah...well, football isn't Ruckle's main sport. He does shot put in the spring. Got a state record in it."

"Well, he should just focus on that and stop desecrating football with his presence."

"Why don't you suggest it to him sometime?"

"Maybe I will."

"I'd pay to see that."

"You would? Okay, fifty bucks. We can go find him right now."

"Madison, you are one crazy SOB." Teddy takes a swig of Gatorade.

I make my eyes big and push the whole second half of my tuna sandwich into my mouth.

Teddy laughs, chokes a little, and wipes his mouth with his forearm. A second later his eyes narrow, regarding me with new suspicion. Teddy tips his head back and raises an eyebrow at me. "You sure know a lot about the Ohkwali football team for a new guy, especially one who acts so anti-sports."

Oh yeah, right...Eric Madison the anti-jock. What the hell is wrong with you, idiot? I spend weeks protecting my personal information like The Beast guarding his stash of baseballs, and now I just start leaking it all over the place. Is the heat melting my brain? Chewing and swallowing the massive mouthful of sandwich provides a second to think, but no brilliant cover story comes to me. I roll my eyes and try to play it off. "You know how much people talk football around here. You can't get away from it."

"Okay..." Teddy's brow creases, only partially buying this excuse. "But, like...that first day when you accused me of being a meathead who gets special treatment from his coach. And now you're all, like, up on our player stats. It's just...weird."

I throw up my hands. "You caught me--I'm weird."

Now it's Teddy rolling his eyes. "Seriously though."

"Would you believe me if I said I got caught up in a wave of school spirit?"

"No," Teddy deadpans.

I sigh and start peeling my orange. "Maybe I figured you had enough people to talk football with."

Teddy half laughs, half groans, "If that ain't the truth... Not that I mind most of the time." He pauses for a long minute. "It kinda sucks though, after a while."

"Playing football?" I offer him a handful of orange slices and he takes them.

"Nah man, playing the game itself is always good. It's more like…" He pops an orange slice in his mouth and sorts his thoughts. I pop one in mine and wait.

He swallows and sits straighter, angling toward me slightly. "Okay, so I've been varsity QB1 since freshman year. And every year we kept winning, then last year taking State…there was all this attention. And now people have all these grand expectations for me. The other guys on the team, the coaches, my parents, my parents' *friends*…hell, even just random people in stores coming up to me, telling me how I'm a credit to the town or whatever and how they can't wait to watch me take the Bills to the SuperBowl someday." He shakes his head and looks out over the field towards the school.

"Anyway, it's a lot, y'know? And the worst part is, it's not *me* they're all interested in--not me as a person--but more like, what I represent. It could be anybody in my uniform, as long as they kept winning games and setting records. And I get that, I do. But it also sucks. Sometimes it makes me wish I could, like, make some android version of myself that I could sub in when it all gets to be too much. Then I could just do other things in life, be whoever I want without worrying about disappointing people or not fulfilling my potential or whatever." He turns his head to look at me again, his expression a little embarrassed and a little hopeful. "Does that make any sense to you?"

It does. I get exactly what he means. Because I've *lived* it—being identified purely through one aspect of your life *does* suck. I guess that's true whether that's being an amazing football player or being a rapist.

Of course, I can't explain this parallel out loud, but it's clear that silence isn't the best response. I can see the subtle shift in his eyes--the fear that he's revealed too much, gone too deep and left himself exposed. It's humbling—him trusting me enough to put himself out there. It makes me wish I could do the same. But it's one thing to admit to feeling boxed in by a single facet of your identity and another to admit you destroyed the life of a kind, innocent girl, a friend who was just trying to comfort you. *I can't...I just can't.*

So instead, I wipe my hands on my cut-off shorts, reassemble my defenses, and turn the questions back on him. "Mackenzie, why are you telling *me* all this? Some weird guy you work with in Chem, who you've only known for a few weeks?" I gesture toward the school. "From what I've seen, you've got plenty of friends in there."

"Yeah, sure, but most of 'um are on the team, and I feel like, as captain, I've always gotta be...positive and sure of everything. To be honest, it gets kind of exhausting."

I grunt my understanding. From daily experience, I can attest that keeping up a front takes serious energy. But Teddy's affable, easy-going charm and confidence has always come off as so natural. And I figured, with everything he's got going for him, why wouldn't he be in a good mood all the time? Now I can't help wondering how many of those smiles were for real and how many for show. *Still...*"If you're in the market for a new friend to confide in, I bet you there are a hundred non-footballers in there who would piss themselves with excitement at the chance."

"Yeah, *exactly*." Teddy's mouth twists into a wry smile.

"Ah...and I wouldn't." I verify by looking down at my hundred percent dry fly.

"I wanna be friends with someone who'd wanna be my friend even if I quit the team tomorrow."

"Uh-huh...and that's your only criteria?"

His brow creases. "No, of course not."

"Okay, so why *me*?" I don't know why I press except I really want to know.

Teddy runs a hand through his hair and glances away, looking uncomfortable. "Look, I know this is weird. I didn't plan to ask you to be my friend, like we've in preschool or something. But..." He takes a deep breath and plucks up the courage to meet my eyes again. "You seem like a cool guy--"

I snort.

"Cool in a very outside-the-box way," he amends. "Like...you don't care about what other people think or what they want from you."

"Oh nice, so you're saying I'm a sociopath?"

"Come on man, you know that's not...I just mean you don't let them put weight on you, load you up with their expectations, y'know? You don't let them dictate who you are. And maybe that means you act like kind of a dick sometimes, but I guess I'm okay with that because... It's like I was saying-- I live with a lot of expectations from most everybody else in my life. I think maybe around you, I can just *be*." He looks out over the field and runs his palms down his face. "God, this is weird. But see--I can't talk about this stuff with other people. Sometimes with my cousin...but mostly I used to with Cass..."

He swallows the rest down. Missing his ex-girlfriend off at college? How deep did the hurt of that break up go? For all his talking, Teddy hasn't once mentioned the girl he'd dated since eighth grade, and I sure as shit haven't pried into the guy's romance-related emotional state.

"I'm sorry. You can tell me to shut up if... But I just think it'd be cool if we could be friends." He turns his head just enough to watch me out of the corner of his eye, trying to read my reaction.

Friends. My gut twists at the word. I cross my arms, then uncross them and shove my hands back in my pockets. "Look, Teddy, I'm..." What? Flattered? It's been almost ten months since every friend I had deserted me like I was patient zero of some humanity-destroying virus. I went from managing constant social attention to enduring complete isolation in a single week. Neither extreme has been healthy for me. But getting pulled into the orbit of someone like Teddy Mackenzie is not without risk. It's like an alcoholic renting the room over a bar.

"...I appreciate your..." *Offer? Consideration? What is this, a job interview?* I start again. "That--what you just said about me being some kind of cool outsider free of social pressures--it's a very generous read on me, but the truth is way more complicated. I'm..." *A rapist? A monster? A rapist monster?* "I'm not the kind of person you'd wanna be friends with."

For some bizarre reason, he looks relieved, smiles even. "Why not let me make that choice for myself? I mean, it's not like we're signing some unbreakable friendship contract. Let's just...be friends. Hang out and stuff, like normal people."

I hesitate, knowing in my bones that being my friend can only end in pain and disappointment. But I want to say yes so bad it scares me. It reveals the truth I've been desperate to deny--how much I still need people to like me, accept me, to want me...and how far I'll go to feed that need. I've been down that slippery slope, and I know who I am at the bottom--EJ White.

"Come on, man. You're new. You *need* a friend. No man is an island or whatever."

Maybe, but that doesn't mean I can have one...or that I deserve one.

Is Kendra making new friends this year? The uncomfortable question squeezes its way to the forefront of my gray matter. My gut twists into an ever-tighter knot as I think of her navigating the halls, head down, trying to avoid notice. Had the online support from classmates translated to invites to sit with them at lunch? ...Or had it all been a public show to make themselves look good and feel morally superior? How much support had even survived those text messages Bronston used to get me off--that *I'd let* him use to get me off? Sure, the community at large seemed unconvinced--surmising I was just another privileged kid whose powerful daddy worked the system. But was it the same story at school? Or had the same classmates who'd always ignored, teased, and taunted Kendra on the regular used "reasonable doubt" as an excuse to go back to their old ways...or worse?

Don't go there! I warn myself. *You can't take back the decisions you made. The best thing you can do for Kendra now is stay as far away as possible and keep a low profile. Follow the plan.*

But how to get Teddy to give up on me? I make my voice as reasonable as possible. "Look, Mackenzie, I'm doing you a favor here. If you knew me..."

"How about you let me get to know you, and then I'll decide if I still wanna be friends?"

"That's not...You're missing the point." I hold my face on either side, pressing against the temples.

"And you're being ridiculous!" He laughs.

From his perspective, I'm sure I am. If I can't tell him the truth, how do I get him to understand that this is for his good as much as mine? I come up blank and let out a long, defeated sigh. "What's the likelihood of you letting up on this let's-be-friends thing?"

"Oh, very low. I'm pretty competitive, and stubborn, and the more you resist, the more I'll take it as a challenge, so...yeah, you might as well give in now." He pulls his phone out of his back pocket, opens a New Contact screen, and hands it to me.

I take it automatically, before my brain sets off the alarm bells. *This is a bad idea. A VERY bad idea*, I tell myself as I type in the number and hand it back. My own phone pings with a notification for the text he's sent me. Now I have his number to add to the four other contacts I have in my phone.

I text him This does not mean we're friends

He reads it and texts back, I'm pretty sure it does SUCKER!

I shoot him a glare, but Teddy's grin is full-fledged, showing off a set of perfectly white, perfectly straight teeth. God, he really is the worst. Except he's not. *Damn it.*

"So, wanna meet up here again tomorrow? My mom makes the best pulled pork sandwiches ever. I'll bring you one--"

"No you won't!" I say, apprehension roiling the tuna in my stomach. "This--" I point between him and me and the bench. "This is not a thing. And we are definitely not eating in the cafeteria together." I command myself not to panic. *He'll get bored of me in a few weeks. And if he doesn't, I'll just start acting like a total asshole to him and he'll drop me. Yeah, that's what I'll do. It'll be fine. The plan is still intact.*

Teddy rolls his eyes. "Okay, fine, relax. I won't cramp your loner style."

"Damn right, you won't." I glower at him, y'know, like an asshole would.

But Teddy just grins and runs backwards in perfect QB form. The empty Gatorade bottle rises and falls in a perfect arch, glinting in the sun before dropping into my hands. Teddy throws his hands up and whoops like he's just completed a touchdown pass. "This is gonna be fun." He says it like a promise, and the corner of my mouth twitches upward, involuntarily agreeing.

Fuck!

Senior Year: Friday, September 20
Pep Avoidance

After lunch, third block P.E. class turns into the pep rally setup crew. A cheerleader with a tight blonde ponytail that splits into two large ringlets assigns me to hang blue and white steamers from a PVC pipe archway the athletes will enter through. When I warn her that a crepe paper curtain will only look good until the first team heedlessly rushes through it, she makes a sour face and asks if I'd rather scrape gum from under the bleachers. I then tell her I *live* to make streamer curtains, grab the supplies, and get busy.

"Hey, Eric!" comes a vaguely familiar voice behind me.

I look over my shoulder, careful not to lose my balance on the school's wobbly, janky-ass stepladder. It's the girl with the locker next to mine, her dark hair pulled back in a decidedly less fancy ponytail. She's already dressed in her soccer uniform, ready for the rally.

"Uh...heeeey there..." I stall, trying to remember her name. Had she ever introduced herself? When nothing comes, I finish with "...neighbor." *Nice one, Mr. Rogers. Very smooth.*

She grins, catching on to my dilemma. "Beatrice DeLuca, but you can call me Bea."

"Hi'ya, Bea. Pleasure to meet you--officially."

"Likewise. Um...I like the update to your look, by the way." She draws a circle in the air around her lips. They're nice lips, I notice. Equally full on the top and bottom and a deep, natural pink... *Stop it, perv! No objectifying!*

"Yeah..." I rub the tips of my fingers over my own bare lips. I just couldn't take the lipstick anymore. It felt weird and left a nasty taste in my mouth. Not to mention it created a visual that could best be described as "corpse mouth." Granted, I'm going for bizarre, but it turns out there are limits. I go ahead and answer her with the more immediate reason for the changeup. "I left my tube of blue in the car yesterday and it kind of...melted all over the cup holder."

"Ah," she nods and braces a clipboard against her hip. "Leaving cosmetics in a hot car--classic rookie mistake."

"Yeah..." *Oops, way to let it slip you're new to the whole makeup thing.* "Well, I took it as a sign. Hey, can you hand me up those strips?" I say before she can ask any eyeliner-related follow-up questions.

She sets down her clipboard and starts handing the cut pieces of streamer up to me. "So how are things going for you here at Ohkwali?"

"Um, good, I guess," I tell her with a shrug and say a silent prayer she doesn't have a string of Teddy-like follow-up questions.

"Are you in any sports or clubs yet? I could help point you in the right direction. I'm the Student Council Athletics Rep, so I know, like, an absurd amount about student activities. What're your interests?"

So much for the power of prayer. "Thanks, but I'm not really the extracurricular type."

"Ah, well, that's okay. There're other ways to meet people."

Guessing that telling Miss Student Council Athletics Rep I'm not interested in meeting people will only prolong this conversation topic and possibly lead to interference, I opt to respond with only a bland smile.

"As a matter of fact, I'm having a homecoming slash end-of-summer pool party tomorrow, if you're interested."

I turn to stare down at her with both eyebrows raised, eyes wide, and mouth slightly ajar. Did this girl I barely know just invite me, weirdo extraordinaire, to a party?

"Just if you're interested, or…anyway, it'd be a good way for you to get to know people."

When I can't yet manage to respond, she shifts her weight from one foot to the other and clarifies, "It's not a kegger or anything. We grill and play kickball and Kan-Jam and stuff like that."

"Um, thanks for the invite, but I'm gonna have to take a pass. Parties aren't really my scene." EJ's scene? Hell yes. And that's the problem. I can't let myself fall back into old rhythms.

"Okay." She smiles a little. With relief? Disappointment? It's hard to tell. "He said you'd probably say 'no,' but I thought I'd ask, just in case."

"Um...who said?"

"Teddy."

"Ah-ha...You're a friend of Mackenzie's?"

"Practically since the cradle," Bea grins.

I should have guessed. No doubt integrating me with the rest of this social group is the next level of his friendship quest. "Right, sorry, I'm still getting used to this small town thing where everybody knows everybody."

She rolls her eyes but keeps the grin in place. "Oh come on, that's such a stereotype. We don't *all* know each other."

"Uh-huh..." I raise a skeptical eyebrow. "So besides me, is there a single person in this gym you haven't known since, like, elementary school?"

She looks around hopefully then laughs. "Okay, fine. But Teddy and I would be close no matter where we lived."

"Oh?" Clearly I'm missing something here.

Bea points to herself and explains, "I'm his cousin."

"*Oh*, right, yeah." I can't stop the surprise from registering on my face. "Mackenzie mentioned he was close with his cousin. I guess I assumed..."

"I was a guy?" Her smile thins. "Nope. Well, I do have a brother but Teddy wasn't talking about him."

"*Ouch.* What's wrong with him?"

"That came out harsher than I meant. It's that...Anthony's younger than us, and has his own...thing going." She gestures vaguely as if her brother exists in a separate dimension. *Kind of like Ellen and I do these days.*

I clear my throat. "Anyway, I appreciate the invite, but I hope Mackenzie didn't make you feel obligated to--"

"No, he didn't!" Now it's her eyes that go wide. "It wasn't like that at all. I mean, I know you two have been, like, hanging out or whatever, and he was saying that you were actually a pretty cool guy, and I was asking him if you were..." Her cheeks go pink under a dusting of tiny freckles. "Anyway, I was curious about you, so he said I should talk to you myself...so I am," she concludes, pulling her shoulders back like she's defying embarrassment to get the better of her.

*Could she be...*interested *in me?* I look back at her, making a quick reassessment. Lips aren't her only good feature. Nice smooth skin. Sea green eyes. The lean, muscled build of a serious athlete. She's cute, though not exactly hot. A bit short...and short on curves. *Don't be so fucking shallow,* I check myself. And anyway, it doesn't matter how attractive she is-- Eric Madison doesn't get to date. Or hookup. Or makeout. Or do anything remotely sexual in nature.

"Here," she says and hands me the last streamer and steps back to take in the effect.

"What'd y'think? Do I get an A...or whatever gold star you guys hand out to your best worker bees?"

"Oh, absolutely." She comes close again, takes the black Sharpie from her clipboard, and draws a star on the back of my left hand. "Student Council thanks you for your service."

"Wow..." I can't help but smile as I hold my hand aloft. "This makes it all worth it."

"For real though, the streamers are going to last, like, ten seconds. You know that right?"

"I may have mentioned as much to one of your colleagues and been threatened with a far less sanitary task."

Bea laughs. "I'll bet it was Christina. Common sense is not her strong suit."

I snort. "Yeah, I gathered that. Speak of the devil..."

Christina stops a few feet back from us and frowns. "The top looks messy. Maybe you can make bows or rosettes or something to cover it up."

"Y'know, you are *so* right." I give her my most brilliant smile and slap a hand over my heart. "And you've come to the right guy, 'cause I make a killer crepe rosette."

"You do?"

"Oh, for sure. Wait, a rosette is where you wad stuff up into a big ball and then take two big pieces of tape and make an X to hold it up, right?"

My task-mistress is not amused and opens her mouth to tell me so, but Bea interjects.

"Maybe we could use those leftover white balloons from the Homecoming Court sign?"

Christina's mouth shuts, lips twisting like she wants to disagree, but after a second she says, "I guess that'd work-- HEY!"

A dodgeball hits her right in the butt to a chorus of laughter from four guys in white football jerseys with blue lettering. Next to me, Bea's eyes narrow at a tall, rangy guy with shaggy brown hair and an enviable summer tan. Through a tensed jaw, she warns me, "Resident asshole incoming."

"Damn, Booth, now that's what I call accuracy," one compliments the thrower while jogging over to grab the ball. He dribbles it like a basketball before tossing it back. Booth catches it with ease and tosses it from one hand to the other as he walks over to us.

Bea turns her back to him and whispers, "If he says anything about...anything, just ignore him, okay? He loves getting a reaction."

Christina gives Booth a disapproving look as he slides a long yet muscular arm around her waist. "Hey'a Chrissy."

"That fucking hurt, Kyle," she pouts.

"Awe, poor baby. You need me to rub it for you?" He slides his arm down so his hand finds the hem of her skirt and slips under it. She yelps and lurches as Booth's hand grips her ass cheek.

Somehow I find myself off the ladder, heart beating fast.

But then Christina laughs and smacks him on the shoulder before stepping away and looking around like she's worried a teacher saw. "You're too naughty," she tells Booth, her smile coy.

He smirks, tossing the ball in the air and catching it without looking. As if sensing my presence for the first time, his head swivels. He notes my spiked hair, currently bright pink with cheap, temporary color spray from the Halloween section at Walmart. "You're that new guy. Eric something-or-other, right?"

I just nod, not caring to offer up my last name.

"You likin' it here?"

"S'okay," I shrug.

"The girls treatin' you right?" he asks, throwing a look back at Christina who pulls a face like Booth just suggested she drink a cup of steaming vomit. Booth and his buddies have a good laugh at that, I look down at the black line painted on the gym floor, praying this small humiliation will be enough to satisfy them.

"What's the matter, Chrissy? Eric here not your type? What about you, Eric? Does Chrissy here get you goin'?" He moves closer and dips his head to try and force me to look him in the eyes. "Huh, man? You like those big, juicy titties of hers? Or you more of an ass man?"

I turn my head away from him, my jaw clamped so tight it aches. My fists clench. I remember this feeling. I remember what it leads to. The rush of adrenaline, the focus, the call to action.

Pause, breathe. The urge to turn his nose into a blood geyser will pass.

His breath is hot on my ear as he laughs.

One...two...three...

"God, Kyle--enough already."

Booth straightens up and looks over my shoulder at Bea, his angular features stretched into a look of mild surprise at her intervention. "Lighten up, DeLuca. Just trying to make sure my new buddy Eric feels welcome."

"I think he got your intended message. Now, unless you guys are helping with setup, you should go wait in the hall with the rest of the team." she says, sounding like an exhausted babysitter.

Booth smirks as he shakes his head. "So protective...Now that makes me wonder. Is he one of your kind? LGBST or whatever?"

Whoa, Bea's a lesbian? Guess I totally misread that whole party invite thing earlier. My shoulders slump. With relief? Disappointment? It's hard to tell.

Bea's cheeks go pink again but her voice is calm and measured as she replies. "He's a cool person who you're making uncomfortable."

Booth takes his time, looking me over from spray-painted head to Pokémon sneakered foot. "Uh-huh, right..." He winks at Bea, his mouth twisted into a nasty smirk. "I get it."

I don't, but I don't trust myself to say anything at this point.

He puts his palms up, nodding sagely to the two of us before craning his neck back to tell Christina, "Sorry, Chrissy, I guess you're not his type after all."

The next second, my whole field of vision turns red as the dodgeball zooms toward my face. I flinch before Booth pulls the ball back mere centimeters from impact. It's a classic playground bully move, but his buddies laugh like he just invented it. Booth presses the ball between his palms like an overripe melon on the verge of popping. "Welcome to Ohkwali." He spikes the ball at my feet, grinning to see me flinch yet again.

Sweat trickles down the side of my face. My chest expands with a ballooning rage desperate to be released, to wipe the smug off his face as I smash his head onto the gym floor. I imagine him scrambling away on his hands and knees, cupping the blood flowing from his broken nose, staining that nice white jersey red. I let myself imagine it. Then take the violent thought and put it into a bubble and let the bubble float away...far, far away. Another Dr. Eduway gem.

"Eric? Eric, are you okay?" Bea is standing in front of me, her hand resting on my elbow.

"Yeah...yeah, sorry, I...thanks."

"Don't take it personally. He's a complete dick to pretty much everybody except his friends. You kind of get used to it."

I can't help but smile a little. "Thanks for havin' my back."

"Yeah, of course. Not a big deal." She shrugs like it's nothing, but the lingering pink in her cheeks says otherwise. "Let's get this finished up, huh? I'll go get the balloons."

With five minutes left until the bell, we complete the entrance curtain and fist bump in honor of our accomplishment (Christina was right--it needed a finishing touch).

Bea pulls out her phone and says, "Teddy already told me you're not on any socials, but what's your number?"

"Uh…" I intone, like an idiot. Is there any okay way to decline? It's not like she's some random stranger I can give a fake number to. But starting up a text chain with her seems like a bad idea, lesbian or not. *Oh shit, if I don't give her my number, will she think it has something to do with that, like I'm a homophobe or something? Shit…* I blurt out my number. Three seconds later, my phone chimes in my back pocket. I pull it out to add her to my contacts and see what she's sent.

"My address," she confirms, "…in case you change your mind about coming to the party on Saturday. The house with the big detached garage--green doors and an American flag painted on the side. You can't miss it."

Then before I can repeat my thanks-but-no-thanks, she adds, "Just for the record, I'm not actually gay. That's a rumor that got started way back. People didn't believe me when I said I wasn't, so I stopped bothering to correct them."

"Ah, gotcha. And neither am I--gay, I mean."

Her eyebrows rise just a fraction and only for a second, but it's enough to make me think my orientation might have been one of the things she'd been asking Teddy about. Is the look on her face, relief? Or disappointment? It's so damn hard to tell.

"Noted." She gives me a last little smile and jogs off to join her team lining up in the hall for their grand entrance.

As I watch her go, I can't help but notice her nice legs...toned and tan and--*STOP! What the hell is wrong with you, White? Why did you feel the need to clarify that for her? Why not let her assume you're gay and keep it platonic and simple. God, so fucking stupid...*

Maybe it was some evolutionary, groin-deep impulse to present myself as a prospective mate. Maybe it was that I'd genuinely enjoyed hanging out with Bea DeLuca. She was easy to talk to, not to mention funny and self-confident and willing to step in to defend a virtual stranger. Well, whatever it was that pushed me to keep that possible-romance door cracked open, I'd have to be more on my guard in the future. For instance, there is no way I can give in to the part of me that wants to show up at her house Saturday. I can easily picture myself in a lounge chair, breathing in the smell of sunscreen and grilled meat, listening to the laughter and squeals from the pool as some guy cannonballs in and drenches everyone. But then the bell rings, and I remember that I don't deserve to have friends or go to their pool parties. Especially not after how I acted at my own.

Summer before Freshman Year: Saturday, August 26
Rejecting Kendra

Mom made me invite Kendra Daniels to my fourteenth birthday pool party. Well, not Kendra specifically. At least five of the 100 kids on my guest list had to be from Youth Group because Mom worried I was becoming "disconnected from the church community" (which I was--on purpose--due to the general lameness of, well..."the church community"). I chose Kendra as one of the five because Mom thought she was a "lovely, thoughtful, intelligent young woman" and the two of them were, like, book buddies or something. They could hang out in the pool house and talk about *Pride and Prejudice* or whatever classic novel no one else read unless a teacher made them. Chaperone distraction? Check.

Okay, so another reason I invited Kendra was because I maybe felt a *tiny* bit guilty. We'd met in second grade when she first showed up at Sunday School with her two long braids, lacey socks, and saddle shoes, getting all concerned because we were taking liberties with our Bible story reenactments. I stood up for her when the other kids teased her about not having a TV and believing that all talking animals were demon possessed or something. And for years we'd build Lego cities and make crazy smoothie concoctions whenever she tagged along with her mom to the Women's Bible Study group at our house. But things got awkward when she switched from homeschooling to public school in sixth grade and seemed to expect we'd partner up in class and eat lunch together and all that. I didn't want to be a jerk, but...she didn't fit in with my usual crew. When she backed off after a couple weeks, I'd felt relieved...but also kinda crummy.

So I figured an invite to *the* party of the summer was a good way to make it up to her. The rest of the guest list was pretty much a who's who of the incoming freshman class. Even guys a grade ahead I knew from sports had been angling for a coveted invite. My birthday parties had gained a reputation over the years--and not without good reason. First of all, my house was dope. It had an entire floor dedicated to recreation and entertainment: a pool table, air hockey, four bowling lanes, a gaming area with multiple screens and specialty gaming chairs, and a home theatre with three rows of reclining seats. Outside we had a custom-built pool with an attached hot tub, corkscrew slide, diving board, and waterfall.

Yeah, our pool had a fucking waterfall.

Then there were all the extras just for the party. We rented a huge tent with a catered buffet table stocked with food and drinks all night long and tables that would get cleared at dark when the DJ took over and the black light came on to illuminate the glow accessories and body paint I'd ordered.

Mom, with her lower-middle class upbringing, always worried us kids were going to grow up spoiled and entitled. But Dad, whose old-money family had literal mansions in Boston and Cape Cod didn't see a problem with us growing up "in comfort." It was an ongoing point of contention between them, but tradeoffs and compromises kept the peace. Like, Mom would go along with the $10,000 birthday parties so long as Dad didn't press about sending us to private school. I liked public school, so it was a win-win for me.

By 5:48 p.m., everything was set to go. The anticipation fizzed through my limbs. I would have liked to burn some of that energy swimming, but I thought it would make a better impression if I positioned myself on a lounge chair by the edge of the pool, all nonchalant, Coke in hand, like all this was no big deal. Ellen sat at the edge of the pool, tilting her head at different angles trying to take a selfie with the waterfall behind her. Mom sprayed sunscreen on Charlie and reminded me and Ellen we better put some on too, even though it was way past midday and I already had an enviable summer tan going. Over at the pool house bar, Dad double checked his mixology supplies. He never missed a chance to schmooze prospective voters, so some of my guest's parents got an ultra-select invite to the "adult" side-party. It was billed as "helping to chaperone," but two drinks in, most of them were having far too much fun to supervise much of anything.

Over the next hour, the guests found their way to the pool, all smiles, hand slaps, hugs, and "happy birthdays." I basked in the streaming light of their attention. As the crowd grew, I filled a plate with Dinosaur BBQ ribs and mingled in the tent awhile before losing my shirt and executing a perfect dive into the deep end.

I joined Gavin Holmes and a group of guys in one corner of the pool to judge which girls filled out their bathing suits the best this year. "Who's that?" One asked, pointing to a skinny girl in a black one-piece. I had to squint to make her out (people look different when they're wet). The suit didn't accentuate much, even if there had been curves to accentuate in the first place, and she looked stiff and nervous, clinging to the pool's edge. She turned towards us and I placed her face.

"Oh, that's Kendra Daniels."

"Who?"

"Wait, isn't she the high school principal's daughter?"

"Dude, EJ, I thought you were only inviting *hot* girls."

I rolled my eyes. "My mom made me invite some people. She thinks Kendra's *nice*."

"My brother says 'nice' is code for boring."

"Yeah, girls who think holding hands is putting out." That gets a good laugh, and I quickly join in.

"So what, your mom's like, trying to set you up with her?"

"Yikes, man."

"No, Mom thinks I'm still too *young* to date."

They burst out laughing, I knew immediately that I'd revealed the wrong thing. My heartbeat pounded in my ears as blood flooded my face.

"Awe, you still mommy's little boy?"

I quirked an eyebrow and hoped I wasn't blushing. "Hey, what my mom doesn't know can't hurt her. I got plenty goin' on."

"Yeah man, didn't you know EJ's been bangin' Lydia Sevanis all summer?"

"Seriously?!"

I shrugged one shoulder and took a swig from my fourth Coke.

"Oh, dude, she is fuckin' hot!"

In truth, Lydia and I had only edged toward third base, over the underwear stuff. But by the end of the summer...who knew?

One of the guys looks back at Kendra and shakes his head. "Well, at least you're safe from bad setups for now, huh? I mean, just look." Kendra was awkwardly hoisting herself out of the pool and running over to a stack of towels.

Gavin snorts. "Yeah, total NBN." No Bra Necessary.

They busted out laughing again. I took another swig of Coke and reminded myself that it was Mom's fault Kendra was in this position, surrounded by people who would never choose to socialize with her.

After most people had eaten their fill of BBQ, I helped Mom cut slices of cake and put them on plates before taking the large, heavily frosted one I'd set aside for myself and looking for the best seat. Which table would I grace with my presence? As (bad) luck would have it, I was standing right in front of a half-full table where four Youth Group kids were sitting. The Baker twins sat on the far side of the table in their matching Sabers jerseys, wolfing down massive slices of cake. On the other side, Kendra and Frankie Gurlance sat next to each other-- her scraping the frosting off her vanilla cake and him sitting with arms crossed, not even touching his. No one was talking to each other. As if sensing me there, Kendra looked up and we made eye contact. My heart sank. Now I was stuck. Mom was standing five feet behind me, so I didn't dare diss. It wasn't worth the flack I'd catch for it later. So I pasted on a smile and sat in a chair to Kendra's right, leaving an open chair between us.

"Hey guys, having fun?" I tried.

"Oh, yeah, for sure," one of the Baker twins (I could never tell them apart) assured me, then remembering their manners, added, "Hey man, thanks for inviting us."

"Oh sure. I'm glad you guys could make it." *Not.*

"Yeah, *thanks…*" mumbled Frankie. He looked bored and irritated. Maybe his parents made him come. Sure, he was a year older than me, and Ellen's best friend's brother, but also he had serious acne and the same bad haircut since he was eight. This had to be the coolest party he'd ever been to. *What a waste of an invite.*

I turned to Kendra instead, who gave me the bland smile she did when she wasn't sure what to say. My gut squeezed with guilt about laughing along with Gavin and those guys earlier. *She couldn't have overheard...could she? No...no, don't be paranoid.* I search my brain for something about her that would make for decent conversation. "Hey Kendra, are you doing the MasterMinds again this year?"

She brightened right away. "Yeah, definitely."

"Cool." *Sooooo very not.* "You guys did really amazing last year, especially that matchup against Fairport."

"You watched our match?" Her eyes widened.

"I caught a bit of it," I admitted. I'd only gone to their lame competition because I had time to kill after school that day before Mom came to pick me up...and I kinda liked to listen to the questions and know that I could win if I were playing.

"You saved it in the second round with the answer to that Sleepy Hollow question. And I bet your team wouldn't have won the final without your lightning math skills," I praised her.

She blushed, never guessing that I was backhandedly calling her a math geek. "Yeah, I like math, but I'm not as good as you. In sixth grade, you never got less than a ninety-five on the homework." Her blush deepened and she quickly filled her mouth with cake.

Okaaay, she remembers my homework scores from three years ago... 'cause that's not weird or anything. "Well," I continued with my compliment, "You were definitely one of the team's top players."

She shrugged and wilted a little. "I was only fifth in overall points."

I smiled reflexively, wanting to put her at ease. "Well, maybe, but for sure you're the number one cutest player there."

Oh God... The blood drained from my skull. *What the hell was that? Damn reflexive flattery!*

Kendra's ears had turned an astonishing shade of red. "Um...thanks, EJ. That's...that's sweet of you to say." She looked down and bit her lip to hide the elated grin that had taken over her entire face.

Frankie, on the other hand, was looking at me like I was a pile of dog poop he'd stepped in.

When Kendra noticed Frankie's expression, her smile faltered. I could tell she was rethinking things, gauging whether I'd been teasing. Deciding that must be it, she stabbed half-heartedly at the globs of frosting she'd scraped off.

A small fist of anger tightened in my stomach. Why had Frankie gone and made her feel bad? And now Kendra was going to think *I* was the jerk.

So I doubled down. "I mean it. Red's your color. You even had that pretty matching headband with the white polka dots and the bow." My voice was nothing but sincere.

Her eyes went wide, astounded that I remembered her outfit. "Wow...you..." she cleared her throat. "Thanks. I do like red."

The truth was, I distinctly remembered seeing her in that candy apple red turtleneck and thinking how much I hated turtlenecks and how I hadn't worn one since my mom stopped dressing me (i.e. a very long time ago). And the headband made her look like Minnie Mouse. But I'd never tell her that. Unlike Frankie, I liked making people feel better, not worse.

Wanting to secure Kendra's good mood, I added, "Love the shorter hair, by the way,"

"Oh, you think? Me too."

Frankie sneered and pushed his plate of untouched cake away. "Ken, you just told me last week that you *hated* it short and couldn't wait for it to grow out again."

Her ears went red again and she didn't look at either of us as she tried to explain. "I donated the hair to Locks of Love, you know, for cancer patients, so I'm still happy I did it.

Besides, I've been trying some new styles with it since then, so..."

"Well, I like *this* style," I attempted to smooth things over.

She gave me a grateful smile and ran her hand through the limp strands of dishwater brown hair, getting stuck on tangles part way through.

Frankie's sneer grew even more disdainful. "Her hair just dried like that after swimming in the pool, so I don't think it counts as a *style*."

Great, thanks, Frankie. Way to make it awkward for everyone. Asshole.

"Sure it counts," I insisted. "It's the natural look, and I like it."

Kendra just stared at her lap.

Damn it... This party was supposed to be a fun thing for her.

Before I could figure out a way to salvage the situation, Mom called me over for a family photo. Once I'd gotten situated under the balloon arch with Ellen on my right and Charlie in front, I looked back over to see Kendra and Frankie arguing. I couldn't tell from that distance what they were saying, but I was pleased to think that Kendra was telling him off for being such a lousy party guest.

By the time the sun set, most people were drying off or getting a final helping of food while the tables got removed from the soon-to-be dance floor. By the time the DJ came on and the dark lights came up, pretty much everyone had found their way back to the tent. I ran inside and grabbed the glow stick kits and body paint and helped a bunch of girls paint designs on their bare backs with the tips of my fingers and tried to manage my proto erection.

Once things got going, I started dancing with a group of girls. Lydia Sevanis, my aforementioned summer makeout partner, was one of them, and the looks she kept giving me while she did her music video dance moves were both turning me on and freaking me out. What if Mom noticed and made an embarrassing chaperone scene? But all the adults were occupied at the pool house on the other side of the yard, talking and laughing over drinks. Even Mom had her back to us, hands gesticulating as she told some story to a group of enthralled listeners.

All was right with my world.

"Help me find your bathroom," Lydia giggled against my ear, her lip gloss sticky against my skin. "I don't wanna get lost." Lydia pulled me halfway across the patio before I got my hand free and looked to see if my parents had noticed our exit. We were closer to the pool house now. Dad had come to stand next to Mom, and I caught the words "Republican Party" over the music. Political talk. Perfect. I still didn't know what Lydia had in mind, but I was sure it wasn't something I wanted my parents to catch us doing.

"Come on!" she called and grabbed my arm so it was pressed against her chest. Her tank-top was damp and one of her bikini straps hung loose down her shoulder.

"Through here." I led her in the back door, past the pool and ping pong tables, past the laundry room to the basement's walk-in storage area. Our old couch was in there, and I was hoping it would be... useful. I'd only opened the door an inch before hitting something heavy propped against it. A muffled gasp came from inside.

"Uh-oh," Lydia giggled again. "I guess it's already in use."

I banged on the door with my fist, my enthusiasm turning to frustration. How dare someone else be using my basement closet for their own make-out session. It was my party, so I wanted first dibs.

"WHO'S IN THERE?"

"...EJ?"

What on earth... "Kendra?"

"Y-yes. I-I'm so sorry. I didn't know—I wanted—I'm sorry." She sounded all choked up.

"Um...are you hurt?"

"No...no, I'm okay."

Lydia rolled her eyes and crossed her arms, clearly expecting me to take care of this as quickly as possible.

I'm trying, I mouthed. "So...do you think you can come out now? I, uh, kind of need something out of there..."

"...Do you think... Can we call my parents to pick me up? I don't have a cell phone, so..."

Shit! I did not have time for this. If Kendra's parents might want to talk to my parents, who might want me to explain what happened and why Kendra wanted to leave early...and I might not get another chance like this with Lydia for weeks-- maybe never again!

"Here, Kendra, why don't you let me in, okay? Please?"

There were some loud snuffling noises and then the scraping noise of something being moved away from the door. When I opened the door though, Kendra was sitting back down on some boxes by the back wall.

I gave Lydia a pleading look. "I gotta check on her quick."

"I'm sure she's fine. Come on, let's just find somewhere else—your house is *huge*."

But it was too late for that. "Just give me a couple minutes to take care of this," I whispered.

She bunched her damp, dark curls in one hand and pushed my shoulder with the other. "Hurry up then." I nodded and motioned for her to wait around the corner.

Then I slipped in and shut the door behind me. In the harsh light of the overhead LED bulb, Kendra's face was puffed and blotchy, like she'd been crying in here for a while.

"What happened?" I asked, infusing my voice with concern and sympathy.

"Nothing. I mean, Frankie was just being so mean. He—said stuff…"

I sat down next to her, put an arm around her shoulder, and doled out my newly 14-year-old wisdom. "You can't let a loser like Frankie get to you. Don't let him ruin your night. Just ignore him; totally ignore him. See, when you don't give him the reaction he wants, he'll shut up and move on."

"Just because he's older, he thinks he knows everything. And just because he's a guy he thinks—" She broke off and looked at me nervously.

"He thinks what?"

"…It's just that he's so bossy lately. Like he always knows better than me."

"Yeah…what a pain. I hate guys like that."

"Like he's my father or my brother or…something. Like I can't tell if someone is a good person on my own."

"You're absolutely right. You should go out there and find him and show him he can't mess with you. That he can't tell you what to do and make you mad or whatever. Y'know—

have confidence." I was saying whatever I thought would get her up and out of the storage room, but she smiled at me like I was her own personal ministering angel.

"You're such a good guy, EJ," she sighed as she leaned her head on my shoulder.

*Oh crap...This is not what I need right now...*I stared at the door, afraid that Lydia would get tired of waiting and leave me sitting here holding the wrong girl.

"Anyway, Kendra, I think you better get back out there. Frankie was looking for you. Maybe he wanted to apologize," I lied.

"Oh, who cares. Let him look." She snuggled even closer into my shoulder.

"Yeah, but uh, you don't want him, like, telling my parents you're missing. They might come looking too...We don't want them to find us in here."

"Oh...right" Her sense of propriety seemed to take over. She was no Lydia.

We both stood up, and I kept a hand on her back to help guide her to the door. But as we reached it, she turned around in one sudden motion and kissed me. It was clumsy and inexperienced, just kind of crushing her mouth against mine, but she was beaming and flushed when we separated.

"I'm sorry," she breathed. "I didn't even mean to. I mean, I did but I didn't." She laughed and put her fingertips on her lips.

"Um, it's okay...We really should go now." I reached for the knob.

"Wait! Um...I was thinking, do you maybe want to come over after church on Sunday? My parents wouldn't let me go out with you alone, but they wouldn't mind if you came and ate with us and we could hang out and…I don't know…maybe we could even go see a Red Wings game sometime. My father takes us to home games, and I can usually invite someone…" She rambled on with date ideas while I tried to not look as horrified as I felt. Clearly, she'd gotten the wrong idea about us—namely, that there was any kind of *us*. Okay, so, maybe all those compliments earlier had given her a reason to think I…but that was just…being nice!

Impatient and uncomfortable, I interrupted her, "Kendra, I'm not allowed to date yet either, so…I don't think any of that is going to work."

"But it wouldn't be *serious* dating…more like, a friendship building to more--someday. I could even ask your mom—"

"No! No…look," I was running out of excuses, and I really did not have time for this. "I'm not really interested in you…like *that*…not as a girlfriend." She just froze there, still and waxy, "Do you know what I mean? I like you as a friend, and that's all…Okay?"

She still didn't move.

"Okay?" I shook her lightly by the shoulder and she jerked away.

"Oh God," she moaned and hugged herself.

"Kendra, I'm sorry if I—"

"Never mind—just, never mind." She squeezed her eyes shut and yanked at the door. It swung open to reveal a guilty looking Lydia, straightening up from listening at the door. A single mortified sob escaped Kendra's throat as she fled.

I hesitated, unsure if I should follow. I may not have *like* liked her, but I still didn't feel right about leaving her a mess…and angry at me now instead of Frankie.

But then Lydia rushed inside and grabbed my arm. "What was all *that* about?"

"Like you didn't hear."

"I didn't get much. The door's too thick. So, spill."

I shook my head. "She...she asked me out..."

"What?! Kendra Daniels? Kendra Daniels asked you out? Is she crazy?" Lydia started laughing.

Again, remembering my earlier comments made over cake, I felt the tiniest prick of guilt. And what had possessed me to tell Lydia the truth? Of all moments my white lies would have done some good. "No...I mean, yeah. I don't know what...I think I should go check on her."

Lydia stopped laughing and tilted her head to one side. She ran her hands over my shoulders before linking them behind my neck. "Awe, you are too sweet, EJ. But that'll just give her false hope, y'know? Best to just let her cry it out somewhere else."

"But—"

She stopped me with her glossy lips, and I lost my train of thought. Hers were wet, grasping kisses, full of tongue and moans—the kind you see in porn videos. Nothing like the pathetic kiddy-smack from Kendra.

Kendra...shit. I felt another pang of guilt strong enough for me to pull back an inch. *I should go check on her. What if she goes back outside and Mom sees her...*

"What's wrong, EJ? Don't you want your birthday present?" asked Lydia as she laid down her folded towel and got to her knees, her fingers unbuttoning the top of my jeans.

If the thought of what was about to happen didn't erase every other thought from my mind, I might have felt guilty for a more appropriate amount of time, might have gone after Kendra

105

and tried to apologize more thoroughly. I might have even bothered to make up a reason to keep Lydia from telling all her friends that Kendra Daniels had asked out EJ White and gotten herself turned down flat because "tens don't date fours."

I might have, but I didn't.

I had no idea what the party-related gossip about Kendra ended up being or how bad it got socially for her because of it. I didn't ask and didn't want to know. But mostly, I just didn't care.

Senior Year: Saturday, September 28
A Risky Invitation

At 12:28, Saturday afternoon, tragedy strikes.

Charlie's blood-curdling scream comes from the second floor, jarring Dad and Ellen from their phones. Aunt Kari--who's already on her feet putting the leftover quiche in the fridge--rushes to the bottom of the back kitchen stairs. "Charlie, what's wrong? Are you hurt? Is Maddie okay?"

We hear the patter of four small feet racing down the stairs.

"LOOK!" Charlie thrusts his favorite--and now armless--Captain America action figure up towards Aunt Kari's face. "Look what she did!" He clutches the dismembered limbs in his other hand.

"Oh honey…" She gently takes the tiny arms from him and tries to pull him in for a hug, but he backs away and swings an accusatory finger towards Maggie where she crouches at the bottom of the stairs, clinging to the railing.

"She did it on purpose," he insists.

Aunt Kari sits next to her daughter on the bottom step. "I think it was probably an accident, right Maggie?"

"I wanted to see how far his arms could stretch," she pouted, gazing up at her mother with those big brown eyes of hers, luminous with imminent tears. "I didn't know he would break."

"LIAR!" Charlie's own eyes overflow with huge drops that cascade down his face.

I take a knee and pull him close. "I'm so sorry, buddy...I know he was special." A bashed-up knee the first day he rode his bike without training wheels. Mom got him Cap as a reward for being so brave when they put the stitches in.

"He's ruined..." Charlie gulped out between sobs. "Ruined!"

"Don't worry, son. We'll get you a new one," Dad assures him.

This promise only makes Charlie wail at top lung capacity.

I glare at Dad, hoping he'll remember, but he frowns at me, clearly not getting it.

Meanwhile, once Ellen saw no one was injured (no human, anyway), she left the kitchen for the relative peace of the living room. She's been glued to her phone all weekend, smiling and giggling and texting at top speed. Any and all interruptions were unwelcome.

"Here, let me see him," I tell Charlie, gently uncurling his fingers from around Cap's torso. White plastic strips stick out from the empty sockets. Maggie must have been pulling pretty darn hard to get them to snap. Aunt Kari holds the arms out to me. She is immobilized with Maggie cradled in her lap, rocking her back and forth. I take them and hold them up to the socket. Yeah--most definitely busted.

"Can you fix him?" Charlie looks up at me, desperate with hope.

"Hmm…" I scramble for some solution and wish I had any fix-it skills whatsoever. "I think we can super glue them back on."

"But then his arms won't be able to move anymore, right?"

When I don't reply, the spark of hope fizzles into whimpering as Charlie collapses on the floor.

Dad bends over Charlie and says, "Come on now. Enough of that. You're too old to be acting like this. I told you I'd get you a new one."

"I don't want a new one. My Cap was special. Now he'll never be the same again…" Charlie curls into the fetal position.

Dad isn't having it. "Get up off the floor. Toys get broken. You're being ridiculous. And you're making Maggie sad."

That does move Charlie to his feet, his tear-streaked face flush with anger, wielding an accusatory finger in Maggie's direction. "She should be sad! This is her fault! She broke him *on purpose.*"

"Charlie, that's not true," Aunt Kari says calmly.

"IT IS! You weren't there. You didn't see," His insists with desperation.

"Charlie…" I put an arm around his shoulder but he shrugs me off, leaving me unsure what to do. I can't fix Cap, so what good am I?

Maggie has started to hiccup. "I'm sorry for--*hic*--breaking him," she says in a small voice, peeping cautiously at Charlie. "It was an accident."

"Liar." He balls his hands into fists and takes a step towards her, his voice and body quivering with the force of his feelings. "*I hate you.*"

"Charlie!" Dad and Aunt Kari say at the same time.

I wince. Dad's heard this sentiment before, but not from his *younger* son.

"That is not the way we speak to one another, young man." Dad moves between Charlie and the object of his ire. "Now it's you who needs to apologize."

The look Charlie gives Dad--face scrunched and eyes narrowed--telegraphs he has some choice words for Dad as well. But whatever they are, he holds them in.

Dad takes a beat but doesn't flinch. "Apologize to your cousin. Now."

"I won't," he grunts through a clenched jaw. His eyes never leave Dad's. "You can't make me."

Dad's face is every bit as hard as his younger son's. His hand moves to take Charlie by the arm, or maybe the shoulder. Whatever the hand's intended destination, Charlie dodges the incoming grip and darts past Dad, through the mud room, and out the back door.

The screen door slams behind him, leaving us in shocked silence, punctuated only by Maggie's hiccups.

Regaining himself, Dad turns to Aunt Kari, "Has this happened before? A tantrum like this?"

Aunt Kari opens her mouth then closes it. After considering, she says slowly, "He gets...very upset sometimes, when things don't go his way...but not like this."

"It's because it was Cap," I try to explain. "Mom gave it to him, after his bike accident. Remember? As a reward for being brave."

This added information doesn't have the softening effect I anticipated. At least not with Dad.

"His mother bought him most of the toys he owns. That's no excuse for this kind of behavior."

"I know, but..." It was scary, seeing my normally sweet little brother exploding with anger like that. Scary because I recognized it from experience. "Forcing him to apologize like that was a crappy solution. Clearly."

Aunt Kari sighs and stands, holding Maggie to her chest.

God, I realize, *what a shit position she's in.* Trying to be a surrogate mom to three messed up kids while raising her own.

"I'm gonna take Maggie upstairs to lay down. And Jim, I think you better give Charlie some time to cool off before going after him."

"Right..." Dad closes his eyes, taking slow breaths in and out as her footsteps fade. On the table, his phone rings.

I look at him. He looks at me.

Then he steps to the table and answers the phone.

And I walk into the living room because I just can't...

Ellen is lounging on the couch, her face radiating delight at whatever's on her phone.

I stand there staring at her, but she ignores me. "Thanks a lot, El. You were a huge help with that."

She looks up, any pleasure wiped from her expression. "What exactly did you want me to do?"

Good question. "Just...something."

It comes out lame and pathetic and I regret saying anything at all. She looks at me until I turn and walk back to the kitchen in search of super glue and rubber bands.

A few minutes later, my phone chimes. I set Cap (now strapped in his rubber band straightjacket) on top of the fridge and check the text.

> **Teddy**--Hey you coming to
> the game today???

I have to give Mackenzie credit for persistence. He's been trying to get me to come to one of his games since we made our deal. That I keep turning down the invitations only seems to make him more determined to get me there.

> **Teddy**-Come on, please?!
> It'll be more fun than
> experimenting on your hair
> or whatever else you're
> doing right now

Considering the afternoon we're having here at *Chez Madison,* it would be nice to get out of the house for a few hours... I could bring Charlie with me, cheer him up a bit... My phone chimes again.

> **Bea**--You totally should!
> We'll save you a seat on
> the 50 yard line

Wait, this is a group chat? I'm part of a group chat now? *Oh God...*

> **Teddy**--There see now you
> can't say no

Bea--Yeah, you owe me for
the other day

Teddy--Owes you for what?
What happened? What did
I miss???

Bea--sorry...it's a secret ;-)

Teddy--You two have been
friends for a whole week
and you're already keeping
secrets from me?
Oh I see how it is--
and I DO NOT LIKE IT

I can't help but smile. *Aw, what the hell...*

> **Eric**--Relax already.
> I'll come to your stupid
> game. Happy?

Teddy--YES!!!!
Come by the sideline and
say hi and explain
why you owe Bea

> **Eric**--Fine
> God you're needy

Teddy--Yup
See ya soon buddy

Bea--Woohoo! Consider
your seat saved :-)

I shake my head as I put my phone back in my packet. *Going to a football game...what the hell are you thinking, White?* Okay, so maybe this is a terrible idea, but it won't be like I'm on the field or anything. Yeah...I can handle sitting in the stands for a football game.

I think.

Maybe...

Well, I guess we'll see.

Junior Year: Saturday, November 17
One Step From States

"LI-ONS! LI-ONS! LI-ONS! LI-ONS!" I chanted and pumped my fist in the air with the rest of my team as we exited the stadium locker room. Our New York State Semi-Final victory was total and complete. 49-21 final score, 286 passing yards, zero interceptions, and a personal best and school-record-setting sixty-two yard pass for the last touchdown of the game. We'd dominated. *I'd* dominated. My system was so pumped full of endorphins.

And it wasn't just a temporary, post-game high. Getting picked at QB1 back in August was like a magic spell that broke the curse. Each victory cleared the heavy fog I'd been surrounded in for the past year, stumbling between shrouded traps like Dead-Mom-Morass, Swamp-of-Existential-Emptiness, and It's-Not-Fair-Flatlands.

Therapy with Dr. Eduway *had* helped some. But even with all the mental and physical exercises, adjustments to my routines, and methods to redirect my thought patterns...God, it had taken months to make any difference whatsoever. Sometimes I felt even shitter when I walked out than when I walked in. It just reminded me of how messed up my life was. How messed up *I* was. Dr. Eduway claimed that my grief needed to take its natural course and that it was important we continue to explore the underlying causes of my behaviors, and that slow and steady progress was better than any temporary, quick fix.

Luckily, Dad had seen through the doc's conveniently self-serving rationale. He wasn't paying a hundred-and-fifty bucks an hour for the indefinite future when it was obvious that I'd found what I needed to get back to good. Winning football games meant winning at life. It was that simple.

A crowd of girls decked out in red and white Lions gear were waiting by the bus. "EJ!" they called over and over until I ran a hand through my shower-wet hair and joined them for selfies. Most were on the young side. "Fresh Meat Freshmen," as some of the guys called them. One with serious curves and a bright red shoulder-length wig shoved something into my pocket while I posed with her. Another swung her leg up so her inner thigh pressed against my crotch. She moved it up and down a couple times before rushing away with her giggling friends.

Some of the other team stars also stopped for pictures. D'Marcus Clay, tight end and fellow team captain, had his arms draped over two girls' shoulders, telling them something that made them giddy. Probably inviting them to his after party.

Coach Bleaker leaned out the bus door and whistled to get our attention. "Alright, gentlemen, wrap it up with your fan club and load in."

I posted a post-game bus selfie with a thanks to my teammates and all the fans then spent the better part of the two-hour ride home finishing off a family-sized bag of Cheese Doodles and scrolling through social media on my phone. There were a total of 102 recent @QBEJWhite mentions and tags. My favorites were Ellen's posts--videos and pics of my best plays; a selfie of her; Dad, and Charlie in the stands; Charlie stuffing his face with a chili cheese dog that made me laugh out loud. But it wasn't just me feeling the love--the whole team was trending. The official school athletics #LionsFootball hashtag had surged to a grand total of 3,879 results, up from 2,682 the week before. Not to mention all the posts using #AllTheWayToState and #LionsPride. Every local station covered the game and posted links to highlights, always featuring my incredible final touchdown pass. It gave me a thrill every time I rewatched it.

Once I finished checking posts (and made sure my own post had gotten plenty of likes), I started reading and responding to the glut of congratulatory texts and DMs. Some included more hookup invites with pics as bait. Most were "top shots"-- waist to head with push-up bras and come-hither looks. A few were closeups of body parts, like a single, hard-nippled breast or a shaved pussy barely concealed under a triangle of black lace. Those would be fun to look through some other time, in private.

But the text that got me the most excited didn't have a visual to go with it. It read:

Hey champ!
See you tonight at

115

dmarcus party
Got a reward for you ;-)
XOXO

Mmm, Tara Kajowski...I imagined her sitting on the cheerleaders' bus behind us--her sun-gold hair loosed from its tight game-time ponytail, her pleated skirt flaring out over her round, ample ass--and contemplated what my "reward" would entail.

Four seats up on the right sat Kevin Markone--my backup quarterback and Tara's ex. When he tore his Achilles tendon last year, I stepped in and led us to the Section V title. Then this season, he'd expected Coach to hand him back his starting position, like it was his right because he was a senior and I was a junior. Thankfully, Coach went by merit, and I outplayed Kevin all through August training. I earned my starting spot fair and square, but Kevin had still spent the whole season whining like a little bitch, trying to get the other players to pressure Coach to swap him back in, to say they didn't respect me as a leader.

D'Marcus eventually put a stop to that bullshit. Winning games was the priority. Attracting scouts, getting players noticed, snagging scholarships--that was key. And D'Marcus knew I'd helped make that happen. But Kevin never got on board. Even now that I'd led us all the way to State, he still managed to pout. It was selfish and pathetic. He didn't deserve a girl like Tara. And if he was gonna be a kill-joy, he should stay home tonight and not bring down the mood at the party.

***

We pulled into the school parking lot at 8:47 p.m., and with my adrenaline spent, I couldn't help yawning as I walked the line of parked cars. Each vehicle was decked out with a variety of "Go Team" type slogans and the names and numbers of specific players. Before the quarter-finals in Buffalo, Ellen, Charlie, and I had painted up Dad's bimmer until the windshield was the only part not plastered with school spirit.

"About to crash?" Dad asked, slapping me on the back.

"Yeah," I admitted, leaning up against the car. "But if we can swing by Starbucks, I'll down some caffeine before you drop me off at D'Marcus's place."

"You sure? I'm ready to pass out myself, and I was only *watching*."

"Dad, the quarterback can't skip the afterparty."

He grunts in grudging agreement. "Well, let's get going then. Your brother's already asleep in the back."

"Where's Ellen?"

"She's going home with Andrea Gurlance for a sleepover. Oh God...John Daniels is coming this way."

John Daniels, Kendra's father, was the high school principal and served as a church elder with Dad. Mom and Dad had always been united in their dislike of him. Mom because he was "the worst kind of mansplainer" and Dad because he micromanaged projects and then took personal credit for group efforts.

"Pretend we didn't see him?" I suggested.

"Too late." Dad grimaced and returned Mr. Daniels' wave. "Be polite."

"Yeah, Dad, like I'm gonna be rude to the principal."

Dad put on his photo-op smile.

"John, good to see you. Oh, hello, Kendra."

Only after Dad greeted her did I notice Kendra there half hidden behind her father, looking down at the pavement.

"Hello, Jim, EJ," Mr. Daniels greeted us. "You played a heck of a game today, young man."

"Thank you, sir."

"He certainly did," Dad agreed. "Let's hope he's got one more like that in him."

"Yes indeed. One more will do the trick. By the way, Jim, I wondered if you'd received the updated architectural blueprints for the new fellowship hall?"

"Y'know, I haven't gotten a chance to stop by the church and look those over yet."

"Ah, well, you're in luck. I have a copy here in the car, just down the row here. We could take a look now. That way you'll be ready to discuss the changes at the meeting tomorrow."

"Ah yes, well, I guess I can take a minute..." Dad managed to keep his smile in place as he followed Mr. Daniels to his car.

Kendra and I stayed behind, silent and awkward. We hadn't really talked since my mother's funeral over a year ago, which gave me the slightest twinge of guilt.

I cleared my throat. "Hey."

"Hey..." She chewed on her lip and took a step closer, like she was working up the courage to say something. The bimmer's headlights illuminated the grease along her unevenly parted hair and an acne breakout across her forehead she hadn't even tried to cover up. And then there were the clothes--too-short khaki pants that sagged around her slim hips and a loose pink sweater with frayed cuffs and a yellow stain down the front. She had a weird sense of fashion, dressing too young for her age. But she'd always been neat and clean and well groomed. This look...it was more like she'd stopped giving a shit.

Mom would have been all over this situation. She always had this way with people, making them feel safe and listened to and cared for. And they would open up to her about this crazy stuff that they'd never told a single soul before. Dad jokingly called her "The Vault" because she never broke a confidence. Yeah...Mom would have known exactly what to say at this moment.

I, on the other hand, managed to come up with "So...thanks for comin' to the game."

Splotches of pink flared on her cheeks as soon as I spoke. "Oh yes, we, uh...the game was...it was great, and um...you played..."

I continued to smile and waited for her to decide on the right compliment. She was even more tongue tied than usual. Maybe she was still a bit overawed by my recent star-making performance.

"You were amazing," she finally managed.

"Thanks."

We lapsed back into silence. I ventured a look toward the Daniels' minivan but saw no sign of Dad's return. *Come on already!*

"So, um...I was wondering..." Kendra began, and I had a strong sense I wouldn't want to talk about whatever came next. "...I was actually wondering how you've been? I mean, besides football, like, in general...without your mom?"

Shit. She had to go there. "Oh...um," I felt a sudden dizziness and put a hand on the hood of the car to steady myself. "Okay...yeah, good. Thanks for asking. How's your year been so far?" I tried to redirect.

"Um, okay, I guess." She dropped her gaze and picked on the cuff of her sleeve, like some kind of nervous tic. "Actually, not so great."

I thought of Mom and made myself ask, "Oh? Did something happen?"

Kendra kicked at some loose gravel with the toe of her Sketchers. "Just...stuff with my parents... They think...they don't want me to... Nevermind."

"No, you can tell me--"

"No, really, I shouldn't have... This is your big night."

So true. I had a party to get to and a hot girl to hook up with. I didn't have time to take on whatever family drama Kendra was going through right now. And yet, my relief at her retreat was tinged with familiar guilt. She'd been there for me at Mom's funeral--letting me literally cry on her shoulder--and I owed her something for that. *Damn it...* "Another time then? I mean, if you need somebody to talk to about...whatever."

Kendra's eyes snapped up to mine. "Really?" Her voice was hushed but intense. Too intense.

Oh God, what did I set myself up for? I keep up the smile as I hedge, "Uh, yeah, really. Like, once the season is over."

"Yes, right, absolutely! Maybe we can hang out at the next Teen Skate or--"

Then, like some miracle, Dad was back, Mr. Daniels striding behind him. I caught Dad's eye and gave a smile I hoped conveyed the right message.

He did not disappoint. "Well, we gotta get going. But we'll see you at church tomorrow--maybe even before! You folks going to the pancake breakfast fundraiser at Applebee's? We're planning on getting there for the 9:00 seating."

"We prefer to avoid the crowd and take the earliest seating at 7:00. I'd highly recommend it. The parking is closer, the food is fresher, and the tables are cleaner." Mr. Daniels counseled us.

I turned away to hide an eye roll.

"Ah, very good to know. Thanks for the inside scoop." Always the politician, Dad was a pro at pretending to appreciate whatever unsolicited advice people gave him.

"As a principal, you get to be a pro at these sorts of things," Mr. Daniels explained with a condescending little smile.

God, what a dick.

Mr. Daniels beckoned his daughter with a hand. "Kendra, sweetheart, time to go."

"Coming!" She assured him without making eye contact. To me she said, "Um...thanks for, um..."

For what? I hadn't actually done anything for her yet. "Uh, yeah, sure. I'll see you. We'll talk." I gave a last little wave, and she returned it with an embarrassing amount of enthusiasm, triggering another guilt twinge.

As we pulled away, I resolved to find a way to be a better friend to the one person who knew what it was like to lose Mom, who lost her too, and who clearly was not having the all-star year I was.

But then my phone buzzed with a text from Tara. Just a preview with a pic cropped in her Victoria's Secret-worthy cleavage. And just like that, all thoughts of Kendra Daniels disappeared from my brain.

Senior Year: Saturday, September 28
Going to Teddy's Game

I'm not sure what Ohkwali's population is, but it feels like a good half of it has shown up to cheer on their Bears. *Good Lord*, I think as Charlie and I navigate our way around a sizable group of college-age looking girls holding posters aloft declaring "Mackenzie is my Mac-Daddy" and "Marry Me Teddy!" *So this is what it's like to be the biggest fish in a very small pond...not bad. Not bad at all.*

I mean, I had plenty of fans--girls and otherwise in my runup to State, but this feels different. Back in Rochester, even stars who get their team to State don't become household names. Now, get put on trial for a rape, and it's a whole nother story. You're not just a big fish anymore, you're a shark, and *everyone* takes notice.

Oh boohoo, cry me a river, White. I catch myself short before sliding into self-pity. *If you didn't want people to hate you, maybe you shouldn't have raped someone. Or here's an idea--maybe if you wanted people to forgive you, you should have stayed in Juvie and served out the sentence you deserved. And what about Kendra, huh? You think she wanted to be known as that girl who got raped by the DA's son? Kendra, who flushed and slid down in her chair like she wished it would swallow her any time the teacher called on her in class?*

"Can we get our hotdogs now?" Charlie asks, hanging off my arm and bringing me back to the present.

"Yup." I hoist Charlie onto my shoulders so we can move through the crowd more easily and have a better view. The concessions line is ridiculously long and slow moving, and after fifteen minutes, my shoulders start to burn. "Oof, you're getting too big for this, buddy."

Charlie giggles, no doubt liking the idea of growing up, but then tightens his thighs on either side of my neck in a preemptive measure should I consider putting him down.

When there's only four more groups between us and the order counter, I'm assaulted by a mustard packet to the side of my head. "What the--" My blood pressure spikes as I whip around to identify my attacker.

Bea waves from about ten feet where she's waiting near the Order Pickup counter.

I take a couple steps towards her but don't dare lose my place in line. When she closes the distance, I say "What the hell, DeLuca?" trying to sound pissed but not quite pulling it off. "Maybe try calling my name next time?"

She laughs. "I did. I guess you didn't hear me."

"Oh…yeah, it's pretty loud around here." *Damn.* I'm still getting used to responding to Eric when I'm distracted.

"And who might this handsome young man be?" Bea redirects her smile up over my head.

"Hello, I'm Charlie Madison," he replies, using his full Super-secret identity name. He reaches down a hand and she shakes it.

"Nice to meet you, Charlie Madison. I'm Eric's friend Bea. I'm glad you like it up high because we have seats way up top." She motions towards the rows right below the announcer's box. Prime fifty-yard-line real estate. *Dang, she must have gotten here super early.*

"Teddy's been talking about you for weeks, so everyone's *very* excited to meet you," she tells me.

Oh fuck. My gut convulses like she kicked me there. "Uh, who's everyone?"

"Just the parents," she shrugs away my concern. "Teddy's and mine. They won't bite, I promise."

"Oh, uh, cool..." *Not cool. Not cool at all.* We move up in line, the strong smell of nacho cheese now less appetizing than ever.

"And this is *my* brother, Anthony." Bea gestures toward a trim, tan, dark-haired guy about her same height. I vaguely recognize him from around the halls at school, very much owning the space with a hot-shit-and-I-know-it vibe. At the sound of his name, he looks up from his phone.

"Anthony, this is my friend Eric and his little brother Charlie."

"Hey," I say with a short, casual wave.

His expression registers slight amusement. A once up-and-down assessment leaves him visibly unimpressed. He looks back down at his phone but says, "You're Ellen Madison's brother."

Not a question. So Teddy was right--our relation is already common knowledge. I paste on a bland smile. "Uh, yeah."

"Huh." Another glance, like he's trying to reconcile my image with Ellen's. "She's cool," he adds, though with such little affect I can't tell if he just means it as a compliment to her or a dig at me by comparison.

I look at Bea, but her creased brow says she isn't sure either.

A girl behind the counter calls, "Order 148," and Anthony turns and claims a tray laden with four cartons of fries and at least eight foil-wrapped cheeseburgers. I assume it's the whole family's order, but then he hands a single burger to Bea and she says, "Okay, bye."

I do a double take at the shiny pile of food and joke, "Just a light lunch for a growing boy, huh?"

"No, Anthony's got a whole harem to feed," Bea replies teasingly.

Her brother's mouth thins in annoyance. "Uh, friends, you mean? Some of us actually have those."

"Uh, excuse me--friend, right here." Bea gestures toward me with both hands as if presenting a prize on The Price is Right.

He gives his sister a weary, pitying look over his shoulder, but only says, "Tell Mom and Dad I'm going to Drew's with everybody after the game."

"Text them yourself!" she calls after him, but he's already disappeared into the sea of blue and white clad bodies.

"He seems..." I try to come up with something complimentary that won't come off sarcastic or a flat-out lie.

"Yeah, I know," Bea saves me the trouble. "But he's family," she adds with a sigh. "And for the record--I have plenty of friends, from soccer and student council...I just don't go out with them *all the time* like he does. And he and these girls are definitely more than--"

A sudden, high squeal of mic feedback sets off a collective groan and ear covering.

"Sorry about that, folks," a deep male voice comes over the loudspeaker. He races through stadium rules and safety instructions and gets to the main event--reading off the names of the Ohkwali Bears' starting lineup as they run out onto the field.

Bea stands on her tiptoes, but we can't see anything from where we are. "I'm gonna go so I don't miss kickoff. See you up there?"

"Right, yeah, see up there."

As she goes, a student trio starts singing the "The Star-Spangled Banner." I put a hand over my heart and try not to wince when one of the vocalists misses the high note on "land of the freeeee."

The jumbotron screen changes from a waving flag graphic to live video of Ohkwali captains, QB Teddy Mackenzie, wide receiver Kyle Booth, and special teams kicker Miguel Sánchez, walking out to meet the ref and the visiting team's captains for the coin toss. The visiting QB calls heads. He loses the toss and Ohkwali chooses to receive the kickoff. It plays out almost word for word like it had at States. Walking across the field with my co-captains for the coin toss, shaking hands like good sports. A solid grip, single pump. Locking eyes with the other team's quarterback, smiling through my face mask, so cock-sure that we were about to rub his team's faces in the dirt. It was EJ White at his most confident and self-assured. The moment before it all went wrong.

Junior Year: Saturday, November 24
States AKA The EJ White Game of Shame

I had never experienced anything quite so euphoric as running onto the Syracuse Carrier Dome field at the head of my pride of Lions as hundreds of red and white balloons launched over our heads. The cheerleaders lined our path, Tara giving a high kick and an air kiss as I ran past. Our side of the stadium was an undulating sea of brilliant red. Air horns sounded. Jugs of rocks rattled. The band blasted out the James Bond theme song. My family was waving to me like crazy people from their prime seats ten rows up on the fifty yard line. I wished I could freeze myself in that moment until my whole body absorbed this intense perfection. But I pulled myself back to focus on the game, telling myself that the only thing better than this moment would be the one after we won and I got named MVP.

Through the announcements, national anthem, more announcements, I was so amped I couldn't stand still. I wanted to jog out to join the Cromwell Central Green Dragons captains for the coin toss, but my co-captains--tight end D'Marcus Clay, fullback Jake Kaminski and lineman Gavin Holmes--set our pace at a chill as y' please mosey. This "makin' 'em wait on us" was one of D'Marcus's psychological power moves.

The ref's voice carried through the Dome speaker system. "Congratulations to our East and West Semifinal-winning teams and welcome to the New York State Class AA Championship Game. Green Dragons, you've been designated the visiting team, so you get to call the toss. What is your call?"

"Heads," replied the Cromwell QB, a scrawny five-foot-eight, 168 pounder whose pass range topped out around forty yards. Yeah, I knew from watching game tape he was fast, agile, and accurate, but none of that would matter. Kaminski may've been as dumb as a box of rocks, but he was six-foot-four and 294 pounds. He was gonna lay this kid out, no question.

The ref tossed the coin. We all watched it go up and fall spinning to the turf.

"It is tails," the ref declared to much cheering from the red-garbed spectators behind us. My stomach leapt. "Lions, you may choose to kick or receive."

"Receive," I say.

"The Lions have chosen to receive…"

Even as the ref was speaking, we turned our backs on the Dragons and strutted off to our own sideline, dancing and pumping our fists in the air to get the crowd going. They readily obliged--another soaring, dizzying moment.

After the kickoff, we were in great position on our own forty-eight yard line.

My fingertips buzzed in anticipation "Hut!" I called for the snap. The ball bounced off my fingertips, just a little, but enough that I lost half a second getting a firm grip on it. Long enough to miss the prime moment to get behind my coverage. So there I was, a sitting duck when Dragon linebacker number ninety-nine somehow managed to get past Kaminski. *Shit!*

The next thing I saw was the sky as my back smacked the turf. The force of the impact left me gasping like a landed fish. By the time I could prop myself up, my view was blocked by the backs of my own players running down the field in pursuit of…someone…someone from the other team who was sprinting the ball towards the Cromwell endzone for their first touchdown of the game.

Oh God…I fumbled the ball. I'd seen ninety-nine coming for me and frozen, just for a second. Instead of dodging or getting rid of the ball, I'd fumbled it. I hadn't fumbled the ball all year. Hell, I hadn't fumbled on a sac since JV. How could I have let this happen? *And on our first play of the game!*

Amid the surprise touchdown pandemonium, I got back on my feet and watched the Dragons celebrating in the endzone. The Lions were scattered across the field, standing where their aborted chase left them. They looked at me, at Coach, at each other. What the hell just happened?

A bad snap—*that's* what must have happened. That linebacker wouldn't have gotten near me if I wasn't trying to get control of a too-low snap. Where was Griggs, my good-for-nothing center?

He hadn't gotten far.

"What the fuck, Griggs?!"

"What?"

"Do you think you can play this off? That snap was shit!" I reached out and gave him a solid, two-handed push in the chest.

"Look, man...I don't know what...I thought it was fine, same as always." He held up his hands palm-out and backed away from me, but I kept advancing until our facemasks knocked.

"Do your fucking job," I warned him through clenched teeth.

"Yeah, man, whatever..." He shook his head before jogging to the sidelines. I balled my hands into fists and cleared the field so that the defense could get out there for the extra point attempt.

You can do this, White! Shake it off and keep your head in the game, I told myself. *Leading a comeback will make the win even sweeter.*

Kevin Markone, QB2, came to stand beside me. "Nicely done, White. A turnover for a touchdown on the first play at States? Couldn't have fucked it up better myself." The corners of his mouth turned up like the jibe was just good-natured humor. *Yeah, right.* I forced a laugh anyway.

"Oh, I'm sure you'd have managed somehow," I assured him with a tight grin.

"Maybe." His own smile widened. "But hey, don't let one total disaster throw you off your game."

"Oh, don't worry, I won't."

"No pressure." He bumped my shoulder pad with the side of his fist in faux solidarity.

He ambled back to the bench--back where he belonged. *What a selfish ass.*

He had a point about one thing, though. The Dragons' last three games were nail biters where they capitalized on their opponent's errors to pull off the win. Our wins had been based on our remarkable passing game. So I had to play the rest of this thing clean and in control.

***

With 48.2 seconds left in the first quarter, the score was still Lions - 0, Green Dragons - 7. It should have been easy to close the gap, but the Dragons had managed to stymie us on every possession so far. So much for our predicted total domination. The game highlight videos hadn't given me a true appreciation for the relentless, well-oiled machine that was their defensive line. And it seemed like their coach had given them one job today--put pressure on the QB--*me*. What started to scare me was how effective their coordinated push was. That first sack was no fluke. I'd been sacked twice more, so hard my ears were still ringing. And when I told Gavin Holmes to do his job and cover my left side. He shrugged. *He fucking shrugged!*

Mom would be freaking out right now. *Concussions, life-long damage...* I pushed away her anxious warnings and jogged to the sideline to get the play. We were third down and eight at Cromwell's thirty-seven yard line--well out of field goal range. Coach called a passing play to try and get some momentum going down the field. I needed to get the ball to

D'Marcus on his route down the left sideline. Otherwise we'd be stuck punting again.

The snap was low, but I got my hands on it okay. I darted backwards and looked for D'Marcus.

Two seconds... He's running his route, but they'd got double coverage on him.

Three seconds... He tried to cut to the inside. The Dragons stayed tight on him. No go. *Shiiiiit.*

Four seconds... I cut back and forth, avoiding loose defensemen and scanning the field for another open receiver.

Five seconds... I spotted an open Lion receiver way down on the right side with nothing but a clear path to the end zone behind him. *Yes!*

Six seconds... I reached back for the pass--THWACK!

Blindsided from the left, I went down hard on my right side. My elbow made first contact with the ground, sending a jolt through my forearm and through my hand, jarring the ball loose before my legs hit the ground. I watched in horror as it tumbled along the ground where a Dragon dove and clutched it to his chest, pinning it to the turf beneath him. Four Lions rushed to pile on top of him...for all the good that was worth.

The officials ruled it a fumble. Some of my teammates tried to argue my right knee was already down when the ball got loose, but no luck selling that lie. Cromwell took possession.

If I'd thought nothing could feel worse than that first fumble, I was wrong. Arm still throbbing and throat tight with fury and frustration, I jogged off.

"White!" Coach barked. When I was close enough to see the vein popping out of his forehead, he laid into me. "If you get sacked, hang on t' the goddamn ball. You understand that? It's quarterbacking 101."

"Coach, Holmes isn't covering--" I let the excuse fade in the face of his scowling displeasure.

"You're the one out there hesitating. The line can't be expected to give you infinite time."

"D'Marcus wasn't open, and I knew we needed a first down--"

"If your intended receiver is covered, find another open receiver quick or run it yourself--you know that!" The edge of his clipboard jabbed at my chest just below my pads.

"I…" wasn't going to help myself by trying to explain or lay blame. So instead I straightened up and said, "Understood, Coach." Besides, he was right. Poor coverage was no excuse for my being slow and indecisive.

"Good."

From the sideline I watched as that scrawny Dragon QB threw a beautiful 22 yard pass, caught on the run by his wide receiver who dodged the tackle and ran the ball down an open field.

Another touchdown.

The stadium exploded with a mixed roar of horror and elation. My whole body went limp, like I was having some out-of-body experience, my limbs too heavy to move. For the first time, I thought, *Oh God, we could lose this thing... How can this be happening?*

"White, look alive!" Coach called through my fog of doom.

"Sorry," I took a quick swig from my water bottle to wash down the bitter possibility of defeat. It didn't work. I jogged back out to the field with the rest of the offense, dread congealing into a ball in my stomach.

Coach called running plays until we were in another third down situation, this time only seventeen yards from the endzone. *You can do this. This is cake.*

"Hut!"

*One second, two...*D'Marcus bolted for the endzone, turned, hands up and ready.

No hesitation. I threw.

NO! A Dragon cut across and side jumped to pick off the pass.

I fell to my knees, gripping my helmet between my hands. If only I'd taken another second to scan, to be sure I had a clear line. *Fuuuuuck!*

Coach was fuming on the sidelines, his clipboard on the ground. "What was that!?"

"I--I didn't wanna hesitate, like you said--"

"There's a goddamn difference between not hesitating and not checking for coverage."

"You're right. I'm sorry, Coach."

He leaned back, crossed his arms, and shook his head. "What the hell's goin' on with you today, White? This isn't peewee. I need a QB out there who can think on his feet and move that ball to the endzone. Can y' do that?"

"Yes, sir," I mumbled.

"No more mistakes, White, you understand me? I need State-Champion-level play from you."

"Yes, sir."

"What was that?"

"YES, SIR."

He got quieter then, more confidential. "Look, we've all got our nerves ramped up for this game. I get it. But we can't let the stakes mess with our heads. Just get in your zone, and go out there and play like you have all season, like it's any other game." He said it like *he* hadn't been the one impressing the once-in-a-lifetime, change-the-course-of-your-life level stakes on us every other sentence for the last three weeks.

I nodded. But there was no way to fool my brain into believing this was just another game.

***

God, no, please, no, please... I watched the ball I'd thrown away delivered on the wings of angels into the waiting hands of a Cromwell cornerback. It was only my tenth interception of the whole season but the fourth in this one crucial game.

With three minutes and sixteen seconds left in the third quarter and with the score Lions - 0, Green Dragons - 28, our chances grew grimmer by the moment and morale was in the toilet. The crowd energy on our side had fizzled. Fans, families, coaches, players--everyone was asking, *Is there any way we can come back and win this thing?* As my teammates cussed me out on our way off the field, I looked above the fifty yard line to my family. Ellen was sitting down, shaking her head, hands over her wordless mouth. Next to her, Charlie was looking back at me and waving his red flag with all the naive faithfulness and optimism of a six-year-old. And Dad, his expression—slight frown with sad eyes and furrowed brow—pity. When this thing was over, that right there was the best response I could expect from anybody.

The coaches talked to each other in harsh, low tones. They looked at me, hunched over and out of breath on the bench. Then they looked at Kevin Markone, warmed up and ready to go.

134

If anybody shared the blame for this disaster, it was Coach, for keeping me in so long. He'd had faith that I'd pull myself together and come through for the team. And I'd failed him and made him look a fool. I didn't need to see his face to recognize the disgust there when he told me, "Bench it, White. Markone? You're in."

Kevin bumped me in the shoulder as he passed, grinning with bared teeth.

"Hey White, you believe in God?"

"...Yes?"

"Because this is divine justice."

Senior Year: Saturday, September 28
Leaving Teddy's Game

What was I thinking, coming to Teddy's game like some normal person? Did I think my new friendships had magically fixed me? Did I really believe being in the midst of all this wouldn't phase me? Sure, the anti-anxiety med was a buffer, a soft filter for the world. But I was still supposed to avoid known personal triggers...like football. I hadn't so much as watched a game on TV in almost a year.

My breath starts coming fast. I hold my tingling hands out in front of me, watching them tremble like I'm OD-ing on caffeine. *Shit...I have to get out of here.*

But it's finally our turn at the window. "A chili cheese dog and fries and a lemonade, please!" Charlie orders.

The girl behind the counter looks at my spiked dog collar and wrinkles her nose as she informs us, "We don't have chili cheese today. The cheese machine is broken."

"Fine. Plain then. Just—here." I pull out my wallet and hand her twenty bucks.

She counts out the change, dollar by dollar, coin by coin before handing off our order slip off to another girl who ambles back to the food prep area and then just stands there talking to the guy working the fryer. It's only him and one other guy back there, who's opening hamburger buns and placing them on a tray...one at a damn time. *You can do this. You took your pill this morning. Just breathe.*

We move to stand in the crowd waiting to pick up orders. Even though I'm not watching the field, I can't tune out the announcer's constant updates on the plays as Teddy completes pass after pass, efficiently moving his team toward the end zone. Cheers erupt all around us, and I don't need the announcer to know that the Bears have scored a touchdown in their first drive down the field.

On our left, a gray bearded guy says to the woman next to him, "The Mackenzie boy never disappoints."

Unlike me. The air catches in my throat at the reminder. Desperate to keep control, I dig at the raw skin bordering my thumbnail. *Where the fuck is our food already?*

I stare at the half-full tray of fries sitting under the heat lamp, along with pre-prepped burger and hots, and imagine hoisting myself up over the counter, grabbing as much food as I can carry, and making a run for it. This escapist fantasy is not enough to impede the wave of intense dizziness that follows. I swing Charlie down off my shoulders, brace myself on the counter, squeeze my eyes shut, and breathe and count and breathe and count...

The girl comes back to the counter to bring out another group's order.

"Excuse me, but how much longer till ours is ready? Order 163?"

"Oh, um…hang on." She walks back to the grill area and comes back to report, "I guess we have to heat up another batch of chili, from the freezer, so like…twenty or thirty minutes."

"Are you serious?" My heart is pounding so hard I can hear it in my ears.

Her eyelids flutter in barely concealed irritation as she offers, "You want a plain hotdog instead?"

"No!" Charlie insists. "It has to have chili."

The next play is starting. In another minute, I'm not going to be able to stand it.

Fuck this. "Sorry, Charlie, we gotta go." I grasp him by the upper arm to lead him away.

"But…why?" He pulls back, heels skidding along the gravel. I thought—"

"I don't feel well, okay?" *Twenty yards to the exit. You can make it. You've got vomit bags in the car.*

"But…you said I could get a chili cheese dog," Charlie's voice quivers.

"We'll get McDonald's instead. You *love* McDonald's."

"They don't *have* chili cheese dogs."

"God, Charlie, stop being such a baby." *Parking lot. Okay…where the fuck did I park?*

"I'm not a baby!" he yells and tries to pull his arm away.

"Oh yeah, well you sure sound like one right now." My breathing is all over the place. Dizziness and nausea swirl together and take over. *Oh shit, I'm not gonna make it.*

"You're just like Dad!" he shouts as he manages to slip from my grasp. "I hate you too!" His little fists are clenched and his face is red and blotchy and scrunched up like he's desperately trying to hold in the tears. A line of snot escapes his nostril and hovers on upper lip.

"Charlie, come on, *please*..." My throat burns from a surge of ascending acid.

"No! I'm not leaving without my chili cheese dog."

"Yes, you are." I reach for his arm again, but he lands a solid kick to my shin.

"Goddammit..." I stumble backward. Equilibrium and vision swirling, I limp towards the nearest solid object--a pickup truck--and crouch there, holding the metal bumper as I puke onto the blacktop.

Eventually, my gut is empty and my pulse slows, leaving me damp all over with cold sweat but steady, back in control of my body. I look to the right to see Charlie staring, scared and round-eyed. I'd been extra careful to keep my panic attacks out of Charlie's view. After what we went through with Mom, he needed his big brother to be strong and healthy.

"It's okay, buddy. I'm okay now. It's no big deal. I just..." *God, how do I explain this to him?*

His wiry little arms dart around my torso, his head lodged under my left armpit. "I'm sorry. I want McDonald's. I want chicken nuggets. Let's go to McDonald's, okay? Okay?"

I hug him tight, disgusted with myself for taking it out on him, my biggest fan no matter what.

"I don't hate you. I'm sorry I kicked you. I'm sorry..." His tears soak through my Paw Patrol t-shirt.

"Okay, Charlie, don't worry. I'm good now. I'm sorry I yelled at you."

"Eric?" Bea jogs towards us and stops short when she gets close enough to see the puddle of vomit. "Oh my God, are you guys okay?" Lines of concern form across her forehead as she approaches.

Charlie grips one of my hands while I hoist myself up by the bumper using the other. "Hey, Bea. I, uh...I'm not feeling the best."

"No kidding," she says, one side of her mouth quirked up. "Was it something you ate?"

I consider saying yes to this. It's a perfectly good reason for what she's looking at. But it feels wrong. Another lie on top of all the rest. So I tell her, "I had a panic attack."

"Oh." She takes it in, nodding, half-smile vanishing. "Do you get them a lot?"

"Less than I used to. I take medicine for them." I sigh and lean against the truck's tailgate. "Sometimes it keeps them from happening, but sometimes it just slows them down or makes them less severe."

She comes closer, stopping at the border of my puke puddle. "And are you okay now? Is there anything I can do to help?"

I shake my head. "I'll be fine. I just...need a minute." Charlie leans against my leg, his head resting at my waist. I wrap an arm around him and gently ruffle his hair.

"Well, at least I can help this guy out." Bea reaches into her tropical fruit patterned hip pack and hands Charlie a tissue for his snot-smeared face.

A cheer erupts in the stadium and we can just make out the announcer congratulating Narby, Ohkwali number fifty-six, on sacking the opposing quarterback. Turnover for Ohkwali!

"You'd better get back in there," I tell Bea. "You'll miss Teddy's next big play."

"Teddy will understand."

"No, really. It's bad enough I'm skipping out. Making his cousin miss out would be the height of bad manners."

She raises an eyebrow and smirks. "Since when were you Mr. Manners?"

"Hey, I have excellent manners...when I choose to use them."

She laughs and I join in, still a bit shaky but glad to be back in control again.

"Tell Teddy I'm sorry, okay?"

"Uh, I think you better tell him yourself."

"Yeah, probably." The evidence of my issues congeals at our feet.

"He'll understand," she assures me.

"Yeah..." I had no doubt he would, and that he and Bea would keep it to themselves. They were good people like that. "I wish I could stay, but...I can't go back in there." Just looking back over at the stadium full of people makes me shudder.

Bea tips her head thoughtfully. "There is another option."

A quick self-assessment makes me very aware of how sweat damp I am, but that's not fatal. "Um...what'd you have in mind?"

"Up there," she points to the small hillside at the school's fence line. A handful of people are up there, scattered around in camp chairs or on blankets. A far less crowded locale. "We can still see the field. Most of it anyway."

"Okay," I agree.

"Okay?" Bea verifies.

"Yeah."

"You sure?" Charlie asks, giving me some anxious side eye.

"Well, it's worth a try. Oh but--" I turn to Bea. "I promised Charlie food. Maybe, um, would you take him back to the concession stand first?"

"Of course! Come on Charlie, let's go get you some food."

Charlie looks at her outstretched hand and back up at me. Though I nod my head in approval, he shakes his head vigorously. "You can take me to McDonalds after the game."

"You sure? I thought you were super hungry?"

"Hang on a sec, I have something that'll help." Bea holds up a finger before disappearing between cars. She returns a minute later with a Scottish-looking plaid wool blanket under one arm, a family-sized bag of Cheez Doodles in the other. "Hillside provisions!" she grins and holds out the bag.

For a second, I stand in awe, taking the bag with reverence. "How did you know?"

"You like Doodles?"

"I adore them."

"Me too!" Charlie yanks away the bag and wraps both arms around it.

"Men after my own heart." Bea laughs. Such a free, untroubled sound that I can't help but grin back.

Then she reaches out and slips her hand around mine. It takes me by complete surprise, leapfrogging my defenses. As she leads us in a winding path around cars, everything else--the crowd noise, the announcer, even the acidic residue in my mouth--fades into unimportance. My mind races.

God, my hand is sweaty. She must be disgusted, but she's too nice to pull away. You should pull away. No, that would make it weird. But weird is better than disgusted. And even if she's not disgusted now, she would be if she knew she was holding hands with a rapist. And what if people see us? I scan the immediate area for familiar faces. *Will they think we're going out? Would that be such a bad thing? She is cute, and nice, and smart, and self-confident and--What the fuck!? Stop thinking about her! There is no way you can date anyone, like...ever. Then she'd be that girl who dated the rapist. You can't do that to her. Not to mention, she'd end up hating you, and so would Teddy.*

My hand is warm in hers, tingling with a pleasant buzz that only increases as I become aware of it. *Wow that feels so good. Fuck! Stop liking it! Why the hell did she take my hand at all? Is it normal for guy-girl friends to hold hands? Maybe it's because of the panic attack, like I'm an invalid or something. Or maybe she's been waiting for a chance to make physical contact without being super obvious about it. Maybe she has a thing for me. No! She can't. I've just made friends for the first time, maybe ever, and that would make everything weird. God, my hand feels amazing--my whole arm is pulsing. Why is my throat dry? STOP THINKING ABOUT IT!*

We're at the top of the rise, and it takes me a second to realize Bea is saying something. "Hmm?"

She lets go of my hand, leaving it empty and aching. "You take one end of the blanket," she repeats as she unfurls it.

We spread it out and take our seats, Charlie plopping down between us, which is just as well. My female physical contact quota for the day has already been exceeded.

It isn't a half-bad view from up here. And with plenty of personal space to be had, breathing comes easy again.

Bea takes out her cell phone and starts texting. "Letting Aunt Tammy know where we are so they won't worry," she explains and puts it back in her pocket.

Another swell of cheers. The distant announcer says "incredible pass by Mackenzie" and something else I don't quite catch. Bea cups her hands around her mouth and Woos. Teddy's linemen have turned to him, hinged at the waist with arms outstretched, mock bowing to him. Sort of a joke, but sort of not. He is their King.

All the admiration, the glory, the physical rush-- everything Teddy Mackenzie has--is everything I craved. And however briefly, I'd had it. Then in a blink, it was one more loss to mourn. Tensing up, I wait for the familiar wave of bitter regret, polluted with the rotting corpses of my erstwhile hopes and dreams.

But nothing happens. Well, I do feel *something*. But it's more like...relief.

Oh my God...I don't want it anymore. As soon as I think it, I know it's true. Hysterical laughter bubbles up inside my chest and I collapse backwards.

Both Charlie and Bea turn to look at me. I clamp my mouth shut, but it's no use. The laughter leaks out until my eyes are watering and I'm gasping for breath.

Charlie looks at Bea, wide eyed and mouth full of Cheez Doodles. "Did you tickle him?" he accuses Bea.

Her own eyes go wide, a blush dusting her cheeks. "No!" To me she says, "Are you okay? Oh no, is this-- Are you having--"

"No, I'm fine. Really," I insist, wiping my eyes with the base of my palms. "I just realized something."

"What?"

"I'd rather be up here than down there."

"Yeah, that's why I suggested it." She tips her head to the side as if she knows there's something she's missing here.

There's no way I can explain the miracle of this moment to her, so I don't even try. Propping my hands behind me, I push myself back up. "Well, it was an excellent suggestion. Thank you, Bea."

The laughter fades from her expression. With matching sincerity, she says, "You're welcome, Eric."

This time, when she rests her hand atop mine, I don't flinch away. And instead of worrying about what it means or if I deserve it, I take a moment to simply appreciate that I've got people who care about me and who aren't phased by my messed-up-ness. Real friends, finally.

Junior Year: Monday, November 26
Pariah

It's fine. It's going to be fine. Just go over and act like everything is normal. The Monday after our loss at States, I gripped my lunch tray like a life preserver as I walked toward my usual lunch table. No one on the team had spoken to me since Saturday. Not even a text. They were mad, yeah, but were they going to shun me in person, in public? I was walking into this blind. But what choice did I have?

As I made my way through the room, I trained my eyes resolutely on the poster of a group of smiling, racially diverse students in graduation caps on the far wall that trumpeted Do Something Today Your Future Self Will Thank You For. My gut was a solid block of cement as I approached my usual table. *Please, please, please*...I begged God, Providence, the tooth fairy, whoever might be listening.

A group of my erstwhile teammates, including my fellow captains Jake, Gavin, and D'Marcus, were in the middle of a heated discussion about the upcoming Bills vs. Patriots game. But when they spotted me, the robust debate quieted into a silence that made my heartbeat sound ten times louder.

Lowering my eyes to my pile of crumbly tater tots, I moved to slide into the last empty chair.

But before I could, D'Marcus swung his leg up to block the seat. "Uh-uh-uh, boy. You think a couple days go by and we're all good now?" His face distorted with disgust and disbelief. He wasn't the only one. All around the table, expressions were hard, unforgiving.

Taking in a slow breath, I tried to steady myself, but anger surged along familiar neural paths. All these years of being teammates, friends and now...nothing? How could they turn on me so completely over one game? If their boy Kevin had screwed up, would they be treating *him* like this? *So fucking unfair!*

"Move along, fool," D'Marcus ordered, just loud enough for me to hear over the cafeteria clamor.

I felt the skin on my neck prickle with awareness of all the eyes on us. How many in this room would take their cue from D'Marcus and these guys on how to treat me? Fear and desperation momentarily overwhelmed the anger. *This can't be--I can't be--They can't--Oh God--*

I leaned down and gripped D'Marcus's upper arm. "Please, man, it was one game. Don't do this to me," I quietly begged, despising the whimpering crack in my voice.

If anything, this show of weakness further repulsed him. He shook me off and flicked his hand at the wrist like he was swatting away an irritating fly.

145

I tried to speak again, but my mouth hung open, as empty as I felt. D'Marcus turned away, and they all went right back to talking about the Bills as if I'd never even been there.

And that was it. I'd been erased. Canceled.

My head swam, vision hazed. I stumbled into a chair behind me as I tried to leave, sending baked beans sloshing up onto my light blue Under Armor tee. *Shit.* I gracelessly swung around to catch myself. As if the moment couldn't get any worse, there she was--Tara, sitting at the table to the right with a group of friends. She'd had a front row view to my summary rejection. This should have been the day I walked into the cafeteria with my arm around her waist, hand resting on her hip. Her official boyfriend. I was supposed to be living the dream, not this bizarre, disorienting nightmare.

We stared at each other, frozen, caught off guard in the moment. Her body was tense and arched away from me, heavily lined eyes wide, plum colored lips twisted between her teeth.

Seconds passed. Neither of us moved.

What was going through her head? Was there a chance she still wanted me? That whatever she saw in me could transcend the shit of the moment and--

"Ewwww," one of her friends pulled a face, eyeing the brown sauce dripping down my front.

The connection broke, and whatever indecision Tara might have felt slid somewhere out of view as a mask of shared disgust slipped into place. She turned to the friends on her right and mouthed *Awkward*, eliciting stifled laughter.

Pressure built behind my eyes--the precursor to fat, ugly, unmanly tears. *Not here!* I scrambled to get away.

My heart pounded so hard my whole body throbbed. The room was a blur. I bumped into another chair, mumbling an apology. *Wake up!* This wasn't real. *Please*... I would give anything--literally *anything*--to wake up back on the bus, on the way to the Carrier Dome. A do-over.

"EJ!" An arm snaked through mine. I instinctively pulled away, but the owner of the arm held tight. Ellen. *Oh thank God.*

"El," I breathed out and squeezed my eyes shut, letting her steady me.

"Here, sit with us." She guided me over to the table with her other freshmen theatre friends, pulling out a chair between herself and long-time best friend Andrea Gurlance. I'd met the rest of them before, too. Their names were somewhere in my brain, if I could get it functioning again. They all greeted me with a bizarre mix of smiling, over-cheery waves, and the kind of extreme frown face you'd wear if a director told your to "Look like you feel really sorry for someone--Make me believe it from the back row!"

I managed a weak, "Hey," and a smile that was more of a grimace. No one said anything after that. What was there to say? What was happening? Was my character's arrival on the scene a cause for excitement or pity? Was I being introduced as a single episode guest star or a new series regular? How long would I be sitting with them? Was this my new social reality-- no friends of my own, lunching with my little sister's castmates? My head swam. *Oh God...I gotta get outta here.*

When I started to stand, Ellen pressed down on my shoulder, keeping me in my chair while she hovered over me, using wet napkins to try and wipe the mess off my shirt. Like a mother cleaning up an infant. In the middle of the cafeteria. This is what I'd been reduced to.

I am pathetic. A joke. A big crying baby. There is no coming back from this. An involuntary, choked moan escaped my lips.

Andrea wrapped both hands around my forearm where it lay limp on the table. Her expression was earnest and intense. "EJ, those people are total jerks. Just forget them. We are here for you, no matter what."

"We" who? I just nodded. Andrea'd had a crush on me since she was, like, ten. Ellen had spilled the beans about it and then made me promise to be nice to her even if she acted weird. Did Andrea still like me? Seemed like maybe. That should have been some comfort, but it wasn't. If anything, it made it worse. Had I fallen so low that she--an NBN freshman with poorly concealed acne--actually thought she had a chance with me now?

No--you will NOT cry!

Ellen finished wiping my shirt and sat close, an arm around my back, head on my shoulder.

"It's gonna be okay," she said so only I could hear. Her mouth formed a smile that didn't match the worried line of her brows. "They'll get over it. Just give it a week and everything will go back to normal."

We both already knew it wasn't true. We just didn't yet realize I was about to make it much, much worse.

Junior Year: Sunday, December 2,
A week after losing State
What Are Friends For?

A full week after States and still nothing was right with my world.

Well, almost nothing. Ellen had been beyond loyal. Checking with me throughout the day at school, hanging out and re-watching episodes of *The Office* after I got Charlie to bed, finding ways to make me crack a smile, to forget my shit situation for a minute or two. And I could always count on her for a blessed distraction during church.

R, I wrote my guess on the corner of the page. Ellen put a slash through it and added an arm to the hanging stick figure.

No phones during service. It's a hard and fast rule that Dad kept up even after Mom wasn't around to enforce it. Probably because it would look bad if an elder's children were so blatantly ignoring the sermon. Paper and pen could be excused as taking notes, dutifully scribbling down choice bits of doctrine and Bible references for later study. *Yeah right.*

I frowned at the ten letter word.

A _ A _ G A _ A _ _

She filled in one blank. **A _ A _ G A _ A T _**

Ah, I think I've got this. **A M A L G A M A T E**

Only SAT words were acceptable for hangman in our family.

Ellen put a grudging ✔ next to it, flipped to the back of the notebook, and added my points to our running calculation. We'd long ago developed our own elaborate scoring system that factored in numbers of letter guesses--correct and incorrect, numbers of vowels (which cost two guesses), and word length. When she finished tabulating, she passed the notebook to me. But before we could start the next round, Dad cleared his throat, the gold tray of flavorless wafers AKA The Body of Christ, in his hands. I took the tray and passed it down, followed by the tray of tiny plastic cups filled with watered-down grape juice AKA The Blood of Christ.

Ellen and I intoned the familiar ritual blessings along with the rest of the congregation. Then we stood for the final hymn, "Crown Him with Many Crowns," and the benediction before the organ played us out and people made their way to the fellowship hall for conversation and light refreshments. My stomach knotted at the thought of more social interactions. Last Sunday, Dad let me stay home from church to lick my wounds, so this week offered a fresh mix of people to avert their eyes, coat their greetings in unnatural cheeriness, and offer condolences on the loss, like someone died. Like *I* died.

"EJ, Ellen, come on." Dad stood waiting for us at the end of our pew.

Ellen slipped her arm through mine and tried to pull me up. But I didn't budge, so she sat back down, giving my arm a squeeze. "I think we're gonna hang out here until it's time to go," she told Dad.

He sighed and walked back to us. "I know this isn't easy, EJ, but it's not as bad as you're making it out to be."

I shook my head. Dad didn't get it. He wasn't the one who'd fucked up. He couldn't feel the shift in everyone's reactions. This was happening to me, not him.

Dad leaned closer, his voice calm but firm. "You'll only prolong it by avoiding people."

Still, I didn't budge. I'd barely made it through last week. My ability to fake okay-ness was tapped out.

"This is ridiculous…" Dad straightened up and tugged at the front of his suit. "You can sit in the corner with your friends, but you need to come to the fellowship hall, *now.*"

Ellen took my hand and squeezed it in solidarity.

"Fine then," Dad said, his tune deceptively light. "If you two can't manage to spend a half hour with people at church, you won't be spending any time with your friends this week either."

Grounded? Big whup. I snorted at the empty threat. Did he not see the irony there? I didn't even have a social media social life anymore, let alone an in-person one.

But beside me, Ellen stiffened. *Oh shit...musical auditions.* They were this week, and being grounded would mean she couldn't meet up with her friends to practice or go out for food after the auditions. Despite what she'd forfeit, she didn't hop up to obey Dad. Instead, she chose loyalty. White siblings forever. I felt a warm rush of gratitude...but I couldn't let her do it.

I stood and she rose with me, momentarily buoyant with relief. Dad nodded, tight lipped, and turned his back, expecting us to follow.

"Thanks," Ellen whispered, her arm still looped through mine. "We'll find somewhere quiet in there, okay?"

"Yeah," I agree, as if that were possible in a room full of 200+ people.

As soon as we got inside the hall, Andrea Gurlance waved us over. She was sitting with a bunch of other youth group kids, including her brother, Frankie and Kendra Daniels.

"I saved you guys seats." Andrea pats the chair directly next to her while flashing me a heavily braced smile.

Before I could sit, Frankie rested his elbows on the table, clasped his hands, and leaned forward. "So, EJ, how's school going for you these days? Livin' the dream?"

I only responded with a mute, stony glare.

"Don't worry...You'll get used to being nobody special, just like the rest of us." His slow smile was pure schadenfreude.

Bastard. I somehow managed not to say it out loud, clenching my jaw and swallowing hard.

"Hey--" Ellen started but was interrupted by the screech of Kendra's chair along the floor as she stood.

"Hey EJ, thanks for offering earlier to help me with the advent hymnal supplements for next week. Is now a good time?" Her eyes flickered toward the exit and I realized she was offering me an out.

My body sagged in relief. *Bless this girl.* "Oh, yeah, sure."

"I can help you, Kendra," Frankie stood and curved a long-fingered hand around Kendra's shoulder.

"Um, it's only a two person job, and EJ already volunteered, so…" Kendra stepped to the side out of Frankie's reach.

I caught the briefest glimpse of Frankie's narrowing eyes and reddening ears and enjoyed my own moment of satisfaction. However far I'd fallen, this paranoid, possessive asshole still saw me as a threat to whatever designs he had on Kendra.

Out in the hallway, I moved to walk beside Kendra. "Hey, thanks for the save."

She gave me a quick, sympathetic smile before going back to her usual gaze aversion. "I know having to be around lots of people can be hard. Well, sometimes it is for *me*, anyway." She rushed on. "I don't mean *you're* like that too. It's just that, today in service you...and in school since...and sometimes Frankie can be...I just thought if you needed--"

"Kendra…" I reached over and pressed my fingertips to the back of her wrist. She let out a tiny gasp and stopped in her tracks. "You're a good friend. Thank you."

Her face flushed to match her maroon corduroy vest. "Well…thanks for being willing to help me with the hymnal inserts."

"Oh, so that's a real thing you need?" I asked, letting my hand drop and fighting back a groan.

Kendra opened the door to the church copy room where six stacks of papers waited.

"Oh wow…" *Holy shit. How long is this gonna take?*

"I'll assemble the pages and you can staple and fold, okay?"

"Yes, ma'am," I saluted. *Suck it up, White. Better here than the fellowship hall.*

We worked at our repetitive tasks in silence, which was kind of nice, relaxing even. After a bit, Kendra started to hum the tune of "It is Well with My Soul," and I found myself joining in. Then, without meaning to, I started singing the words. "When peace like a river, attendeth my way, When sorrows like sea billows roll…" It had been one of Mom's favorites, written by a man who'd lost his wealth to the Great Chicago Fire and then lost all four of his daughters in a shipwreck. Turned out, I knew all five verses by heart. And so did Kendra. By the time we reached the final chorus, I'd stopped folding as I struggled to push the words through my straining throat. It was no use. The words morphed to sobs, and Kendra came and wrapped her arms around me. I let her, leaning in, my face pressed down against her shoulder.

"I miss her too," she said in a voice that also sounded close to tears.

Her words, her warmth. It felt nice to have someone hold me like that. Not having to hold it in and pretend to be okay. Knowing, for once, I didn't need to explain or make excuses.

After a while, when I'd mostly cried myself out, my phone buzzed in my pocket: Ellen telling me to meet them at the car. I wiped my face on my sleeve and told Kendra, "I gotta go, my family's leaving. Sorry I can't finish helping you."

She waved away my concern and handed me a much-needed tissue. "It won't take me long."

"Uh, thanks for..." I moved my hands in a random motion, trying to encompass the whole encounter.

She smiled in that full, unworried way she used to when we were kids. "Of course. What are friends for?"

"Right..." So Kendra Daniels still considered me a friend, even though Lord knew I'd been a piss poor one to her since, like, puberty. "Well, I'll see you at school?" I offered. "We still haven't gotten to talk about...You were gonna tell me about something, right? That day in the parking lot...?"

"Oh...we don't have to talk about that. It was nothing." The smile stayed in place, but something changed in her eyes...dimming, closing off. Then she blinked, locking away whatever thought she'd been having. "Maybe we can eat lunch together, though. If you want. I eat in Ms. Cathaway's room. I'm sure she wouldn't mind if you came too."

Shit. "Um...yeah..." *If I wanted to put the final nail in my reputation's coffin.* Ms. Cathaway's was known as the last refuge of weirdos and outcasts. If I showed up there... *God no. Fuck no. Just...no.* "But, the thing is, I kinda eat lunch with my sister, so..."

"Oh, of course, nevermind. I only thought...if you needed somewhere...nevermind." Her eyes dropped again.

God, I'm an asshole. "But hey, maybe we can hang out again next Sunday? Catch up on...whatever."

That earned me some returned eye contact. "Really? That would be...yeah, I'd like that."

"Okay, it's a date." *SHIT.* "I mean, not a date-date," I quickly revised, my face flushing to match hers. *God, what is wrong with me?* "Just, like, it's a plan or whatever."

"Right, no, I knew what you meant," she assured me.

"Okay, well, cool...um, see you next week, Kendra." I gave her a little floppy wrist wave, like a total dork, and jogged all the way out to the bimmer.

Everyone else was already inside, belted and waiting. Ellen flashed me a look of wide-eyed warning as I jumped in the back next to Charlie.

"You're grounded," Dad informed me as he shifted the car into gear with more force than necessary.

"Grounded? What the hell, Dad! Kendra asked me to help her with--"

"I'm not interested in excuses, EJ. I told you to stay in the fellowship hall, and you left. Plain and simple. One week."

"But I was *helping*--"

"We can make it two."

I pressed my face between my hands and groaned. Apparently no good deed goes un-fucking punished.

Senior Year: Tuesday, October 22
Workout Rituals

The Ohkwali Battle Harks weight room got updated when the stadium did, so it's pretty well equipped. But like all high school weight rooms it still manages to smell like a combo of Axe body spray, BO, and feet.

Teddy convinced me to join him for pre-dawn lifting Tuesdays and Thursdays when team attendance is optional and only a handful of people ever show up. Since I've kept up morning runs and basement home gym lifting sessions since becoming anti-jock Eric Madison, I expected to jump right in and keep pace with him. Yeah, no such luck. Teddy is a strength training *machine*. We've done pullups, barbell squats, dumbbell bicep curls, and tricep extensions, and he hasn't even sweat through his tank top.

It's fucking annoying.

Now we're on the *coup de grâce* of masculine comparison, second only to dick measuring--the bench press. But instead of showing me up by adding weight when I hit my 220-pound ceiling, Teddy says that's "almost" his limit too. Which is bullshit. A fib to save my pride. If he was a better liar, he'd have thought to put on a show of straining a bit more. He doesn't even need an assist when he lifts off or replaces the bar between sets. But I spot him to keep up the ruse.

"Dude, what's with this workout music?" I have to raise my voice to be heard over the sentimental pop coming through the weight room's Bluetooth speaker.

He looks up at me, eyes narrowed as he effortlessly reps. "Dude, you better not be hating on my girl Selena right now."

"Oh, your girl, huh? You're a Selena stan?"

"We prefer the term Selenators, thank you very much. She was my first celebrity crush," he admits with a wistful smile as he finishes his set and sits up. "You're judging me right now, aren't you?"

"What? Not at all. Selena slays." I gasp and grasp my chest, staggering like I've been shot. "Lose You to Love Me" plays the soundtrack to my mock pain, just in time for me to join Selena on the second verse. "...In two moons, you replaced us, like it was easy." Dropping to my knees, my face distorted into a fake cry as I mouth, *Why?*

Teddy laughs. "Dude, you look like you really have been crying. Your eyeliner's, like, all over the place."

I lift fingertips to my sweat-damp face. They come away charcoal gray. *Lovely.* I pretend to cry even harder and reach out toward Teddy's face with my now liner-contaminated hand.

"Ooooh, no, don't even think about it," he warned, dodging out of my reach.

"Hey, are you insulting my bodily fluids? How rude. I thought we were friends?" I grin as I cross my arms and grab the bottom of my shirt, yanking it up over my head. Wadding it up in one hand, I use it to dry my face, no doubt smearing the black liner worse than ever. Though plenty also comes off on the shirt. I stare at the nasty ball of fabric. Teddy eyes it too, nose wrinkling. His expression shifts to one of horror as he realizes what I'm planning.

"Oh no no no no no."

"Awe come on, Mackenzie, what's a little perspiration between friends?" I jump the bench between us.

"I'm warning you... Don't you fucking dare." Teddy tries to back up but is stopped by a rack of dumbbells, arms windmilling to keep his balance. I manage to catch him, keeping him from falling back with one arm while shoving my smelly, sweaty, liner-smeared, shirt in his face with the other. Teddy yells into the fabric as I *whoop* in triumph.

"Aw, aren't you two cute."

It's a voice that sucks all good feelings from the room. I let Teddy go and we instinctively step further apart.

"No, no, don't let us interrupt your, uh...playtime," Booth insists, his mouth twisting into a satisfied smirk. Worse yet, he's not alone. Six or seven guys stand behind him staring at us. All football players, Teddy's teammates. How long have they been there? Of all moments to catch out of context. *This is not good. Very, very not good.*

For one, despite transitioning past the "trial" phase of our friendship, we've still kept our distance in public spaces. Per my insistence. Ohkwali's QB1 buddying up with the bizarro new kid would draw too much attention. Bad for me, and as I had argued, bad for Teddy as well. Did he want to field all the inevitable, intrusive questions? No. And neither did I. And now here we are all of a sudden doing...what? At the very least, something weird. And if Booth's tone and sly smile are any indication, something far worse in his book. Something unacceptably un-straight.

But Teddy seems unfazed. He crosses his arms and raises an imperious brow. "Well, well, well, what a pleasant surprise. My teammates getting their asses out of bed in time for optional morning strength training--for once." Eyes slide away from the stinging heat of QB1's judgment. "You're only..." Teddy checks the wall clock, "32 minutes late."

The briefest tightening in Booth's facial muscles betrays his irritation before the smirk slides back into place, unwilling to let this opportunity pass. "Yeah, looks like we been missin' out on the fun. Face painting and everything, huh boys? Come on Mackenzie, aren't you gonna introduce us to your, uh, new buddy here?"

Teddy turns to me with a smile that has got to be fake but manages not to look it and says, "Guys, this is my new friend Eric Madison. He may sweat like a pig, but he benches 220 and doesn't complain about my taste in workout music."

That earns a smattering of laughter, so Teddy's Selena obsession must be a running joke.

"Madison, this is Herrera, Narby, O'Connell, Burdett, Springsteen--spelled the same but no relation--and Sánchez there in the back." Teddy points them out and hands raise as each teammate identifies himself. Booth clears his throat, drawing attention to the oversight. "And Booth...though Bea tells me you two already met." Teddy lowers his chin and gives his fellow captain a hard look, one that sends a clear warning that there will be no repeat of that bullshit here, or anywhere for that matter.

Booth jerks his head back and makes a *tch* sound like he's going to make an excuse or throw out some dig about that day in the gym, but something makes him stop short. Instead, he runs a hand through his shaggy hair and sniffs before holding a hand up and spinning two fingers in the air. "Alright, boys, let's get this started already. I got dibs on the vertical leg press."

"Yeah, don't waste the whole--" Teddy checks the clock again, "23 minutes you've got left."

The rest of the guys hustle over to various stations. Narby holds up his phone towards the speaker and makes a sad, pleading face at Teddy, who sighs and says, "Fine." Selena is shortly replaced by Zac Brown Band.

Question now is how to make my exit without it looking like a retreat? Maybe if I move slow and casual enough...

But when I turn, someone is standing in my path. "Hey, I'm Miguel. Nice to meet you." He's got a slim build, a slight accent, and a friendly smile with a small gap between his two front teeth.

"Uh, yeah, you too." I take his offered hand.

We've never spoken before, but Miguel Sánchez first showed up on my sports radar last year when Ohkwali was making its way to States. His name showed up in the news right alongside Teddy and Booth's. They were--are--the Ohkwali Eagles victory trifecta. Miguel is currently the best kicker in the northeast, stat-wise for distance and completion. And he's the only Ohkwali team member to get a full ride to a D1 school--so far, that is. Come fall, he'll be off in Idaho scoring field goals for Boise State Broncos.

From what I've picked up since starting school here, Miguel is a well-liked, good-humored guy, if a bit on the quiet side. I've seen him and Teddy hanging out at lunch and the halls and such, so I figure they're friends, though Teddy rarely mentions his teammates or anything else to do with football.

"So, uh, how're you liking it here? I came to Ohkwali in junior year, so I know it can be kinda tough to break in, you know?"

"Yeah, I know..." I can feel Teddy on the right a few feet behind me, hovering. "People have been pretty cool though."

Miguel's eyes do a quick circuit, first over my shoulder to Teddy, then over his own shoulder to Booth at the leg press before going back to me. His smile seems more forced than before when he says, "Nice, well…Mackenzie's a good guy to have on your side."

I swallow and make myself smile as well, remembering my first, less-than-cordial encounter with Booth in the gym. Would being friends with Teddy keep Booth and Co. from messing with me…or would it only put a target on my back, a proxy in whatever power struggle the quarterback and wide receiver have going?

Either way, it's best for both of us if I make myself scarce. Out of sight, out of mind, and all that.

I walk over to Teddy, rubbing my left shoulder. In a voice loud enough to carry, I say, "Uh, hey, I know we had a couple more stations to go, but I think I mighta strained my upper trapezius. I'm gonna go put some ice on it."

Teddy's head shoots up, eyebrows raised in some combination of surprise, worry…and perhaps a little relief? "Oh no. You okay?"

"Yeah, yeah. No big deal."

"You, uh, want me to show you where the ice is?" He raises his eyebrows extra high, like he's asking me something else. Maybe checking if I'm okay.

"No need. Just tell me where it is." I assure him, then raise my own eyebrows. *Are you okay?*

He flicks a glance over my shoulder at his interloping teammates before clearing his throat. "It's in the freezer, in the equipment room next to the tennis rackets."

"Thanks. See ya."

"Hey, um…" Teddy puts an arm out to stop me but then lets it drop. His ears have gone pink, and I can tell he wants to say more, but another look past me changes his mind. "Yeah, see ya later in Chem."

161

Smart move. Whatever he's got to say, now's not the time and this isn't the place.

So I find my sweaty, wadded up shirt on the floor and pick it up before heading to the locker room, making my own escape.

Junior Year: Friday, December 14,
Two weeks after losing State
A Way Back In

"Hey, White, you decided not t'come out for basketball?"

The sound of D'Marcus's voice behind me raised the hairs on the back of my neck. But I managed to ignore it, not missing a step as I made my way down the hall to AP Lang. *What kinda stupid question is that anyway?* Varsity tryouts were last week, and I didn't go, so the answer was obvious. Was D'Marcus trying to rub salt in the wound? He and Gavin Holmes would likely be captains this year. If they didn't want me at their lunch table anymore, they sure-as-shit didn't want me on their team. And I wasn't stupid enough to make myself an easy target for their taunts and trash talk. Plus the coaches would no doubt be worried I'd fall apart under pressure, leaving me on the bench when it mattered. Or hell, I might not have made the team at all. That would have been the absolute worst outcome. At least by not showing up, not playing was my choice.

At my silence, D'Marcus jogged a few steps to catch up. "Hold up, man." He put out an arm to block my way then turned so we were facing each other.

I tensed up, not sure where this was going. "What d'you want, D'Marcus?"

"Relax, man, I just wanted t'check in with you or whatever." He claimed, his stance loose and casual. Like the whole public shaming scene in the cafeteria never happened.

Still suspicious, I looked around for more of my former teammates lurking around as backup, but with the bell about to ring any second, the hall was mostly empty. "What d'you care?" I scoffed, ignoring the ping of hope in my back brain.

"Aw, come on, don't be like that." Marcus swatted away my skepticism like it was an invisible ball floating between us.

"Be like what? *You're* the one who--forget it. I gotta get to class." I stepped around him, careful to avoid contact, but he spun and walked with me.

"What I'm sayin' is, now that we've all had time to cool off, and I figure, you've prob'ly done some thinkin' while you been in Time Out. Am I right about that?"

I stopped short as the bell rang. Did he just compare getting practically the whole damn school to shun me to putting a naughty child in fucking Time Out? Choking back the reflexive outrage, I made myself consider what else he implied--that my so-called Time Out could be over.

"Am I right?" D'Marcus repeated. "Have you had some time to think?"

I shifted to face him. He was already turned towards me, waiting with arms crossed, chin out, and eyebrows raised. My mind raced, weighing what was on offer--a way back in--against what it would cost--an admission of...what was D'Marcus looking for? Me taking on sole blame for the flaming garbage fire of States? Or looking for some added contrition? To know that I wasn't trying to play it off like no big deal, like

163

some privileged asshole whose daddy would cover his college costs.

Aw, what the hell. My pride could survive the hit if it meant getting my friends back. I cleared my throat and mustered my best version of sincere and reflective. "Yeah, guess I kinda acted like a dick," I admitted, leaving it open-ended for him to apply it as he liked. "Sorry about that, man," I added for good measure. My heart pounded as he considered me in silence, making his own mental assessments.

Come on, man... The hope I'd held back earlier surged, becoming a small, frantically flapping creature in my chest.

A slow smile spread across D'Marcus's face. "Okay, we cool."

I released a ragged breath I didn't know I was holding and quickly tried to convert it to a laugh. "Yeah, okay, cool. I'll uh, see you around then?"

"Yeah..." D'Marcus rubbed a hand over the stubble on his chin. "As a matter a fact, I'm hosting one of my little gatherings tonight. If you wanna come, that'd be alright."

Holy shit, a party invite? Already, just like that? "Dude, are you sure? I mean, just because you and me are cool doesn't mean--"

He batted away my concern. "Don't worry about the other guys. I'll take care a'all that tonight. You good with me, you good with them, see?"

"Uh, wow, okay...cool." If this turned into any more of a miracle, I was gonna cry right here in the hall and ruin everything. "Well, I better get to class."

"Oh sure, sure, you go be good," he mocked and punched me lightly on the shoulder. "And hey, for what it's worth--we did have one hell of a season, y'know, up till then."

"Yeah, we sure did." There was an unspeakable relief in having him acknowledge it.

"So you're comin' tonight, right? No excuses. If you don't show, I'm gonna take it personal." He rested a hand on my shoulder leaning to make sure he had my complete attention, his playful smirk doing nothing to mitigate the hard look in his eyes. "You wanna make good with the resta the boys, this is your one shot."

My neck hairs got the message. This party was my second chance. If I blew it, there wouldn't be another. "I'll be there. Count on it," I assured him.

His smirk broadened into a true smile. "Alright then. I'll see you later, White."

We bumped fists and went our separate ways. Once he'd gone, I allowed a grin, though the unfamiliar expression made my cheeks ache. It was all I could do not to take a running leap, let out a whoop and fist pump the air. Ellen had been right all along. It just took a little time...and a willingness to eat some crow on my part.

It only then occurred to me that I was still fucking grounded.

I spent the rest of eighth period distracted, trying to come up with a viable way to get to the party. Even if I managed to sneak out, D'Marcus's house was too far to walk or bike. And since the Uber and Lyft apps on my phone used Dad's account and credit card, I couldn't order a ride anywhere without him knowing. I'd need to get permission and transportation. Dad could be a stickler about punishments, and he wouldn't agree to un-ground me for anything remotely resembling a party. I'd have to make something up, something that didn't sound *too* fun but not so dry he'd be suspicious. I

165

didn't have a job that I could pretend needed me to cover a last-minute shift. Maybe a pretend school project? Dad would suggest my group members come over to our place like usual. The time-honored need to go study at the library cliché? Not viable in the age of the internet. I even looked up a list of events going on around the city, but I highly doubted Dad would believe I had a desperate need to attend a metalwork sculpture gallery opening or a free ska band concert. Not under normal circumstances and certainly not while grounded.

If only I had friends to coordinate the lie with, to back me up, to give me a ride... Figuring it was worth a shot, I texted five former teammates I thought would be going to the party. Saying D'Marcus had invited me, seeing if I could grab a ride. *Hey...would Tara be going? Was there a chance she'd...? Oh God...* My already roiling stomach lurched with a mix of fear and excitement at the possibilities the night held. Maybe I should text her, let her know I'd be there. It couldn't hurt, right? Just a casual **Hey, see you later at Dmarcus place?** Yeah, that would be fine...

By the time I got home off the bus, no one had texted me back. I was fresh out of ideas and frustrated enough about it to kick the trash bin outside the garage door. It made a satisfying *Thunk* before tipping over and spilling its contents over the lawn and pavement. I kicked one of the bulging, white kitchen bags, splitting it down the side and sending coffee grounds, potato peels, and various other debris down the driveway. A strangled, inarticulate yell broke free as I stomped my foot through the remains of a rotisserie chicken.

Breathe, I reminded myself, sucking air in through my nostrils and holding it, letting out slowly. *Take back control of your emotions.* I breathed and held and counted until my heart slowed.

When I went into the kitchen to get rubber gloves and a new garbage bag, my phone buzzed with an incoming text. My heart jumped to my throat as I fished it out of my back pocket and dropped again when I saw the message was only from Ellen to say

Ellen--I GOT KIM!!!

>**EJ**--Cool. Is that a good part?

Ellen--YES! It's the lead teenage role Anne-Margret played Kim in the original Bye Bye Birdie movie

>**EJ**--Congrats sis! You deserve it When will you be home?

Ellen--Not sure We've got costume fittings then out for pizza Why?

>**EJ**--Dmarcus invited me to a party at his place tonight

Ellen--OMG!!! I knew you guys would make up YAAAAAAY

>**EJ**--Yeah but I'm still grounded Any ideas?

Something Dad will
buy?
I REEEEEALLY need to
get to this party
Starts at 9

For a minute, nothing. Then--

Ellen--Leave it to me ;-)

EJ--You got an idea?
TELL ME

Ellen--I'll let you know when
it's for sure.
Just trust me XO

Not like I had much of a choice. Redemption was so
damn close yet I could already feel it slipping through my
fingers. It was so fucking frustrating! *Breathe*, I reminded
myself, *and trust Ellen to work her creative magic.*

Senior Year: Sunday, October 24
Semi-Platonic Hang

Maggie makes chocolate chip smiley faces on the
pancakes' bubbling surface, getting them ready for Charlie to
flip. His technique still needs work, but he's getting there. Eight
out of ten land somewhere on the griddle. Not a terrible ratio for
an eight-year-old. As I wipe stray batter off the stovetop, Ellen
saunters into the room.

"Whoa, you look extra nice today, El," I tell her. She's
done some elaborate crown braid with half her hair and curled

the rest. The makeup's more shimmery than her "natural" school look. Her tall brown leather boots, dark green velvety pants, and flowy print top are all new from our Syracuse mall stop the day before. She's got jewelry on, too--the dangly gold teardrop earrings that used to be Mom's and a long chain with an emerald-studded E pendant Dad gave her for her twelfth birthday that she hasn't worn in ages. "Going somewhere?"

She replies with a clipped, "Yup," as she passes the table set for six, steaming scrambled eggs and wonky pancakes ready and waiting. Grabbing her coat off the hook, she calls into the living room, "Ready, Dad," and heads out the front door without waiting for a reply.

Still wearing my red, batter stained apron, I walk over to Dad as he sits on the entranceway bench putting on his shoes. "Where you guys goin'?"

"I'm just dropping Ellen off to meet up with some friends," he says without looking up from his laces.

Uh-huh, riiiiight. Ellen wasn't putting in hours of self-prep for a casual friends hang, not unless there was someone in the mix she wanted to be more than friends with. But I don't clue Dad in on this point. Instead I huff and say, "You guys didn't even eat yet."

Dad tilts his head at me, brow furrowed like he's confused, but also amused. "I'll only be 20 minutes."

"Yeah, but then Ellen won't be here. I mean, it's Sunday. Shouldn't we be all together, at least for part of it?"

Dad lets out a sigh as he pulls on his jacket. "I don't know why you're worked up about this all of a sudden. We had plenty of together time in the car yesterday."

"Yeah, but…" *Ellen had headphones on, Charlie played games on my phone, and you listened to NPR the whole way.*

But I couldn't say that without Dad taking it as criticism and complaining, two of his least favorite behaviors. So I tried, "Aunt Kari and Maggie weren't there then, and I think it's important for us all to sit and have at least one meal--"

"Okay, noted. We'll try for that next weekend."

The car horn beeps, and Dad is out the door.

What's Dad's deal these days? Why do our family traditions seem to mean less and less to him? Is it because we don't all live in the same house anymore? How did I end up the only one who misses our Sunday routine? The going out to brunch, the lounging around watching whatever game was on, the board game after dinner. Hell, I even miss the *church* part.

I hear the back door open, Aunt Kari coming in from the barn. "Hey, I've got a litter of eight-week-old goldendoodles here for their first grooming. Anyone want some puppy play time?"

"Me!" Charlie and Maggie reply through mouths full of pancake, their chairs screeching along the floor in their rush to leave the table.

"Hey, what about breakfast?" I gesture with both hands at the prepared table. "Everything's ready."

"Oh, right..." Aunt Kari slaps her forehead with her palm. "I've gotta get started, but you kiddos finish your food first." She gives me an apologetic smile. "It smells great in here, Eric. Thanks for cooking. Save me a plate for when I'm done?"

"Yeah, sure thing." I say, trying not to sound annoyed.

Charlie and Maggie both stand in front of their plates, stuffing their mouths like they're in a professional eating contest, then scramble out the door after her.

With a resigned sigh, I eat my own breakfast. *All alone. Exactly the kind of Sunday I was looking for.*

170

After clearing the table and using four Clorox wipes to finish cleaning the mess left behind from the littles' syrupy exuberance, I grab my coat, and go sit on the front porch. The rusted folding chair creaks in objection as I drop down into it and pull up the group text with Teddy and Bea. Over the past weeks, we've racked up a total of 245 messages. Just looking at the number sends a buzzy warmth through my chest. Maybe it wouldn't be impressive to EJ White (who could hit that number on an average weekend) but to Eric Madison (who hadn't expected to exchange a single message outside his family) it feels like some kind of achievement.

I make it 246 by texting my crew of two to see if they're up for doing something. Teddy makes a big deal out of this being the first time I've initiated an activity and what a friendship milestone it is and blah, blah, blah, but he has to decline because he's got the recruiter for UB coming over. Still going through the motions until it's "safe" to break the news of his football-less future. Bea is in though, and she knows exactly what we should do. She texts me her address.

Hanging out with a girl. A girl I kinda maybe have a thing for, and who kinda maybe has a thing for me... *Is this a terrible idea?* Maybe. I hesitate for a few seconds, my thumbs hovering over the screen. Ohkwali has been full of nice surprises so far. Sometimes my life here seems almost normal. A way different sort of normal than before. In some ways, a better normal. There are even moments...like balancing equations in Chem with Teddy while we debate the likelihood of multiple universes or the unfairness of the school's ban on "energy drinks," or watching cartoons with Charlie and Maggie from inside our prodigious blanket fort...that I forget why I had to flee to Ohkwali in the first place. These lapses make me giddy and guilty all at once. I deserve to be back in Cell 4B, not enjoying my senior year.

But still... The pull of that normalcy, the friendship, the maybe-something-more with Bea...it's hard to resist.

And it's been a shitty day so far. And I need a distraction. I need something good.

So I text Bea back, telling her I'm on my way.

***

"Have you seen *Firefly*?"

"Nope."

"Any of the *StarTreks*?"

"No, and no thank you."

"Don't be so prejudiced," she scoffs. "There's a lot of deep philosophical thought and sociological theory in *StarTrek*."

"Ooooo...double no thank you."

"Okay, how about *Battlestar Galactica*?"

"I feel like I've heard of that… Is that the one from *The Office*? The identity theft prank Jim plays on Dwight where he says--"

"Bears, beets, *Battlestar Galactica*," Bea recites in a surprisingly decent imitation of Jim imitating Dwight. "And yep, that's the one."

We're hanging out in the DeLuca's finished basement. It's a nice space with cream plush carpeting and a comfy, oversized red sectional couch facing a generous sixty-five inch screen. There's also a kitchenette and bar area fully stocked with snacks and soda. There's beer in there too, but Bea warns that her dad keeps track of the can count. We polish off two bags of microwave popcorn before we even agree on what to watch. Bea has deemed my Sci-Fi/Fantasy viewing history to be "severely lacking." And, no, my countless Marvel movie viewings with Charlie don't count. Too mainstream, apparently. Though she's impressed with my on-theme hairstyle--three Rey Skywalker-esqu loop buns in place of my usual gelled spike creations.

"I still think new *Doctor Who*. It's essential viewing for any Sci-Fi noob. And it's my house, so I get final say," Bea declares and grabs the remote.

For the next 44 minutes, I watch the most bizarre, most British show I've ever seen. Its special effects are laughably terrible...and somehow I kinda like it. Or at least I like watching it with Bea, who keeps getting excited and explaining the significance of various objects and characters.

"Well?" she asks, waiting for my final verdict as the credits roll.

"Mmm...I dunno."

Her face falls a little.

"Okay, I guess I could hatewatch another couple episodes with you," I tell her with a smirk and a shrug.

"YAY--I knew you'd get hooked!" Bea springs from her side of the couch to mine and throws her arms around me.

On instinct, my free arm wraps around her while the other braces against the arm rest so we don't slide to the floor. Her shirt has slid up a bit, exposing the curve between her waist and hip, right where my thumb and forefinger land. I feel her soft, warm skin shiver at the point of contact, and my heart launches into my esophagus. We both go still, our chests pressed together, heart beats escalating. I inhale sharply and try to sit up without dropping Bea. In the next second, she's on her feet, flushed but smiling and looking right at me.

Am I smiling too? I can't even tell. My brain and body have disconnected.

"Time for a snack refill," she announces. "What're y' hungry for?"

Dude, say something. "Do you have any more of those Cheez Doodles?" My voice cracks on Doodles. *What the hell?!*

Her smile goes as wide as humanly possible, but she doesn't laugh. "Let's check." She reaches out a hand to pull me up.

I take it, but she lets go once I'm standing, which is both a disappointment and a relief. I give myself a few seconds to regain composure before following Bea to the kitchenette. She opens the fridge and asks, "You want a drink?" opening the door wider for me to peruse the selection.

"I'll take a root beer, I guess. Thanks."

She hands me a can and picks lime sparkling water for herself before checking the pantry for the Cheez Doodles. "Sorry, looks like we're out. How about...peanut butter filled pretzels?" She pulls out a Costco-sized container.

"Even better," I say. Bea sets the pretzels on the bar and hops up on one of the bar stools. I stay on the other side of the bar, putting a solid barrier between our bodies.

She props her chin on her hand and watches me take a handful of pretzels, the slightest of smiles forming on her lips. "It was a nice surprise to get your text this morning. It's fun to finally hang out somewhere besides school, y'know?"

"Yes, agreed." *Yep, exactly, just two, platonic friends hanging out and binge-watching campy sci-fi. No crackling sexual chemistry going on here.*

She lifts her can and we toast. As if to confirm today as a casual friend thing, she adds, "Maybe we can hang out again next Sunday when Teddy can make it. I know he was bummed to miss out today.."

"Oh, yeah, definitely. I mean, maybe--depending on what my family has planned."

"Yeah, of course." Bea takes another sip then licks her lips.

It's probably not some kind of unconscious signal that she's thinking about kissing, but my mouth goes dry anyway. *Don't stare at her mouth.* I stare at her forehead instead, counting the freckles for a distraction.

It takes me a second to realize she's saying something. "...get started on 'The End of the World.' Such a good episode," her eyelids flutter in pleasure. "Way better than the first one," she promises. "It sets up so many cool characters and storylines. You're gonna love it."

"Okay, we'll see," I hedge, not wanting to get her hopes up.

"I'll make a geek of you yet!" Bea calls over, already getting herself cozied in.

I shake my head and reclaim my own corner of the couch. "And here I had you pegged as a jock when we first met," I tease Bea.

"Well, I'm that too. I'm a...gock."

"A gock?" I laugh.

"Yeah, a geeky jock. It's a thing...that I just made up."

I laugh harder and she throws a pretzel at me. I grab it out of the air, toss it about three feet up, and catch it in my mouth.

"Showoff. Okay, okay, let's see what you got, Madison. Open up." She gently tosses me another and I snatch it out of the air with my jaws.

"Nice! You've got hidden talents, Madison." Bea pops the pretzel she was about to throw into her own mouth and winks at me.

So simple, yet so hot. Before my groin can get further activated, I say, "Alright, let's cue up round two."

I admit the second episode is better, or maybe I just know what to expect this time. But I get distracted half way through when Bea stretches out and the back of her calf slides across my shin and stays there, warm even through the fabric of our pants. *Don't think about it*, I command myself. *It's nothing. Don't make it weird.* So I leave my leg where it is and pretend I don't notice and certainly don't enjoy it. When episode three starts, Bea doesn't suggest we get refills. She doesn't move. Neither do I.

Twenty-some minutes later, the sound of the door opening at the top of the stairs sets off a jolt of adrenaline. I prop myself up, swing my legs over Bea's, and plant my feet on the floor. I'd assumed it was one of Bea's parents coming to check on us, but the voices are too young, a guy's and a girl's. As they descend, I see Bea's brother Anthony. He's holding the hand of a giggling girl. When Anthony stops at the bottom of the steps, she comes up behind him, sliding a hand around his waist and kissing him on the neck. I recognize her immediately from the distinctive hair.

Bea hits pause but stays laying and cranes her neck to see the newcomers. "Hey, bro."

"What're you doing down here?" Anthony asks Bea, looking none too pleased to find the space occupied.

"Watching TV with my friend," she tells him, the *duh* heavily implied.

"Hey." I raise my hand and give them a single wave. The girl--the redhead I'd seen Ellen with a bunch of times at school--blushes and steps back.

Anthony rolls his eyes and asks, "Are you guys almost done? Megan and I were planning to hang out down here, so…"

"Well, feel free to join us." Bea indicates the empty side of the couch with a wide sweep of her hand.

He sneers like she's told a bad joke then clamps his mouth shut and opens his eyes wider, communicating wordlessly with his sibling. I can't see the expression on Bea's face, but whatever it is, it's not the reply he was looking for.

Anthony gives us an annoyed grunt before he turns and pulls Megan back up the stairs.

When the door snaps shut behind them, Bea and I make eye contact. Her eyelids flutter as she takes a long breath in through her nose. "Sorry about that. Anthony acts like such a prick when he's around girls. I don't get it…but it seems to work for him." She shakes her head in bewilderment.

"And we've co-opted his favorite make-out space," I surmise, remembering the many girls I'd snuck in and out of our basement over the years.

Bea snorts. "Something like that. Don't worry, he'll live." She wiggles even deeper into the cushions and presses play.

After a few minutes of internal debate, I tentatively reposition my body as it was, slipping my legs between Bea's legs and the back couch cushions. No big deal, right? Just…sharing the space. Out of the corner of my eye, I catch her lips forming the briefest of smiles before she sucks them in between her teeth. *God, those lips… No, stop it. Watch the show.*

We manage to fit in two more episodes before Bea's mom calls down to say dinner is here, her announcement accompanied by the aroma of pizza.

"Wanna stay for dinner?" Bea asks. "We can keep watching while we eat."

I feel myself smile in response, but an alarm bell sounds in my back brain. This whole thing with me and Bea laying on the couch...I'm already pushing my limits. The longer I stay, the higher the chances I do something stupid and ruin the perfectly time nice we've been having together. Not worth the risk. "Thanks, but I actually have a bunch of homework to get to tonight, so I better get going."

I catch only the briefest moment of disappointment before Bea's smile is back in place. "Another time. Maybe next Sunday?"

When Teddy could be here too. *Perfect.* "Yeah, that'll be great."

"Great," she agrees. "I'll walk you out then."

At the door, we both slip on our shoes and she pulls on her soccer team warm-up jacket. My black Grand Prix sits over on a large paved parking/basketball area down from the green four-car garage. Bea's house is newer and gloriously spacious compared to the Mackenzie's but pales in comparison to my own house--the one I grew up in, not Aunt Kari's ramshackle farmhouse where everything creaks and you're lucky to get ten straight minutes of hot water.

By some silent agreement, we take our time getting to our destination. A pink and gold sunset illuminates the scene. A foolish part of me wants to backtrack and accept her dinner invitation. Tell her the homework can wait. No, this was the right decision. *Keep walking, White.*

I sense her watching me and glance over. She gives me a shy smile and tucks a loose strand of brown hair behind her ear. Without consciously deciding to, my arm arcs outward, my knuckles grazing hers. She doesn't need further encouragement to slip her hand around mine, interlacing our fingers.

There it is again, that fantastic buzz under my skin. *How does she do this to me with a simple gesture? Fuck... I should say something, compliment her--no, bad idea.* Just holding her hand again was probably a bad idea. Especially since I couldn't write it off as some post-panic attack gesture of comfort. *What the hell do I say right now?* Something safe and generic. "Thanks for having me over," I blurt.

"Of course," she squeezes my hand. "Any time."

Is my palm sweaty? Oh God...

"Sorry if we threw off your brother's routine." My voice cracks again on routine, like some middle school virgin.

Bea snorts. "Are you kidding? That was a bonus." After a pause, she adds, "To be fair, it is an ideal make-out space. My parents, like, never go down there."

Why is she telling me that? Holy shit... "No kidding," I manage, praying she won't notice the uptick in my pulse. *Has Bea hooked up with many guys down there? What kind of guys has she gone for in the past? Not that it matters and not that it's something I have any right to feel jealous about right now.*

She goes on, her tone blithe but her cheeks pink. "But like, the weird part is, if we have someone in our bedroom, we have to keep the door open. They're super strict about it, which makes no sense to me. Like nothing naughty can happen unless there's a bed in the room."

"Yeah, weird." I swallow hard, desperately trying not to picture Bea laying on her bed. The image transitions into her laying on the couch, then laying on top of me on the couch...*the warm, heavy weight of her pressing me into the cushions, her face so close I can feel her breath on my cheek.* When I manage to pull myself back to reality, it's only to realize my palm is fucking on fire, the pulse in my wrist hammering against hers. We're almost to the car though. *Thank God.* Reaching in my pocket for my keys gives me an excuse to pull my hand from hers.

"Um, thanks again. I'll see you tomorrow," I say without looking at her, fumbling to get the right key in the door lock. *Ancient piece of shit.*

"Yeah...Eric?"

"Hmm?" *Why do I have so many goddamn keys?*

"Um, there was just one last thing."

When I turn, she's maybe three feet from me. Her shoulders are squared, feet apart, jaw set, with a determined look in her eye. She flexes her fingers out long into wide fans before drawing them into fists. If I didn't know better, I'd say she was working herself up to take a corner kick. Or to punch me in the jaw.

"I wanted to say, I think you're really great, and I like having you as a friend..." She pauses to gulp down air before letting it all rush out with the rest of her declaration, "and I kind of hope we can be more than friends."

Well, there it is.

"And I've kind of gotten the sense you feel the same?" she asks, voice tentative but brows arched hopefully.

Not like it came out of nowhere. And I have lines ready. I've rehearsed this in my head. Versions of *Sorry but I don't like you like that. Let's stay just friends.* But would she buy that at this point? I'd just been holding her hand, heart beating like crazy. Would she think I was nuts? Accuse me of leading her on? *Fuck.*

I swallow and open my mouth, not sure what will come out. As the moments pass, nothing does.

Bea's intense green eyes lock with mine. The pink tip of her tongue flicks out, coating those gorgeous full lips with a hint of shine.

God, that's hot.

She takes a step closer. Still, I don't say a word.

Oh God, is she going to... My head swims. The cold, solid frame of the car door steadies me.

She takes another step. There's maybe six inches between our bodies. *I should stop this. It's my fault for letting it get this far, for letting her think--*

She lays a palm on the bare skin of my neck and slides it upwards until her finger lace through the hair at the base of my head, applying just enough pressure to make it clear what she wants.

My head dips obediently.

She tips her face up and closes the distance.

WHAT THE FUCK ARE YOU DOING? I scream at myself.

But her lips pressing gently on mine silence all protest. They are every bit as lush as I'd imagined. My own lips soften and kiss her in return, answering her question without words. She sighs against my mouth, her frame relaxing before she kisses me again, this time with confidence, knowing she won't be rejected. Her tongue teases at the entrance to my mouth and any lingering objections dissolve in a rush of oxytocin. I lean my back against the car and pull her with me, our bodies pressed together through multiple layers of fabric. Still, I can make out her small, firm breasts against my ribcage. When I suck her lower lip, she moans and grips my bicep.

Oh God...

I grasp her around the waist and roll us so I have her pinned up against the car. She rakes a hand through my hair, dislodging the bottom tie before taking the loosened waves in her fist and pushing my face even more firmly against hers. Our mouths seal together, tongues exploring the new terrain, unbothered by the trace hints of peanut butter.

Eventually desperate for a deep drag of air, I release her mouth but keep my lips close, breathing against her jaw, kissing my way to her neck. When I locate the pulse point just below her earlobe and probe it with my tongue, she moans a long, low "oooooh" and arches against me, her fingertips pressing into my scalp and shoulder. My own lower body answers, already anticipating the endgame.

Shit. I freeze, my throat closing up. Too much, too far, too fast. *Get it under control, White.* I force myself to pull away slowly, keeping my hands around her waist until I'm sure she's steady. Her expression is dazed but pleased, with a grin she tries to force into something smaller and less goofy. But it's no use. She lets go of me and raises both hands to cover her mouth.

I take another step back, giving us both some space. The fall evening air is blessedly cool against my overheated skin.

Bea lowers her hands and stares at me. "Wow...just, wow. That was...I mean, *wow*." She covers her mouth again and giggles at her own lack of articulation.

What have you done, White? "Bea, oh God, listen, I'm...I'm sorry."

Her eyes go wide, blinking rapidly, "Sorry for what?"

"I really...I shouldn't have…"

"Wait--oh my god--do you have a girlfriend back at your old--"

"No! Nothing like that."

"Okay then…" She looks even more confused than before, and newly suspicious.

"What I'm trying to say is, I didn't mean to go all...zero to sixty on you like that."

She tilts her head to one side like she's trying to figure me out. "Um, I was right there with you. I mean, I *started* it. And you didn't do anything I didn't want you to, so no need to apologize."

That's right. It was all consensual. That was something. Not just something--that was key.

Still… I squeeze my eyes shut and rub my palms over my face, trying to force my rational mind back into action so I can remind myself of all the other reasons starting something with Bea is a very bad idea--the ongoing need for deception, the risk of exposure, the likelihood she ends up hating me, the public hating her for dating me. *If you like her, all the more reason to protect her from all that. You can't date. Period.*

"Eric, you okay?"

I open my eyes. She's standing there, the aroused flush gone from her skin, waiting for me to explain why I'm trying to backtrack from the great thing that happened between us.

Sorry, Bea, I'm a recovering rapist. And clearly still a hormonal, out of control, asshole. Okay, so I won't be saying that. Better go with, "I do like you, Bea, like--*a lot.* But my life is kind of a mess right now, for lots of reasons. And I don't exactly have the best track record, romantically speaking, so I just think…" *you should stay the hell away from me, for your* *own good. Whatever you're feeling for me, fight it...*Is what I should finish with.

But I look at her standing there, hands braced against my car door with that confused frown and wide, vulnerable eyes, and all my good reasons feel like these far away if/then hypotheticals compared to the very real and present hurt I could inflict with my next words. And there is still the sensation of her lips on mine and the strong desire to feel and taste them again.

So instead of the harsh but safer course, I say, "...I think we need to take things slow."

"Oh..." Her expression clears. "That's totally fine. Whatever you need. We have plenty of time." With a supportive smile, she takes a slow step toward me and squeezes my forearms lightly.

"Right, okay, great." I manage a twisted side-smile, my innards jumping with a combination of fear and delight as her fingertips slide down to my wrists, leaving goosebumps in their wake.

"Okay, well...I'll see you tomorrow, first thing?" she checks.

"Yup, see you then," I confirm, now wearing a goofy grin of my own.

She walks backwards a few steps before sticking her hands in her pockets and turning to jog back up the drive.

I locate my keys on the pavement (dropped in mid-kiss delirium), get in my car, and sit with my hands on the wheel a minute, making sure I'm calm enough to drive. My hands are shaking a little, but I'm not nauseous, so I don't think it's The Black Hole coming for me. I haven't had a full-blown panic attack in...weeks. Not since the football game. Either my medication is doing its job better than before, or *I'm* doing better than before. Like maybe one day The Black Hole can be something I leave behind with the rest of my fucked-up past. *Wow, if that's true…*I let myself consider then stop myself. It's only been a few weeks. Too soon to know…*Then again, it's the longest you've gone since they started almost a year ago. This new life, this new you in Ohkwali, maybe it's working. Building real friendships is healthy, a sign of healthy growth. And this thing with Bea, maybe that's the right next step too.*

I start the car and pull away, my mind spinning in new directions, like I'm on the verge of an epiphany. I made out with a girl and my body had reacted in a fairly normal-for-a-teenage-guy way. Do I still need to work on control? Yes. But I pulled back before anything went too far. That's, like, huge! And not for nothing, it's a sign I can have healthy physical interactions with a girl again. Until now, that was still a big question mark in my life. Since that night with Kendra, I can barely masturbate or fantasize, can barely even look at girls without being overwhelmed by nauseating shame and self-loathing. I start worrying, *What if I lose control and hurt someone again the way I hurt Kendra?*

But with Bea, everything seems possible again. She's an amazing person who I already have an actual relationship with. The kind of girl I'd've been excited to introduce to Mom. She's easy-going and patient and comfortable in her own skin and makes me feel good about myself. She makes me want to be a better person, the kind of guy she deserves.

And it just feels so right.

Since day one in Ohkwali, I've let my past control me--second guessing my instincts, overanalyzing every action, every conversation, keeping people at arm's length, worried they'll peek behind the curtain and find EJ White lurking there.

Maybe that's the problem. I've been thinking about this all wrong, playing Eric Madison like he's only a short-term cover identity, like he's the lie. But maybe he can be the real me, the better me. I have a second chance here, with a new name, a new life, new friends--even a possible girlfriend. The only way to get the life I want is to start living it. Start being the kind of man Mom and Dad and Ellen and Charlie can be proud of. This life in Ohkwali is a gift, and it would be stupid-- morally wrong, even--to keep living in fear of what might happen in the worst-case scenario.

Lying awake past midnight, I let myself think about Bea. I relive our kiss and fantasize about what would have happened next if I hadn't put on the breaks. My body responds. The Bea in my mind presses even tighter against me. She knows what I want, and she wants it too. We're braced up against my car...the car...the back seat... And then it happens like it has a hundred times before--the body under my hands is Kendra's and she's crying and... My body tenses. Cold floods my gut and proceeds south.

But this time I force myself not to recoil and force Kendra from my mind. Instead, I try something new. I fast forward and imagine Kendra out there going about her life and how much better things are getting for her. I see her at the grocery store with her mom, relieved knowing that she won't randomly run into me in the produce section. And the people at school who used to tease and ignore her think she's brave for coming forward about what I did to her and treat her with respect, friendship even. She goes to the fall multi-church Youth Group retreat and meets a cute, nice guy who loves classic literature and makes her smile and listens when she needs to talk and holds her when she needs to cry and who doesn't pressure her to do anything physical she isn't completely on board with. I imagine she's getting on with her life and is able to think of me as little as possible.

This year is a second chance for *both* of us.

All we have to do is make the choice to shed the past and step into the future.

Junior Year: Friday, December 14, Two weeks after losing States The Night in Question--What Happened at the Party

When I opened the passenger side door of the Honda minivan, I was unpleasantly surprised to see Frankie Gurlance behind the wheel. "Oh...hey." Based on his complete lack of eye contact or verbal response to my greeting, I'd say Frankie wasn't particularly pleased to see me either. Lord knows how Ellen and/or Andrea managed to convince him to transport me. To a party no less.

I turned around to Ellen and mouthed, *Frankie?*

"Beggars can't be choosers," Ellen reminded me in a whisper as she got in the back with Andrea.

"Hi, EJ," Andrea cooed, her head cocked to the side and chin tipped down like she was posing for a selfie. The dome light did her makeup job no favors, accentuating already heavy blush, bright pink lipstick, and mascara clumped lash extensions.

"Hey Andrea. You ladies look, uh...fancy." Through unzipped coats, I could see her and Ellen's sequined dresses and chunky plastic beaded necklaces.

"Why thank you." Andrea smiled and gave her straightener-fried red hair a little flip. She'd been laying it on thick all week, making it clear that she was ready and willing should my lonely self need female companionship. All I had to do was say the word.

I smiled back and noted, "You got your braces off!"

"How sweet of you to notice." She beamed, showing off bare teeth and too much upper gum.

I cleared my throat. "So uh, what're you guys up to tonight?" i.e. Where'd you tell Dad I was going that convinced him to unground me?

"It's the Winter Youth Group Teen Skate tonight," Ellen explained as she used a compact mirror to apply her own lipstick.

"Ah, cool…" *Yuuuuck.* A couple hundred kids from local churches hanging around the Northwinds Christian Academy gym, skating to "contemporary" Christian music from two decades ago. No thanks. But I had to hand it to Ellen. It was exactly the kind of event Mom and Dad always "strongly encouraged" us to attend. I hadn't been to one in years, and Dad'd never believe I'd want to go if I *wasn't* grounded. It was a brilliant plan.

"The theme is 'Be Bold,'" Andrea further explained, tucking her hair behind her ears to reveal mini disco ball earrings.

"As in--be bold in your faith, like 'the righteous are bold as a lion,' but we decided to take it literally for costume purposes." Ellen's now crimson lips curve into a less-than-righteous looking grin.

Andrea leaned forward and put a hand on my bicep. "EJ, you must be so proud of Ellen getting a lead role!"

Frankie clocked the physical contact and frowned.

"Oh totally. My crazy-talented sister is one step closer to Broadway." I twisted further in my seat to wink at Ellen and break away from Andrea's touch. No sense in pissing Frankie off when he was doing me a huge favor. "So, Andrea, what part did you get in the musical?"

"I'm Helen! She's one of the teen characters and has a solo in 'The Telephone Hour' song. Ellen and I are in a bunch of scenes together!" Both girls squealed and grasped each other's hands. Then they were on to *Bye Bye Birdie* talk--who had a fit on social media about not getting the part they wanted, ideas for hair and makeup, whether so-and-so's girlfriend will be jealous over the stage kiss...

Unable to join in, I tried (like an idiot) to make small talk with Frankie. "So uh...are you going to the Teen Skate too?"

"Yes," he replied in a tone that let me know how stupid my question was.

"Nice..." I forged ahead anyway. "So you like to skate?"

He let out a long, annoyed sigh. "Sure."

"He likes to skate with *Kendra Daniels*," his sister clarified.

"Andrea..." Frankie growled in warning.

But it did no good. "What? It's true. When she's there, you follow her around the whole time, and when she's not, you sit on the bleachers and sulk and make us go home early."

Andrea turned to me and added in a conspiratorial tone, "That way he can spend time fantasizing about her in the privacy of his room."

"Shut up!" Frankie glared at her in the rearview mirror as she sat back, a small, satisfied smile on her lips. Frankie clamped his mouth shut rather than say more, his chest heaving, breathing heavily through his nose. It had to sting his pride. All these years going after Kendra...but she'd never buckled. Apparently she had the good sense to see the drawbacks outweighed the benefits of dating a scowling, controlling douchebag like Frankie. And I had the good sense to keep my mouth shut about it and feign interest in something out the window while Andrea and Ellen went back to their own conversation.

Fortunately, it only took a few more minutes to get to D'Marcus's place. When Frankie pulled up by the end of the driveway, I unbuckled and pasted on a smile. Even if he was doing this under duress, I still appreciated it. "Thanks for the ride."

There was no response.

"Okay then...so I'll see you back here a little after midnight, once the skate's over?"

Frankie looked momentarily uncomfortable and ran a hand down his long, angular face. He glanced behind me at the house, his brow creased. *Oh God, he's not gonna give me some moral lecture, is he?*

But all he said was, "12 o'clock *sharp*. Be outside. We're not coming in for you. If you're not out here waiting, we'll leave. And don't text us to pick you up any earlier. That's not happening."

"He must already know Kendra will be there," Andrea told Ellen in a loud whisper.

Frankie's jaw tightened but he otherwise ignored her.

"Don't worry, I won't wanna leave early," I assured him. "In fact, the longer I can stay the better. So if you guys decide to go to McDonald's or something after--"

"We won't."

Beggars can't be choosers. "Midnight it is. Thank you soooo much, man. I owe you big time."

He snorted. "You can pay me back by not getting drunk and puking in the van."

"Clean and sober. You have my word." I made the Scout's Honor sign.

He looked over at the house one more time, a tight little smile forming on his lips. "Enjoy the party. You deserve it."

Um...okay. "Thanks, will do." Though it would be harder to enjoy the party while sober and having to leave just as things really got going.

The minivan's wheels screeched as Frankie pulled away.

I took in a deep breath of cold air and readied myself. It was only 9:16 p.m. but there were already fifteen cars parked in the driveway and along the street, and I could hear the music from the sidewalk.

As soon as I walked in the door, I scanned for D'Marcus, not sure who he'd talked to already or what the plan was to reintroduce me to society. But he was nowhere to be seen. Instead, I spotted cornerback and NHS President Chris Turrik, coming out of the kitchen with a red SOLO cup in each hand. His scraggly red eyebrows went up and he gave me a nod. "Hey, White. Didn't expect you yet."

At least Chris knew I'd been invited and was willing to speak to me. That was a good sign, right? Especially since he was tight with Kevin Markone. I nodded back and gave a slouching, casual shrug. "Yeah, my uh, ride was on their way somewhere else, so..."

"Ah, no worries, man. Glad you could make it. When D'Marcus filled us in, we were all on board." He smiled and jerked his head toward the living room area. "Follow me."

I felt the tightness in my chest that had been there for weeks finally ease. I sent up a silent thanks to the Holy Trinity-- D'Marcus, Frankie, and Ellen White for making tonight possible.

Chris and I made our way to where Gavin Holmes was on a couch between two freshman girls. Chris handed each girl a cup and leaned down to say something to Gavin I couldn't hear over the music. Gavin glanced at me over Chris's shoulder then looked back at Chris and said something in response, his lips barely moving. Chris nodded and turned to go. As he passed, he slapped me on the back harder than was strictly friendly but gave a reassuring nod. "You hang with Holmes. I'll let D'Marcus know you're here."

Gavin thrust his own full SOLO cup at my chest. "Hey, man, welcome back. Have a beer." I grabbed for it before its frothy contents sloshed all over my letterman jacket but it ended up dripping all over my jeans and shoes instead.

Oh for fuck's sake... I would reek like a brewery by the time I got back in Frankie's car. And I'd be wearing clear evidence of my non-Teen Skate activities if Dad was still up. Still, any heat I'd take from those two afterwards would be worth it to get back into these guys' good graces.

"Oops. My bad," Gavin laughed, not sounding sorry at all.

Whatever. He's probably wasted already. "Thanks..." I wiped at the wet trails on my thighs.

"Here, have a seat." Gavin pulled one girl onto his lap and scooted over so there was a spot between him and the other girl.

It was a tight fit. My upper arm pressed against the other girl's left breast until she managed to shift and put her arm between us. They were nice breasts, I noticed. "Hey, I'm EJ. What's your name?" I tried. But she only looked away and raised the beer to her lips. *Okaaaay...* I turned to Gavin instead, planning to ask about how basketball practices were going so far, but he was already making out with the girl on his lap. *Perfect. I'll just...sit here then.*

I took a sip of beer just to have something to do and scanned the rest of the room, noticing others noticing me, the glances, the smirks, the poorly concealed curiosity. A group of sophomore girls looked my way, then leaned in to whisper and laugh. About me? Or was I being paranoid? I could feel my face heat. *Relax, just get through this part.* D'Marcus would be here in a minute to make a public show of reconciliation and people would take their cue from him.

That's when I spotted her. Tara Kajowski--over in the far corner, hard to miss in a skin-tight, bright yellow dress-- sitting on Kevin Markone's knee. Kevin Markone who was back on top after nabbing a starting spot on the varsity basketball team with D'Marcus and Gavin. Tara was laughing at something he'd said, but when she caught me staring, her smile faltered. She looked surprised and almost...disappointed, maybe? Either way, it wasn't the reaction I'd been hoping for.

Kevin's hand moved up under her skirt as he buried his face in the crook of her neck. Talk about being quick--two weeks and she was already back with her ex. Had she wanted him back all along, or was she the type who spread her legs for whatever guy was currently King of the Mountain? From an uncomfortable mix of emotions I latched onto disgust. *What a slut. You're better off without her. She's probably carrying multiple STIs...Fuck, I better get tested.* I'd used a condom that night after our semi-finals win when we'd hooked up in the back of Holmes's Tahoe, but it didn't always protect you from herpes and genital warts and other disgusting shit.

Wiggling a little deeper into his lap, she leaned over and whispered something in his ear. He craned his neck, looking for me. Seeing me put a smile on his face, which was definitely not a good sign.

I peered into my now half empty cup of cheap keg beer. *What's one beer? I'm not gonna get drunk on one beer. It'll help take the edge off, that's all.* I downed the rest in three long pulls.

The girl with the nice breasts was still angled away from me, swiping through images and videos on her phone. She looked kinda familiar now that I took a minute to focus on her. I especially remembered her flashy purple acrylic nails with rhinestone tips. Where had I seen them before... Ah yes--they'd been (barely) covering her nipples in a picture she'd sent me a few weeks ago. What was her name again? Latoya? Lamara? Something like that. Should I remind her of her previous interest in me? There was plenty about me still to like, right? Besides, at this point, it wasn't as if something was gonna happen with Tara, so what did I have to lose?

I leaned close to her ear to say, "Hey girl, I liked that sexy pic you sent me the other day."

"I don't know what you're talking about," she replied, still scrolling, liking, scrolling...

Oh, it's like that, is it? I could feel my neck pulse with a surge of angry heat. Where did this freshman bitch get off looking down on me, a good-looking upperclassman? Did she realize my house was a fucking mansion compared to D'Marcus's place? *I guess athletic performance is really all that mattered to these jockstrap fangirl whores.* When you're a starter, they'll happily suck your dick, but once that spotlight's gone, so's their interest.

Well, at least I could call her out on an obvious lie. I pulled out my own phone and found her pic. It had been hot enough that I decided to save it.

I reached over so my screen was a foot from her face. "This is you, right?"

She frowned at the picture, lips pursed in annoyance. She pushed my phone away and claimed, "Somebody musta forwarded that to you."

"Nice try. You sent it to me right after--"

"And I'd appreciate it if you'd delete it," she added as she stood and walked off, hips swinging.

I watched her go. Angry, stunned, confused, blood pumping in my ears. Never, in my entire life had I been so completely brushed off by a girl. I'd been wrong. Turned out I did have something left to lose--the last ounce of my pride.

Across the room, Tara was still hot and heavy with Kevin. Right next to me, Gavin was focused on groping his plaything's ass. The room felt warm. Stifling. How long had I been sitting here? I checked the time on my phone. Only 9:28. *Goddammit. Where the fucking hell is D'Marcus already?*

I leaned my head back and closed my eyes in an effort to reset. *Relax. Give it a minute. Don't worry about that freshman bitch. She's just one girl. And you knew chances of getting back with Tara tonight were slim. There's plenty of pussy to be had.* I counted to ten once, then twice, then a third time until I felt back in control.

Well, sitting there waiting with an empty beer cup wasn't going to make anything better. I stood and walked around the room, trying to look like I was going somewhere. Everyone seemed to notice me—until I got within speaking distance. I tried to join in with a group of girls who'd started dancing, but when I got in close, they looked at me like *As if, loser,* before closing ranks and boxing me out. Two girls even straight up walked away, leaving me to dance on my own, like some pathetic, zit-faced reject.

Frustration burned a line down my throat to my gut. This was all wrong, and I didn't know how the fuck to fix it without D'Marcus. *Beer...I need one more beer...to get a buzz going. These things are always shit when you're sober.*

I headed to the kitchen and almost ran into Chris Turrik coming in from the back porch holding six SOLO cups by the rim. "Whoa, watch it," he snapped.

"Sorry," I put my hands up in apology.

Chris's face relaxed, like he just remembered he's not supposed to hate me anymore. "Oh, hey, White. You havin' fun?"

"Not especially," I admitted and shoved my hands in my pockets. "Most people are actin' like I'm not supposed to be here. D'Marcus made it sound like he was gonna..." *tell people to be nice to me again.* God, that sounded pathetic. "...let everybody know we'd made peace or whatever. You said you were gonna find him?"

Chris grinned and set the cups on the breakfast bar. "Yeah, he's uh...finishing up with something," Chris winked at me to be sure I caught that some*thing* was some*one*. "Don't worry, he'll be down soon."

"Yeah, but like, what's 'soon'? 'Cause you and Gavin are the only people willing to talk to me so far. And Gavin's a little...distracted, so--"

"Dude, you expect us to hold your fuckin' hand or something?" Chris sneered.

I looked away. "No, but...nevermind." *Do not cry, loser--DO NOT CRY.* "Maybe I shouldn't have come. Prob'ly still too soon."

Perhaps realizing how harsh he'd come off, Chris switched modes again and fixed an easy smile on his face. "Relax, man, you're too tense." He stepped behind me to squeeze my shoulders, pressing hard with his thumbs into the muscles. "Loosen up, huh? You need another drink," he suggested, slapping my ass before grabbing two of the beer cups he'd brought in and holding one out to me.

"Cheers, man--to setting things right." He bumped the plastic edge of his cup against mine and downed half his cup in one go.

"Yeah...cheers." I took a less enthusiastic sip of mine. When he raised an *Oh please* eyebrow, I took another, longer chug.

"There ya go," Chris nodded approval. "Hey, why don't you...play beer pong or something? Enjoy yourself!" He made a sweeping gesture at the increasingly packed party scene around us before taking the remaining beers off the counter and heading to the living room, leaving me once again on my own. Another time check--only 10:06. Two whole hours to fill.

So I halfway took Turrik's advice and went over to the beer pong table in the dining area. Watching at least gave me something to do that didn't make my ongoing pariah status too obvious. After a couple of rounds as a spectator, my second beer was gone, and I was getting bored, so I called dibs on the next round. But as soon as the cups got refilled, some couple stepped right in and started playing. *They must not've heard me*, I reasoned. So I called out, "I got next ups after these guys," a bit louder this time. But next round, it was the same thing all over again. There was always somebody else who'd step up for the next round, claiming they'd been ahead of me. Which was bullshit, of course.

Whatever. Even with my blood already at a simmer, I wasn't stupid enough to pick a fight in the middle of a hostile crowd. My bladder was starting to ache anyway, so I walked away and ditched my empty cup. It was 10:42 and the house was now bursting at the seams with people. Squeezing through the throng, I made it to the top of the stairs only to find eleven other people waiting in line for the bathroom.

Sixteen agonizing minutes and a long piss later, I put the toilet lid down and sat, using the private moment to consider my next move. Only one thing was for sure--coming tonight had been a mistake. But here I was...so what now? Without knowing when D'Marcus would make a public appearance at his own damn party, my options were limited. I could stick it out, spend the rest of the time until midnight giving people yet more opportunities to shun and humiliate me, or...I could leave. The map on my phone showed a shopping plaza about a half a mile away with a Walmart that was open until 2:00 a.m. I could text Frankie the address and wait there until midnight.

Hiding out at a Walmart... very cool, White. A success all around. I groaned and bent over, elbows braced on my knees, face in my hands. Feelings of anger, disappointment, embarrassment, and powerlessness oozed together in a churning brew that made me dizzy. *You could have been home with Charlie, eating warm brownies and watching a movie.*

Someone banged on the door and I forced myself to stand and give my hands a quick wash, splashing water on my face as I did. Looking at my blotchy, dripping face in the mirror, I made a final choice. *I'm done with this shit. Time to go.*

But when I opened the door, both Chris and Gavin were standing there waiting for me.

Chris delivered the good news. "D'Marcus sent us to get you."

"Oh..." *Fucking finally.* I sag against the doorframe in relief.

"Yeah, he's got a fun surprise planned for ya," Gavin said as he moved to my right side and dropped a heavy arm over my shoulders.

"A 'fun surprise'?" I repeated, not sure what to make of this after how D'Marcus had left me hanging for hours.

"Yeah...*very* fun," Chris concurred. But something about the way the corners of his mouth twitched with suppressed glee made my innards clench and blood run cold. Whoever this surprise was gonna be fun for, instinct said it wouldn't be for me. *Shit...* My mind raced as they brought me down the stairs, Chris in front and Gavin behind. *They wouldn't really force me to stay, would they? No, that'd be crazy.* But they might not make it easy. I'd have to be quick. *When we get to the bottom, it's only ten feet to the front door. Walk over, open it, and leave. Simple as that.*

I took the final step at a rush and ducked out from Gavin's arm. He stumbled and reached for me then had to grab the railing when I stepped out of reach.

Chris had wasted no time moving himself between me and the door.

"My ride texted me a few minutes ago they're on their way. They'll be here any minute," I explained.

"Who's your ride?" Chris asked in a casual tone.

My mouth had gone so dry I could barely get the words out. "Um, a friend."

"Cool...so they won't mind waiting a few more minutes."

"Uh, they will, actually. They told me to wait outside, so I better--" I tried to sidestep Chris, but he'd been joined by Jake Kaminski, his solid bulk covering the door knob. "Oh, hey…excuse me, I gotta..." I tried to smile at him, but he just glowered, not bothering with Chris and Gavin's friendly veneer. *Oh shit, they're really gonna force me to stay. Shiiiiit...* I glanced over my shoulder toward the sliding glass door in the kitchen--the only other exit. *Maybe if I walk with them toward the living room and then make a dash for it...*

But the look gave my thoughts away. Kaminski looped his thick arm around my right arm and held it vice tight. Gavin followed suit with my left. Chris stepped out in front, taking up my field of vision. "Don't even think about it. We've got that exit covered too," he warned.

Fear spiking, I reacted on animal instinct and tried to wrench myself out of their grip. Precious little good it did against our two biggest lineman. *Fuck.*

Chris was still talking low and close. "Don't fight it, White. You'll only make it harder on yourself."

My breath started coming fast and shallow. *Oh God, Oh God...fuuuuuck...* Dizzy, pulse racing, and out of ideas that wouldn't end in me getting the piss beat out of me, I sagged in defeat.

"That's better," Chris cooed in the slow, ominous voice of a serial killer to their chloroformed victim. I shivered, the hairs on my neck rising as he went on. "Just come with us to the living room, get your surprise, and then you can go, okay buddy?"

I nodded.

Still, they weren't taking any chances. My two guards held me tight and frog marched me through the assembled crowd, all watching us pass, waiting for whatever was about to happen. Waiting in anticipation. I was to be the centerpiece of tonight's entertainment. *God, please, please, please, no...* I pressed my lips shut and swallowed back a traitorous whimper.

As we passed through the dining area, I saw the last person I ever expected to see--Kendra Daniel. She was near the back wall, looking stricken, her eyes wide and helpless as she watched them escort me past. Dear God, was everyone I'd ever known gathered to witness whatever fresh humiliation my former "friends" had concocted for me?

Still holding me by the arms, Jake and Gavin maneuvered the three of us onto the empty couch, which had been turned to face a blank wall, the framed jerseys that had been there before leaning up against the floorboard. I gave an involuntary jerk as a third arm snaked around my neck, pressing against my Adam's apple, hard enough to hurt but not enough to stop the air flow. "It's payback time, cock sucker." Kevin Markone, of course he'd be in on this...whatever this was.

Cheers and claps started up in the kitchen and spread as the mastermind made his way front and center. D'Marcus Clay put his hands in the air, one of which was holding a phone mounted on some kind of tripod. The assembly made a last exuberant rush of noise before falling silent. Someone cut the music so D'Marcus could be heard through the whole house.

"Hey everybody, glad y'could make it here tonight. We got a special film to premiere. And we're lucky enough to be joined tonight by the star of the show, Mr. EJ White." A smattering of claps, laughs, and boos went up at my name. D'Marcus looked directly at me for the first time to say, "We all know how much you like the spotlight, so we knew you'd wanna be here for this."

There it was, confirmation of what I'd already figured out--that the offered reconciliation and party invitation had been false lures to get me here. I'd walked myself right into the Lion's Den, not as a returning member of the pride but as prey. I choked on a sob as it sunk in how big a fool I'd been.

D'Marcus stepped up to the couch and lowered his voice. "I had D1 scouts callin' me before State. Then after, the only offer I got was SUNY Buffalo--fuckin' UB, man. You know how many players got drafted from UB in the last two decades? *One.*" We stared at each other, both struggling for breath. I wanted to apologize again, plead the case the D1 teams wouldn't have passed on him just because of a single game. But I could barely form clear thoughts, let alone words.

D'Marcus turned away and got the tripod set up, the phone's projection attachment aimed toward the blank wall "Alright, somebody hit the lights!" he called out.

The space went dark except for a five-foot-wide projection of a YouTube video titled "EJ White Game of Shame: EJ on His KNEEEEES!!!" Though my vision was blurring worse than ever, I could tell from the thumbnail picture that there was footage of my failure at States. I squeezed my eyes shut, unwilling to watch what I'd already replayed a hundred times in my head. But Kevin wasn't going to let me take the copout. "Hey now, don't be ungrateful, White." He increased the pressure on my neck, making me gag. "It took *days* to put together this tribute, so sit here like a good boy and watch." He shifted so his hands were on either side of my face, his thumbs forcing my eyelids to stay open and my head to face straight ahead.

Sure enough, the footage rolled, showing each sack, each interception, each fumble, and shots cut together of me running back and forth, looking like a chicken with my head cut off, all to matching sound effects. But that was only the first minute and a half. Then came the real cutting edge of the tribute to my failure. The screen froze on a still shot of me fallen to my hands and knees right after I'd thrown that last interception. A second later, the image added a Green Dragon player photoshopped directly behind me. A player's face was pasted over the helmet—Aaron Rogers, the first interceptor. And my pained face behind the facemask was replaced with a smiling shot from the team pictures. One of Aaron's arms looked edited to be grabbing the side of my ass. The picture moved, jerkily, back and forth, thrusting, accompanied by voiceover sex noises and the occasional taunt in a husky male voice, like "Oh, EJ, you're soooo good to me. Just like that. Throw me another one." Every ten seconds, the face on the player would change. It was even the face of Dragon's head coach at one point, but by then I was already mentally numb, my hands and feet tingling, my whole body covered in a cold sweat. There was no need to hold me down anymore. I could barely move, let alone run.

The video ended to more laughter and applause.

Kevin tilted my face back before releasing me and whispered in a ragged hiss. His face was right above mine, a mix of rage and satisfaction. "This is what you get, you arrogant little prick. This is what you get for stealing my senior year and then fucking it up for everyone."

Whack! I'd somehow mustered the strength to jolt upwards and head butt him in the nose. He stumbled backwards and started swearing, blood starting to stream down his face. Broken, I hoped. Capitalizing on the distraction, I pulled my arms free and staggered to my feet.

"Let him go. We're done with him," I heard D'Marcus say. He probably didn't want an all-out brawl in his house. They'd already gotten what they wanted, and blood spatters and broken furniture would be such an inconvenience.

Bodies moved out of my way as I wove and teetered towards the door. I felt hands push me back as I stumbled in the wrong direction. I reached out for something to steady myself on but found only air and tumbled to the floor, landing hard on my side.

Laying there immobile, unable to control my limbs, the first wave of nausea hit me. Vomit filled my mouth. I choked and gagged and spit out as much as I could. Someone had come up behind me and laid a hand on my shoulder. "Help! Somebody help me get him up!" It was Kendra's voice.

"Get 'im outta here before he gets sick all over the carpet," another voice concurred and multiple sets of hands pulled me roughly to my feet, half carried me out the door, and dumped me on the frozen ground.

Senior Year: Saturday, November 2
Ain't No Party Like a Halloween Party

Eric--I'm not a party
person
Really not my scene

Bea--Ah but you've never
been to a Halloween
BARN party!
They're the best!
There is a corn maze!!!

Eric--Well I don't have
a costume

Bea--No costume required!

Teddy--Oh come on dude
You wear crazy shit every
day and you can't put
together a costume for
Halloween?
LAME

Bea--No big deal if you

don't want to dress up you
can wear whatever

Eric--I don't do so well
in large group settings

Bea--It's not a kegger
or anything crazy like that

Eric--So there's no
alcohol?

Bea--Its BYOB but you
don't have to drink
No one will pressure you.

Eric--How about I meet
up with you
guys after and we watch
a horror movie?

Teddy--COME. It'll be fun.
I promise

Eric--Dude don't
promise that.
You can't guarantee my
level of fun

Teddy--What I promise is
that the party will be fun
even if your lame ass
doesn't enjoy it

Teddy--I didn't mean that.
You are not lame
Please come.
I really think you'll have a
good time

I'm not just saying that

Eric--Okay fine, you win

Bea--YAAAAAAAAAY!

Teddy--Nice! I promise you
won't regret it!
And don't worry we'll all
hang out together the
whole time

Teddy--Unless you two
lovebirds want some
privacy ;-)

Bea--What's the matter, cuz?
Has our PDA been getting
too intense for you?

Definite sarcasm since our PDA over the past week has
consisted of linger looks and finding excuses to casually touch
hands…and maybe lower backs…and the occasional quick
shoulder massage or tucking a stray hair behind the ear or
bumping hips during between-class locker meetups. But nothing
approaching cousin gross-out levels. In fact, far from being
weird about it, Teddy has taken credit for matchmaking and
keeps goading us to "make it official already." But Bea has
been true to her word, letting me set the pace based on my
comfort level. And amazingly, with Bea, I *am* comfortable
taking the leap into couplehood. I'm just waiting for the right
moment…and this barn party might be it.

One trip to Savers later, and I've even got a costume that's just over-the-top enough to fit my vibe. When I pass Ellen in the upstairs hallway, her eyes boggle at my attempt at 70s Elvis: shiny gold pants, black wide lapel shirt, pompadour hair, and mutton chop sideburns drawn on with one of Aunt Kari's old eyeliners.

"Not bad," she offers after looking me over.

"Thanks," I reply, trying not to sound as pleased as I feel. From someone with Ellen's theatre background, I take it as high praise. It's also the first compliment she's paid me since...God, I don't even remember when.

She glances down to see my Fender case hanging from my left hand.

"Prop for later," I explain.

"Hmm," her lips purse as she considers. "Wouldn't Mom's guitar be more Elvis accurate? It's a Gibson, like the kind he played."

My eyebrows rise at her unexpected guitar trivia knowledge. Then I remember that last spring Ellen was starring in the Elvis parody musical, *Bye, Bye, Birdie,* and she'd always started any show by meticulously researching the show's history, influences, and time period. As her lips thin, I can tell she's remembering that whole situation ended for her...and whose fault it was.

Not wanting to let this rare interaction go sour, I pull us back to the present by answering her question. "I, uh, didn't want to risk Mom's getting damaged." It's not *un*true. No need to get into the reasons I still haven't been able to so much as open the case since Dad brought it. For levity I add, "Who knows how crazy these backwoods barn parties get."

"Wait, *barn party?*"

"Yeah, uh…is that where you're going tonight?" Even as I ask it, I know the answer. Of *course* Ellen is going to the barn party, and of *course* she doesn't want me there.

Face already blotching red, she steps around me, yanks her bedroom door open, and slams it shut behind her.

Maybe a few weeks ago I'd have slunk off and left it at that, but Eric Madison is a bridge builder. Or repairer, or whatever. I wait a few seconds before knocking. "El?"

"Fuck off, asshole!"

I take a few steadying breaths and rest my forehead against her door, wishing I knew what to say to her. As the root source of her pain, I deserve any venom she needs to get out of her system. The summer apart was supposed to help us "reset" our relationship, but it was clear from the get go that the time, space, school, and name change made no difference whatsoever. Not that she's spent any real one-on-one time with me to notice the changes.

Enough tiptoeing around. Time for a new strategy.

Through the door I tell her, "I'm sorry. I didn't realize you'd be going. I should have, but I didn't, and now I've committed to going with my friends."

The only response is the sound of a drawer slamming shut.

"Actually, El, there're some things I need to talk to you about. Stuff going on with me I think you should know."

"I don't care." Another drawer slams.

"Well, it may affect you, and I'd rather you hear about it from me than somebody at school."

Her room goes silent. I've got her attention now.

"Eeeeriiiiiiic!" Charlie calls up the stairs. "We're ready! Don't forget your pillowcase for candy!"

"Be right there, bud!" I turn back to Ellen's door. *You're not the same person that hurt her. She needs to understand that if you're ever gonna fix this.* "El? You can ride with me to the party, and we can talk on the way, okay? ...Please?"

More silence, which I take as tacit agreement.

Then I head down to join the part of the family that actually wants my company.

***

Several hours later, Maggie and Charlie are fast asleep and Aunt Kari is on the couch watching some true crime docuseries while Dad sits in the recliner with his laptop, half watching, half working. I go up and knock on Ellen's door to check if she's ready.

"Almost. Meet you in the car," she says in a clipped but not entirely hostile tone.

I go back down and pull on my latest thrifting find--a bright blue down jacket with a white faux fur trimmed hood. "We're heading out," I tell Dad and Aunt Kari. We've already had the discussion about me and parties and risks involved and laid out expectations for my behavior while there, so all I get now is a narrow-eyed look from Dad that says "don't make me regret this" and an audible "be safe and have fun" from Aunt Kari.

If it felt like fall earlier when the sun was out, it now feels like we've jumped all the way to winter. I rub my hands together as I wait for the car to warm up, wishing I had a pair of gloves. I'll have to ask Dad to bring the rest of our winter stuff next weekend.

Ellen comes out the front door in a long, black and white checked wool coat she must have borrowed from Aunt Kari, but from the painted-on whiskers and two ears poking out from her hair, she's got a cat costume going on underneath. I have the urge to quote the Ellen of two years ago who said, "dressing as a cat for Halloween shows a complete lack of imagination." But I manage to keep my mouth shut. After all, that Ellen was still a "theatre kid" with access to the drama club's costume closet.

Google Maps say it'll only take six minutes to get to the party, so I need to make them count. "Okay, spit it out," Ellen says as soon as we pull out of the driveway. "What's so major and complicated you couldn't text it to me?"

"So, I, uh…" I readjust my hands on the steering wheel and clear my tightening throat. Just say it. "Teddy Mackenzie and I have, uh...we're kinda...friends now."

She curls her lip. "Yeah, no kidding. You think people haven't noticed? You think people weren't talking about it and asking me what the deal was with you guys? If you wanted to warn me, you're a few weeks too late."

"Oh, sorry, I didn't think--"

"As usual." She rolls her eyes and turns her glowering expression toward the window.

I shift in my seat, ill at ease with the confirmation that my friendship with Teddy is a current hot topic of the Ohkwali gossip mill. Not to mention feeling like an idiot for not realizing or even considering how my relationship choices could affect Ellen. She's right--I should have looped her in earlier.

Clearing my throat again, I restart, "That wasn't actually what I wanted to say. It was leading up to… So you know Teddy's cousin Bea?"

"Bea DeLuca, Anthony's sister?" Ellen turns back to me, both brows arched.

"Yeah. We uh, we have lockers next to each other, and once Teddy and I started hanging out, Bea and I started to get to know each other and…"

"And?"

"And we're exploring a romantic option between us." *God that sounds stupid.* "We're kinda…together."

"Like, dating?"

"Yeah, basically." *If all goes well tonight.*

Ellen's brow knits together. "Isn't Bea a lesbian?"

"No, she isn't. That's just an old rumor."

"Oh…okay, whatever." She shrugs and checks the notifications on her phone.

That's it? My shoulders release a tension I didn't realize they were holding. I'd expected more of a fight, at least a lecture about how I'm not supposed to be having friends, let alone a girlfriend. But this was almost *too* easy.

After a few seconds, she smirks and adds, "You know, I've had a couple people ask me if *you* were gay."

"Oh yeah?" I say, though this surprises me not at all.

"Yeah. It's not like you can blame them with the way you dress and act these days. But don't worry, I told them 'No,' you're just a weirdo freak."

"Oh, gee, thanks."

She shrugs. "I thought that's what you were going for."

"Yeah, well…" *that was when Eric Madison was just a one-year cover identity I'd drop after graduating and getting the hell out of Dodge.* "I guess, but that's another part of what I wanted to talk with you about. I've decided to take this year in Ohkwali more seriously, as a chance to distance myself from…myself, my old self, I mean. To embrace being Eric Madison, y'know? To really becoming a better person who treats people with consideration and respect and has real friendships and acts--"

In five hundred feet, your destination will be on the left.

"Up there, where that other car turned, by the cart of pumpkins," Ellen points.

"I see it. So um, like I was saying--"

"Yeah, I heard you. You wanna forget the past and go ahead and have friends and a girlfriend now, and you want me to be okay with it too. Clean slate time. That about right?"

"That's not... I'm trying to explain that I'm working on being a better person as Eric, like a real permanent change. And part of that is getting rid of EJ."

"You sound like you have some dissociative identity disorder."

"It just helps me think of it that way, okay? To like, separate the version of me who thought and did messed up things from the version who recognizes that and is trying to change."

"Fine, great, got it. Thanks for the update. RIP EJ. Past erased. Poof." She snaps her fingers. "Who knew it was that easy?"

"Come on, that's not... Look, it's gonna be a process." I pull my car off in the grass next to three Ford F150 pickups. "Maybe we can talk more about this later? I'd really like to explain--"

"No, really, no need. Go ahead and do what you want. You're going to anyway." She gets out of the car and walks off toward the barn as fast as she can manage in high heeled boots.

***

Is it worse for my sister to hate my guts or not give a shit? I wonder as I sit and watch more cars pull in and people emerge in a mix of costumes, Carhartt's, and letterman jackets.

This isn't the time for a pity party, I remind myself, taking the key out of the ignition and forcing my feet to walk up to the barn. *You'll be fine. Nothing bad will happen. Teddy and Bea won't ditch you. You won't have any alcohol. You can leave if you need to.* Color-changing lights and country music stream from the wide open doors, which makes me remember the guitar I brought...and left in the car. *Nevermind. It would be my way anyhow.* On one side, flood lights point out at the corn maze with its tall viewing platform. On the other, strings of lights crisscross above a patio with picnic tables and bales of hay arranged for seating around a fire pit.

I pass the DeLuca's Lexus so at least I know Bea is here somewhere already. Most people seem to be keeping warm in the heated barn, dancing, drinking, bobbing for apples, and getting pics with their friends peeking out through the face holes of painted Addams Family characters. Ellen has already found her friends hanging out in a back corner, the girls all dressed as cats, each a different color scheme. Redhead/green-leotarded Megan is sitting on Anthony DeLuca's lap, fishnet-stockinged legs crossed, suggestively pretending to lick the back of her hand/paw.

The cranked volume and close pack of bodies in the barn has me on edge already, so I make a quick exit, welcoming the bracing cold. If Bea is in there, better to text and ask her to meet me out here instead of wandering around on my own. I reach for my phone but spy Teddy out at the fire roasting marshmallows on the end of a long stick. When I get closer, I see Bea at the fixins table assembling a s'more.

Teddy notices me and waves. "Hey, there he is! Welcome to the party, Madison."

Bea, who has just taken her first bite, sees me as I step onto the patio and rushes over. "Hey! Oh wow, Elvis, right?"

"Yup." I unzip my coat and pull a pair of oversized, white plastic, bejeweled sunglasses from my pocket, adding them to complete the look. "So glad I put the effort in so I wasn't the odd man out. How long did it take you to put together that varsity athlete look, Mackenzie?"

Teddy, standing there in his usual letterman jacket and jeans, laughs. "Hey man, it's taken me years to perfect this look." He gestures to letters and patches on the front, back, and down the sleeve. He's even got the J with gold bars to testify to his academic honor roll streak. It makes me think of my own letterman jacket: black, red, and white, and still hanging in my closet back home, never to be worn again.

"Don't worry, I'm wearing a costume," Bea assures me, misinterpreting my frown. "It's just too freaking cold out here." She takes her coat off, spreads her arms, and does a 360 degree turn to display a long gray hooded raincoat type thing over a navy shirt with stripes across the chest and swingy blue pants that end mid-shin to reveal her tall soccer socks.

"Ah, you're from *Doctor Who*, right?" All that *Doctor Who* meme searching is coming in handy again.

"Yes! I'm Jodie Whittaker's thirteenth doctor. Wow, good for you. I didn't even have to pull this out." She takes what I recognize as a sonic screwdriver out of her pocket. "I special ordered the whole outfit, though it feels like kind of a waste now." She struggles to get her coat back on with a s'more still in one hand.

"Here, let me hold that a second for you." I offer, but she steps beyond my reach.

"Oh no, I trust no one with my perfect, double mallow s'more," she says and crams it all into her mouth.

I laugh. She laughs. Graham Cracker crumbs escape and stick to her lips. Marshmallow goop oozes out the sides of her mouth.

"You got a little…"

"Here?" She tries to wipe the left side of her face, but her hand is sticky too and it makes it worse.

"It's more like…" I draw a circle around the bottom half of her face.

"Hmm, I guess you better help me," she says for only me to hear. There's a suggestive lilt to her eyebrow, and I'm ninety-nine percent sure she's thinking about us eating ice cream sandwiches above the soccer field, me using my thumb to wipe the chocolate from the side of her mouth.

I take my sunglasses off and hang them from the neck of my shirt. Our eyes connect as I lick my thumb and slide it across her upper lip. She breathes in and tips her chin up, on purpose or on instinct I'm not sure. *You know what to do.* Her eyes don't leave mine as I lean in, my hand cupping the side of her face. Inches away, her gaze drops to my mouth before her lids fall closed.

A gentle press transfers some of the crumbs from her lips to mine. I lick my own lip clean before pressing them to hers again, this time tracing a line along the swells of her top and lower lip with the tip of my tongue.

Someone wolf whistles, and I pull back to see half the people on the patio looking our way, their faces register surprise at this plot twist. Apparently, generating fodder for the gossip cannon is a special talent of mine. Did you hear? The lesbian and the weirdo new guy are hooking up. For real or for show?

Y'know what, who cares what they think.

Bea, flushed and bright eyed under the string lights, slides her non-sticky-handed arm through the un-zipped front of my coat and around my waist. "Come on," she says, turning me around and guiding me toward the barn entrance. "Let's go inside and get something to drink. I brought root beer for you!"

People continue to look at us. One girl says something to her two friends as we pass. They laugh behind their hands, triggering my muscles to tense and making me second guess myself. After all, I'd effectively announced our relationship to the whole school without checking with Bea if that's what she wanted. *You didn't get consent! Come on, Eric, you're supposed to be able to handle parties better than EJ. You don't even have beer in your system.* I lean down and say, "Sorry I kissed you in front of everybody like that. I wasn't thinking about how it was like going public, and I shouldn't have without talking to you first."

Her hand drops lower to rest right above my waistband and she steers me to the left, away from the crowded barn and toward the corn field. "Are you going to apologize every time you kiss me? 'Cause it's super unnecessary. I've never had an issue with people knowing about us. You were the one who wanted to go slow, so I figured we'd tell people when you were ready."

"Oh, okay, cool then." I let my shoulders relax.

"And I like it when you kiss me, in case you couldn't tell." She gives me a still-sticky smile and a playful bump with her hip.

"Yeah," I allow a slow smile to spread across my own face. "I got that sense."

"What is it then? Are you worried because…" She looks around to make sure no one else is within listening distance. "…you think I'm super inexperienced or something?"

"Oh, um…" While that wasn't my concern, it is a better answer than the real explanation. And it does make me curious. "Is this the conversation where we talk about dating histories?" That's okay. We can do that. I knew we'd have to eventually. And leaving out Kendra won't be a lie since technically we never dated.

She takes in a deep, fortifying breath. "Yeah, sure, I guess it can be."

Oh shit. Does she want to talk about this or not? I can't see her face well enough in the dark. "Hey, I mean, we don't have to if--"

"No, it's fine. I can go first if you want."

"Um, whichever. It doesn't matter."

Bea's warm arm disappears as she steps away and pulls her coat back on. She stands straight and clasps her hands in front of her. "So my last boyfriend was named Dan. We met at US National Soccer Training Camp the summer before my sophomore year. He was gonna be a senior and lived in Cleveland, so after the six weeks at camp it was long distance except for a couple of visits. Like, I went out there for his prom. That's when we started sleeping together, and I know losing your virginity on prom night is cliché and whatever, but it seemed fun and romantic at the time."

"Don't worry, no judgment here." *Not a virgin. That's some pressure off.*

She quickly adds, "I was also curious what sex would be like and knew Dan would try and make it good for me."

She pauses a second, but I have no idea if she expects a response to that or what to say, so I just nod and stick my hands in my pockets.

"So, um, yeah, we went to the same camp together that summer and it was really great and I was super happy until he broke up with me the week he got to college because he didn't think the whole long-distance thing would work out. He wouldn't admit it, but I think he'd met someone else he was interested in."

"Ouch."

"Yeah, it was rough for a while, but I got over him. We're even friends now."

"Okay, cool," *Is it?* Yes. Eric Madison is not the jealous, possessive type.

"And before that I dated Kyle Booth," she blurts out.

A mix of music, chatter, and laughter play behind my stunned silence. "...Are you serious?"

"Yes." She rocks forward and back, eyes on the ground.

"What the...*Kyle Booth*?" I sway on my feet, stunned by this new revelation.

"I know, trust me, I do." She steps toward me then back again. "It started at the end of eighth grade. I hadn't gone out with anyone, like, ever and word got around that Booth liked me and everyone was saying I should date him because he was popular, and I was kind of flattered and wanted to see what it was like to have a boyfriend and...it was such a huge mistake. Like, he would be all nice one minute and an asshole the next, and I knew after a week I wanted to break up with him, but my friends kept saying I wasn't giving him a fair chance and how hot and popular he was…"

She groans and covers her face with her hands. "So I kept dating him for most of the summer, but I was miserable." She lowers her hands and checks the area again to make sure no one is close enough to overhear. "For weeks, he kept wanting me to give him a blow job, and even though I didn't want to, he told me it's what girlfriends were supposed to do. So I tried, but he was so…and then when he…" she shivers. "I'll spare you the details."

"Thank you." I shivered too.

"Anyway, I got so grossed out that I threw up, like, on him. Like, literally. It was soooo bad."

"Oh God. I can imagine," I say while trying not to.

"I was super embarrassed, and like, fled. Since it was summer, I didn't have to see him and we didn't talk or text or anything. I hoped that would be the end of it--and it was the end of us, thankfully--but then I found out he'd started telling everyone that I was a lesbian."

Ah, and there's the origin story of that rumor. That Booth's behind it is perhaps the least surprising discovery of the night.

Bea looks over toward the crowded barn. "And then when people started asking me if it was true, I said it wasn't, but no one believed me except Teddy, and it was…really difficult. A lot of people were horrible to me, like it was some game to get me to admit it." She hugs herself and scuffs her shoe through the dirt. "And after a while I thought maybe they were right, that Booth was right, and if I was straight, I should have been thrilled to have his smelly dick shoved down my throat." She pulls in a ragged breath and expels a gasp, the sort I recognize as a precursor to tears.

I close the distance and wrap my arms around her. "Hey...I'm so sorry that happened to you. People are assholes. And Kyle Booth is king of the assholes. Rolfing on his dick was exactly the right response, and I for one applaud you for it."

She laugh-cries against the puffy down of my coat. "It was years ago, and I'm over it, really I am, mostly. But sometimes it just...hits me, y'know?"

"Yeah, I get it. Of course."

"Sorry about the crying. I hadn't planned to tell you all that, but once I said his name, and you...I just felt like I needed to explain."

"Bea, please do not apologize to me right now. I'm so sorry if I overreacted. The name Kyle Booth kind of sets me off."

"I guess we have that in common, huh?" She looks up at me, and I can make out a hint of a smile in the darkness.

"Yup, and from now on, we can loathe him together," I say, trying to lighten the mood.

She gives a weak laugh-sniffle and steps back, taking my hand. It's her sticky one, but I don't care. We walk slowly along the edge of the field back towards the barn. "I never told people the whole gross truth about what happened with Booth. I mean, I told Teddy, but--"

"No worries, my lips are sealed." I mime locking them and throwing away the key.

"Thanks. And to be clear," she says with another sniff, "no one is more disgusted by my fourteen-year-old self's dating choices than me."

"Ah, well, prepare to be far more disgusted by a different fourteen-year-old." I square my shoulder and brace myself to present the unflattering truth. "He lost his virginity at a Labor Day party to his quasi-girlfriend Lydia. The sex had been the endgoal of the relationship. That, and being able to tell his friends he'd sealed the deal. So, mission accomplished, he promptly dumped her a week later for Aliah, a sophomore dance team member with twice the cleavage." I glance to the side, nervous to see how she'll react to discovering she's dating a former asshole.

Her eyes are wide as she nods slowly. "Oh wow…so this guy's a total dick."

Hmm…maybe I should have sugar coated it a little more.

Bea just bumps me lightly with her hip and adds, "Good thing I never ran into him. He'd a been chasin' after these major melons for sure." She uses her free hand to pat both sides of her chest. "Hmm," she frowns and pats again. "I'm sure they're hiding in there somewhere."

An unexpected laugh breaks through the tightness in my throat. *A self-deprecating joke, that's a good sign! You can do this, Eric.*

I swallow hard and go on with my cringeworthy romantic history. "So, uh, it didn't get much better from there. Lots of hookups, a few girlfriends he had little-to-no emotional connection with. And then…" *She was totally open and vulnerable with you...* I look to my left, and we're close enough to the flood-lit area for me to see her expression--the encouraging smile belied by a worried crease between her brows. *...but it's still way too soon for the whole truth.* I can't let finding out who I was that night color her perception of who

I am now. It's one thing to admit to being a shallow asshole, a whole nother thing to admit to being a rapist. "...Let's just say, the young man in question ended up sad and alone and finally realized cup size is a terrible criteria for choosing a girlfriend."

It's Bea's turn to laugh. "Glad he had that epiphany." She squeezes my hand. "So, what are his new criteria?"

"Oh, he's got a whole list of new criteria now."

"Wow, so now he has a whole list of body parts to rate before a girl makes the cut?"

I groan at her well-aimed jab.

"I'm just teasing," she assures me.

"I know..." My feet shuffle to a stop. "Listen, Bea, I..." How do I make it clear that I've been paying attention, listening to her and taking the time to know her like I never bothered with any other girl? That I'm having so much fun discovering what's uniquely amazing about her. And that on top of that, I think she's beautiful. That I am honored and excited to be her boyfriend. *But how do I say stuff like that without coming off as corny and over the top and--*

"I'm listening." She turns so she's in front of me again.

I manage a dry swallow. My chest hurts, and I'm not sure if that's a bad sign or a good one. "Bea, I want you to know that things are different with you. They're better--*way* better. I know we've only been dating for, like, six days at most if you even count this last week as us dating--"

"Which I do, but go on."

Aw, what the hell. Just say it. "I need you to know that even though I've had a long, storied dating history, you already mean more to me than any other girl I have been with. You're more than just physically beautiful. You are kind and funny and positive and you have this amazing energy--"

She stops my mouth with her lips, standing on her toes and grabbing the fur of my hood to pull me close. I hold her around the waist and respond with slow, lingering kisses. We don't need more words. We are completely in this moment together, where neither of our pasts matter.

Loud, screeching laughter from somewhere in the maze shatters the illusion of privacy, and Bea lets her heels drop with a sigh and a smile. She bites her lip as she looks at me. I can't help but smile too, relieved that we've gotten over the relationship backstory hurdle. And it even ended in kissing! Bea has got to be the coolest girlfriend of all time, and with her, I can learn to be the kind of boyfriend she deserves. Deciding to date her was definitely the right call.

"Hey, where did you guys go? Did you get lost on your way to get drinks?" Teddy asks with mock concern, meeting us halfway back to the campfire. "Or did someone decide to hide the coolers in the corn maze? Those bastards." He shakes his head.

"Corn maze time!" Bea throws her hands up in the air. "Let's go, you guys!"

I groan, but Teddy says, "Hell yeah!"

He and Bea high five and she jogs off to go grab those drinks and a bag of kettle corn to take along.

When she's out of earshot, Teddy drops his volume and says, "Tomorrow, Dad and I are going to Syracuse University. Their scout invited me to tour the facilities and meet with coaches and all that."

"Holy shit!" I punch him lightly in the arm. "That's fantastic. I mean, right?"

"Yeah, um…" He looks around to make sure we're alone and says, "I haven't told anybody yet, but…I'm not gonna play football in college."

"You're not…Wait--are you screwing with me?" That has to be it. This guy is on ESPN's list of Top 100 High School Quarterbacks to Watch. He can't just decide--Oh, D1 college football wants me but, eh, no thanks.

Teddy clears his head and squares his shoulders.

"You're serious. Like, you're not playing at all?"

"Nope."

I gape at him, my brain trying and failing to process what's happening. "But don't you need an athletic scholarship to pay for school?"

His second eyebrow lifts and I can feel my face heat. *Nice one, White. Real Smooth.*

"I didn't mean--I figured…"

Teddy laughs and waves away my discomfort. "You're not exactly wrong. I told you my dad's a mechanic, right? Well, he had an accident in the shop a couple years back. His right shoulder and hip are still messed up, and he's got all sorts of chronic pain to deal with, so he's on disability. And Mom works as a secretary at the VA hospital for sixteen bucks an hour. So yeah, we're poor. So poor it makes me eligible for a buttload of financial aid. Plus I'll be the first in my family to go to college, so there's a bunch of scholarships for that too. SUNY, Ivy, whatever--if I get in, I'll be covered."

"Oh, okay then…cool." To cover my mind melt, I ask, "What's the plan then?"

Teddy's smirk morphs into a sad smile as he looks out over the corn field. "Y'know, Cassidy and I had a whole plan-- We'd go to the same college--whatever one I picked to play ball at. After that, we'd get married, make a life in whatever city's NFL team drafted me, pay off my dad's medical bills, buy my parents a house near us. They'd retire early, help out with the grandkids." His Adam's apple bobs as he clears his throat. "But then…"

"…she dumped you." I fill in the known conclusion of their relationship.

"It wasn't that simple. I'd been…" He waits several long seconds before turning his head to look at me. "Last year, some stuff happened…and after, she wasn't sure--*neither* of us were sure… And then she got into FIT for fashion design, and yeah, she made the final choice. But only because I'd been too afraid to." Teddy's eyes close against some painful memory.

When he opens them, he seems calmer again. "Anyway, once she left, I had to rethink our joint life plan. And I love playing football--don't get me wrong--but the pressure and time commitment for college ball is on a whole new level. I couldn't take on a demanding major or do internships." He grimaces and runs a hand through his hair. "And the whole star athlete thing…it's not who I wanna be anymore. I'm not sure it *ever* really fit me right."

"So what is it you wanna do now?"

He slips his hands into his jacket pockets and shrugs. "Not sure yet. Maybe major in mechanical engineering. I grew up fixing old cars with my dad, and I kinda like the idea of designing the cars of the future." He shrugs again, but I don't miss the tentative, hopeful smile that forms. "Keeping my options open for now though."

"Hey, nothing wrong with that," I encourage him.

Teddy's smile fades and a concern line forms between his brows. With a glance towards the barn, he adds, "I'm not really ready to deal with the fallout yet. When family, Coach and the rest of the team finds out, the school, all the businesses around town with my fucking poster on the wall..." He mimes pulling a grenade pin then a shrapnel fist hitting him in the chin.

I nod. All that disappointment, disbelief, frustration, anger even--I know from experience, letting people down just plain sucks.

On the other hand, this revelation opens up new possibilities. I have a fleeting vision of us together at one of the big SUNYs--Buffalo or Binghamton.

"But I hate the feeling like I'm wasting these college's time, letting these coaches think I'm seriously considering their offers. Not to mention how excited my Dad and Coach Norris are getting. And I can't even tell Bea--I mean, I love the girl, but she's got no poker face." He runs his hand over the light stubble on his jaw, looking as weary as he sounds. "It's not like I'm lying to everyone...but I kinda am, right?"

My mouth goes too dry to reply. Oh the horrible irony--asking that question of a liar and fraud like me. I swallow and remind myself, *Eric Madison isn't a lie or a fraud. Not anymore. I'm making him real.*

"Into the maze!" Bea calls out as she approaches, armed with popcorn balls, cans of Coke, and headlamps.

Teddy and I share a quick look of understanding--conversation to be continued--and put on smiles appropriate to the festive occasion.

We spend a better part of the next hour navigating the winding paths by the light of the headlamps corn-maze-pro Bea brought along. At the central haybale tower, we finish off our provisions and sing "We Are The Champions " obnoxiously loud and off key, and I have to admit it was more fun than I expected.

Back at the barn, Teddy goes in search of pizza while Bea tugs me in the other direction. "Come on, let's snag some good pie before it's gone."

"Pie? That's a high school party food here?"

"It is at the Halloween barn party! Each cheerleader brings one. It's a tradition."

Pie tins are assembled on a long table amidst a variety of gourds and a witch doll that shakes and cackles when you press the wart on her nose (Bea demonstrates for me).

"Oh look--there's still apple crumb pie left." She rubs her hands together in anticipation. "It's the very best of the fall pies, don't you think?"

"As a good boyfriend, I agree one hundred percent with your bizarre and objectively incorrect pie assessment."

Bea punches me in the arm.

"Ouch!" I rub my down-padded bicep. "Well, if that's the way it's gonna be, I might as well speak the truth--*Pecan* is the ultimate king of the fall pie world, as any human being with functioning taste buds knows."

"How dare you speak such heresy..." A mischievous glint in her narrowed eyes, she picks up one of the Costco-sized canisters of whipped cream and shakes it, preparing her weapon for battle. I try to back up, but she uses her prodigious soccer skills to block my retreat and trap me against the pie table, holding the can aloft.

"Hey now, there's no need for more violence. We can agree to disagree." I plead a moment before a burst of whipped cream hits me in the face.

My eyes squeezed shut against the incoming confection, I grasp blindly, searching for the can so I can disarm her, but she's too nimble. "Aarrr, okay, okay, you win. Apple crumb reigns supreme."

"That's more like it," she suspends her attack and stands on her toes to lick whipped cream from the tip of my nose, sending a burst of fizzy excitement from the point of contact all the way to my groin. Is this going to be our thing--erotic food-on-face stuff? I'd be cool with that...*especially if we're alone, stretched out on that massive couch in her basement instead of surrounded by--*

"Quite the show you two're puttin' on."

I have to wipe the cream out of my eyes before I can see the speaker, but I already recognize the voice.

Booth is standing behind Bea, a beer in one hand and a paper plate full with pepperoni pizza in the other. Bea turns to look at him but stays close to me, her shoulder pressed against my chest. I automatically slip a protective arm around her waist. Booth's mouth curves up at one side with mocking amusement. But the muscle that jumps at the edge of his jaw betrays something else. Could it be...jealousy, even after all this time? Like some kind of the-one-who-got-away thing?

"The thing is though..." He takes a quick glance right then left before leaning in conspiratorially and saying in a loud whisper. "Nobody's buying it."

I feel Bea tense against me, her face a rigid mask.

As Booth leans back, his smirk morphs into the satisfied smile of a marksman who's hit his target. Looking from me to Bea, he takes three steps backward before turning. As soon as he does, my own body surges into action, lurching forward,

ready to pummel that subhuman piece of scum. "That piece of--
"

But before I can take a second step, Bea stops me with a hand on my chest. I take a long, steadying drag of air in through my nostrils. *She's right,* I reason with myself. *Don't give in to the anger. He isn't worth it. Let him walk away.*

But that isn't what Bea has in mind. She slams the whipped cream can down on the table, pivots towards Booth's retreating back, and reaches him in five long strides.

"Hey, Kyle," she says loud enough that Booth and everyone else in the immediate area can hear her above the music. Heads turn toward her. She plants her feet and puts one hand on her hip. "Just because I didn't want your dick, doesn't mean I don't want anyone's." Her delivery is pure disdain. While I can't see her face, I have a direct view of his, and the contorted shock there is priceless. So are the reactions from those nearby, everything from blinkered amazement to outright giddy delight. Taken together, it's ten times better than any physical punch I could have thrown, though my fists still itch for impact.

As Booth's mouth opens and closes like a malfunctioning robot, Bea whirls around with athletic grace and comes back to me, slipping an arm around my waist. Grinning, I drape my arm around her shoulder and we walk off, our pie mission forgotten.

"That was…" I look down at Bea in awe, "the most incredible smackdown I've ever seen."

"Wasn't it?!" Bea's face is alight with excited energy. "I don't even know where it came from. Maybe because we were talking about the whole thing earlier…All I know is, I feel incredible! Like I just won Sectionals or something."

"Uh, you won at *life* back there."

"Right?! God, I've wanted to do that for like, *ever*." She presses her side tighter against me. "Thank you."

"Uh, that was all you."

"Yeah but...I don't know. It's hard to explain, but like, something about tonight--knowing you were right there with me. It made a difference."

I nod, knowing what it's like to be facing your problems alone. "I got your back, whenever, wherever."

The way she looks at me with those green eyes... God, the level of trust there. *I swear I'm gonna earn it, Bea. Your trust, your love, all of it. You won't regret--*

"Cotton Eye Joe" starts blasting and Bea squeals and rushes us toward where half the barn is lining up, Teddy included. Since it's one of the few line dances I know, I don't bother objecting. The three of us continue to dance and sing along to "Monster Mash," "Party in the U.S.A." "Uptown Funk," and (God help me) "Achy Breaky Heart."

Still buzzing with energy, Bea wants to bob for apples. While I have no interest in ruining my Elvis hair by sticking it in a barrel full of freezing water fifty other people have contributed their saliva to, I do agree to film the two of them bobbing...which reminds me that I left my phone in the car. Bea says I can use hers, but I'm worried Dad or Aunt Kari might try and check in and freak out if I don't respond. So I jog back to the Prix.

As I walk through the haphazard row of cars, I notice black and white check fabric pressed up against a backseat window. The coat Ellen borrowed for the night. In the back seat of the DeLuca's Lexus. Without thinking, I step closer to the vehicle. A palm slaps up against the glass. A jolt goes through my body, like I've been hit by a shockwave. It's a male palm, and it doesn't take a genius to figure out who it belongs to. My sister is in the back seat of that car with Anthony DeLuca.

Senior Year: Saturday, November 2
Girls in Cars with Boys

I bang my fist on the glass.

Anthony looks up and snarls "Fuck off" through the Lexus's soundproofing at whoever's dared to interrupt.

Like hell I will, you little player piece of shit. I bang on the window, this time with both fists and standing so close that the breath from my nostrils fogs the glass.

His eyes go wide, features contracting when he recognizes me. He hauls himself up and off my sister. The next second, Ellen twists and pulls the coat further down to see out. Her expression quickly morphs from confusion to fury. Behind her, a bare-chested Anthony gropes around for his shirt and jacket. Ellen moves the coat again, this time to block my view.

I step away from the vehicle, clenching and unclenching my fists.

The door opens and shuts on the other side and Anthony comes around the back, still zipping up his coat. He doesn't even spare me a look as he starts to walk away towards the party.

Oh no you don't. Blood thrums in my ears as I call after him. "Hey, Anthony. I think Megan was looking for you." When he doesn't react, I take a few steps after him. "You think it's cool to cheat on your girlfriend with my little sister? What the fuck, asshole?"

He slows then stops, hesitating another second before turning. He looks around before walking back. "What's your problem, man?" he asks in a low, harsh whisper. "I haven't butted into whatever it is you've got going on with *my* sister. So maybe do me the same courtesy, huh?"

"Don't try to compare me dating Bea with you messing around with my sister--who you are *using*, not dating," I practically spit in his face.

"Look, man, I'm not dating *anybody*. Megan and I aren't exclusive. Nobody in our group is," he explains with slow condescension. "We hookup with whoever. It's no big deal."

"Oh, okay, I get it," I slap my forehead. "So you're sampling your way through the friend group, and Ellen's the next flavor on your taste test? That's fine then."

"It's not like that," he scowls.

"Oh yeah? What's it like?" I demand, fists clenched so tight my fingernails bit into the skin of my palms.

"Y'know what..." He leans in like he's about to share a secret. "It's none of your fucking business."

My whole body pulses with the need to grab this little punk by the neck and watch his eyes bulge in fear while I teach him to stay the hell away from sister. But I settle for stepping in even closer, forcing him to lean back, letting my height and muscle mass advantage send a warning. "You mess with my little sister, it *is* my business, shithead." I bite back a few more choice names I'd like to call him, reminding myself he's Bea's brother, not some random jerkwad I can completely avoid after this.

Anthony swallows hard and takes a long step back. He's not fool enough to think he could take me in a fight. But he still tries to play it off like he's got the moral high ground, looking me up and down, lip curled in disgust. "You've got issues, man."

"Yeah, and one of them is *you*."

"Your sister's not a kid. She doesn't need your permission to have fun with someone at a party. And trust me, she's already had plenty of fun when you're not around to bust in on it."

I try to blink away a sudden brain glitch. Did he just call Ellen a slut? "You keep your fucking mouth shut, you son of a--"

Behind me, a car door slams shut. "Eric--*enough*." Ellen slips between me and Anthony. Over her shoulder, she says, "Go. It's fine. I can handle this."

He shoves his hands in his pockets and spares me one last disdainful look before walking off.

Punk. I watch him go even as I ask Ellen, "Did you hear what he just said about you?"

"Come on." She hauls me further down the way toward the Prix.

Good. Home is exactly where we should be going.

"Ellen, are you--" I start, but she lets go of me, crosses her arms, and starts walking faster so she's out in front. Her braids have come loose, her careful curls mussed and tangled. How far had they gotten before I found them? God only knows what he said to get her to get in that car with him, what he pressured her to do... *Don't think about it. Just be grateful you found them at all. Now you can keep it from going any further.* My pulse starts to slow. I roll my shoulders to release the tensed muscles. *Deep breaths*, I remind myself. *Calm down so you don't lash out at Ellen.*

We get to the car and I fish out my keys.

Ellen glares daggers at me as she gets in and slams her door shut. "Where the fuck do you get off?" she hisses through clenched teeth.

"Listen, El, it's not your fault. Anthony...he's not a good guy, okay? He's been playing you. Using you as some side piece while he's dating your friend--"

"They're not dating," she insists, as if that completely excuses him.

"Does *Megan* know that?"

"He's honest with her too. It's not his fault if she wants more." Ellen shrugs.

Wow, I gotta hand it to the guy--that is some true bullshit artistry right there. I let out a guttural laugh. "Ah, got it, so he's not a cheater. He's a guy who goes around screwing a rotating crew of girls. You're right. My bad. He sounds like a prince." I grip the steering wheel and shake my head, all out of sarcasm. "God, El, if you already knew what he was... Why would you ever wanna be with a guy like that?"

She rolls her eyes and lets out a short laugh. "It's not like I'm in love with him or something. We have fun together, okay? That's it."

I wince, remembering Anthony's hint that he isn't the only one my sister has been "having fun" with lately. *That's not Ellen. I know her. She's a total romantic. She wouldn't... Would she?*

Ellen twists in her seat so she's fully facing me. "And where do you get off judging him? Or me? Or anyone for that matter?"

I angle myself towards her as well, still clutching the steering wheel with my left hand. "I can judge him because I *was* him."

"Um, no, you raped a girl. He didn't." She leans in a faction. "I was fully consenting."

Touché. Familiar guilt tightens in my gut. I sit back in my seat and stare out the windshield into the dark. "What I meant was, before...Kendra, I had plenty of so-called fun hooking up with 'fully consenting' girls who I didn't give a shit about as people. And I don't wanna see my sister getting used the same way I used them."

Ellen shakes her head but doesn't reply. Instead she shifts to stare out the window and crosses her arms over her chest. I take this as a sign something I've said hit home and venture to rest a hand on her shoulder. "Hey...I get that it feels good to have a guy other girls want interested in you. And I get that you're embarrassed. But--"

She twists away from my touch. When she looks at me, her eyes have glazed with tears. "No shit, I'm embarrassed! *You* embarrassed me. My brother banging on the window like a crazy person. Like he's got any right--like he's got a say in what I choose to do with my body and who I chose to do it with." She pauses to choke back a sob. "What was this, some kind of do-over? You raped a girl in the back of a car and this time you wanted to rescue one?"

"No, I..." That wasn't it, was it?

"Well, I didn't need rescuing." Her breathing goes loud and ragged. "All I want from you is to stay the hell out of my life. Don't you get that?"

"Okay, yes, I get it. But it's not like I can just...stop caring about you. You're my sister."

Her laugh is like splintering wood. "If you really cared about me, you'd have gone to Deerfield Academy instead of insisting on moving here so you can fuck everything up and ruin my life--*again*."

"That's not fair, El." I clutch the wheel with both hands again, knuckles whitening. "You know I promised Charlie we'd stay together, that I wouldn't leave him again."

"Charlie would've been fine. He's got plenty of people looking out for him. He doesn't need you hovering around on a daily basis, playing parent. A few minutes of video chat before bed would have been plenty to keep your promise, and you know it. You came to Ohkwali because you're selfish and scared."

My face feels hot from a bloodrush of indignation, but I try to keep my voice even. "Yeah, well, if anything is gonna ruin your life here, it's sleeping with the guy your friend is most definitely into. You think those girls are happy to have extra competition for his attention? What if they decide to drop you, huh? Is he worth it, to lose all the new friends you've made?"

Ellen manages to laugh and bare her teeth at the same time. "Those girls aren't my real friends. They're who I hang out with so I'm not all alone here. They're a social Band-Aid. I had friends--*real* friends--back home. Friends who I'd known since elementary school, who I'd been in shows with for years. Friends I mostly lost because of you--because I defended you every chance I got. I even…" She shakes her head in disgust. "And the couple who stuck with me, I never get to see anymore because we moved to the ass end of nowhere."

I press my head back against the headrest. She's right that her loyalty to me cost her plenty in the past. But I've also already admitted as much and apologized a dozen times. What we both need to focus on is the life we're building here and now. Turning to her, I say, "Hey…I get you miss your old crew. But writing people off because you haven't known them long or they live in a small town...that sounds kinda like self-sabotage to me."

She lets out a single, sharp laugh. "You'd be the expert on anything with the word *self* in front of it."

"Yeah, yeah, I only care about myself, I get it."

"Oh, I think you care about other people, just never more than you care about your own happiness and comfort. Case in point--the new friends and girlfriend you've gotten for yourself."

"Okay, go ahead and enlighten me." I angle toward her, spreading my arms in invitation. "How does forming a few healthy relationships with people make me some kind of selfish monster in your book?"

"Because you can't have 'healthy relationships' based on a lie." She tips her chin and regards me down the length of her nose. "At least Anthony's been honest with me about who he is and what he wants. You on the other hand, have been lying to his sister this whole time."

My chest constricts. "I'm not lying to her--to them...I'm just not telling them everything yet."

"Secrets are a subspecies of lies," she says, sounding every bit a lawyer's daughter. "Ever since you got here, it's all been some level of cover up. You've lured them in, tricked them with this idealized, reinvented version of you. News flash, brother, fake people can't have real friends."

"It's not fake! *I'm* not fake. That's what I was trying to tell you earlier. This is me now--a better me, one who's trying to make different choices, to grow and learn from--"

"You can't erase the past by putting it out of your head, EJ." There it is again, that pitying smile of hers. Talk about fake.

"What good does it do us to dwell on the past?" My voice comes out high and sharp. "I can't undo what I did then. I can't make myself decide not to go to that party, to not ask you to work up a plan to help me get there. I can't make myself not get in that car with Kendra. I can't get you your friends back or make any of our lives go back to how they were before. I can't, okay?" I throw my hands up in helplessness before pressing the base of each into my throbbing temples.

"Yeah, well, you also can't hide it forever either. You think they'll never find out? You're gonna grow up and marry Bea DeLuca and be best man at Teddy's wedding and your kids will all grow up together?" she mocks. "It's a fantasy. A delusion."

"I'm not an idiot. I'm going to tell them eventually. Once they know me well enough to…understand that's not who I am anymore. I just need time to prove I've changed." *To myself and to them.*

She lets out a dismissive *pft*.

"I told you before--It's a process I'm working through, okay?"

"So while you 'process,' you're going to string them along, get 'em good and emotionally invested, and then--BAM-- the big reveal! Wow, you're right, that doesn't sound like the plan of a selfish monster at all."

I shake my head. "You don't get it. I'm not...Bea asked *me* out, okay?"

"Yeah, based on a lack of info," she snorts. "How does that make it better? Is that what she'll be thinking when you get around to sharing the truth?"

Enough of this. She's just trying to get back at me for interfering with her and Anthony. "Yeah well, guess what, you want me to reserve judgment on your questionable romantic choice, how about you do me the same courtesy?"

"That works for me." She flips the visor down and checks her makeup in the mirror, pulling a tissue out of her coat pocket to wipe the gray tear streaks away.

"Are you...going back to the party right now?" I can't help but shake my head in wonder. Is she planning to find Anthony and pick up where they left off?

"Yep. And you're going home now. I'll get my own ride later."

"Wait, what?" I can't help but balk. "Why would *I* have to go home now?"

"So I can be sure you won't find some other way to mess up my night."

"Are you serious right now?"

"Completely." She reapplies her glossy pink lip color. "And you're gonna do exactly as I say. Because if you don't, I'm gonna tell your new friends and girlfriend exactly who they're dealing with, and I won't paint a flattering picture."

I stare in disbelief. "That's... You wouldn't. At the beginning of the year, you were terrified someone would find out and people would turn on you like they did before."

She puts the tube of gloss back in her pocket and presses her lips together before giving the mirror a practice smile. "Turns out this isn't a mutually assured destruction kind of situation. Back at our old school, we were tied to each other. I was on the record defending you. Sibling solidarity and all that bullshit. But here, it's the opposite. Everyone knows I can't stand you. So if you blow up..." she mimes the explosion, "I'm already way outside your blast radius."

Stunned, my body goes limp against the car door. "Who even *are* you anymore?"

Her photo-ready smile widens, sending a shiver through my limbs. "I'm Ellen Madison, the new and improved Ohkwali edition. RIP Ellen White."

I force my dry throat to swallow. "Mock all you want. But I'm just trying to move forward in a *positive* way, not letting the past dictate my whole future. And I hope you can too. You and Kendra and everyone else my actions affected."

Hand resting on the door handle, Ellen pauses and turns to me with wide eyes. "What do you hope Kendra can do?"

"Just...that she can work to move beyond what happened to her--what I did to her. Move on as a happier, healthier person who doesn't let her trauma define her." I can tell by Ellen's slowly dropping jaw that I've said the wrong thing. *Shit. Why did I even bring up Kendra?*

"Oh God, do you even hear yourself? What bullshit pop psychology podcast did you get that from?"

"Nevermind, I shouldn't have said--"

"No please, this is some fascinating Grade-A rationalization. So you imagine she's gonna come through her rape experience as a stronger, better human being? That it'll improve her confidence and social skills, and she'll be like, all empowered and ready to take on the patriarchy?"

Hearing Ellen say it out loud like that makes it sound absurd, but it's possible, isn't it? "I mean, not like, right away or anything, but maybe eventually, something like that. It's possible."

Ellen lets her hand drop from the door. "Holy fuck, you really are delusional… So the way you see it, maybe you ended up doing her a favor by raping her? Like, she'd use it as some kind of pivotal growing experience?"

241

I shake my head and put my hands out like they can block her words. "God, Ellen, no, that's not what I think. You're twisting things."

She leans towards me and asks, "Do you wanna know how Kendra's senior year is going so far?"

This time it's my turn to be shocked. "How would you know that?"

"Andrea Gurlance is one of the only people back home I'm still close with, and she sees Kendra sometimes."

"Oh…" Cold spills through my abdomen, my body's panic triggers responding to the bad news that's coming. Because of course it's bad news. If it wasn't, Ellen wouldn't be offering it up right now to shatter my optimistic illusions.

Ellen leans even closer, eyes fierce. "Her parents pulled her out of school after the second week. Apparently she got caught self-harming--cutting her arm in the bathroom during lunch or something. So now she has a tutor who comes to the house."

Holy shit. I squeeze my eyes closed as my vision blurs, but it can't unhear the words as Ellen goes on.

"Andrea says when they went to the Daniels' for Game Night, Kendra looked and smelled like she hadn't showered in a week. She still goes to Youth Group stuff, but she doesn't interact with anyone and people have basically given up trying to talk to her. Except Frankie. He's as obsessed with her as ever. It creeps Andrea out. He even decided to take a gap year and asked Mr. Daniels for a list of which colleges they're having Kendra apply to so he can apply to the same ones. That if her parents even *let* her go away to college. Kendra's mom mentioned they may have her do an online program, so she can 'stay where she's comfortable and cared for.'"

I start to shake as the cold spreads. My hands and feet tingle.

"So that's *her* bright, better future. College as a virtual shut in or off at some uber-strict conservative school her parents choose with Frankie Gurlance hovering over her. He'll probably convince her to marry him eventually, and that'll be the rest of her life. Awesome, right?"

"Enough, please…" I curl forward, hiding my face between the steering wheel and the door.

But Ellen's on a roll, her voice harsh and jagged. "Her life was kinda crappy before you raped her, but now it's become well and truly shit. And it's not likely to get better any time soon. Maybe ever."

"For the love of God, *stop*." I grip my churning gut. "Go back to the party."

"You need to hear this, *Eric*. If I have to live with the truth, so do you. You don't get to imagine Kendra's got some great new life going on so you can go on your merry way guilt free."

I can't handle this right now. "Get…out…" I manage between short, hyperventilating breaths. Groping blindly in the center console, I manage to find one of the paper bags I keep on hand and press my nose and mouth into the opening.

"Fine." She opens the passenger side door and gets out. Before she goes, she leans back in to say, "Oh, and so we're clear, my threat to expose you stands from now on. The next time you interfere with my life, I blow up yours. Got it?"

I'm too deep into The Black Hole to reply, but she closes the door anyway. Her point is irrefutably made.

Junior Year: Friday, December 14,
Two weeks after losing States
The Night in Question--What Happened with Kendra

I crouched on my hands and knees by the shrubs in front of the porch as my stomach lurched again and any remaining beer-swilled stomach contents made their exit. Kevin's blood dripped down the left side of my face and off my chin, falling like drops of red food coloring in the beige vomit pool. My arms shook so bad I worried they wouldn't hold me up much longer. So I spit a few times to clean my mouth, shift away from the mess I'd made, and let myself collapse. Rolling onto my back, I lay there trying to regulate my breathing, focusing on the billowing streams of fog I created with each exhale.

"EJ, are you okay?" Kendra hovered nearby, but my ears were ringing, making her voice sound distant and distorted. "Should I...call someone?"

"No, I'm alright...I think that was the worst of it." I replied, though speaking required an unusual amount of effort and my words came out as a raspy croak. Did Kevin's chokehold do something to mess up my vocal cords or was this just another symptom of...whatever the hell that was? Losing control of my body, my mind even. Whatever it was, it was fucking scary. At least what I told Kendra was true. Getting outta that house and emptying my gut had brought some relief. My heart no longer felt like it was trying to beat itself out of my ribcage, and objects in view were re-solidifying.

"Are you sure there isn't someone we can call? Someone who can take you home?" Kendra asked, coming to kneel beside me.

"I'll be fine. I have a ride coming soon."

"Um...how soon?"

Good question. I fumbled for my phone in my jacket pocket. 11:24. *Fuck.* It was too damn cold to sit and wait out here for another half hour, but with the state I was in, there was no way I could walk to that Walmart. I'd have to text and ask them to come get me.

I shot off a text to Ellen with a plea for transport ASAP before rolling onto my side and using my elbow to prop myself into a seated position. "There--hopefully Frankie'll be here in ten minutes or so."

"Frankie...*Gurlance?*" she asked, brow furrowed. "Frankie Gurlance gave you a ride here tonight?" Her shock didn't surprise me. She more than anyone knew Frankie's intense, long-standing dislike for me.

"Crazy, I know. He musta owed his sister a huge favor or something. They're at the Teen Skate. My sister too."

"Ah..." was all she said in return, her thin lips pinched. She stepped in front of me and offered a water bottle from her purse. I accepted and swished some around in my mouth before spitting it out.

"Thanks," I told her and handed the bottle back. She put it away and reached out both hands for me to grab. With her help, I managed to get to my feet, still a bit dizzy but much better than earlier.

With careful steps, I made my way to the curb and lowered myself onto it before asking the next obvious question: "What the heck are you even doing here, Kendra?"

She came and sat next to me, smoothing her knee length jean skirt and stretching out bare legs. She had on a pair of pink high heeled shoes with a thin strap that buckled over the ankle. Not stilettos, but a step up the maturity scale from her favorite saddle shoes. "I, uh…heard about the party from…someone who was in the art Mac lab during senior study hall. D'Marcus and some of those guys were in there too. They were working on the video--though I don't think he knew what was in it--the person who told me," she added quickly, "Just that they were planning to…make the party go badly for you. To embarrass you."

So everyone had known it was a setup. Even someone as out of the gossip loop as Kendra Daniels had known. And I was the world's biggest chump. Shaking my head slowly, I asked, "Why didn't you warn me? You could have texted me or something."

"I uh, wanted to, but…" I can barely make out her blush by the light from a nearby streetlamp.

"Oh shit… You don't have my cell number. Sorry, that's…I'll give it to you now." I pulled my phone out right as it chimed with an incoming text from Ellen--

Sorry I tried but frankie says 12 as
planned. Kendras not even here so
not sure why he won't leave grrrrr

What a jackwad… I considered texting back that Kendra was here with me, but decided to let Frankie see for himself when he got here. I wanted to see the look on his face.

"Ride'll be here at 12," I shared the update with Kendra.

"So that's…" She checked her wristwatch. "A while. Do you want to call a taxi?"

I shook my head. "Dad has Uber and Lyft on his phone, but I don't yet. Can't until I get my own debit or credit card."

"Um, I meant, like…a regular taxi?"

I blinked at her. "Are those still a thing?"

"Oh…" She blinked back. "I thought so, but I have no idea."

I shrugged. "Either way, by the time one got here, my ride'd be almost here." Then I asked, "So anyway, what's your number? I'll send you a text."

She tugged the sleeve of her oversized pale pink knit sweater, her shoulders curved inward. "I don't have a real cell phone… Not like everyone else has." After a slight hesitation, she reached into her purse and pulled one of those chunky plastic, drop-proof phones they market for elementary age kids. It looked like the one Dad got for Charlie in case of emergencies that only lets him make or receive calls for a set of pre-programmed parental-approved numbers.

"Oh…so you can't add new numbers unless..."

"Yeah. My parents...they don't want me 'wasting my time' on my phone, so…"

God, how embarrassing. Yet her willingness to reveal this sad detail of her life made me feel oddly comforted, less alone in my own mortification.

"What numbers do they let you have?"

"Um...ones for family members, and my cello teacher...oh, and Frankie's, because my parents think he's a good influence."

I snorted. Of course the ultra-pious Daniels would love that self-righteous brown noser.

Stowing the kiddy phone, Kendra went on, "And I still had your home phone number from when…" *your mom was alive*, she didn't need to say. "I tried to call a couple of times earlier. No one picked up, so I left a message...but I doubted you'd get it in time."

No shit. Who the fuck listens to their family's landline voicemail? Out loud I said, "We just keep it for emergencies. No one but telemarketers call it anymore, so we keep the ringer volume low and ignore it."

She ran both hands down her legs to her shoes before resting them on her knees. "To be honest, even if you did get my message, I wasn't sure how seriously you'd take it. It wasn't like I had details or overheard them planning."

I opened my mouth to protest, but she might have been right. I'd been so desperate for this party and everything it promised to be, I'd likely have written off whatever Kendra'd heard as unreliable hearsay. So instead I cleared my throat of lingering acid and asked, "Is that why you came here tonight? To like, warn me in person?"

She flicked a glance toward me, her blush deepening. "I knew it was too late to keep you from coming, but I thought...I don't know." She looked back at me again, this time forcing herself not to look away. "I didn't have some big plan figured out. I just had this feeling like...I knew whatever they had planned would be terrible for you. So I thought I could do...*something*. Give you an excuse to leave or...at least be here so you wouldn't be all on your own."

I knew I should have been grateful. It was sweet, her wanting to help me. But somehow it managed to compound the night's shittiness. *This is what my life has come to--getting pitied and rescued by Kendra Daniels. That's bottom-rung level pathetic.*

Not that I could tell her that. I managed a weak, "Well, thanks for trying, I guess..." and asked, "How did you get to the party?" It was hard to imagine her crazy strict, won't-even-let-their-sixteen-year-old-daughter-have-a-real-cell-phone type parents allowing her to come, even if she knew D'Marcus's Dad's cell number for them to call and get the bullshit line that he was here supervising. And there was zero chance they'd driven her here and let her walk into a house polluting the air with throbbing, obscenity-laced dance remixes.

"Jackie Rodriguez--you know, the cheerleader?--she's my neighbor, and I'd heard her saying during last period Spanish she was going to D'Marcus's 'thing' later. So when you didn't pick up, I...walked over to her house and asked if I could go with her."

"You did? And she said *yes*?" Yet another shocking twist.

Kendra's lips twisted into a wry smile. "I offered to be the designated driver on the way home." From her purse, she pulled a set of keys on a huge gold J keychain.

"And your parents were cool with that?" I asked, still incredulous.

"I told them I'd invited Jackie to the Teen Skate and she was driving so she could pick up more friends to come along."

Oh God, that damn Teen Skate, without which neither of us would be here right now. I tried to smile at the irony, but it wouldn't come.

"I meant to get here earlier, but Jackie...she said it was lame to show up before eleven, and I had to sit in her room waiting for her and her friends to finish their hair and makeup."

"Looks like they did yours too," I told her, noticing the difference for the first time. It wasn't much--hair clean and brushed with a slight curl at the ends, lipstick that lent a bit of fullness to her thin lips, some mascara and liner, eye shadow maybe...it was hard to tell for sure in the semi-dark.

In a bold, surprise move, she reached down and set her hand on mine in the space between us. "I'm glad I came, even if it was too late to change anything." Her hand was cold but still warmer than the air. It felt...nice. At least a nice distraction from trying to process what had happened inside.

For a moment, neither of us spoke. I shifted my gaze to her legs and thought of how long and smooth they looked, just inches from mine. *Were her legs that long when she asked me out? Had her lack of chest kept me from noticing her other assets?*

It occurred to me that maybe Kendra's efforts to get here, even lying to her parents, weren't so much about her pitying me as about romantic feelings she still had for me. Even after rejecting her before the start of freshman year and the teasing it must have led to, did Kendra Daniels still have a thing for me? I thought about all the times she'd lingered, sought me out, even if it was just to say hello and make awkward small talk for a minute. How she'd stayed with me after Mom's funeral. And last week at church, how she'd held me as I cried about Mom again. This whole time, had she wanted more than friendship and stayed close, waiting for another chance to tell me how she felt? Sure, Frankie had some weird, possessive crush on her, but I'd never seen her encourage him at all. Maybe that was because she'd never gotten over me.

The possibility soothed my raw self-loathing a fraction. The thought that a girl--any girl--who'd just borne witness to my ignominy was still into me. Kendra wasn't Tara by any stretch, but she wasn't...ugly. *At least those legs sure aren't. She should show them off more instead of hiding them under long skirts and baggy pants.* Then I thought, *God, she must be freezing.* I was cold myself, and I was covered everywhere but my head and hands. She didn't have a jacket on either, only the bulky sweater that probably did little to protect from the windchill.

But at the same time I said "Are you cold?" she said "They're such assholes."

Hearing Kendra, principal's daughter, good-girl extraordinaire use that word snapped my eyes back up to her face, bare legs momentarily forgotten.

"I can't believe they did that to you. And then how everyone joined in, clapping and cheering and... As if you'd personally hurt them by losing a game."

"Yeah, it sucked," I underrated. "I'd rather not rehash it right now, if you don't mind."

"Right. Sorry, sorry, of course..." Kendra squeezed my hand, and I thought she was done. But after a few seconds, she felt the need to add, "You should really report this to someone. My dad, maybe. I bet the ringleaders would be in huge trouble for this. In school suspension at the very *least*."

Ha! A few days in ISS, some missed practices...yeah' that'd show 'em. I sighed, wishing she would drop it and let me be distracted by her nice legs. "That would only make it worse," I tried to explain. "Whining to the adults, your dad or my dad..." My dad would be worse than hers, wanting to press charges, file lawsuits and all that shit. I might have been able to talk to Mom, but...yeah, not an option anymore. "Trust me--It'd only make everyone even more pissed at me. It's not worth it."

"But they're already angry at you, so could it really be that much worse if you turned them in?" She hesitated before adding, "What about telling the basketball coach? There's a player code of conduct, right? Making that video, holding you down like that… It would get them kicked off the basketball team."

I leaned away and regarded her with wide eyes. "Are you insane? They'd *murder* me if I got them kicked off the team."

She blinked in alarm and confusion, like she wasn't sure if I meant it literally.

"Look, I just gotta figure out a way to make it through this year, then most of those guys will graduate and my fuckup at States will be old news and I can start fresh senior year." *Hopefully.*

"So you're not going to do...anything?"

I shrugged, trying to tamp down a surge of anger at her for forcing me to admit my own helplessness. "I'll flag the video on YouTube, hope it gets taken down quickly." Though by then it would already be uploaded again on another account or ten. Anything uploaded to the internet was basically immortal.

Her expression settled into resigned disappointment. "So...they get away with it."

"So they get away with it," I echoed, tingeing the words with my own bitterness. "What d'you care though? It's not like any of this bullshit affects you."

A flicker of hurt appeared on her face, but she blinked it away, glancing down where her hand still lay atop mine before shifting to study her pink heels. My instinct was to apologize, but the urge subsided in the next moment. *Why should I apologize to her for making me feel even worse?* I'd asked her to stop talking about it, and she kept going anyway. I was barely holding myself together, my emotional tank running on fumes, and now I was supposed to redirect my energy to cheering *her* up? No. That wasn't fair.

Then, seemingly out of nowhere, Kendra said, "Tara Kajowski's such a bitch. You're better off."

Whoa, "asshole" now "bitch"? Who was this girl and what had she done with the shy little Sunday School friend who'd told everyone saying "jeez" was taking Jesus's name in vain?

Without looking at me, the new, profanity-using version of Kendra lifted her hand off mine to rest on my thigh, midway between knee and groin, fingers perched on the inside seam of my jeans. So I didn't move. I didn't do anything else either. Normally, I would have taken this as an invitation to return the gesture in some way. I mean, this *had* to be confirmation that she still wanted me. But this was also Kendra, the virginal, awkward, holy ice-princess.

"Kendra..." The angle of the light made it impossible to read her facial expression.

She started to move her hand, stroking tentatively, so lightly I could hardly feel it through my jeans.

"You're different from them, EJ. Better. I've always known that." Her leg was right against mine now. "I care about you...care that you're hurting. And maybe I can't fix anything, but...I just want to do something to...make you feel better."

My throat went dry. "Yeah?"

"Yeah..." She reached with her other hand to cup the side of my face.

Our faces came together like magnets.

At first, her lips were as tentative as her hand, testing my reaction.

I hear her words over again in my head. *You're different from them...better...make you feel better...* My lips moved against hers, pressing, begging her to prove she meant it. *Yes, this feels better.*

I reached with my own hands and pressed them to her face and hair. Kendra became reassured, enthusiastic even. And I fed off it, increasing the intensity, letting my hand slide down her side, waist, hip...all the way to those long legs to her bare calf. She pressed closer and slipped a hand inside my jacket, stroking my chest back and forth over the thin fabric of my shirt. Emboldened, I slid my hand up her calf, across her knee, and over the warmer skin just under the hem of her skirt.

I was cognizant enough to have thoughts—however fleeting—like: *This is a bad idea. Frankie could show up at any second, or someone might come out that front door. And what am I doing with Kendra freakin' Daniels? Was she planning this? Will she think we're dating now? Oh God, does my mouth still taste like beer and vomit?* But my body's physical reactions were far more pressing and intense than any second thoughts.

Both Kendra's slim arms were inside my jacket, wrapped around me, her upper torso pressed to mine. Were those...her breasts? Far larger than I'd expected. *Wow, so that's what she'd been hiding under all those baggy layers.* From NBN to a decent handful in two and a half years. Maybe she'd let me unfasten her bra and...

As I moved my hand to reach up the back of her sweater, she tensed and broke the kiss.

"Wait..." She was breathing heavily. "Keep doing what you were..."

I put my hand back to her left leg. My fingertips moved higher, brushing small circles along her inner thigh.

"Yes, like that…EJ…I've wanted…for so long…" She trailed off into a breathy moan as I moved my mouth to her neck, letting my tongue flick over the skin below her earlobe.

"Jackie's car," she whispered.

"Hmm?" I pulled back far enough to see her face.

"It'll be warmer in there…" Her breath was still coming in small gasps, but she looked me right in the eyes when she said it. Everyone knew what it meant to invite your makeout partner to move to the back seat of a vehicle. She knew what she was offering me.

At least I thought she did.

Did I want to? Any other night I'd've balked at the idea of having sex with Kendra Daniels. I'd never even seriously considered the possibility before, and that was saying something. But tonight, everything I thought I knew had been turned on its head. Why not this too? My body's answer was clear. Within a stretch of fifteen minutes, I'd gone from barely being able to walk to being up and ready to have sex in the tiny, cold back seat of a VW Jetta. I'd been emasculated in that room in front of all those people, and it felt so good having Kendra stroke my face and chest. But even better was how she stroked my ego. *You're better than them…* Telling me, showing me, that I still had some measure of power. That I was still someone wantable, despite what had just happened back there.

I kissed her once more and said, "Okay, yeah…yeah, let's go."

After starting the car and cranking the heater, Kendra joined me in the back seat but stayed on her own side. Her smile was shy again, now that we'd had a break in momentum, but I was already primed and impatient to get things moving. I pulled her in for a kiss and slipped my tongue in her mouth and my hand back up her skirt, higher this time, brushing the wet fabric of her cotton panties with my fingertips. She gasped, her breath catching. "EJ...oh, I...oh..."

I kept going for another minute, making sure she was good and ready, before I shrugged out of my jacket and shirt, tossing them over the passenger seat. But when I reached for the hem of Kendra's sweater, she wouldn't let me take her sweater off. "I uh...I'm still too cold," she claimed, tugging her sleeves until her hands were barely visible. I wasn't going to waste time arguing, though the heater had more than done its job. So I moved on to her lower half. After some uncomfortable grunting and maneuvering, I gave up on getting her jean skirt off and just bunched it up around her waist. But when I tugged at her underwear, she clenched her thighs and trapped the fabric midway. "I, um...I'm not...this isn't something I...EJ, I don't know--"

"Sshhh, I know. It'll be fine. Don't worry," I tried to sooth her worries, taking a minute to stroke the inside of her leg like she'd liked earlier. It was obviously her first time. Which I'd usually consider a drawback--the extra time and care required, worrying it would hurt her and all that. But in this case, this moment, it made it more thrilling. I wasn't just having sex with a girl; I was taking her virginity. There was a special power in that. And I wanted that power.

I kissed her as I continued to stroke, relaxing her until I could get her panties off without resistance. Then I gripped her by the hips and tried to get her in position for easy access.

"Ow—EJ, my head." I glanced up to see her neck squished up against the door at a funny angle.

"Oh, sorry..." I moved back so she could rearrange herself, but she didn't move. Just laid there like an uncomfortably posed doll. So I went ahead and took hold of her hips to shift her body down. "That better?"

She nodded slightly, her eyes following my hands, widening as I unzipped my fly and yanked my pants and boxers down to my knees. She let out a stuttering sort of gasp that sent a warm electric pulse over my skin. *Is mine the first dick she's ever seen outside of art textbooks? Yeah, I bet it is, and now it always will be.* My heart hammered. I was so ready.

But there was one more required step in the process--the condom. I awkwardly extricated my wallet from the pocket of my bunched-up jeans, wishing I'd thought to take it out before pulling my pants down. I slipped out the Trojan I kept stashed behind my library card and rolled it on, tossing the foil to the floor. By the time I got myself wrapped, she was shivering and hugging herself. I leaned down and kissed her neck a few more times and rubbed her body from waist to knee with my right hand.

"EJ...I'm sorry, but...I don't know if..." She squeezed her eyes shut.

"Don't worry. It'll only hurt for a few seconds, then you'll like it. I promise."

"I just...don't know if I'm...ready...for this." She continued to tremble, tears starting to pool at the corners of her eyes as she stared at the back of the driver's seat.

My anticipation crackled with a bolt of anger. My mood soured in a split second. *What the fuck? Seriously?* First public humiliation and now this? Rejected by a reject, at the last fucking moment? "This was *your* idea." My voice came out in a strangled bark. "Hey, look at me." She obeyed and I reminded her, "You asked me to get in this back seat with you. You're the one who said how long you've wanted me, and now you get your chance and what...you wanna stop?" I motioned to my erection. *"Now?"*

My breath came in angry puffs as I waited for her to respond. But she just stared back at me, wet trails running down her temples. she closed her eyes and mouth tight. Did that mean she was ready, bracing herself? Well, I was ready. I needed this to feel like I was still myself.

So I pushed her tensed thighs the rest of the way open and took what I needed.

The act itself was over in less than a minute.

When I pulled out, she just lay there, all limp, her head propped up against the door handle.

"Kendra?"

A shudder moved through her, ending with a sob. I reached out to touch her face, but she pushed my hand away and began groping around the floor for her underwear. So I settled for redressing myself the best I could. My gut clenched and felt like I might throw up again.

"Look, that was...Are you okay?"

She said nothing.

"Kendra?"

"Just get out."

"But—"

"Get out, get out, get out, get out..." she kept saying as she curled into a ball against the door, as far away from me as possible.

My gut clenched. *Was it that bad?* "Hey, are you--"

"GET...OUT!" She shouted between sobs, snot running down her upper lip.

"Okay, I'm going!" I scrambled out of the car, dropped the used condom by the curb, and stepped into the street to

watch for my ride. 11:54. *Not long now, thank God.* All I
wanted now was to go home, take a bunch of Advil PM, and
fall into my bed.

Even outside the car, I could still hear Kendra. I glanced
back at the house door, wondering momentarily if I should go
back and try to get Jackie or one of those girls to sit with her or
get her cleaned up or whatever she needed to stop crying like
someone had...had tortured her or *forced* her or something.
Which wasn't what happened. I gave her the chance to stop
things, and she didn't. I mean, from the screaming afterwards, I
got that she hadn't...enjoyed it. But it's not like I'd been rough
with her or something. First times could be like that for some
girls. She couldn't blame me for that.

Still, better to let her process whatever issues in private,
without witnesses. None of those girls inside were her friends
anyway, and she might not want anyone else to know we'd...
Oh shit, she won't tell people, will she? My social stock was
rock bottom as it was, and word getting out I'd gone from
scoring with Tara Kajowski to settling for Kendra Daniels
would cancel any already slim chances of recovery. Not to
mention, her dad would kill both of us if he ever found out, that
was for sure. I could still see the look of pride on his face when
he watched his only daughter sign her Abstinence Until
Marriage Pledge the Sunday before we both started high school.
The pledge had mostly been a show for the parents, and by then,
already a moot point for me. But for Kendra, she'd played the
whole thing so seriously, like the vow to God it was supposed
to be. Now she'd broken it. A choice she clearly regretted.

I regretted it too--the uncomfortable, disappointing
backseat sex, not breaking my abstinence pledge for the
umpteenth time. That fantastic sense I'd had of regaining

control, that rush of power and excitement and strength...gone again. Poof. If anything, I felt lower than ever. Why should I worry about her when my own wounds were still stinging and fresh? However bad she was feeling, didn't I have twice as much reason to be miserable? *She* was the one who asked *me* to get in the back of that car and then managed to make my already supremely, unbearably miserable situation worse.

But it was hard to make my anger at her stick as her muffled weeping combined with the party noises. I turned back to the car, at a loss for what, if anything, I could do to smooth things over with her.

That was when Frankie finally pulled up. Relief flooded my whole body, making me sway. As soon as the van came to a full stop, I got in the back, not wanting Frankie to see the disheveled state I was in and start asking questions. Andrea was sprawled out, eyes closed in the third seat, so I took the second row seat next to my sister.

"Oh God, EJ...you're a mess..." Ellen stared open mouthed and reached toward the side of my face with streaks of dried blood on it.

"It's fine—It's not mine. Hey, Frankie, can we get out of here already?"

Instead of pulling away, Frankie was stock still, staring at the Jetta parked along the side of the road less than five yards away. He lowered his window, listening.

Shit... Why didn't I walk further away to wait? Could he hear her from here over all the noise?

"Who's in that car?" he asked in a calm but strained voice.

Panicked bile rose in my throat. "What are you talking about? Let's go."

"I asked you—" he turned stiffly to fix his stare on me. "Who's the girl in Jackie Rodriguez's car?"

"Whose car? What girl?" I looked where he pointed and was relieved to see that from here, Kendra was only a dark silhouette, indecipherable from any other human in the dark.

"You mean you've been waiting out here all this time and didn't notice the girl crying in a car parked ten feet away from you?" His tightly controlled calm set my heart hammering.

"The party's too loud to hear anything." I lied.

He turned back to the parked car. "Is it Kendra?"

"What?" I faltered, blood deserting my brain. "Kendra *Daniels*? You think she'd be *here*? God, you really are freakin' obsessed with her. Forget it, okay? It's just some girl. None of our business."

His hand moved to unbuckle his seatbelt.

My heart beat so fast my chest constricted, my breath coming in short puffs as my vision swam again. *No no no no no, not again. What the hell is wrong with me?* "Dammit, Frankie! *Drive*, would you! I feel like shit, okay? I threw up in the bushes, and I've been freezing my ass off waiting for you guys."

He turned to study me. "What happened to you in there?"

Not, "*Did* something happen to you?" Not, "Your fault for getting wasted." *Holy shit... He knew... He fucking knew. He'd known all along. He's gotta be the one Kendra said overheard them in the computer lab. Then he agreed to give me the ride so I'd be sure to get what I "deserved."*

I leaned forward and hissed through clenched teeth, fury overtaking every other emotion. "I think you already know."

Frankie blinked and leaned away, not prepared for my knowledge of his part in the night's events. On the defense now, he adjusted his hands on the wheel and glanced back at the possible Kendra, conflicted.

He'd made the whole miserable night possible. Even Kendra showing up. I'd never wanted to strangle someone so much in my whole life, but I gripped the sides of my legs hard enough to leave bruises.

"What happened? EJ, what's going on?" Ellen prodded, shaking me lightly by the arm, probably frightened by my edginess and the blood.

"It was some seniors giving me crap, still upset about States. Don't worry about it."

"But--"

"Frankie, get me the fuck out of here," I ordered him with my own ominous calm.

After another moment of indecision, Frankie faced forward, shifted into drive, and pulled away.

Senior Year: Saturday, November 2
Seeking Refuge

I come to in the grass next to the Prix, my door still open, dome light on. I must have gotten out to throw up. *Yep. There's my partially digested pizza and pie.* After rolling in the opposite direction of my vomit, I manage to stand and get back into the car.

My cell, still in its hands-free holder, buzzes three times in a row.

It's Bea, wondering where I've disappeared to. *Shit.* There's no way I can go back in there. I text her the partial truth.

> Had a panic attack
> Need to head home and sleep
> Really sorry
> Call you tomorrow

The phone buzzes with more incoming texts, but by then I'm already pulling out and driving down the pitch-black road at breakneck speed.

My brain goes as fast as the car, replaying and analyzing the new information about Kendra. The cutting, getting taken out of school, more isolated from the world than ever, Frankie still lurking, insinuating himself into her life with her parents' help and approval, how withdrawn and miserable and alone she was. *And it's my fault.* The road in front of me blurs. *Oh God, oh God, oh God...Why the hell isn't the Lexapro helping?* I take my foot off the gas and focus on regulating my breaths. *You will not lose control. The Black Hole will not take you. Not again. Not behind the wheel. Think about something else. Something relaxing*...swimming, playing pool basketball with Charlie...Kendra in the pool at my birthday party, climbing to the edge, me laughing with Gavin and the others about her flat chest. *No, stop it, stop thinking about her or you'll lose it again!* ...Her chest that night at the party, how she wouldn't let me take her top off. The cutting, when had that started? Was the pool the last time I'd seen her bare arms? All those drapey, oversized sweaters, always tugging at the sleeves... I'd thought it was a modesty thing combined with a nervous habit, but what if...? Did it start after the whole thing at my pool party? *Because* of

263

the whole thing at my pool party? Or had it started later, because of something at home or at school? No way for me to know for sure, and I guess it doesn't matter. Even if she'd already been self-harming, getting raped could only have made it worse.

Oh God, Kendra, I'm sorry. I'm so sorry... The tears come as I gasp for breath and grip the steering wheel like it's a life preserver. I'm driving too slow now, not even sure where I am anymore. At a stop sign, I turn in the direction I think leads back to town so I can get my bearings with landmarks. After a few miles of nothing but farmhouses here and there, it's clear I've gone the wrong way. I pull over, put my four-way flashers on, slump forward, and rest my forehead on the wheel as I let myself cry in earnest.

Ellen had talked about being outside the blast zone when my Ohkwali life exploded. She'd meant if and when people found out about what I'd done to Kendra. But for me, the bomb has already dropped, and she's the one who dropped it. A reality bomb. Ellen was right--I'd worked so hard to construct this ideal life for my "new self," an alternate reality where that pesky guilt and those bothersome consequences belonged to a different person and could be conveniently relegated to the past. It was a world constructed of popsicle sticks glued together with rationalization and built on a foundation of wishful thinking. And the sad truth of Kendra's current life had induced a structural collapse.

I'd needed to convince myself that the pain I'd caused Kendra was also a thing of the past. That it was a terrible episode we'd both moved on from, lived through and come out stronger. If she was rebuilding a better life for herself, then I could too. And in the absence of any actual information, I'd let myself believe it was true. Because I'd so badly wanted--needed--it to be true.

Delusional.

"But if Eric Madison was willing to ignore the truth to get what he wanted in life, willing to perform mental gymnastics to justify hurtful actions, then deep down, was he--was I--really so different from EJ White, the guy who'd taken when he wanted from Kendra that night in the car?

No. I was the same person I'd always been and always would be.

Selfish.

And what was I doing now to my new friends? Had I truly believed that Bea would take the news that I'd raped a girl better the longer I waited to tell her? That lying longer would lead to less hurt? That if she loved me more she'd give me some sort of pass? Overlook *rape*? Was I fucking insane? And Teddy...God, I'd had this image of us having some deep conversation months from now where I'd finally open up to him about my past and by the end he'd hug me and thank me for trusting him with my secret. But there's no way it will play out that way in real life. Teddy will be horrified by who he's let into his life, into his family's lives. The trust will be broken. The relationships damaged beyond repair.

What now?

The more I consider the situation I've created, the more doomed it seems. I am a toxic human being who cannot be trusted to know what is right or what to do next without inflicting more damage on the people around me. I'm helpless to fix any of the messes I've made...on my own at least. I need an objective sounding board, someone to walk me through this, help me assess my options.

I need Dr. Eduway.

Releasing my phone from the holder, I open up my email app and compose a message to Dr. Eduway that I hope conveys the serious, time-sensitive nature of the situation and beg him to fit me in for a session. Like, in days, not weeks, please please please. Once I hit send, my body relaxes a fraction, relieved to have taken some small action.

The phone buzzes in my hand. Another text from Bea, along with one from Teddy. I open up the group chat with the two of them and shoot off a quick reply.

I'm okay now. Just need sleep.
You guys have fun
Please don't worry about me

Then add,
Can you make sure Ellen gets
home okay?

They both reply within seconds with assurances that they will and that they'll check on me tomorrow. Such good, attentive friends, concerned for my welfare. My stomach clenches with guilt over how little I deserve them. *Don't worry, you won't have them for much longer.*

I bring up my maps app and as soon as I go to type in my destination, it gives me the option for Home, which I select without thinking, before realizing I've never updated the address and it will send me *home* home, to Rochester. Seeing the old address, the one I'd learned to write on envelopes back in kindergarten, sends a pang through me. It's been so long since I slept in my own bed, surrounded by walls I'd picked the color for, shelves with sixteen years' worth of my favorite books, and a closet full of my own junk. Wouldn't it be nice to be there again, even for a night or two? Maybe it would help me get my head sorted… And if I make a special trip back to town, I can tell Dr. Eduway I'm there, ready and waiting, and it'll make him more likely to make a spot in his schedule for me ASAP. Is this tactic manipulative, demanding, and inappropriate? Probably. Just one more in my string of bad decisions. But I'm desperate.

Decision made and second email sent off to Dr. Eduway, I hit Start on the map, put the phone back in its holder, and let the computerized female voice lead me to the highway. Dad and Aunt Kari aren't expecting me back for another hour. So by the time I text to tell them what I've done, I'll have a good head start. Not that I think Dad will drive after me in the middle of the night to drag me back, but if I'm still close, he might try and order me back. But no matter what he says, I'm not turning around. Having a plan is the only thing keeping me stable and focused right now.

Junior Year: Friday, January 3,
Three weeks after the Night in Question
Aftermath

It didn't take long after the party for my real life to become a surreal nightmare.

"EJ White Game of Shame: EJ on His KNEEEEES!!!" got 5,348 views on YouTube before it got blocked…only to be reposted by a different account, then another. I spent the rest of the weekend playing virtual whack a mole replying to tracking down posts, flagging them, and replying to comments.

Engaging the trolls and assholes was stupid, I knew, but I couldn't help myself.

Monday I stayed home "sick," spending most of my time lying in bed with my laptop, monitoring my transition into digital punchline and plotting my revenge on D'Marcus and Co. That's where I still was at 7:13 pm when the doorbell rang.

It was the police, asking if I was Eric James White, informing me I was charged with the forcible rape of Kendra Daniels, putting me in cuffs, reading me my rights, marching me across the lawn. Ellen held back a crying Charlie as Dad walked a step behind, reminding the arresting officers I was a minor and not to question me without him present and warning me not to say anything until he got there with the lawyer.

Six hours later, after supplying a written statement and undergoing a thorough questioning by the detective in charge, they released me into my father's custody. Dad didn't need me to repeat my story. He'd read my statement and been present for the questioning, so we drove home in complete silence, both half in shock, trying to process this turn of events. Over the next few weeks he'd have plenty to say, of course. Plenty of anger and disappointment. With me for lying, breaking the trust we'd rebuilt, for involving my sister in this mess for God's sake! With D'Marcus, Gavin, and the rest for turning on me in such an extreme and even criminal way. With the Daniels for overreacting and going to the police instead of coming to him first. With himself for not realizing what had been going on with me since States. With me again for not calling him for a ride as soon as I got out of that house. Then with himself for not making me feel able to talk to him about my problems or call him in my hour of need.

Though what surprised me most was the one thing he *wasn't* angry or disappointed with me about--what had happened in the car with Kendra. He was certain his son would never--*could* never--have 'forcibly raped' a girl. Certainly not a childhood friend. When he was feeling generous, he was sure it was all a mix up, a miscommunication, a misunderstanding. It was possible Kendra misremembered the situation, thinking of what she'd *wanted* to say rather than what she'd said out loud. When he was feeling less generous, like after the pastor and three of the other elders came to ask him to step down (since as 1 Timothy 3:4 states, "an elder must be blameless...one who manages his own household well, keeping his children under control with all dignity") he'd contend that Kendra had lied to her holier-than-thou parents rather than admit she'd voluntarily given up her virginity before marriage. And Mr. Daniels--who'd been the one to actually report the rape--simply could not face the idea that his precious, cloistered little girl had grown up into a hormonal teenager with a developmentally normal interest in sex.

I'd stopped saying much in return, instead spending the Christmas holidays in a haze--eating too little, sleeping too much, listening to music about how miserable life was, and barely touching the backlog of lesson materials my guidance counselor dropped off. Somehow, I couldn't bring myself to care about my Music Theory grade when my whole world was dissolving.

In the new year, the school switched me to online classes and suspended D'Marcus, Gavin, Chris, and Kevin for three games over the video and party, which was some little comfort. And Bronston Aster, Dad's old school friend and now hotshot NYC-based criminal defense attorney, arrived to take over my case from the family lawyer who specialized in wills and house closings.

Bronston was the embodiment of the entitled, ivy league legacy type. I didn't like him. Hell, I wasn't sure Dad liked him that much. But he was, "a master of spin and storytelling," as Dad put it, "and the guy I'd *least* want to go up against if I was the one prosecuting this case." And he made it clear to me how much we needed Bronston and how grateful we should be for his help. So I reminded myself that having a lawyer renowned for defending big time criminals and creeps didn't make me one. I was an exception to his usual clientele, which must be a nice change for him, to be on the side of truth. And yet...he didn't make it easy to like him.

Whiskey glass in hand, Bronston reclined against the couch. His athletic, six-foot-three frame swathed in an Armani suit took up most of the space there. We met in the formal living room reserved for important company, me off to the side in an elegant but uncomfortable chair, required to be there though two of them talked like I wasn't.

"Look, J-Bird..." I winced a little whenever Bronston used Dad's old and now somewhat ironic nickname, though Dad allowed it without a blink. "We've got a solid case. Per New York State Penal Code, Article 130 Section 25, it all comes down to the clarity piece. If the 'reasonable people' of the jury can't be positive that her continued silence in the dark was a clear message to stop--then how could they expect a traumatized kid, who just had a fucking panic attack, to make that determination? So if she wasn't clear--"

"It wasn't rape," Dad finished.

"It wasn't rape," Bronston agreed, holding up his glass toward us to punctuate the point. "*But* the legal verdict will only be half the battle. Like it or not, we're living in a post-MeToo world, my friend. And the optics are against us. Your position as DA, your background and family money, hell--even your last name." He leaned forward and rested his elbows on his knees. "People are clamoring to sacrifice EJ on the Altar of Social Justice. They won't take it too kindly when their target escapes."

Dad ran a hand through his hair and let out a ragged exhale. "So, if we win in court, we get a PR crisis?"

"Bingo, J-Bird." Bronston nods and leans back, one arm stretched out along the top of the couch as he takes a drink. "Even if EJ served a full prison sentence and all the rest, plenty of people out there wouldn't feel he paid enough for it to be 'justice.'" Bronston added an eye roll to his use of air quotes. "Like the only fitting punishment is life-long exclusion from society. You remember that swimmer kid from Stanford's rape case, the whole girl-unconscious-by-a-dumpster thing? The one where she wrote a bestselling memoir afterwards? The kid got convicted, served his three months, is on the Sex Offender Registry for life, *and* was kicked out of college, but is that enough? No. People still go after him like it's their job to exact retribution for a girl they don't even know. Now *there's* a proxy war for you."

So, either way, I'm well and truly fucked? I looked over at Dad, who looked back and shook his head as if I shouldn't let Bronston scare me. But the grim set of his forced smile wasn't reassuring.

"Anyway, my point is, if you want any kind of career and normal family life on the other side of this, we need to start working up a strategy now for how to handle the fallout. For a start, move outta this sad little rust belt city. You only moved here for your wife, right? So go back to Boston, where your family name still means something. Forget this politics and all that public servant bullshit, and go into the private sector. It's where the real power and influence is anyhow."

"I appreciate your advice, Stoney," Dad told him, using Bronston's boyhood nickname. "But let's focus on winning the case before worrying about what comes after."

Agreed. I sat limp-limbed in the wing-backed chair, dinner a leaden weight in my stomach as guilt threatened to burn a hole through my gut.

"Alright, fair enough." Bronston knocked back the last of his whiskey before pulling out a folder marked Expert Testimony and flipping through its contents. "The key will be presenting EJ as sympathetic--just another victim in all this. Now, I've got the form from the family physician, Dr. Holder, diagnosing EJ with Panic Disorder--Again, sorry about that. I know getting slapped with a label stings, but it's important for the case." Bronston told Dad, who nodded with a tight jawed air of resignation. Getting his son categorized as "mentally ill" had been a hard pill for Dad to swallow. I'd mostly been relieved to finally have some clue what was happening to me.

"And we'll need the psychologist--this Dr. Eduway--to establish past trauma, how the events leading up to the night in question would affect his state of mind."

"Right...EJ hasn't been to see him since..." Dad flickered a glance my way and shifted uncomfortably. "He'd been doing so much better since he got made QB1, so we thought--"

Bronston swats away the explanation. "Get the kid an appointment. And I'll have my office call. We need the shrink on the stand. Our defense depends on--"

The alarm sent out its friendly triple beep. Ellen home from rehearsal.

"EJ, could you check and make sure your sister's had dinner?" Dad asked then turned back to Bronston, "Unless you had any other questions or instructions for him?"

"Not at the moment. J-Bird, you're gonna set up an appointment with the psychologist, and I gave you the stylist's number... Oh, kid--you've been staying off social media--no posts, no text, no nothing, right?"

"Right," I forced my eyes not to roll. Like I needed a tenth reminder that anything I put out online, even in private messages, could be used in court.

Plus, I'd figured out that checking my accounts was guaranteed to send me down a misery spiral. At the beginning there'd been ones mocking me and Kendra both. Stuff like, "You know you've hit rock bottom when even the ugliest girl in school doesn't want your dick," which got taken down when people flagged them and clapped back in Kendra's defense. Lately most of my mentions were stuff like "There's a special place in HELL for RAPIST SCUM like you" or people pissed about the athletic suspensions venting "That pussy tanked our basketball season cuz he couldn't take a joke!!!" Oh sure, there were some supportive shoutouts, but they were from strangers, and based on the other stuff on their accounts, not the kind of people I'd ever want to be associated with.

It was so fucking unfair. Why was *I* the one getting strung up as a sex offender? How many of the guys blasting me on social media had done way worse and gotten away with it?

But what good would engaging the mob of haters do? Would anyone care if I tried to set the record straight? Doubtful. Better option was to stop caring about those people and what they thought of me. Easier said than done, but I was trying. Keeping my phone on silent in my desk drawer instead of my pocket helped.

As Bronston and Dad took the case materials and their empty whiskey glasses into Dad's office, I went to the kitchen where Ellen was pouring herself a glass of milk to go with the open pack of Oreos on the counter.

"Is that dinner or dessert?" I asked, dropping onto one of the breakfast bar stools.

"It's the food I want right now," she deflected, not making eye contact with me.

"Okay…" As an Oreo binge was a sure sign of a bad day, I waited for her to launch into the story, but instead she asked, "You want some?"

"Uh, sure, I guess."

She put four cookies on a napkin, filled a second glass, and slid them across to me. I dunked an Oreo in the milk and popped the whole thing in my mouth.

"How's the trial prep going?" She pointed with her chin in the direction of Dad's office.

I swallowed and offered a shrugging sigh. "It's hard to tell. Good, I guess, if Dad's mood is any indication. What about you? How's rehearsal going?"

"Oh, fine." She stared down into her milk.

"It was a vocal rehearsal today, right?"

A nod. More milk contemplation.

This had been a trend over the last week. She'd gone from never shutting up about rehearsal happenings and reporting on other cast members' interpersonal drama to offering scant detail even when asked. But this was the first day of absolute zero info to share. "El…" I prompted, bracing myself for the answer. "Is everything okay?"

"Mm-hm," she nodded, not looking at me. But I couldn't miss the tear that spilled down her cheek and off her chin.

Oh shit. I knew it. "El, what happened? Did the director yell at you or something?" It was the *or something* that worried me. While Ellen claimed her friend group had rallied around her at school, shielding her from the assholes who tried to take their feelings toward me out on my sister, I knew it was impossible that she could completely escape the fallout. Not when she'd been defending me to anyone who'd listen.

"No, she…" Ellen hesitated, flashing a brief look my way before inspecting her milk again.

With a sick feeling I already knew the answer, I asked. "El, come on, you can tell me. Was it…was it because of…everything with me?"

She spared me another quick look, like she was weighing the pros and cons of admitting the truth. Definitely something to do with my mess then. *Fuck.* I got up and walked around to the other side of the bar and pulled her in for a hug. She sagged against me and let the tears come, the story spilling out along with them.

"Ms. Denning asked me to stay after rehearsal, and she and Mr. Cassara told me the majority of the cast and crew had signed a petition saying they 'did not feel comfortable taking part in a show that highlighted a rape apologist in a lead role.'"

"What? How can they--what the hell is a 'rape apologist'?"

"Anyone who supports somebody accused of rape I guess."

"That's total bullshit!

"I know. It's like people can't fathom that I know my own brother better than they do. That I know you would never rape someone, let alone Kendra. But pointing this out makes me some kind of pro-rape, gender traitor."

It was just like Bronston had said--no more assumption of innocence in cases like these. Apparently guilt by association was a thing now too. My fingers tightened around the fabric of Ellen's hoodie. "I can't believe the directors didn't just ignore their stupid petition."

"Well, that wasn't an option, because the petition threatens that if I'm not replaced by next week, they're all going to quit the show on principle. Like a strike or something."

"Holy shit...Can they do that?"

"I guess so, if there's enough of them that they can't be replaced. But the directors can't just kick me out of the show because, like, school policy won't allow them to unless I've missed three rehearsals or broken the student code of conduct. And I think they were kinda scared that if they did try and force me out, Dad would sue them."

"Not an idle fear," I agreed.

"Yeah, well, that's why they put it on me. Asked me to give up my part voluntarily. Ms. Denning said it was my choice if we had a show this year or not. Can you believe that? And Mr. Cassara even said, 'I know it's difficult for you individually, but sometimes the hardest thing to do is the right thing to do.' And I just sat there nodding like I understood and trying not to fall apart in front of them. But I couldn't keep it together and started balling, and they're like, rubbing my back and saying they understand how hard this is for me. Like fuck they do!"

"God, El, that sucks. How can they... It's cruel, when you've done nothing but be a good sister." *Why is life so completely and utterly unfair? What kind of system for existence is this?* I wondered, bitterness settling on the back of my tongue. I wrapped my arms tight around her. "I'm so sorry."

"It's not your fault, EJ. You're the victim here too," She told me, her words muffled against my shoulder.

I didn't reply. Partly because my throat had constricted and partly because as many times as I reminded myself it hadn't been rape, that me and my family were being unjustly accused and persecuted, I couldn't completely tamp down the pestering bit of conscience that said none of this would be happening if I hadn't been so desperate to make nice with those assholes. If I hadn't begged Ellen to get me to that party, she'd still be basking in the glory of a lead role instead of standing here gutted, forced to give it all up. So maybe technically it wasn't my fault. I wasn't the proximate cause, but still...I wasn't sure I deserved for her to let me off the hook.

A single, harsh laugh escaped Ellen's throat. "I shouldn't have been so surprised. Andrea had already told me there was a cast group chat going over break about who was telling the truth, and lots of people agreed that believing and supporting Kendra was the right thing to do, like, on principle. Even though most of them know you but couldn't pick Kendra out in a crowd. It makes me so mad!"

This echo of Bronston's earlier warning chilled me from head to toe. Would it matter how good our defense argument was when everyone was primed to believe the accuser? Especially with a model victim like Kendra Daniel. My heart kicked into overdrive as the cold dread settled in my center. *Goddammit, not again.* A panic attack, as the doctor had now helpfully diagnosed. But that didn't quite capture the force that hijacked my mind and body, swallowing me, taking me over until my insides ejected their contents. I'd have to think of another name... I steadied myself with a hand on the counter. "Um...are you okay, El? I gotta..."

Ellen nodded, recognizing my pale, sweat-sheened face as a sign of things to come. "I'm fine. Go."

Without another word, I bolted for the stairs, locked myself in the bathroom, and sat propped against the door, waiting for the black hole to suck me in. *Ah, The Black Hole...that's what I'll call it.*

Junior Year: Thursday, January 10, Four Weeks after the Night in Question State of Mind

Dr. Eduway's office was exactly the same--the row of dusty African masks mounted over a tightly packed wall of books, the huge mug with cracked blue glaze in the same spot on a coaster under the side table lamp, even a green slip of paper peeking out from under a stack of books on his desk I'd swear was in that exact position six months ago. And that same frustrating expression of neutral consideration. It was probably part of therapist training--keeping any moral judgements off your face--but it drove me nuts, never being able to tell what he was thinking. Especially now, when I'd just recounted the whole shitshow leading up to and including that night with Kendra.

I shifted awkwardly in my big, leather chair as Dr. Eduway looked back over his notes. Sensing my agitation, he peered at me over his wire reading glasses. "A lot to unpack here," he says.

A nervous laugh escaped my lips. "Yeah, no kidding."

You've got this. I encouraged myself. *Whatever concerns he has, you've got a response.* My fingers pressed tight against the brass buttons of the armrests as I marshaled my array of responses to his possible concerns. *He may need some convincing,* Bronston had warned me. I swallowed hard, ready to do my part, recruiting the key witness for my defense. "I want you to know, I'm here to do the work, Dr. Eduway. Committed to the process. For however long you think necessary."

Dr. Eduway offered only the slightest of smiles in return. "I'm very glad to hear that, EJ." Then he tipped his chin down to peer at me over his readers. "Though I wish it hadn't taken such...drastic events to bring you back to my door."

I swallowed as the pace of my heartbeat accelerated. "Yeah, uh...me too."

His eyes held mine for a long second, both of us likely recalling my last session in this familiar office. Me blithely claiming that football--the friends and focus it provided--had been the solution to the "rut" I'd been in after Mom. Him cautioning me that for one, football was seasonal and temporary, "a Band-Aid over a still infected wound." Not to mention, the "competitive, aggressive, hyper-masculine behaviors that locker room culture encourages" that could ultimately increase the "emotional volatility" I struggled with and blah, blah, blah.

It boiled down to him thinking I needed to continue therapy and me thinking nearly a year was plenty. This therapy thing had been fine. Sometimes even good. Really good. The strategies for managing my anger and risk evaluation and all that stuff were legit helpful. And it'd been nice having a person to vent to about literally whatever and whoever was bothering me. Someone I could tear up in front of without worrying he'd laugh or call me a pussy. Who was interested to talk through concepts of the afterlife and souls and the slow fade of memory and all that out-there philosophical stuff that sometimes kept me up at night. But I'd had months to cry it out, and honestly, I didn't want to talk about missing Mom anymore. Why keep focusing on the horrible part of my life when the rest of my life was fucking amazing? Time to focus on all the good stuff in my life. That was the key to my happiness.

Or so I'd thought at the time. Now here I was, having to eat some serious crow. He'd been right all along. I was already one seriously messed up kid, and the amped-up assholery of high-stakes high school football had only made things worse. If only I'd stuck with therapy, maybe I would have been able to handle what happened that night differently. But I hadn't, so I didn't.

"EJ, before we go on, I think it's important that we are both open and honest with what we hope to achieve from this session--"

"Not just *this* session," I insist. "However many you think I need to get, y'know, better. Be a healthy, well-adjusted person."

"That's...a great attitude to have..." The implied *But* hung heavy in the moment of silence that followed.

Shit. Blood pumped thrummed against my eardrums. "I'm serious. I get that I still have, like, trauma from losing Mom and now from all this shit--sorry--I mean, this stuff that happened with football and the party and with Kendra and all."

Dr. Eduway's gaze was steady as he forged ahead. "EJ, before we get into any of that, I want to be clear that I will not be participating in your upcoming trial."

My breath hitched as my stomach dropped from the attic to the basement. "What do you mean?" I asked once I could speak again, falling back on an instinct to bluff it out. "That's...that's not why I'm here."

"EJ..." For the first time the whole session, Dr. Eduway's face shows something akin to disappointment. "Your lawyer's office already called asking me to testify on your behalf, and I declined. I think you know that."

Shit. "Well...yeah, but...you said you couldn't because, like, I wasn't your patient anymore, so, since I'm seeing you again, we thought..."

"Yes, I know. And that's why I wanted to take this chance to clarify the situation."

My head bobbles on my shoulders, somewhere between a shake and a nod. "I mean it though, about being committed to therapy. I wasn't lying to get you to testify."

"I didn't think you were." Dr. Eduway unfolded and refolded his hands atop his closed notebook. "While I'm more than willing to resume your therapy, that won't change my decision not to testify."

I blinked, thrown off by the seeming finality of his refusal. *No...no, no, no.* He had to tell the jury about my cumulative trauma. My state of mind or whatever the hell Bronston called it. It was key to our defense. *Fuck.* I choked on the air making its way out of my lungs.

"Are you alright?" Dr. Eduway asked. "Would you like some water?" He reaches into the mini-fridge next to his desk without waiting for an answer and hands me a bottle.

I squeeze, hoping it can serve as a receptacle for my rising, prickling panic as I fight to keep my voice level. "But I don't get it. You're the one who said I was still processing my grief."

"Yes, I did, and while that's part of--"

"You thought if I got in a 'triggering' situation, I might get overwhelmed and not be able to handle it in a healthy way." I forced myself to sit back up and look him in the eye, dare him to deny it.

"Yes, that's true, and the panic attacks you've started having could tie into that as well, an escalated response in your body."

"So you were right. A hundred percent right, okay?" The muscles in my neck tightened as anger started to edge out the panic. "So why won't you just come and tell the jury that? Tell them how messed up I was--I am--and that's why I couldn't perfectly process everything that was going on in the car and, like, read the nuance of Kendra's non-verbal signals. You called it, Doc. Why not get up on the stand and say so?"

"EJ..." He closed his own eyes for several seconds, pinching the bridge of his nose. "I take no pleasure in knowing my concerns were justified. But..."

"But *what*?" I leaned forward and released my vice grip on the water bottle, freeing up my hands to gesticulate. "Don't you think the jury should know all that when they're trying to figure out if I'm, like, some kind of depraved sex predator?" I jabbed a finger in his direction. "You won't take a couple hours out of your day to explain that--as an expert, as my therapist, who is supposed to care about me?"

If any of my hurled words hit a nerve, he didn't show it. "EJ, you know that I care about you," he replied with infuriating calm.

"Yeah, well, you don't seem to care if I end up in jail. So much for our therapy sessions then, huh?"

Dr. Eduway leaned forward, resting his elbows on his knees, his hands extended, palms up. "I want you to know that I'm willing to continue supporting you as your therapist, wherever that might be."

Something about the quiet, matter-of-fact way he could talk about the possibility of visiting me behind bars hit me like a suckerpunch to the gut. "You think I *should* end up in jail, don't you? You think I'm guilty."

Dr. Eduway raised his hands in a placating gesture. "This isn't a courtroom, and I'm not a judge or jury. My role as a therapist isn't to determine guilt or innocence under the law. And that's essentially what lawyers like yours want me to do."

"Oh, don't fuckin' give me that. If you believed me, you'd want to help make sure I didn't get my life derailed because of some...some...misunderstanding." I stared across at Dr. Eduway, envying the preternatural control he had over his emotions as my own spilled out. Squeezing my eyes shut, I slumped forward, fighting off the creeping dizziness. *Not again, not now...fuck.*

Dr. Eduway immediately recognized what was happening. "EJ, try to regain control. Focus on your breathing. Four seconds in, hold for seven, exhale for eight. Just like we practiced."

No, a stubborn, pissed-off part of me thought. *Let him see me get sucked into The Black Hole. Then maybe he'll have an ounce of compassion.* Then the tingling started to creep up my fingers, leaving that cold, numb, bloodless sensation behind as it made its way up my hands and wrist. Dr. Eduway was right--if didn't do something to regain control right now, it would be too late. This would end with me vomiting on his zigzag patterned area rug. He'd call Dad, the session would be over, and I'd have completely failed in my mission.

So I took a measured breath. Dr. Eduway counted the seconds for me. Inhale--hold--exhale, repeat...over and over again until my heart rate fell, I had full feeling back in my extremities, and the room returned to sharp focus. It might have taken five minutes, or maybe fifteen. All I knew was that I had limited time left to try and get Dr. Eduway to change his mind.

Leaning my head back and gazing towards the ceiling tiles, I took a moment to reassess my approach. Getting angry, defensive, and accusatory hadn't worked so well, big surprise. I needed to stay calm. Let him ask me his questions. Be more vulnerable, own up to my fuck ups. *Yeah, he was always big on taking personal responsibility and all that.*

"Feeling better?" Dr. Eduway asked.

I nodded and took several gulps from the water botting I was still clutching.

"I wonder, have you noticed anything in common about the situations that trigger them?"

I rolled the water between my palms as I pretended to consider, as if I hadn't already gone through this with Dr. Holder a couple weeks ago. "It happens when I feel like...like I've lost control of a situation. When it's too much or...when I have to make a quick decision and I don't know what to do or how to react. I get, overwhelmed, I guess. And...not trapped, exactly, but..."

"Powerless?"

"Yes, exactly." I pointed the water bottle in his direction.

Dr. Eduway nodded and finally opened his notebook again. "So was that how you felt that night at the party, when they showed the video?"

"Yes! God, it was like...they knew exactly what to do-- what to *take*--to break me down, y'know? Everyone packed into that room, watching, laughing. They made me a joke. Pathetic. Even Kendra felt sorry for me..." I trailed off, worried I'd get carried away and say something wrong, unsympathetic.

Dr. Eduway latched onto the mention of her anyway. "Hmm, did it help, having Kendra, a friend, show up to support and comfort you?"

Are you fucking kidding me? I stopped an eye roll just in time. "Yeah, sure, I guess."

"You guess?"

I shrugged.

"Can you explain to me a bit more how her presence there affected you?"

"It...I mean...I appreciate what she was trying to do and all, but like, at the time, it wasn't..." I shrugged again. There wasn't a way to explain it without sounding like an asshole.

Dr. Eduway nodded like he understood something I didn't, then said, "Maybe we shouldn't try to go any further today."

My fingers tightened around the water bottle again. "What? Why?"

He closed his notebook again. "It's probably best if you go home and get some rest. Give your mind and body a chance to relax and recharge before we--"

"No, I'm good now." I strained to keep the bubbling frustration out of my voice.

"Still, if you're not ready yet to examine--"

"No, I am, really." We held eye contact for a long second, and I could tell he wasn't buying it.

"EJ...I'm getting the sense you don't feel able to be open and vulnerable with me. At least not right now. Not about what happened that night."

Yeah, no shit, Sherlock. "I just don't feel comfortable doing therapy with someone who doesn't believe what I say."

"EJ, it's not that I disbelieve the version of events you laid out earlier." He put a hand over his heart to emphasize his sincerity. "But examining those events--getting to the *why* behind them--is a necessary part of the process. As I told you in our very first session, a therapist isn't a sympathetic ear who gives you all the reactions you're looking for, always telling you how right you are. I must ask the difficult questions, challenge your perspective by asking you to shift your point of view."

"Yeah, I know. I remember. It just feels...different now that a judge and twelve strangers, and everyone I know, and basically the whole fucking city are judging me."

Dr. Eduway briefly lifts his palms. "And what you choose to tell all of them is up to you. But what you say here, to me as your therapist, that needs to be the truth. That is, it does if you meant what you said earlier about being committed to 'getting over your trauma and being a healthy, well-adjusted person' was it?"

Damn he's good, using my own words against me. "Okay, fine then. Go ahead and ask me your questions."

"Alright…" He adjusted his glasses and then cut right to the chase. "When Kendra kissed you, and then when she asked if you wanted to get into the car with her--How did the possibility of having sex affect your sense of power?"

Oh God… My innards felt like a dishrag getting rung out. *This is a mistake. He's not gonna testify. I should just get up and go. Who cares what my old shrink thinks of me?*

But apparently, *I* cared, because in my next breath, the answer came spilling out. "Yeah, it helped, okay? It felt good to have someone want me, even if it was only Kendra." My whole body shivered with the admission.

Dr. Eduway took this information in stride. "That's a very natural reaction--especially right after the loss and embarrassment you'd experienced."

"Yeah? Oh…okay." My clenched intestines eased a fraction.

"And when she told you she wasn't sure she wanted to have sex after all?"

Like she'd floored the gas on a race car then stomped on the breaks and expected it to make the turn. A wave of frustration hit me along with the memory. "It felt shitty! She shouldn't have started it if she wasn't sure. It felt like another trick. Like I needed one more humiliation added to the worst fucking night of my life."

Hands still draped loosely over his closed notebook, he gave a slight nod, like we were talking about the fucking weather or some shit. *God, how does he do it?*

"Did you think that Kendra owed you sex at that point?"

"No!" *Maybe.* "That's not what I'm saying. I'm just being honest, like you said. What--was I supposed to feel good that she wanted to back out? That I was getting rejected by a girl who most guys wouldn't even pity fuck? How pathetic. How--" *Shut up!* I clamped my jaw against the torrent of angry words. *You sound like an asshole. Like the kind of guy who'd...*

No. He's getting you all twisted around. "She didn't actually back out," I clarified. "She just got nervous. I gave her the chance to stop, and she didn't take it, okay? She only had to say the word, and I'd have backed off. If she'd really changed her mind, then she needed to make it clear. I'm not psychic. It's not my fault if she thought one thing and did another." The legal defense sounded wooden and practiced coming out of my mouth.

Dr. Eduway looked from me to his hands then back again. "EJ, do you remember the empathy exercise we've done--where you take on the role of someone, your father for example, and try to recount the situation from their perspective?"

I swallowed, not liking where this was going. "Yeah, I remember."

"I wonder...have you tried viewing that night from Kendra's perspective?"

Hell no...why would I ever want to do that? I have enough misery of my own to sort through.

"EJ? Is that something you would be willing to do? Maybe together, at our next session?"

But if I won't, what does that say? There it was again-- the spike in my pulse. *Fuck. I can't do this. I can't be here anymore.* I splayed my finger through my hair, pressing my thumbs against the base of my skull. "I'm not a bad person. I'm *not a monster*," I managed to croak out, needing him to acknowledge that.

"EJ...it's not just terrible people who do terrible things. Human behavior is complex, and by examining our experiences in new ways, we may discover truths that are buried deep in here--" he tapped two fingers on his temple "and in here." His hand dropped to rest over his heart.

"My truth isn't buried anywhere. I'm crystal clear on what happened that night. So thanks for nothing." I set the near empty water bottle on the stand beside the chair and walked out without a goodbye or backward glance.

"How'd it go?" Dad asked when I joined him in the Psychology Department's lounge. The hope in his voice was painful to hear. "Will he testify?"

I shook my head.

Dad's expression fell, but only for a second. "Well...It's alright. Forget him."

I stared at Dad, mouth ajar. Whatever reaction I'd expected from him, it wasn't this. "I thought he was crucial for my defense."

Dad moved his head back and forth noncommittally. "Since he was your therapist before all this, it would have been ideal. But Bronston already got someone else lined up in case Eduway wouldn't play ball. There's a psychologist his firm has worked with on these kinds of cases before. She's a trauma specialist of some kind out in New York City. A female psychologist might play better on the stand anyway."

Dad took out his phone and started texting, setting up Plan B. Getting me in with someone who wouldn't ask too many uncomfortable questions. Who would tell my story the way we needed it told. The version that would keep me safe and protect my future.

The true version...or just the one I wish *was true?* I could feel the seed of doubt that Dr. Eduway planted, pressing uncomfortably at the back of my brain. *No, stop, enough!* I gritted my teeth. *Forget Dr. Eduway and his psychology mindfuck bullshit. It's Dad and Bronston I need to trust, the ones who believe me and are willing to do whatever it takes to help me out of this mess.*

Junior Year: Friday, February 22
Kendra's Testimony

"Do you swear to tell the truth, the whole truth, and nothing but the truth, so help you God?"

"I do."

It was the first time I'd heard Kendra's voice since she shouted at me to get out of the car. It was far quieter now, but no less jarring.

"You may be seated."

Kendra removed her hand from the Bible and smoothed her long, navy skirt under her before sitting down. She pulled at the cuffs of the white turtleneck she was wearing under an oversized blue and green argyle sweater vest before folding her hands in her lap. She was the picture of demure modesty. If it weren't for the braids hanging over each shoulder, she'd look almost matronly. I was pretty sure it was the same outfit she'd worn for school pictures back in September.

Bronston leaned over and gave me a final reminder to "Sit up straight. Don't look down--it makes you seem guilty. Keep your face neutral. Go somewhere else in your head if you need to. Or do that counting thing you like--" He cut off as

Jessica Gresham, the Special Prosecutor brought in to avoid a conflict of interest within the DA's office, approached the witness box and offered her nervous witness a reassuring smile.

"Kendra, we've already heard from Frankie Gurlance, who found you that night outside the party and drove you home, as well as from both your parents and the court-appointed counselor about what occurred in the days and weeks after you were raped--"

"Objection, Your Honor," Bronston was halfway to his feet when the judge replied,

"Sustained." And then to Ms. Gresham, "Watch yourself, counselor."

"When you were *allegedly* raped," Ms. Gresham corrected with the slightest flick of her eyes towards the six men and six women in the jury box. "So today, I want to focus on the most important piece of this case--what went on between you and the defendant in that car."

Kendra gave her the smallest of nods. No doubt they'd prepared her for this, just like Bronston and I had rehearsed my testimony over and over for the last week.

"But before that, I'd like to ask you some questions that will help put that night in context for the jury." Ms. Gresham turned to look directly at me before she asked, "How would you characterize the relationship between you and the defendant?"

"We were friends." Kendra did not look at me, which was no surprise. Instead she stared at the polished wooden rail in front of her like she was determined to memorize the pattern of the grain.

Ms. Gresham waited for Kendra to elaborate, but when she didn't, the lawyer prompted, "How long had you been friends?"

291

"Since elementary school. Since I moved here in second grade."

"And how did you meet?"

"At church."

"And were you also friends outside of church?"

"Um...not so much. Not once we got to middle school. He was...a lot more popular than me, so... But he was never mean to me. I got teased a lot by...people, but he never... And he would talk to me, if there weren't a lot of other people around. It may not sound like much, but it...meant a lot to me."

"And did--"

"Like this one time in eighth grade..." Kendra lifted her eyes but didn't focus them anywhere. "I was rushing to get to class after lunch and somebody bumped into me and I dropped my binder and the papers went everywhere...and people just laughed and stepped around me. The bell was about to ring, and I started panicking that I was going to be late, and...there was EJ, crouched down next to me, helping me pick the papers up. It was..." She shook her head as if in wonder. "It was...the kindest thing..."

"So even though you weren't close, you still considered the defendant a friend?" Her lawyer summed up to end this off-script reminiscence of me at one of my better moments. Though Kendra gave me more credit than I deserved. I remembered the day I helped her, and I remembered how I'd checked up and down the hall to make sure none of my friends were around before helping her.

Pulled back from the memory, Kendra's eyes dropped back to the polished wood. "Yes...I did."

"And was there a point you wished he was more than a friend?"

Kendra's cheeks flushed so suddenly it was like a drop of blood spreading through a bowl of milk. "I...yes...I had a crush on him."

"When did this crush start?"

"I, um, I'm not sure. I always liked him...but by the end of eighth grade, I started to think about...what it would be like...to be his girlfriend, but...I knew I wasn't the kind of girl he usually dated, so...I didn't expect--"

Next to me, Bronston jots something down on his legal pad as Mrs. Gresham cuts in again. "And did you ever make the defendant aware of your romantic interest in him?"

"Yes..." Her chin dipped so far down it pressed against her concealed collarbone. "I...at the end of that year, at his fourteenth birthday party, I...told him and I..." The last part of her answer was almost inaudible.

"I'm sorry, Kendra, but can you repeat that last part?"

"...I kissed him," she says just loud enough to hear.

"And how did the defendant respond to your expression of feelings at that time?"

It was all I could do not to curl forward in my seat.

"He told me...he wasn't...that he only liked me as a friend."

"At the time, did other people know you had a crush on the defendant?"

"Yes, well, afterwards they did. There was a girl at the party who saw us right after he...and she guessed about...me liking him and him not liking me the same way back and...she told people at school and they...made fun of me about it."

I'd heard Lydia spread the story of Kendra fleeing the storage room in tears and that people had mocked Kendra about aiming too high and getting shot down, but I'd told myself it would pass, that people would forget and move on. Had they? I didn't know. I hadn't wanted to know. Knowing would have meant having to feel guilty.

Ms. Gresham gave her a sympathetic smile. As did several members of the jury. One jury member, an older woman with short salt and pepper hair looked in my direction and frowned.

Neutral expression, I reminded myself though I could feel my face burn. *Relax...just relax.* I started doing my breath-counting exercise to keep my composure as Ms. Gresham asked Kendra a series of questions I already knew the answers to-- what she'd heard about the party, her attempts to warn me by calling our landline, lying to her parents and offering to be the DD in order to get to the party, how she was too late to warn me, going outside with me afterwards to make sure I was okay, waiting for my ride together, our conversation, the kiss, how unlike the last time, I'd reciprocated, how cold it was, how as the DD, she had the keys to the car, and how she thought it would be warmer and more private...

"And by asking the defendant to move to the back seat of the car, was it your intent to signal that you wanted to have sexual intercourse there?"

"No, it was not."

"Were you at all aware that 'taking it to the back seat' is commonly understood as a suggestion of sex? As in, going to a place where the parties can lay down...to get in a more comfortable, horizontal position for sexual intercourse?"

"No, I didn't."

"And how is that?"

"We don't have a television, and we only have one computer at home, and it's only for homework...and I mostly read classic novels, so…"

"Not a lot of cars in those books, I'll bet," Ms. Gresham joked, coaxing the tiniest of smiles from Kendra's lips.

"No, not really."

It was just like Bronston had guessed--them playing up how sheltered and innocent Kendra was of contemporary teen hookup culture. And Bronston was letting Gresham roll along without objection, planning to build on this established naivete during cross, that in Kendra's cluelessness, she hadn't made her wishes clear.

"At what point did you realize the defendant was expecting sex?"

"Um…when he…"

"I'm sorry, Kendra, but I need you to talk a little louder for the jury to hear."

Kendra lifted her chin a fraction, attempting to make herself audible. "When he unzipped his pants and...put the condom on."

As soon as she said it, I could feel the foil of the wrapper between my fingers and tried to scrub away the phantom sensation on the side of my pant leg.

"And how did you react once you realized what he intended?" Ms. Gresham went on.

"When he started to pull down my underwear, I pressed my legs together. And tried to say...to explain that I didn't…" Kendra shook her head. "I wanted to explain to him that I wasn't...experienced with...sex. That it wasn't something I was ready for. But I had trouble figuring out how to say it without making him think that I was...rejecting him or something. And as I was trying to get it out, he stopped and said he knew and it'd be fine and not to worry."

"And what did you think he meant by that?"

"I thought it meant he understood I didn't want to have sex and that he'd only been pulling my underwear down to…" Kendra leaned so far forward her forehead nearly rested on the railing.

Ms. Gresham put a comforting hand on Kendra's shoulder. "We all understand it's difficult to relive a traumatic experience, especially in this context." She takes a moment to frown in my direction before . "Take a moment if you need to."

Bronston shifted in his chair as if he didn't much like Gresham characterizing the "sexual encounter" as a "traumatic experience," but he must have decided objecting would backfire and let it pass.

Several long seconds later, Kendra straightened and glanced at her parents before dropping her eyes again. "I thought he was just planning to touch me…there, between my legs…with his fingers."

"And what made you think that was his intent?" Ms. Gresham asked, her tone light and curious, absent any sense of judgment.

"Well, that's what he'd been doing right before, but…over the fabric, so… And when he said, 'I know' I though he meant he knew I didn't want to have sex, that I was waiting for marriage… I mean, he was there when I took the Purity Pledge, made an oath before God to…and he'd taken the Pledge too." She shook her head as if she still found our crossed wires in that moment incomprehensible. "He *knew*, we'd both vowed…so I thought…and I liked…the way he was touching me…and I thought, as long as it's just his hand, it's not sex, not breaking the Pledge…" Kendra squeezed her eyes shut and covered her mouth with a hand, fighting back a surge of emotion.

I felt my own chest tighten as heart hammered against my ribs. Of course she'd think that I, of all people, would understand and respect her limits. I, who knew what the church taught about abstinence, who'd taken the same oath she had. If only I had taken a minute, thought the situation through from her perspective, I would have realized… *But you did realize, didn't you?* A small but insistent voice reminded me. *Yow knew how inexperienced she was and why. That was part of the appeal. It made you feel powerful, thinking she wanted you so bad she'd break her promise to God for you.*

Kendra's chest rose and fell heavily as she went on. "I knew I shouldn't be letting him… That even if it wasn't technically…we were crossing a line. Being intimate in a way only a husband and wife should and that we had to stop. And I kept trying to think how to tell him, how to backtrack to just kissing again without…making him mad or having him think I didn't…that I didn't like him enough to…"

My chest rose and fell in time with hers, synched by some invisible tether. Kendra was giving me the answers to the homework problem Dr. Eduway had set for me, the one I'd scrupulously avoided, sensing the outcome might be self-damning.

"Because I did like him, so much, for so long, and I always hoped that…maybe someday…he would be…my husband…and then we would…"

Oh God, she actually thought we'd…that I could be her husband? Oh God…

A sickening electric shock went through my body as Kendra unexpectedly turned to look at me with a focused intensity. Like her next words were for me alone and she needed to be sure I heard them. "I was so afraid that if...I said or did the wrong thing he'd...that I'd mess up my chance...at a future with him..."

She looked away again, allowing me to draw breath. But the breath didn't come easy. My throat had constricted. I gripped the edge of the table as I forced the stale courtroom air down into my lungs without making a scene.

"Hold it together, kid," Bronston whispers, "It's all part of their plan to unsettle you and gain sympathy with the jury. I've seen it a hundred times."

I didn't respond, couldn't respond. Maybe he was right about Gresham coaching Kendra, but that didn't mean she was faking her reactions or calculating each action for effect. The downcast eyes, the unsurety, the pauses, sudden intensity of emotion...that was the same Kendra I'd known for more than half my life.

Ms. Gresham's tone was gentle and coaxing. "Considering that fear you describe of saying or doing something that would hurt or upset the defendant..." She paused while Kendra tugged at her sleeves. "Did you consider going along with what he wanted? Once he exposed his erection and it became clear to you what his intentions were?"

Kendra dropped her chin and shook her head. "No, I...when he...I was so...I'd never seen a man's...and it was like I couldn't move. I was scared then, *really* scared...and he tried to move me so he could...get me in position to...and I knew I had to figure out a way to stop it happening, but it was like my body wasn't responding..."

I remembered it--the look on her face when I pulled down my underwear, the way she'd gone limp when I tried to shift her into position, her neck pressed against the door at an uncomfortable angle. How could I not have registered...? *But you* did *register her shock, and it excited you--your dick being her first.*

Ms. Gresham looked to the jury members--many of whom were visibly uncomfortable or upset--before positioning herself to the left of the witness stand and placing a hand on Kendra's shoulder. "It's okay if you need a moment," she told her witness.

Kendra nodded then shook her head, lifting her visibly trembling chin. "I can keep going."

Ms. Gresham looked to the jury once more but then withdrew her hand, stepped away, and continued. "Once the defendant put the condom on, what did you do?"

"I knew I was out of time...and I told him... 'I don't know if I'm ready for this.'"

"Kendra, if you were sure that you wanted the defendant to stop what he was doing, why didn't you state it more definitively? 'I'm not ready' or 'I don't want to' or something along that line?"

"I didn't want to...embarrass him. He'd already had such a terrible night... And I still hoped that maybe, he'd be interested in me...afterwards. So I tried to be...gentle."

"And how did the defendant respond?"

"He got...upset. Told me it was my idea. That I'd suggested getting in the car, in the back seat. And that I'd said I'd wanted him for so long, and...something like, this was my chance, and did I really want to stop now that he was..." Kendra made a vague gesture towards her lap.

"He was what, exactly?"

"Um, he pointed to his...penis, with the condom on."

"And what did you take the defendant to mean by that?"

"That he was...that it was too late to ask him to stop."

Maybe it was the familiar bleakness in her tone, or the way whole body sagged with some invisible weight of defeat, but I recognized what underlied her words. *She felt powerless. I was the one in control of the situation, and I used that control, that power to...* A familiar cold sensation trickled from my stomach to intestines. *Have you tried viewing that night from Kendra's perspective?* Dr. Eduway had asked. I hadn't then-- had purposely avoided it--but now...*Oh God...how could I...what've I done?*

"And how did you respond?" Ms. Gresham went on.

"I just looked at him and I...didn't say anything. But I started crying. I couldn't help it. I knew I'd ruined any chance...that he'd never want..." Kendra hid her face behind her hands and choked back a sob.

It was all I could manage not to do the same as my breaths came short and quick. *No no no no...not now.* I tried to slow my inhales, but it just made me feel suffocated. My vision started to blur. *No, please not now...*

"--And then he just...pulled my legs apart and...pushed...inside me." Her chest heaved as she fought valiantly to keep her composure. "It...hurt...so much...but it was like...the rest of me...went numb... I couldn't even..." The tears took over then. Kendra buried her face in her hands again and leaned as far forward as the railing would allow.

It wasn't only Kendra who was crying by then. Not a single juror had been unaffected by Kendra's halting, anguished narrative. There were tissues dabbing at wet eyes, a mouth covered in horror, multiple heads shaking with mounting anger on her behalf. Six sets of eyes were on the witness where she sat trembling. The other six were on me, their expressions loaded with judgment, their minds made up. We'd have our chance to mount our defense after this, to shift the blame for any unwanted outcomes onto Kendra's naivete and "lack of clarity." I'd have the chance to get on the stand and contradict...what, exactly? What had she said that I could truthfully point to and call a lie or an exaggeration or even a sad, tragic misunderstanding?

Maybe I had let myself believe she wanted to have sex when she suggested we move to the car. But once we were there, I'd disregarded each and every sign of her reluctance and distress. I'd taken the comfort and validation Kendra offered me and used it--used *her*--to fulfill my own twisted needs. By the time I pushed her thighs apart, any "misunderstandings" on my part were willful.

"Jesus..." Bronston muttered beside me and pressed a tissue into my hand under the table. "You're dripping sweat. Turn this way and mop your face."

I probably looked like shit, but I didn't move. I couldn't. My focus was frozen on Kendra's hunched, crying form...almost exactly as she'd been in the car after--

"Your Honor," Ms. Gresham stepped toward the bench. "I'd like to ask for a brief recess--"

"No!" Kendra straightened in her chair, gasping for air, eyes wide and bloodshot. "I can finish. I need this to be finished," she said. From the ragged desperation in her voice, it was clear she was talking about more than just her testimony.

Ms. Gresham, opened her mouth, hesitated, and looked to Kendra's parents sitting in the small gallery area. Mrs.

Daniels' eyes were red and swollen, her lip quivering, clutching her husband's arm. But Mr. Daniels sat rigid and unmoved, buoyed by rage and righteous anger. He nodded for Ms. Gresham to continue. The prosecutor checked her notes, swallowed her reservations, and cut to the chase.

"Kendra, at any point, did the defendant ask for your consent to engage in vaginal sexual intercourse?"

Kendra swallowed and sat poker-straight. "No, he did not."

"At any point, did you verbally consent to vaginal sexual intercourse with the defendant?"

"No, I did not."

"And when you told him you were not ready for intercourse, indicating that you in fact *did not* consent, did he respect your wishes in any way?"

"No..." she paused for a shuddering breath. "He did not."

Ms. Gresham took her own steading breath before asking, "And did the defendant forcibly have intercourse with you after you had told him you did not think you were ready? Did the defendant rape you, Kendra?"

Kendra's tear-glazed eyes met mine. Her features were taunt and stricken, but her answer was resolute and decisive. "Yes, he did."

Yes...I did. Oh God...

Ms. Graham touched Kendra on the shoulder and said, "Thank you. You've been very brave today. Almost done, okay?" Then she turned to Bronston, her smile fading. "Your witness."

Bronston cleared his throat and adjusted his tie as he stood. I gripped his arm as he moved to step out from behind the table. "Call a recess," I begged, swaying precariously in my seat. "I need...the bathroom..." My vision was too far gone for me to make out the expression on Bronston's face, but I heard him ask for a fifteen-minute recess and the judge granted it.

Thank God... I staggered as I stood and turned down the center aisle. Dad caught me under the right arm and kept hold of me as we made for the exit.

While I threw up in a stall. Bronston came in and said, "Well, that was a disaster."

Dad replied with a heavy sigh of agreement. "We knew she'd be a strong witness."

"God, tell me about it. Those waterworks... She's got the jury primed to come after us with pitchforks. But it's not just that. The kid was sweating like they had his feet to the fire. And the hyperventilating... Quite frankly, he looked guilty as fuck."

I spat out the last dregs of vomit and slumped against the side of the stall as Bronston and Dad discussed how to spin my hobbled flight from the courtroom to bolster our defense narrative. How it's fortunate I got the official panic disorder diagnosis. Bronston will talk to the psychologist we're flying in to testify about my trauma and have her work my reaction to Kendra's testimony into--

I swing the stall door open. "Don't bother...I wanna change my plea."

Bronston scoffed and rolled his eyes. Dad just looked sad. He stepped close and placed his hands on my shoulders. "Son, I know it was hard to hear Kendra say those things about you, to see her in pain. Kendra was saying what she was coached to say--not just by the prosecutor but *by her father*. You saw how nervous she was up there? Well, I guarantee you she wasn't half as scared of the judge and jury as she was of *him*. She gave the explanation of her actions that John Daniels wanted to hear."

It wasn't that what Dad was saying didn't make sense or sound convincing. But the thing was, I couldn't dismiss her as a puppet or a liar. Because I'd been in that car with Kendra. And the story she'd told up there, how she'd explained it...it all *fit*. It was true. I knew it down to my bones.

"Dad, I..." the rest of my confession dissipated before it left my tongue. I swallowed hard, and tried again, but as I looked into Dad's face, so full of confidence and faith in what he believed to be the truth of things, I just...I couldn't.

"Just hang tight, okay, kid? I saw how the jury was looking at you back in there, but you'll get your chance to tell your side. And once the psychologist testifies, the jury's sympathies won't be so one sided. Trust me, I know how trials play out."

I nodded. *Okay...let the jury decide and the judge pick my punishment.*

So when it came my turn on the stand, I did as I was told. But I wasn't fooling anybody in the jury box. Maybe because I wasn't even fooling myself anymore either.

Senior Year: Sunday, November 3
Indefensible Offspring

The first thing I do when I wake up is check my email to see if Dr. Eduway has replied.

He has and is willing to make a trip to his office this afternoon so we can meet. *Thank God...* Tension in my chest releases like a rubber band gone slack. I roll over onto my back and stretch. It's 10:43. The last time I remember seeing on my Cornell wall clock was 4:26, so I got some sleep. Not nearly enough, if my aching limbs and fuzzy brain are any sign.

After emptying my bladder, I head downstairs, praying there's something to eat in the kitchen because I am painfully hungry.

But there is more than breakfast waiting for me in the kitchen. Dad is sitting at the far end of the breakfast bar. He looks up from his laptop as soon as I enter. We both just stare at each other for what feels like a long minute before I say, "Hey."

"How are you feeling?" he asks, shutting his laptop.

Wow, he's not going to try and multi-task this conversation. He really is worried.

I shrug, continue to the fridge. It's scant pickings, but I find an apple and a jug of milk that passes the sniff test.

Strain shows in the creases around Dad's eyes. "EJ..."

Maybe it's being back in our house. Maybe it's the recent realization that a new name can't make you a new person. Either way, I let the reversion to the old name slide.

"You can't drive off like that in the middle of the night. And you can't just show back up in Rochester all of a sudden. If you recall, people here think you're away at boarding school. Where, quite frankly, I still think you should be." He slides his hands over the cool marble in self-soothing circles.

I snort, almost choking on my milk. "Being isolated from my whole family off at boarding school wouldn't have fixed my problems, Dad. Or was the idea of sending me away for everyone else's benefit? Out of sight, out of mind?" I accuse, knowing the barb will hurt, a reminder of his own quasi-neglectful parents who shunted him off to boarding school at the earliest acceptable age to make their own lives easier.

305

His head jerks back like I've landed a physical blow, eyes searching my face, trying to gauge if I really believe what I've said. *Or maybe my jab hit home because deep down, he knows it's true. Deep down he does want me gone.* This new thought sets my heart beating at double strength against my ribs. But before the fear can take root, Dad is hugging me tight.

The side of his head pressed to mine, he says, "I know it's been hard these past few years, for all of us, but for you especially. And I worry about you, that's all. I only want what will make life safer and easier and better for you. I want you to be healthy and happy. That's all. Nothing will ever change that."

He steps back far enough to look at me and holds me by the shoulders. His eyes search mine, checking that I understand, that I believe him. He cups the side of my face like he hasn't done since I was much younger and at least three feet shorter. "I know I get too focused on my work sometimes, especially since your Mom isn't here to remind me to be in 'Dad Mode' when I'm home. And I know I've done a pretty piss poor job of keeping everything going like she did. But...you know I love you. You know that, right?"

And I do, mostly. At least I know he is doing the best by me and Ellen and Charlie as he knows how. It isn't fair to expect him to change his whole personality to become Mom. Neither of us can fill her shoes.

I nod my understanding and he lets his hand drop to my shoulder again.

"I just worry about you. You can't go driving off in the middle of the night on a quest to see your old therapist and not expect me to be scared you'll..." His fears go unspoken, but we both know what they are.

I step away, trying not to be annoyed by his persistent fear that I'll go off the deep end, literally and/or figuratively. "Dad, I'm fine. I mean, not really *fine*, but I'm not going to hurt myself or drive over to the Daniels' house or anything insane like that, so you can relax."

The mention of the Daniels makes him grimace. "Ellen shouldn't have told you any of that about Kendra. Her situation is not your responsibility. It's sad, yes, but if anything, it's her own parents' doing." Dad's expression tightens. "John Daniels seems to have a talent for making any bad situation worse with his need to control it, and his wife only ever follows his lead."

His tone gentles as he adds, "That's why your mom took such an interest in Kendra, you know. She saw how they stifled every creative thought the girl had, even punished her for them. Your mom used to sneak her fantasy and poetry books, things her parents wouldn't let her get from the library. I warned her there'd be hell to pay if the Daniels ever found out, but Abigail couldn't stand to see a bright mind go to waste..." Dad's eyes peer into the middle distance, reliving some long-ago conversation with Mom.

"Anyway," he comes back to the present with a slight shake of the head. "Ellen understands it was wrong for her to lash out in that way. There'll be no more talk of Kendra or any of that from now on." Dad puts both hands on the outsides of my shoulders. "It's done. You can't let misplaced guilt over a deeply troubled girl pull your life any further off track than it already is."

"Dad..." I step out of his grasp and take in a deep, fortifying breath before trying one more time to make Dad face the truth about his son. "I know you don't want to hear it, but I *am* responsible for what Kendra's going through. Not all of it, but still. And I need to--"

"EJ, we've been over this. The legal impetus was on Kendra to communicate her wishes. She didn't *clearly express* that she wanted you to stop. She even admits as much in those texts she sent saying it was consensual."

"But those texts were most likely her trying to--"

Dad raises his volume to talk over me. "They were statements made directly after the incident and clear evidence of her thoughts at the time, before friends and family got her to question her own understanding of events. Now...was what happened with Kendra a tragic misunderstanding? Yes. But that doesn't make it forcible rape." His words are infused with decisive confidence and emphasized with precise hand motions. It's like I'm an undecided jury member he's targeting during closing arguments.

I spread my arms in a plaintive shrug. "Alright fine. Maybe you're right that based on the evidence the court had, there wasn't enough to make it clear-cut forcible rape under New York State Law. *Maybe*," I allow, knowing it's pointless to debate him yet again on the legal front. "But technicalities and burdens of proof aren't what matter right now. Not to me, and not to Kendra. This isn't about what she did or didn't say or do--It's about what *I* did."

"EJ..." Dad tents his finger and presses them to his lips a moment before continuing. "It's okay to feel some regret about the encounter with Kendra. Given all that followed, I think it's safe to say we all regret it ever happened. But this false guilt you've had since your acquittal..." He frowns and shakes his head. "It's not right. It's not healthy. To take this burden on yourself to...to do what, exactly?"

"I don't know. That's part of what I wanna talk to Dr. Eduway about."

Dad steadies himself with a hand on the counter and manages to keep his tone low and even. "I don't like the idea of you going to a therapist who encourages you to believe a distorted, self-recriminatory version of events. He used his bag of tricks to confuse you before the trial and--"

"That's not how it was," I insist. "Dr. Eduway didn't make me... He got me to look at more than one point of view, and understand why people act--"

Dad stops me with a raised hand, face slightly flushed with the effort to keep his temper under control. "Well, I'm no psychologist, but even I can tell that making you question your own memories, making you see yourself as some sort of sexual predator, has only hurt your mental health. And that's what matters here." He lets out a long breath and there is an undercurrent of pleading in his next words. "You're doing well in Ohkwali--getting good grades, making friends, having fewer panic attacks...Don't let yourself lose that by getting bogged down in the past."

He offers me the smile of a parent looking out for their child's wellbeing. He's been on my side, through everything. Protecting me, even when I didn't deserve it. And I love him for that. I do. It would be so easy to let him keep doing it. But I can't...not anymore. I close the distance and wrap my arms around him. "Dad, I appreciate that you wanna make my life better and easier and happier. That you wanna save me from the fallout of my decisions, but--" My voice catches. "But I need to face what I did and be accountable for my actions." I release him and nearly choke as I force my lungs to take in air.

"Son, you don't--"

"*I knew.*" Desperation gives my voice a ragged edge. I need to make him understand, to believe me. "I knew Kendra didn't want to have sex, to have her first time be there in the back seat of that car. And when she tried to tell me, I got angry. I yelled at her, made her feel guilty, like she was a bad person, a tease for wanting to make out but then not wanting me to go ahead and shove my dick in her."

Dad's head snaps back at my crude but accurate description.

I rush on before he can summon a reply. "And then I gave her what, six, maybe seven seconds to summon up the courage to tell the boy she'd had a crush on since forever that she doesn't want him after all? She knew my life had just gone to shit. She came there that night to help me. She showed me that someone still cared, that I wasn't alone, that those assholes' opinions of me didn't change the way she felt about me. And I took advantage of that, of her. Dad, I knew she wanted to stop, she'd basically already said so. But all I cared about…" I pause, close my eyes, and take a steadying breath. "After everything at State, at the party, I wanted to feel powerful again. In control. And right then, I thought having sex with her would give me that. So I went ahead and did what I wanted, not caring about Kendra or what she wanted or how my actions would hurt her. "

"EJ…" Dad wraps a hand around a fist I'd formed without realizing. "You'd been held captive, traumatized..." He repeats Bronston's defense from my trial. "You weren't in any state of mind to make clear-headed interpretations or decisions about--"

"Yeah, I was messed up! I was in pain. But that doesn't excuse what I did. I was still in control of my actions."

"EJ, you say all that now, but at the time, you--"

"Dad, please just listen to me, okay?" I wrench my hand out of his and force both hands to unclench. They shake at my sides, but my voice doesn't waver. "It took me a while to face it, to be honest with myself. I didn't try and tell you the truth until after the verdict got thrown out, but I knew even before that--by the end of the trial, after hearing Kendra testify...I couldn't lie to myself anymore. She'd wanted me to stop...and I knew it. There in the car, I knew it. And that's what it comes down to. Kendra's parents may be responsible for plenty of shit in her life, but bottom line, what happened to her in that car is on me."

Dad's mouth opens, closes, then opens again. "This isn't...if you'd *known*...you wouldn't have..."

"But I *did*. I raped her. I'm guilty." I think back to Ms. Layton confronting me in the restaurant at our get-out-of-juvie celebration dinner, how conflicted I'd felt, how afraid I was of admitting my guilt, of what would happen if I did. "I was too scared to face it back then, but I need to now. Deal with it, face it, own it. No more hiding and pretending. It doesn't work. Not in the long run."

Dad closes his eyes and shakes his head in short, jerky movements, like my words are a buzzing fly trapped inside his skull. "Enough...enough," he mutters angrily, and I'm sure I've failed. The next thing out his mouth is going to be a directive to cancel my appointment with Dr. Eduway, get in my car, drive back to Ohkwali, and never say another word of this garbage ever again. But a second later, his mouth closes and his face sags in the defeated way I haven't seen since we watched Mom's casket being lowered into the ground. The rest of his body follows, dropping onto the nearest stool.

With a pang, I realize what forcing him to hear the truth means. It's removed his whole operating framework. He knew how to be a father protecting his son from trumped-up accusations. It wasn't far from his courtroom comfort zone. But what is he supposed to do if he isn't allowed to protect and defend? If his son is, in fact, indefensible? Now he has to look at his own son and see someone capable of rape. This is why in the past I've backed down and let him have the final word on the subject. I didn't want his view of me to change forever, stained with a permanent, unalterable shame. But some truths have to be faced, no matter how much it hurts both of us.

"Dad?"

"Hmm." He's looking at the wall, instead of me.

I swallow hard and force myself to go on. "I'm sorry. I'm so, so sorry...for everything I put you through. I know how hard you fought to protect me, and...I only wish I'd deserved it."

He gives his head a small shake. I'm not sure what it means. That he doesn't accept my apology? That he thinks it's not necessary? Maybe he doesn't know yet either.

Senior Year: Sunday, November 3
Paths Forward

"Every time I think I'm doing the right thing, it turns out I'm fucking things up worse than ever. My sister is right--I keep finding ways to justify what I want even when there's a high chance it could hurt other people. I'm still selfish. I'm still angry. Still scared." I sigh and slouch, letting my head tip back and eyes close. "Sorry," I tell Dr. Eduway. "I know the last time

312

we met I was pretty messed up and kind of an asshole to you. Hell, you were probably relieved I didn't come back." I put my hands up before he can object. "No, I know you want to help me. Otherwise why would you have made a special trip in on the weekend to see a *former* patient."

"Not a former patient," Dr. Eduway says. "I always hoped you would be in touch one day. When you were ready."

I tip my head up and look at him. "Yeah well, I tried going it alone. And I thought I'd been doing better, y'know? Like, a lot better. Making real progress. Despite the lack of professional help. Realizing I'd made yet another mess of things...it's thrown me."

"EJ--or would you prefer me to call you Eric?" Dr. Eduway asks.

"Whichever," I shrug. "Turns out it doesn't matter."

"Actually, from what you've told me, I think it might. A sort of psychological goal-setting tool. So--Eric, in many ways, I think you *have* made progress."

I regard him with narrowed eyes. "You're not goin' soft on me now, are ya Doc?"

"No fear of that," he chuckles. "But it seems to me you've already identified your personal and behavioral goals and recognized what's gone wrong in your attempts to reach those goals. That in itself shows progress from the young man I first met."

I snort and let my head drop back again. "I no longer drink half a bottle of 40 proof vodka, almost accidentally kill myself, and then insist I'm fine. So, yeah, that's progress I guess. Glad I've cleared that high bar."

Dr. Eduway nods as if deciding to take my jibe seriously. "Recognizing your own emotional distress and grappling with its underlying causes *is* a high bar for many, especially on your own. Don't discount it. For instance," he looks to his notes, "your fear of rejection if people knew about your past is very understandable. Rational even. And you have already figured out that using secrecy as a shield against rejection is only a temporary solution. Useful for surface-level relationships perhaps, but not for the deeper, lasting friendships and the romantic relationship you've started to form. And you've come today because you want to make better, healthier choices going forward, choices that consider the needs and feelings of others and avoid doing harm. That, too, is progress."

"Yeah, but how does that make anything better *now*?" I press him. "And how do I go from recognizing my mistakes after the fact to not making mistakes anymore?"

"Eric…" He sighs in a way that makes me think it's covering a laugh. "Mistakes are part of life. And progress isn't strictly linear. Not for anyone."

It's tempting to stay quiet and let the positive feedback slide like warm honey down my aching throat. But I didn't come here for encouragement and reassurance. I shake my head at him. "Yeah, maybe, but what can I do to, like, mitigate the damage? Make amends or whatever?" I cross my palms over my forehead, trying not to feel overwhelmed by the thoughts of how much damage I've done and how much more I stand to do. "I need you to help me get my next move right. Figure out what to do…"

"Do about which part, exactly?"

"All of it. Any of it." I groan and let my hand drop to the armrests. "My new friends, my girlfriend, my sister, my dad...Kendra. God, it's the worst thinking about Kendra, knowing how shit her life is and not knowing what I can do to make up for it, to make it better, to fix what I broke...Is there any way to make amends for raping someone? And then for letting Bronston use those texts to get me out of juvie, even though it meant people might think she was lying at the trial. I mean, is there something I can do, or do I just, like, hate myself for the rest of my life?" I pause and look at him, hoping he might have some brilliant idea I haven't thought of before.

But he just tilts his head to the opposite side and asks, "When was the last time you had any direct communication with Kendra?"

"Well, not since...the car. I mean, after my arrest, Bronston warned me not to...and after my conviction got overturned, I figured she wouldn't want to hear from me, right? I wouldn't, in her shoes." I'd wanted to contact her so badly, all through that spring and summer. Sometimes I'd even laid awake at night and played out the whole conversation in my head. Spoiler alert--it always ended badly.

"Well, it might depend on what you have to say and on your motivation for saying it. If the apology is about being able to clear your own conscience, then It's ultimately self-serving, and not of much use to Kendra."

I nod, suspecting the me who'd once practiced apologizing in the mirror, making sure to get the repentant face just right, had been at least partly guilty of this. "So then, what's the right kind of apology?"

He purses his lips, looking pensive. "What kind of apology would *you* want? Say for instance, that D'Marcus Clay were to contact you. What would you want him to say?"

The specter of D'Marcus sent my neck hairs into high alert. Eyes closed, I imagined it playing out. "I'd wanna know he got how fucked up all that revenge shit was, that he

315

understood how bad it hurt me. The party and the video and all that, but also how like, he was supposed to be my friend, but he just turned on me like that..." My voice goes thin and I have to take a deep breath before I can go on. "I'd want him to lay all that out. And no excuses. No putting it back on me, making me feel like somehow I'd deserved it, like I'd lost State all on my own. And even if I had, that still wouldn't make it right. And I wouldn't want him bringing up how he and some of the other guys got kicked off the basketball team over the video and the party. Just because he faced some consequences for the shit he pulled, that doesn't, like, make us even."

Dr. Eduway tilts his head to the side and asks, "And if he did all that, said everything you wanted to hear, the way you wanted to hear it, and you believed him to be sincere, would you forgive him?"

I want to say yes. But even after imagining it all play out, I still feel that hot-blooded rush of anger that makes my ears ring. "Maybe," I say more truthfully. "But maybe not right away...Is that wrong?"

Dr. Eduway nods and taps his pen on his notes. "No, forced forgiveness isn't really forgiveness, is it? So remember that she doesn't owe you closure or absolution any more than you would owe it to D'Marcus."

"Right...okay, yeah."

"So then, knowing what *you* would want, how can you apply that to your own apology to Kendra?"

"Well..." I think back through my example and start breaking it down. "Be clear and specific about exactly what I'm apologizing for--lay it all out. Don't make excuses. Acknowledge the damage and pain my actions caused. Be sure not to use me and my family's troubles to try and gain her sympathy or earn her forgiveness… But then what? I want to offer to…I dunno, fix it? But I have no idea how or if it's even possible. It's not like I can undo the rape. I can't put myself back in juvie. I can't erase the whole thing from everyone's collective consciousness so her life can go back to normal. So what can I do for her?"

"Ah, that is a good question, but you're asking the wrong person. Kendra is the only person who decides what, if any, amends can be made. It's about what she needs from you, not the other way around. And when you ask the question, be ready to listen to the answer. In fact, be ready to listen to whatever she may need you to hear, however painful it might be." His voice is gentle, and he lets me sit with that for a minute.

I swallow hard. What will she want from me? How far am I willing to go? *I* deserve whatever penance she may require, but what if what she needs will result in another major disruption for the rest of my family? I imagine the look on Dad's face if I announce I'm going to make a public confession and post it to YouTube. And Ellen…God, something like that could put the final nail in the coffin for our relationship.

That's a worry for later, I remind myself. *You've got more immediate problems.* "Speaking of apologies, how should I handle things with my friend and my…girlfriend? I never wanted to hurt them…and I don't wanna lose them."

Dr. Eduway's brow creases. "There's no way to completely avoid causing pain. But you can do your best to minimize it. You can be honest and open with them and allow them to react honestly as well. Answer whatever questions they have." He sighs and spreads his hands out to the side. "As far as if they'll want to remain friends…there are no guarantees in these sorts of situations. But they deserve to make that choice with full knowledge. And even if they decide they want to maintain the friendship, it may be on different terms. Trust is a fragile thing and takes time to repair."

I try to ignore the twisting in my gut. *At least when it's family, they're kinda stuck with you. Technically, anyway.* Swallowing, I tell Dr. Eduway, "My Dad knows everything now. I told him the whole truth today before I came."

"Today?" Dr. Eduway's eyebrows rise in surprise. "Had you tried to discuss it with him before?"

"Oh yeah, a bunch a times, but it never got far. Until today."

"And how did it go?"

"Um...jury's still out." I give a nervous laugh. "He's in shock or something. Like, he barely said anything after. Then as I was heading over here, he's in the family room watching the Bills pregame show and replying to emails, and he calls me in and says, 'I think your car's due for an oil change, so why don't you stop by Delta Sonic after your appointment and get that taken care of.' Like everything was totally normal. But...how could it be?" I sigh and let my head lean against the back of the chair. "I don't know. It was weird."

Dr. Eduway nods like Dad's nonreaction to the fact that his son raped someone is perfectly normal. "Everyone processes information in different ways and at different speeds. For now, I'd recommend giving your father time. If down the road, he's still struggling to find a way to respond to what you've told him, I'd be happy to work with the two of you jointly," he offers with the flicker of a smile.

"Ah, more joint sessions," I give him my own rueful smile. "Dad just loved those. I'm sure he'll be on board for more."

Dr. Eduway chuckles and gives a little shrug. "There is a time and place for everything. Maybe this time he will be ready. But that will be up to him. Not me, and not you."

"Right, we can't control others' decisions or behavior, only our own," I repeat a maxim from one of our first sessions.

"Exactly," he taps his pen in the air as if awarding me a gold star.

I shake my head and stare at my hands folded in my lap, at the pink, smooth, healing skin at the edges of my thumbnails. "I'm scared, Doc."

Dr. Eduway leans forward and extends his hands to me. I hesitate only a second before extending my own. His skin is warm and dry against mine. He squeezes tight and says, "When we are afraid is when we have the chance to be brave."

I know he's right, and I know what I have to do...but I'm not sure knowing will make it any easier.

Senior Year: Monday, November 4
Telling Bea

Monday morning, I wake up back in my bed at Aunt Kari's. The level of bright sunlight in the room alerts me that I've overslept even before I check my phone and see it's 11:46 a.m. *Oops.* I must have forgotten to set my alarm. Aunt Kari's left me a note saying she thought the sleep would do me good and that she's called me in sick to school. *Cool.* That at least saves me from spending the day pretending to Bea and Teddy that everything is normal before I have a chance to go through with my big reveal.

While waiting for coffee to brew, I reply to Bea's early morning text wondering where I am.

> **Eric**--Stayed home.
> Needed sleep

True, technically.

> **Bea**--Oh, you OK?

> **Eric**--Yeah no worries
> Catching up on
> homework now

After a few seconds hesitation, I add,

> Talk later? You free
> after school today?

> **Bea**--Have indoor soccer
> practice till 6 then it's my
> month to attend school
> board meeting as student
> council rep
> Tomorrow?

Part of me wants to say sure. Have one more day of Bea sending me sweet, goofy texts, believing I'm the kind of guy who's worthy to be her boyfriend. And really, I've spent months hiding and pretending, what's a couple more days?

It does feel different though. More like lying than it ever did before. And now that I've decided to come clean, my anxiety level is only going to build until I've gone through with it.

Eric--What about after the meeting?
I could pick you up?

Bea--Oooo totally!!
8:30ish? Bring food?
Class now GTG
Miss you XO

I pull up in the loop outside the Ohkwali School District Administration Building at 8:58 pm. My feelings of dread intensify as I wait for Bea to come out. The car smells like McDonalds I picked up for Bea on the way over. She mentioned over text she'd only had a sleeve of Ritz crackers and cheese for dinner, so I thought it would be a nice surprise. Also something that will soften the blow when I give her the bad news that she's been, y'know...dating a rapist.

Oh God, I need air.

The night air is cool in my lungs and tastes like exhaust from the Ford Bronco idling in line ahead of me. I move a few steps further from its tailpipe and lean against my trunk. I'm wearing normal-ish clothes, a white tee with the Dunder-Mifflin logo and navy basketball shorts. Nor have I done anything crazy with my hair, which falls halfway between my ear and chin in black waves. I did put my contacts back in and put liner around my eyes. I didn't want to take the chance she'd recognize me as EJ White on the spot. Or have her not recognize me as Eric. No need to shock her twice.

Bea beams and waves when she sees me. "Hey! Oh my gosh--your hair. I love it!" She rushes over to run both hands through it. "Oh my gosh, it's soooo soft and silky. And that wave...I'm completely jealous. That's it--you're never allowed to super-gel-sculpt it again. Just kidding. I like how creative you are with your hair. And being your girlfriend does not mean I am in charge of your body. Thanks for offering to pick me up, by the way."

"Yeah, no problem." I smile and try to ignore the anxious fluttering she's set off in my stomach.

She wraps her arms around my neck and gives me a kiss. A quick, sweet greeting kiss. Brief enough that she doesn't seem to notice the way I tense in response.

"I've missed you. And I was kinda worried after you had to leave the party all of a sudden. It's good to see you in person." She sighs and rests her cheek against the hollow of my shoulder.

"Yeah, I know. Missed you too." I raise a tentative hand and slide it down the length of her ponytail.

She spies the McDonald's bag in the passenger seat and gasps. "Did you bring me food?"

"Yup. Quarter-pounder with cheese--hold the pickles, fries with BBQ sauce for dipping, and an iced tea--half sweetened, half unsweetened."

"Ohmigod, you memorized my order! You're the best boyfriend ever," she says before pushing off my chest and practically wrenching the door off its hinges to get to the provisions.

"*Mmmph*," she moans through her first bite of burger.

"I thought maybe we'd go somewhere and park while we talk?"

I pull out and head for the soccer hill. One of our first-ish date locations, a reminder of the good times. *Is that emotionally manipulative? Should we go somewhere new and neutral? Oh shit...* We come to a stop sign. I take too long trying to think of another location and Bea realizes where I was taking us. "Oooo, our spot at the soccer hill. How romantic." She drops her chin and flutters her lashes at me, then ruins the alluring effect by taking another huge bite that leaves mustard dipping down her chin. It's so...Bea. I can't help smiling.

She leans over to kiss me on the nose. "Oops!" Laughing, she uses her thumb to wipe away the mustard she left behind. "Did you get anything for yourself? You wanna share the fries?" She dangles a long, floppy fry in the air like a lure.

"Nah, I'm good," I say as I pull into the narrow dirt strip at the top of the hill and put the car in park. It's dark, so I turn on the dome light.

"You sure? We can eat from both ends, like the spaghetti thing in Lady and the Tramp. I've always wanted to do that." She grins, puts one end of the fry between her teeth, and wiggles her eyebrows.

A few days ago, I would've been happy to play sexy food games, no question. But it feels like anything I do here and now--any kiss, any touch--would be taking advantage, even more than it was before. *I am never going to kiss those fantastic lips of hers again.*

She takes the fry out of her mouth and tilts her head. "What's wrong? You seem...sad." She slides her finger over the worry crease between my eyebrows.

"Yeah, so, um…" I take a steadying breath and hold tight to the wheel. *This is it.* "I need to tell you about something that happened before I moved here. Something I should have told both of you--but especially you--before we…got together." My breathing gets shallow as my heart accelerates.

"Hey…" Bea puts her hand over mine on the wheel. "Whatever you have to tell me, it's gonna be okay. I promise."

323

Oh God, she has no idea, no clue...would never suspect I'd be capable of...

"Is there anything I can do to help?"

I shake my head, squeeze my eyes shut, and count, taking in air nice and slow through my nose, holding my breath, and letting it out again, over and over until I can feel my heart calming to match.

When I open my eyes, Bea is watching me with a concerned but patient expression. "Eric, whatever it is, if you're not ready to tell me, that's okay. I don't want you to make yourself sick."

"No, you need to know." It was bad enough to keep my kind of secret from a friend but far worse to keep it from someone I was in a romantic relationship with. I knew that, but I let my feelings for her, my attraction to her override my better judgment. *Selfish*, Ellen's voice chides.

"Okay then…" Bea slides her hand over my forearm in a soothing motion. "Take your time. When you're ready."

I take a few more breaths to make sure I'm back from the brink and begin. "So last year, there was this party…" I tell her how desperate and stupid I'd been, how it was all a setup, how the only person who'd come to my aid was a childhood friend, a girl who'd always been kind to me even when I hadn't been much of a friend to her in return. How we'd started making out while we waited for my ride. How she suggested we go to the car where it was warmer.

Bea listens and nods and squeezes my arm encouragingly as I stop and breathe and start again. I keep waiting for a sign that she suspects what's coming.

"And then, by the time I got the condom on, she was all tensed up and she says that she doesn't think she's ready,

324

y'know, for sex. And I knew how sheltered she was, how little experience she had with guys...God, I mean, she was starting to cry. It was so obvious she wasn't ready, that she didn't want to go any further. I should have...but I was so worked up from the party, so angry at everything and everyone."

Bea's hand goes slack before she slowly removes it, like someone who thought they were petting a house cat and discovered it's a bobcat.

I rush on, wanting to get to the conclusion before she does. "I wasn't thinking about Kendra and what she wanted or how she felt. So I--"

"Hang on." Bea raises both hands, her unblinking eyes fixed on mine. "Kendra...do you mean Kendra *Daniels*, from that case in Rochester where that rich football player's politician father got him off on some bullshit technicality?"

And the penny drops. I swallow. "That's exactly who I mean."

"So you... That means...you're EJ White?"

"Yeah, it does."

Bea moves her head in a slow arc from side to side, unable or unwilling to accept her own conclusion or my admission. "But you don't... I remember in the pictures, he had these, like, dramatic blue eyes."

I pull the travel contact holder out of my pants pocket and hold it up. When she just frowns at it, I set it on my leg and reach up to remove one brown contact and then the other. Even with the eyeliner still on, the "dramatic" blue eyes are enough to remove any doubt. Bea blinks and it's as if I can see her brain overlapping the image of the guy in front of her with any one of the pictures of me that had been pilfered from my own accounts and circulated far and wide after my arrest.

Her blinks become rapid. "Oh my God, oh my God...I thought--when you were talking I thought you were gonna say you'd fathered a kid or... I never even considered that...*Oh my God.*" She turns toward the windshield and wraps her arms around herself. "I remember reading...everyone was talking about it. On the team group chat...we compared him--you--to Kyle Booth and how he gets away with everything and how brave Kendra was to report it and go through all the publicity. Because that's what scares so many girls--that if you put yourself out there, everybody will know what happened to you. And even if people believe you, everybody looks at you and sees a rape victim for God-knows how long. Maybe the rest of your life? And is that worth it?"

There's plenty there to unpack in what she's said, but my brain gets stuck on one piece in particular. "Um, is Booth...I know you said you'd agreed to, but...did he rape girls?"

"That's not the point." She gives me a sharp look and shakes her head in a way that might be denial or just annoyance with me for diverting focus off myself. Either way, Bea is quick to redirect. "So like, you're admitting you're guilty, that you raped Kendra Daniels?"

"Yeah, I am."

"Oh my God... This is insane." It's her turn to struggle for breath.

"I know. I'm so sorry that I kept it from you. I convinced myself it was okay to...that if you got to know me, saw that I'm not the same guy who did...what I did then." I sigh and pull my hands down my face. "Whatever my reasons, hiding something like this from you was wrong and selfish and stupid, and I'm sorry, Bea. So sorry. I never wanted to hurt you." First Booth hurt her and now me, maybe even worse than he did, though in a different way. She cared about me, trusted me, and I've betrayed that with my deceit. Shame and regret tangle inside my ribcage, pressing against my lungs.

"So you raped her and then claimed you didn't so she had to sit there in a courtroom and relive it all in front of a judge, twelve strangers, her parents, the guy who raped her, and God knows who else? And you just sat there and listened?"

"That wasn't...I mean, yes, partly, but I wasn't lying the whole time. At first, I didn't believe what I did was rape. I was so focused on my pain and how unfair and fucked up my own life was, and I used what happened to me at the party to excuse myself. But mostly, I let myself put the responsibility back on Kendra, that since she was the one who started it, who suggested to move things to the car--"

"That's total bullshit. Kissing you and wanting to keep making out somewhere warmer doesn't mean she owes you sex."

"Yes, I know. But it took me awhile to get it, to really understand."

"Oh yeah? And did you understand what you'd done before or after you took the stand and called her a liar?"

The word, heavy on my tongue, is barely audible. "...before."

Bea and I look at each other for a long moment. "Well then..." She nods with finality and turns away.

Sensing the last of my time with her slipping away, I rush ahead. "Bea, I know what I did to Kendra was horrible, unforgivable. And I don't expect--but I want you to know that I've learned since then, that I never would--not to you or any other girl ever again. And I'm working on making amends, to

Kendra, to everyone who I've hurt...including you, so whatever I can do to--"

"I don't wanna be on any list of yours." Even in profile, I can see her lip curl in disgust.

Oh course she hates you now. What did you expect? Still, with my last embers of hope, I attempt to leave the door open for some kind of reconciliation between us. "Okay, I respect that, but if at some point you change your mind and want--"

"I won't." Bea fumbles for the door handle, swings it open, and almost trips as she gets out.

"Bea, wait!" I get out and start to follow after her as she starts down the hill to the unlit field. "Please, let me give you a ride home, or at least back to--"

"Get...the fuck...away from me," she chokes out in a low rasp.

I slow and then stop, watching as she marches across centerfield in the direction of the school, gradually disappearing into the dark until I am completely alone. Already I miss her.

My head swims, my legs buckle, and I let myself down onto the grassy hill. The stars are so numerous and bright that I can see them through my tears. *Mom...Mom...I miss you so much. I need you. I needed you* then. *If only you'd been there--* I catch my train of thought and groan and rub my eyes with my fists. *Now you're blaming your dead mother? Nice. Real nice.* Laying there, looking up, I wonder, *Can Mom see and hear me up there? Is heaven literally "up there" or is it some alternate dimension overlapping ours so she could be right here next to me but I wouldn't know? And if she is watching, what does she think of me and all the pain I've created in the world? All from one terrible mistake... Ah, but it wasn't just one mistake, was it?*

There were so many others, both before and after. So many missed chances to do better, to do right. Like the failure Bea had honed in on--my failure to own up to my actions in court once I'd recognized them for what they were.

Senior Year: Tuesday, November 5
Telling Teddy

I lie awake coming to terms with the increasing likelihood that Bea will hate me forever. It's not as if I hadn't understood from the start that it was the most likely outcome of confessing. But there's a big difference between understanding something horrible *could* happen and knowing that it *has*. Like a vending machine rejecting a wrinkled dollar bill, my brain won't accept my new reality. I've lost Bea, and tomorrow, I'll probably lose Teddy, too.

Teddy...oh shit.

I didn't ask Bea not to tell Teddy yet, that I wanted to tell him myself. *Shit.* I grab my phone off the nightstand. He hasn't texted me with a bunch of all caps expletives saying he never wants to see me again, so that's a good sign. Right? We're supposed to meet at the weight room in the morning like usual. Maybe he's waiting to chew me out in person, maybe even get a few punches in. Though that doesn't seem like Teddy's style. I've never seen Mr. Congeniality come even close to losing his temper.

If anything, his game is *avoiding* conflict...which means Bea might have told him, and his plan is to avoid me, cut me off and hope I get the message to steer clear. *Shit...would Teddy ghost me?* But I can't exactly text Bea to ask. Should I just text

Teddy and ask him if he's talked to Bea? But if he hasn't, that could make him suspicious and backfire. Because if I don't want to lie and if I refuse to explain over text, he could decide to ask Bea and then...*fuck.*

Around midnight, I finally decide that either way, the only thing to do is show up to the weight room the next morning.

I get there early, hoping to catch Teddy on his way in so I can ask him to talk in private. But his truck is already in the lot. *Well, so much for that plan.*

When I get to the locker room, I can already hear his Selena Gomez playlist going. I pause for a second, hand on the doorknob. *Okay, you can do this. You* have *to do this.* With one last steadying breath, I enter the weight room. There's Teddy, doing warm-up lunges. It must be a leg day. Blessedly, he's the only one there.

Not wanting to waste what could be a brief window of privacy, I move into Teddy's line of sight. He freezes mid lunge, his eyes going wide before narrowing, his expression hardening.

He knows. Shit... I swallow and call out over the music, "Can we talk?"

Teddy scans the room then slowly stands straight, his hands balling into fists as he does. He's not taller than me, but the cords of honed muscles in his neck and arms visible just beneath his skin are plenty intimidating. I try to ignore the writhing in my gut--a warning to retreat while I still can.

"You've got some nerve showing up here, Madison--or White, or whatever the fuck your name is." His chest heaves as he fights for control, the same way I've done far too often when my temper threatens to take over.

My eyes involuntarily drop to his white knuckled fists. He wouldn't use them, would he? *No, not Teddy Mackenzie. He doesn't have my anger management issues. He's better than that.* Still, I proceed with caution, palms spread, not moving any closer. "Please, I just wanna talk. To apologize for--"

He cuts me off with a slice of his hand through the air between us. "I'm not interested in your apologies, or anything else you've got to say. Bea already filled me in about how my new best friend not only raped a girl last year, but then let his lawyer make her out to be a liar so he could get outta jail early instead of paying for the crime--screwing her over, yet again. Have I got that about right?"

I ignore the desire to add in any context that might soften the harsh reality of what he just said--of what I did. With a long, slow breath, I let my hands drop to my sides.

Something like disappointment shows in his face, like some part of him had hoped I'd tell him it was all a huge misunderstanding, to explain things in a way that wouldn't necessitate the end of our friendship. Then whatever it is passes, and his anger and disgust resolidify. "Well then, we have nothing more to talk about, *EJ.*" He says through a clenched jaw before turning his back on me.

That's it? Maybe I should be grateful for how quick and simple it had gone. But instead, a dizzying sort of desperation surges from my gut to my brain, making my ears ring. *No...that can't be it.* "For what it's worth, I'd planned to tell you myself this morning. I wanted you to hear it from me." I call out over the music.

Teddy's shoulders tense. He turns and comes two strides closer. "Because hearing it directly from the source would make it better somehow? Oh yeah, turns out my new best friend raped a girl last year, but as long as he fesses up, admits it to me man to man, we're all good?"

"No, of course I didn't expect…" *but I'd hoped that it would be worth…something.* "I just felt like I owed you that much."

Teddy swallows hard, Adam's apple bobbing. "What you did to Bea--letting her fall for you, pretending like you two could be together--that's messed up, man."

I want to explain that it hadn't felt like pretending. It had felt intensely real. More real than with any girl ever. But I can't say that without it sounding like an excuse, so instead I say, "I know. I should never have started anything with her. I convinced myself…it doesn't matter. It was wrong."

"And *she* trusted you because *I* trusted you." He thumps his chest in frustration. "And we told you things--personal, private stuff that we never would have…"

His self-recrimination intensifies the guilt twisting my guts. I tip my head back to look up at the exposed ventilation shafts. "I know. And anything you guys told me in confidence will stay private. I promise."

He lets out a choked laugh. My promise is a worthless joke now. And no amount of assurance here and now can prove otherwise. So I only say, "It was wrong to deceive you guys, and I'm so, so sorry."

"Right…*you're sorry.* Fat lot of good that does us." His initial fury has burned down to raw hurt and regret.

He's right, of course. I'd made selfish choices--again. And hurt people who cared about me--*again.* More crimes against humanity to pay for. Except this time around, I'm willing to pay. "If there is anything…any way I can make amends--"

He laughs again then shakes his head. "You can't fix this. Unless you've discovered the secret to time travel. Then you could go back and warn me to steer clear of..." His face goes slack. "Oh shit...you *did* warn me, didn't you? That day we had lunch out at the bench. You said something about how you weren't the kind of person I'd wanna be friends with and you were doing me a favor by steering clear. But I kept pressing..." Teddy slowly sits on the closest bench and lets his head drop into his hands. "God, I'm such an idiot."

"Teddy, don't blame yourself," I plead, voice wavering.

He groan-screams into his palms.

My limbs are heavy with pooling guilt. Still, I take a tentative step closer.

"Teddy..."

"Just get out."

"You could never have guessed how bad--"

"*Get. Out.*" His head snaps up, face contorted and blotchy, eyes glistening tears threatening to spill over. A shaking finger points me toward the exit.

I hate that he's blaming himself. But at this point, nothing *I* say will be a comfort. The best I can do is respect his wishes. "Okay...I'll go."

Teddy tips his head back, squeezes his eyes shut. It feels like a full minute before he wipes a fist roughly over his damp cheekbones. "And stay the hell away from me and Bea," he adds in a hoarse voice.

There it is--the unequivocal cutting of ties. I close my eyes and swallow the lump blocking my windpipe, adding it to the familiar stew of regrets churning in my gut. "I will. I promise."

I'm halfway to the door before remembering there's one more thing we need to discuss. "Hey, I uh, I'm sorry to have to ask this, but…are you guys going to tell people? I'll understand if you do, but I'd just like a heads up…so my family doesn't get caught off guard." I worry it sounds like I'm using them to protect myself, but it's just the reality of our situation. My life inevitably affect theirs--a lesson I now carry deep in my bones.

Teddy's nostrils flare as he takes a deep breath before answering. "Bea already thought of that--how people finding out could really mess things up for the rest of your family. And we agreed to keep it to ourselves. She'll say she found out you were still dating a girl back at your last school. That should explain why we're not talking anymore either."

"Thank you," I exhale in relief.

"We're not doing it for your sake." His Adam's apple bobs again as he looks away.
"Just make sure you follow your original, loner game plan, got it? If we see you cozying up to anybody, we'll fill them in."

"Fair enough." *It's more than fair… It's grace.* I deceived them, took advantage of their kindness and trust, and even after finding out the horrible truth, they're both willing to protect my family by lying for me. *I don't deserve either of them. Not yet, anyway.*

Teddy stands and offers me a final nod before turning away.

Tears well behind my eyes, I turn to go before I lose it.

As soon as I step through the door, I'm stopped short by a body in my way. Booth's body.

Seriously? This is the last thing I need right now.

The smirk on his face sets my neck hairs on end. "Hey there, Madison. Trouble in paradise?"

I let confusion mask my fear. Did he overhear anything? We weren't yelling at the top of our lungs or anything. Plus we were standing a good fifteen feet from the door, and the music in the background would have covered anything we said...right? But then why did he just make that comment? Can he tell from my face?

No reply seems safe, so I roll my eyes for effect and sidestep right to get around him. But me mirrors me, blocking my escape, our chests inches apart.

The smirk widens into a malicious grin. "Let me guess-- you finally dropped the straight act and made a move on Mackenzie."

"Wait...what?"

"And from the look a' you, it didn't go so well."

I laugh. I can't help it. Warm relief floods my emotional slurry and makes me light headed. With a shot that far off the mark, Booth obviously didn't catch any of the conversation's content.

Booth's grin morphs into a sneer. The same one he had on that night at the barn party right before Bea stood up to him. *If only more people called this guy out in his assholery...*

Maybe my brain is an over-marinated mush from days of intense emotions and hormones. Whatever it is, reason and self-preservation desert me, and I poke the bear. "What's your deal, Booth? Are you just some textbook bully overcompensating for his own insecurities? Or are you jealous that your ex-girlfriend from junior high would wanna date me? Or, wait, I've got it--maybe you're jealous because of *Teddy*? The smacking girls' asses and homophobe bullshit is all a cover so no one suspects that *you're* the one who's into guys. Is that it?"

For a full second, Booth looks stunned, and I feel a kind of fizzy euphoria of triumph. Then his nostrils flare and chest swells as his hand shoots out, twisting the collar of my t-shirt in his fist, knuckles pressing into my throat.

I should be scared, but instead, my muscles ease and I go slack against the door at my back. Maybe this is what I want right now--what I *need*. Someone to throw a punch at me, the one Teddy wouldn't, the one I deserve.

I glance down to see Booth slipping his phone and AirPod case into his pocket, freeing his right hand for action.

Go on, do it. Take your shot. I let my mouth form into the kind of glib smile I know will only goad him further.

Booth's morning breath is warm on my face, his voice all quiet intensity. "You don't get to talk shit about me--or Bea or Mackenzie either. We all grew up together. You think you can show up here and act like--"

A burst of loud, tangled voices carries over the banks of lockers as Miguel, Narby, and the rest enter. Booth's grip loosens as he takes an automatic step back and glances over his shoulder. Their sudden arrival snaps me out of my masochistic moment, and I capitalize on the distraction and get the hell out of there.

Senior Year: Tuesday, November 5
Ellen's Confession

"You want this or what?" Ellen asks from my bedroom doorway.

I wipe my eyes, pause the breakup music station on my phone, and roll over so I can see her, a bowl of teriyaki stir fry dangling from one hand. "Not hungry," I mutter. Not true, but when indulging in a full-day regret wallow, physical hunger pangs are the perfect complement to the mental misery.

I expect her to close the door again, but she stands there, staring. "You actually went through with it then?"

"Yeah...it's done." *In every sense of the word.* And if I'd subconsciously expected doing the right thing to feel good somehow, I now know better.

Ellen surprises me again by setting the bowl on my dresser and sitting down in the middle of my big, purple shag rug. I sit up cross legged in the middle of my creaky, antique bed. We stare, but neither of us seem to know what to say next. We're too out of practice at this. After a few seconds, Ellen scans the room, assessing the hodgepodge of lacy, floral-patterned items that came with the house when Aunt Kari bought it and bizarre thrift finds I'd added to represent my Eric Madison ethos, like a Sonic the Hedgehog cookie jar and hat rack hand painted with a black and white checkerboard pattern. And the shag rug, of course. It's certainly a different vibe than my spacious room back home full of Pottery Barn furniture and sports paraphernalia. The only constant between the two rooms--the two lives--is my cobalt blue Fender.

As Ellen takes it all in, I realize it's the first time she's even been in my room here and my heart convulses with a familiar ache. "You were right," I tell her.

She gives me a side-eyed glance. "About what, exactly?"

I lean forward, resting my elbows on my knees. "All of it, I guess. You knew from the beginning that my coming here was bound to get messy, *yet again*. I tried not to let it, but...I keep making selfish choices, like you said."

She tilts her head, more curious and less gloating than I expected. "Do you regret it though? If you could go back, would you choose differently? Go to Deerfield or somewhere instead?"

I let my imagination play out the alternatives, asking the same question I did back then. Would it be worth it to break my word to Charlie, worsen his fear of abandonment in order to protect Ellen's restart?

And now there are new questions--If I'd known I'd make great friends and fall for an amazing girl, only to hurt and lose them, would I choose never to meet them at all? Was my personal growth worth the pain I'd caused Bea and Teddy? Because if I'd gone off to boarding school, I'd likely have found other ways to ignore the guilty memories--and had no sister around to call me out on it.

Finally, I tell Ellen, "Even if I wanted to, I can't go back and make a different choice about coming to Ohkwali. But I *can* offer you something else, something that may matter even more."

She lifts one carefully sculpted brow, waiting.

I take in a breath and let out the word on a rush of air. "Cornell."

Her second brow shoots up.

"I won't even apply. You'll never have to share a campus with me again."

Her eyes go wide, lips parting as she takes in the enormity of what I'm offering. Cornell--the university the Whites have attended for generations, where our parents met and fell in love, the campus grounds we visited every summer as a family. The stairway wall at home features framed photos documenting each year's visit with Mom, Dad, and kids dressed up in "Big Red" gear. But I'm offering to abdicate my rights to that legacy.

"Eric--no, that's...Dad would freak. He'd *make* you apply to Cornell."

"Dad doesn't have the final say on where I go to college. I'll be eighteen. It's my choice."

"Yeah, but..." Ellen brings her knees up to her chest, looking almost...afraid.

"What's wrong?"

"Nothing. You're just being stupid. As usual." She mutters.

"Cornell isn't the only good school in the world, okay? I'll be fine," I say with a brash confidence I hope sounds convincing. Truth is, without the legacy boost, my next-best option is *way* down the prestige ladder. My post-arrest grades took a major dive when I slept half the day and stopped doing any assignments.

Too savvy to buy my bluster, she shakes her head. "You'll end up at a SUNY."

"Yeah, maybe I end up at a state school. So what?"

She juts out her chin. "You think giving up Cornell will make up for what you did?"

"No--look, I don't think there's anything I could do to make up for how badly I fucked things up for you, let alone Kendra. But, El, you deserve to be at a school without me and my mess there threatening to screw it up for you all over again."

Ellen swallows and closes her eyes.

"El?"

She opens her mouth like she's about to reply, but then lets out a soft moan and slumps forward, face hidden.

"El, *what* is *wrong*?" I repeat.

339

"Just stop, okay? I don't want your sympathy or your thanks or your grand gestures. If our lives suck, it's because that's what we deserve. *Both* of us."

Completely confused, I get down from my bed and sit facing her. "What are you talking about? You were innocent in all this. Let me do this for you. Please."

In one sudden motion, she launches to her feet and blurts out, "I'm the one who told Bronston about the text messages Kendra sent Frankie."

I stare up at her. "You...what? How did you even--"

"I got them from Andrea Gurlance."

"Oh my God..." The mysterious source of my so-called exonerating evidence, revealed at last. Frankie's little sister Andrea. She'd always liked me--maybe even had a crush on me. And the texts would have fit perfectly into the narrative she had from Ellen, proof that her gross, controlling, weirdo brother-- who'd always had it out for me--had taken his jealousy over Kendra too far. "How did she even get them?"

Ellen hesitates a moment, crossing her arms over her chest and rubbing them like she's cold, but then explains, "She knew his passcode, and she thought he was...it doesn't matter. She was looking for something else." Ellen shakes her head, unwilling to share more of her friend's secrets than she already has. "So when she was in her brother's phone, his message string with Kendra was open and she got curious and...yeah, so, she took screenshots and forwarded the messages to herself, but she didn't tell anyone."

"Wait, so when did this happen?" I ask, pushing myself up to sit on the edge of my bed.

"Like, a week after the trial."

My eyebrows shoot up in surprise, and Ellen rushes on to explain. "Andrea didn't want to get her brother or Kendra in trouble for perjury, and she didn't think you'd actually get convicted. But when you did..." Ellen pauses for a deep, shuddering breath. "She felt guilty and showed me the messages. Asked me if she should go to the police, if they'd be enough proof to fix things and let you come home."

Ellen sags, her arms dropping to her sides, then sits back down in slow motion. "I could have told Andrea that you'd confessed to me and had her delete everything. But instead, I had her send me the screenshots, and I used an encryption app to send them anonymously to Bronston. He alerted the police, who seized Frankie's phone and found the original messages and...you know the rest."

I always wondered who turned the messages in. Even thought maybe Bronston had done something shady, like hacking or putting spyware on Frankie or Kendra's phone. But I never guessed my sister could be involved. "El...I just can't believe you'd...I mean, that night after Kendra's testimony, when I confessed to you, you told me..."

"That I hoped you'd get gang raped in prison?" she recalls with a sardonic edge.

"Um...yeah."

Ellen sighs and stares into the middle distance. "All the years I looked up to you, believed you were the best big brother of all time...and then...finding out you were just another asshole who..." She closes her eyes. "Finding out what you did, how you'd lied about it and let me defend you...it fucking *broke* me."

"I know...I know, and I'm so sorry...so sorry I wasn't the brother you deserve." The words strain to pass through my constricting airway.

"And after you got sentenced, everything was so messed up. Charlie was refusing to eat anything me or the babysitter cooked because we didn't make it right--how *you* made it. He'd throw a screaming fit anytime we tried to get him off his video games. And at night, he refused to brush his teeth or put his PJ's on because *you* were the one who always--" Ellen's voice cracks and she shakes her head. "And Dad--God, he was wrecked. The night before Andrea showed me the texts, I'd found Dad still in his office at midnight, smelling like whiskey, with his eyes all bloodshot and puffy. He was all, 'I failed my son. I failed this family,' and then broke down crying right in front of me."

"Wow...shit." I'd guessed things had been tough at home while I was locked up, but once I got home, I hadn't asked for details. I hadn't wanted them. I'd been totally focused on moving on, planning our exit to Ohkwali. "I didn't realize..." I abort the half-formed excuse and simply acknowledge, "That must have sucked."

"Yeah, pretty much." Ellen pulls her legs up and wraps her arms around her knees. "So when Andrea showed up and offered me a way to get my family, my life back to some version of normal...I took it." Her voice thins at the end, emotion pushing against her control.

"Not that it worked, at least not like I hoped it would. Knowing the truth about you...I thought I could push past it, pretend, for the sake of the family. But it made me sick-- watching Charlie go back to hero-worshiping you and Dad acting all vindicated, then jumping on board with your plans to

342

change our names and go hide in fucking Nowheresville…" she lets out a long, shuddering breath ending with a sad, single laugh. "Turns out I'm not that good of an actress after all."

I run a slow hand down my face, processing this new understanding of Ellen's aversion to my presence…and family time in general. And could this be the real reason why Ellen completely dropped theatre--the thing she loved most--and morphed into the kind of person who hung out and hooked up with shallow placeholders? Has it all been some sort of self-punishment? The possibility guts me. I swallow and tell her, "Listen, the choice you made, it's not on you, El. You'd never have been in that position if I hadn't--I'm the one who started all this shit, so you're not the one ultimately responsible."

Ellen shakes her head as tears well in her eyes. "Look, it's great that you're all gung-ho to take responsibility for everything now. And don't worry, I blame you for plenty--but this part was on me. Kendra got justice in court, and *I* took that away from her. I knew you were guilty. I knew Bronston could use the texts to make Kendra out as a liar, but I sent them anyway. That was *my* choice."

"El…" I want to contradict her, but I'm not sure how to without it sounding like I'm making excuses, the same kind of excuses I've stopped making for myself. But there is something I *can* tell her that she needs to hear and that I know to be true. "El, you've got a good heart. You care about other people, about their happiness. And about doing the right thing. That's why you've never let me off the hook, and why you're not letting yourself off the hook either."

She sniffs and wipes her wet cheek with the back of her hand, a hint of a smile on her lips. "Is that what your therapist would say?"

I roll my eyes in return, and for a moment, it feels almost like old times. "I have no idea what Dr. Eduway would say. But hey, maybe you should ask him yourself."

That earns me an eye roll before she stands. "Look...I appreciate the offer--about Cornell. But it's time I stopped letting other people's choices direct the course of my life. Time I figure out what kind of life I even want."

I nod in understanding.

She nods back and walks out the door, leaving it open behind her.

Senior Year: Wednesday, November 5
Should Have Seen It Coming

After taking two "sick" days, Aunt Kari insists I get my "sad ass back to school." Though I try to argue for another day, I know she's right. I'm only delaying the inevitable discomfort. So I ultimately get said ass showered and dressed and into the Prix.

From halfway down the hall I see Bea at our neighboring lockers. As if she could sense me, she frowns and looks around. Like a coward, I duck into the nearby bathroom, close myself in a stall to do my breathing exercise, and wait for my heartbeat to slow. Has she told anyone but Teddy that we've broken up? If not, she'll have to soon. I'll have to ask Ellen what story starts going around. Or maybe Teddy will be willing to fill me in today in Chem. *God, the whole rest of the year as lab partners...* That's going to be pretty fucking awkward. At least the break up with Bea will explain why we're not chummy anymore.

You'll get through this. One day at a time, I repeat over and over as I wash my hands for show then jog down the hall to make it to my first block Civics class before the bell.

At lunch, I manage to ignore the way my stomach convulses when I see Teddy sitting with his teammates and their assorted girlfriends at their usual back corner table. No more of his finding reasons to wander over to my sparsely populated table of solitary randos. Glowering and telling him not to had only made him do it more. It was annoying. Except it wasn't, not really. And now it was one more thing I'd miss.

Don't cry, don't cry... I lower my head and stuff my face with cold leftover stir fry.

Teddy's words from yesterday float through my mind like they have innumerable times since he said them. "... some nerve showing up here, Madison--or White, or whatever the fuck your name is." I swallow and close my eyes, seeing Teddy's hurt, angry face as he said them.

Then I hear my own voice answer, "Please, I just wanna talk. To apologize for--" *What the...* I've heard Teddy's voice in my head plenty of times, but never my own. Spoon paused an inch from my mouth, I shift focus to my surroundings, tracking the origin of the voices as our conversation continues, not coming from inside my head but behind it.

Shit. Oh, shit...

Slowly, I turn to see a girl staring open mouthed at her phone. On her screen, a particularly douchey picture from one of my old EJ White social media accounts next to a candid picture of me from the barn party, grinning like an idiot, and despite the different eye color, clearly the same guy.

The girl's head jerks up and swivels to catch me staring right at her. "Holy shit," is all she says before she whips back around and starts telling the table to "check Kyle's post."

Kyle...Booth. Phone in hand, skulking right at the door. He may not have overheard what we said in person, but if he'd recorded it, filtered out the background music...it'd take some tech skill, but it's all too possible. My pulse accelerates, pounding in my ears.

"Bea already filled me in..." Teddy's voice starts up from a guy's phone at the table on my left. It's a domino effect from there until the usual lunchroom chatter is drowned out by the overlapping cacophony of our private conversation.

As I hold a breath then let it out slow, I remind myself, *You always knew exposure was a risk of coming clean.* But I hadn't imagined it would go down like *this*--all at once, exposed in every sense, surrounded by half the student body.

One of the two older ladies assigned to monitor the cafeteria realizes something is going on and walks over to a student, watching over his shoulder, her face going from confusion to shock. The room's volume escalates again as people react. People start standing and craning their necks to pick me out of the crowd. The bright red streaks I sprayed on either side of my hair today don't exactly help me blend. Fingers and phones start pointing in my direction.

"Booth had no right.." I hear Teddy's voice punctuate the din. "...private conversation..."

Teddy, oh God--what are people gonna do to him and Bea for keeping my dirty secret? As if I haven't messed up their lives enough... I stare at the brown sauced noodles and try to pull my thoughts together. At least Bea has second lunch, so no chance for a spontaneous cafeteria mob to turn on her. Booth doesn't have this lunch either. So while he's timed his post for maximum impact, it also means he can't witness his revenge in person. Unless he's got someone recording it for him.

I make the mistake of scanning the room again and see no less than six phones pointing straight at me. *Yup, this is definitely getting documented, maybe even live streamed. My cover is well and truly blown.*

If any situation was going to send me careening down the Black Hole, this should be it. And yet, an unexpected calm comes over me instead. My heart rate slows and my hands are steady and tingle-free where they rest on the tabletop. My lungs fill and hold to full capacity. While I'd love to sit and appreciate this unlikely state of Zen, I have no idea how long it will last and there's no way I'm sticking around here to find out.

Re-covering the Pyrex, I slide it back into the Moana thermal lunch bag I borrowed from Maggie and get to my feet. After pausing a second to check for any signs of dizziness, I swivel toward the exit and take the most direct route possible. I can feel everyone watching but focus on taking one step at a time at a steady walk. Because I'm done running. Though a few people call out for me to "get the fuck out" of their school and the like, no one throws any food or confronts me directly. I guess I should count myself lucky that Booth didn't have a plant in the audience to force a conversation. Maybe he hadn't thought of it…or with State only weeks away, none of his crew would risk suspension for a stupid cafeteria brawl. *Besides, nobody except Booth has a personal ax to grind with me,* I think, right before two hands shove me from behind.

"What the hell'd you do to my sister?"

I catch myself on the end of the ice cream case. *Oh shit…Anthony DeLuca.* With all the other people I've had to

347

worry about lately, I haven't given him a thought since the barn party. He *definitely* has an ax to grind with me. Multiple axes.

"Bea's been a mess for days. Locked herself in her room. Didn't even come to school yesterday. Because of something *you did.*"

Hold shit, does he think I... My throat goes dry as my brain tries to formulate something that isn't a lie or denial but also makes it clear I'm not some serial rapist predator. "I...It isn't what you think. I told her the truth about me. That's all, I swear I didn't touch her."

"Bullshit." He hurls the word at me, jagged and sharp, but I don't miss the way his face contorts and Adam's apple bobs. I recognize the pain he's fighting to cover with anger. Anthony and Bea may not be close, but he's still a brother whose sister has been hurt, a sister he loves and failed to protect. "You touched her plenty before she found out what you are." Anthony's volume escalates even as the room has quieted to listen in. No one wants to miss a word. "How's that okay?" He shoves me again and I stumble a little, twisting to keep hold of the ice cream case.

An anonymous voice calls out, "fight" and others quickly join in. With a glance toward the exit, I see one monitor on the corded phone behind the cash registers, likely calling for backup. But who knows how long it will take to get here... *Guess Booth is getting that big confrontation scene after all.*

"Anthony!" Ellen's voice, sharp and commanding, surprises us both. She steps between us, one hand pressed to his chest and the other on mine. "Not here," she says more quietly now that she has his attention.

His eyes narrow, but at least he follows her cue to drop his volume. "What, you're *defending* him *now*? When it finally makes sense why you can't stand your own brother? After what he's done to my sister?"

Ellen's voice holds steady. "Maybe you should talk to *her* before jumping to conclusions." She arrows her own eyes and drops her voice even lower before leaning in to add, "And it won't help Bea to have a viral video of her brother white knighting."

"Video?" Anthony blinks to her, then looks to his right, out at the audience, phones in hand. His lips part and I see the *Oh shit* realization right there on his face.

Ellen moves her hand so it's resting on his arm. "Teddy went to find Bea. Go meet them at the counseling office. Be there for her, yeah?"

After a second, Anthony swallows and nods. Without another look my way, he steps around us and is gone.

"Come on." Ellen takes my hand and walks with me the last length of the cafeteria and out the nearest building exit. She lets my hand go and leads the way, staying close to the side of the building and crouch-walking so no one will see us from the classroom windows. When we make it to the Prix, she starts towards the passenger side but pauses to ask, "You okay to drive?"

"Uh..." I check my senses--no dizziness, vision clear, breathing steady. "Yeah, I am...but it doesn't matter. My keys are in my locker."

"Shit..." she mutters, eyelids flutter closed. "You couldn't have said that earlier?"

"Sorry. Escape logistics weren't at the forefront of my mind."

Ellen rolls her eyes. "You have your phone at least?

I pull it out of my pocket and hold it aloft, glad to have done something right.

"Good. Call Aunt Kari for a ride. I'll text Dad, give him the heads up and send him Booth's post."

"Right...okay, good idea." When Aunt Kari answers, I fill her in on the basics and she tells us to "sit tight," that she's on her way.

"Dad says not to say anything to anyone," Ellen reports. "He'll be here as soon as he can...and to expect a call from Bronston, which you *will* answer and follow *all* his instructions."

I wince but nod. "You don't think Dad will, like, lose his job over this, do you? If it dredges up all the corruption accusations..."

Ellen purses her lips as she considers. "His term is almost up, and he's already agreed not to run, so...probably not." She shrugs. "And at least the recording doesn't have you actually admitting to the rape."

"Wait--what? Yes I do--or I did. That part's not on there?"

She shakes her head but suddenly doesn't seem so sure anymore. "Hang on..." She holds her phone up between us over the hood of the car. I steel myself to listen again as Teddy lays out the facts of my past, the enormity of my betrayal. Then after he asks me for confirmation with "...Have I got that about right?" there's a three second pause before he goes on with, "Well then, we have nothing more to talk about, *EJ*."

"Right there, he responds like you said yes, but you didn't."

Hadn't I? It takes me a moment to refocus on myself in the memory. "I guess the look on my face was answer enough."

"Plausible deniability then. Lucky break for you."

"No kidding…" Guilt and relief mingle in a way that's become all too familiar. A part of me wishes I had admitted it out loud, in my own voice. No more hiding or lying or avoiding accountability. But then Kendra would assume my apology and willingness to accept the consequences was only because I'd already been exposed by some leaked recording. She could never trust it was authentic, that I was willing to confess publicly if that's what she wanted.

"…already been viewed 653 times," Ellen is saying. "Shared 48 times. And the comments…Oof" She shakes her head as she scrolls. "Safe to say that was our last day at Ohkwali High."

There's no need for me to see what she's reading to know she's right. I look across at my sister, who has every reason to hate me, but who is standing out here with me nevertheless. Gratefulness wells in my chest and lodges in my throat, giving my words that tell-tale emotional wobble. "Hey El, thanks for helping me out back there."

"Your welcome," she says, tone dry, still checking something on her phone.

"But…why did you though?"

She sets her phone aside to give me a withering look. "Why did I try to keep my brother from becoming the star of another take-down video? Hmm, lemme think."

"Yeah, but I thought…I mean, you said before how you made sure you'd be, like, outta the blast radius if my secret identity blew up. You could've said, 'now you all know why I hate him' or whatever and people would've been sympathetic, right?"

"Yeah well, I don't really deserve their sympathy, now do I?"

"Ellen..." I stop myself from repeating that she was only in the position to make the choice about those texts because of me.

"Besides..." She leans forward against the car, resting her arms on the roof and resting her chin on the top of one hand, "It matters that you got yourself caught because you were trying to do the right thing." The glimmer of a smile she offers sends warmth spilling through my chest. The truth may have ended things with Teddy and Bea, it may be the saving of me and Ellen. Or a start at least.

She raises an eyebrow and adds, "Though it was royally stupid of you to stage your confession *at school*."

"I know, I know." But there was no guarantee he'd ever have agreed to meet...and waiting to find out would have required the kind of patience I wasn't used to practicing. So I'd taken the riskier route--ambush. A bad idea on multiple levels, as it turned out. I mirror her position and reach out a hand over the top of the car. "I'm sorry, El, for screwing things up for you, again."

She hesitates a moment but then takes my offered hand. "It's okay. It's not like my life here was anything great."

"Yeah, well...still."

"Still." Her smile is almost wistful as she looks back over at the high school's deteriorating brick facade. "What are you gonna do now?"

I hold air in my cheeks and let it out slowly. "Well, for one, write Kendra an apology letter, including a full confession to do what she wants with."

Ellen's face swings back to me, lips parted in surprise. "Because of Booth's post?"

"No, I'd already decided. Dr. Eduway is helping me."

Her gaze slowly drops as she plays out the possibilities. "You can't get reconvicted--double jeopardy and all. But she could go public with it. Go to the media."

"Yeah, she could," I acknowledge. "It wouldn't be the kind of justice she got before with my conviction, but at least she could prove she wasn't lying."

Ellen nods and I can see the wheels turning in her head, the hope sparking in her eyes when she realizes that giving Kendra the power to prove the truth might also help undo some of the damage Ellen's own actions caused.

After a few seconds though, Ellen frowns. "Problem is, Kendra might not be allowed to make the decision for herself. I'm betting they monitor her email, and it's not a stretch to think they'd open her mail. And if they get ahold of your letter…they could even take us to court again in a civil suit, ask for millions in damages. Seems like something Mr. Daniels might do, doesn't it?"

My stomach drops at this possibility I hadn't considered before. "Yeah…shit." It was one thing if Kendra was the one wanting to take me back to court, another if it was her dad forcing her back there. After a few seconds of consideration, I say, "If money would help Kendra, if I knew it would go to *her*, and not give her parents another reason to keep her shut away in that house…"

Ellen "Mmmm"s in grim agreement.

"What if… Do you think Andrea'd agree to give her the letter in private? Without knowing what it said?"

Ellen's mouth twists. "Maybe...I could tell her you showed it to me, and that I think it will help Kendra. And it's totally up to Kendra if she wants to respond. I can ask at least."

"Okay...yeah. Once I write it." A task that loomed ever larger in my brain. I look down at Ellen's hand still resting on mine. "And what about you? What do you do now that you've hitched your boat to my sinking ship?"

Ellen laughs out a single puff of air. "Not stay at Ohkwali, that's for sure." After a long pause, she says, "Deerfield is still an option...for the both of us."

My eyes jump up to meet hers. "You'd be okay with that? Me being there too, I mean?"

She rolls her eyes but her mouth twists as she hides a smile. "Don't make a big thing about it. We both need a new school pronto and Dad would be thrilled. Plus, a diploma from there would help you on college apps... It just makes sense."

"I guess...but who's to say if they'd even let me in."

"Oh, they would. Didn't Mom used to say something like, half the reason boarding schools exist is so rich families have somewhere to send their problem children? I'm sure you're not the first rapist they've admitted," she adds dryly. "And I bet a half million donation to their latest building project would override any objections."

"Half a million? Fuck..."

"Yup, and it's coming outta *your* share of the inheritance, bro." Her mouth quirks up at the corners.

I laugh, then groan and drop my forehead to rest on the cool metal of the car. For all my objections to elitist boarding schools, it might not be half bad if Ellen and I were there together. And yet...

Straightening up, I clear my throat and say, "Deerfield might be a good idea...for you."

Her smile thins, but she doesn't look surprised. "But not for you. Charlie?"

"I promised him." It comes out part apology, part plea for understanding. "And if both of us left now, he'd be a mess."

"I know. You're right. You have to stay." She squeezes my hand before drawing hers away.

I hate that it feels like choosing one sibling over the other, but I don't know what else to do. Forcing some brightness into my voice, I tell her, "Besides, you'll be better off without me there to complicate things."

"Very true," she agrees, matching my tone. "So what, you get home tutored, or enroll in one of those remote learning academies?"

I shrug, unable to conjure any enthusiasm for the isolating necessity of my options. "Something like that. I'm sure the school'll be happy to set something up, avoid any parental fears about having a possible sexual predator roaming the halls with their daughters."

"Well then...I guess, we've both got a plan then." Ellen manages a convincing enough smile, I can't help but note the tension around her eyes. Sure, Deerfield makes sense for her, but it's still gotta be scary thinking about leaving her family completely behind and starting from scratch.

"And it's a good plan," I assure her. "But I'll miss you... I've *been* missing you."

She blinks rapidly then looks skywards. "Now why you gotta get all sappy on me? You know I'm a sucker for that shit."

"Sorry, sorry, I wasn't trying to… it's true though. El, you're the best friend I ever had. And there's no one more important to me."

"Oh yeah?" She drops her eyes to meet mine, brows arched in skepticism.

"Yeah, and from now on, I'm gonna do a way better job of showing that."

We hold each other's gazes for a few long seconds before she starts to raise her right hand to rest over her heart, three middle fingers splayed in a W. Our White sibling symbol of solidarity.

Rendered speechless by the sudden surge of joy that wells in my throat, I mutely raise my own W in response.

And then we both start to cry. Turns out we're both a couple of saps.

Senior Year: Saturday, November 8
Finding the Words

I'm still a minor, a fact Bronston mass-emails every local news station from Buffalo to Albany as soon as the Rochester station contacted him for a comment about Booth's post. He'd also pointed out that I've been legally cleared of all charges, and any reporting to the contrary opens them up to a libel lawsuit.

As for Dad and me, we make a deal. I agree to go radio silent--let him handle any public statements and handle the necessary meetings with the school, the Mackenzies, and the DeLucas. And in return, Dad won't interfere with my planned apology letter to Kendra. If she uses it to bring civil charges against me, he'll do his best to settle out of court so Kendra doesn't have to testify again.

His agreement to back down from a legal fight strikes me as a sign that he's at least beginning to accept the reality of what I'd done. Whatever else he's feeling on the subject of my guilt he camouflages well, keeping busy with the various logistics of crisis management. He's also latched onto Ellen's transfer to Deerfield as a "silver lining" to an otherwise disastrous week for the White family.

After they leave early Saturday morning for Massachusetts, Charlie spends the rest of the day snapped to me like a magnet, as if unbroken physical contact is the only way to ensure my continued presence. Aunt Kari and I are bracing ourselves for high drama when he has to go back to school Monday. Hopefully an offer to drive him and Maggie to and from school every day will help ease some of his separation anxiety. Plus he's going to be meeting with the school psychologist on a regular basis now.

I glance up from my desk to where he's sprawled out asleep on my twin bed, mouth ajar and bare feet dangling over the edge. There's a rip in the knee of his too-small Spider-Man PJs, yet another relic of his early childhood he's refused to part with. Soon enough, I'll be off at college somewhere, and he'll be...a not-so-little kid anymore. Just thinking about our inevitable separation makes me nostalgic for this moment.

After a deep, centering breath, I force myself to refocus on the task at hand--my letter to Kendra. Even though I'm pretty sure I can recite it from memory by now, I stare at the apology guide Dr. Eduway helped me put together.

❏   Clearly outline what actions you are sorry for

- ❏ Acknowledge the hurt you caused
- ❏ Explain why/what was in your head, but don't make excuses or use your own troubles to play for sympathy
- ❏ Make it clear you understand that she doesn't owe you closure or forgiveness
- ❏ Let her know you are willing to do whatever SHE may want or need to make amends--and mean it
- ❏ Leave the next step up to her

The problem I keep running into is how to make my remorse come across as genuine and sincere. Not like some apology form letter with a bunch of sentence starters. I am sorry that I (fill in your crime/harmful action here). And how far back do I go? Do I focus in on that night? Go back to how I treated her at my fourteenth birthday party? Even further, to the beginning of middle school when I started to avoid her in public? And how do I acknowledge the hurt I've caused without making assumptions? I don't know all the exact details of how I've hurt her or the extent of the damage. Not yet anyway, not unless she decides to tell me.

I reread my current draft, notice it has the word sorry...sixteen times, ball it up, toss it in the garbage, and start again. Except I don't get past **Dear Kendra,** Am I allowed to call her *Dear*? I mean, it's just a common writing convention, but still. What if she reads into it, thinks I'm taking liberties or being disingenuous or... Oh, I don't know. I scribble out the greeting, toss my pen to the side, and rest my forehead on my desk. *I thought I was ready to do this, so why is it so fucking hard?*

After a few minutes of controlled breathing, I lift my head, stare down at the next piece of blank copy paper, and think, *You only have one chance to get this right.*

But the pressure only makes the whole effort seem doomed. Let's be real--no matter how good the letter is--*if* she even reads it--most likely her response will be to tell me to go to hell and never contact her again. Or maybe her reply will be the form of reporters with cameras showing up on the doorstep again...

And that will be Kendra's choice, a Dr. Eduway-like voice reminds me. *This isn't just about the letter. It's about you finally being willing to accept the consequences of your actions.*

I know, I know... A break, that's what I need. And a snack.

My ancient desk chair creaks as I stand and Charlie, semi-waking, rolls onto his side and groans.

"Hey, bud, you ready for your own bed?" Another groan, and I worry that he's going to insist on being my wiggly bedmate for the night. But after a few groggy blinks, he sits up and lifts his arms for me to pick him up, then wraps his legs around my waist when I do.

After depositing him on the top bunk in the room he shares with Maggie, I head down to the kitchen. The sound of Saturday Night Live carries through from the living room where Aunt Kari is relaxing with a glass of Pinot Noir (or so I assume from the quarter-empty bottle on the counter). While waiting for my microwave s'mores melt, I check my phone. There's a pic from Ellen--a wide-eyed selfie, the dorm room wall behind her covered in posters of Broadway shows. Her text reads,

My roommate Trisha's side.
Think we'll get along just fine!!!

I text back with laughing and eye roll emojis. *Good for
her*, I think, realizing the ache of missing her is somehow less
even though she's physically further away.

My pulse jumps when I see there's finally a reply from
Teddy. Multiple replies, in fact. I'd texted Wednesday afternoon
to check how he and Bea were doing and again yesterday with
the update that I'll be finishing high school through an online
community college program.

Word already going
around that you're not
coming back. Some girl
whose mom works in
guidance knew you'd
unenrolled

Still plenty of drama to
deal with. Bea's soccer
teammates have been
playing defense for her
telling the fake sympathetic
gossip fishers and assholes
to fuck off

Btw I appreciate you not
leaking my football
retirement news
That coulda taken the heat
off you by giving people

something else to talk
about

And fyi I'm gonna tell my
parents and coaches right
after state
Wish me luck!

I read and re-read his text as I eat, trying to gauge tone,
figure out if he means them as closure--tying up loose ends--or
as an opening to keep the conversation going. By the time I'm
washing the marshmallow and chocolate off my hands, I decide
to err on the side of optimism, going with a reply that's
supportive but not too pushy.

Thanks for the update
Glad Bea's got a good
support system.

And LUCK, dude!
Let me know if you
need someone
to talk to afterwards
Cuz I know all about
letting down parents
and coaches

Returning to my room (and to my own pending
confession), I silence my phone again and turn off the overhead
light before flopping on my bed. I close my eyes to see if I feel
sleepy, but I'm still too wired. What can I do that isn't letter
writing or homework? I drag my hands down my face, the tips
of my fingers pulling my cheeks, forcing my eyes open. In my
direct line of sight is my Fender resting in its stand. It's too late

to turn on the amp and risk waking up the kids. And unplugged electric guitars sound like shit. My gaze shifts involuntarily to the scuffed and cracked black leather guitar case covered in stickers, like stamps on a passport. Mom's acoustic. My inheritance. Still untouched. Entombed.

I shiver, the hairs on my neck and arms bristling. *What are you waiting for? Some magic moment that lets you accept she's gone? Some cosmic sign of her approval that signifies that you've sufficiently redeemed yourself? That you're finally worthy to receive her gift? Ha! Never gonna happen, White.*

I pull my legs up to my chest and press my eyes against my knees to block the tears.

God, I miss her so much...How pathetic. Practically grown and back to hiding in bed and crying for Mommy...

Overcome by the need to feel her close, to summon her, I push myself off the edge of the bed and kneel on the hardwood floor in front of the case. I lay it down and flip the two metal latches. My throat tightens at the sight of Mom's once-treasured instrument. Tentatively, I run my fingers over the cool, smooth wood to the faint scratches made by the music note charm bracelet Ellen and I had gotten her for Mother's Day one year. I breathe deep and pick up the guitar.

And when I do, I see it laying there against the worn-down red velvet lining...

An envelope, with her cursive handwriting on it.

To My Eric James

Open at Rock Bottom

As I stare at it, my heart rises into my throat. All this time I'd believed I'd heard the last of my mother's words. There would be no more, nothing new. But here... I reach out and skim the lettering with the tips of my fingers. If I'd been waiting

362

for some sign from Mom in order to open the case, the joke is on me--the sign was on the *inside*. It's almost laughable, though the sound that escapes my mouth is more of a cry, breathy and aching. I lift the envelope with care, like some ancient piece of papyrus that might disintegrate if not handled properly.

Taking the guitar and envelope back to my bed, I set the instrument at the end and sit in the middle, keeping hold of the precious, unearthed missive. It isn't heavy, so it can't have more than a page or two of paper inside. I flip it over to the side with the sealed flap and probe the slight gap at one edge with my pinkie. *This is it...once I open it, once I read it, I really won't get any more new words from her... Maybe I should save it until...* I turn it back over and reread what I take to be instructions:

Open at Rock Bottom

...at rock bottom, huh? She must have assumed I'd find this letter long before now, soon after losing her. Though God knows I've been at "rock bottom" more than a few times since she wrote it. Should I save it until I'm at the lowest moment of whatever crisis comes next? Though if anything, I'm late getting her message, so what's the sense in waiting and making it even later? Or--*Don't fucking overthink it!* Before I can change my mind, I stick my pinkie in further and pull it down along the lip of the envelope. There are two sheets of lined paper inside with writing on both sides. The right corners have rounded edges, but the left side is rough like it was torn from a book binding. Hands shaking, I begin to read.

My Dearest Eric James,

You just left the room a few minutes ago after spending an hour playing the guitar for me. I'd tried to play at first but couldn't manage it. Realizing I'd never play

363

again came as a terrible shock, though it shouldn't have. But you, my kind, caring boy, softened the blow by asking if you could play for me instead. You started with "This Little Light of Mine," the first full song I ever taught you to play. The tears in my eyes turned to joy at seeing two pieces of my legacy--my music and my child--come together. It feels right that my instrument should belong to you now, and the thought that you will use it to make music long after I'm gone gives me great comfort.

I also think you should know the history behind your inheritance. It's a story that comes with a confession. I bought myself this guitar with money I got from pawning the necklace my parents gave me for my 16th birthday.

Perhaps I should start by explaining that I'd been playing a school-issued guitar since 4th grade and was desperate for one of my own. One made of wood, not plastic with a fake wood grain. I begged my parents, but they didn't see the difference and weren't about to "waste good money" on something the school lent us for free. Nevertheless, I continued to ask, and when I turned sixteen, I was positive the time had come. I'd spent my teen years so far being the obedient, straight-laced, straight -A daughter and believed the guitar would be my reward.

But when the day came, the box my mother presented me with was far too small. Just the right size to contain a gold cross with a small ruby at the center. As I stared at it, stunned by this no-doubt expensive gift so different from the one I'd begged for, Mother explained how the ruby was to remind me of Proverbs 31:10 "Who can find a virtuous woman? for her price is far above rubies." They were both already so proud of me and the Godly woman I was becoming and blah, blah, blah... I could barely take her words in as the blood pounded in my ears. They wouldn't spend money on the instrument I desperately needed but would spend it on useless jewelry? How unbelievable, how unfair! Despite my simmering fury, I was able to look up and smile for the camera and say convincing lies like "I will treasure it always" even as I began to think of ways to convert the gold into a guitar.

Four months later, (and several weeks after the necklace got "stolen" from my gym locker), I got my friend Ruth to drive me to a pawn shop to exchange the gold for cash. Then it was on to the House of Guitars (the very same place I brought you to pick out your own guitar when you turned twelve). That night, I came home with a new guitar in a deceptively battered case and passed it off as a hand me down from Ruth's Army-bound brother. Such was my parents' trust in me that they never suspected a thing. Any guilt I felt at these deceits was eclipsed by the joy I felt holding the instrument, so beautiful and all <u>mine</u>.

It wasn't until almost a month later that my sin found me out (Ruth never was the best at keeping secrets). My parents were more shocked and disappointed in me than angry, and I couldn't believe it when they didn't punish me. Later that night, shame and regret filled me as I listened to my mother crying with my father down in the kitchen and heard her describe the necklace as an "irreplaceable heirloom," a gift from her Great Aunt Nancy (a tidbit I must have tuned out). In the morning, I biked eighteen miles to the pawnshop with the guitar strapped to my back, hoping to make a swap. But I was too late. My necklace was already sold.

On my dejected return journey, I passed the nursing home where our church choir went to carol at Christmas time and an idea struck me. Maybe I couldn't undo what I'd done or the hurt I'd caused, but maybe I could redeem my ill-gotten prize by using it to do some good in the world. So I walked up to the reception desk and offered my musical services. And from then on, Sunday nights I played hymns and Wednesdays I played old-timey country songs. I became an important part of the seniors' lives and they of mine. We sang and talked, laughed and cried together.

Those two years of volunteer experience gave me a sense of purpose, fulfillment, and self-determination, not to mention a trove of amazing stories to draw from when writing my college application essay. When I visited Cornell and met with the admissions counselor, they informed me that it was my essay that caught the panel's attention. And at Cornell I met and fell in love with the wonderful young man who I married and had three amazing children with.

You may wonder, if I ended up with a happy life and family I love, am I now glad of the plots and lies? Nope, not a bit. What I did was wrong and purely self-serving. What I can recognize now, as a parent myself, is that my own mother hadn't wanted to hurt me or ignore my wishes when she gave me that necklace. She meant it as a sign of her love and approval. Pawning that symbol of her love hurt her deeply. I can't be glad I did something that caused such pain, that damaged relationships. But I'm sure glad I got caught.

Yes, you read that right. I'd fibbed plenty of times before the guitar incident and gotten away with it. And if I hadn't gotten caught this time either, it'd only have reinforced the lesson that lies are a successful strategy for getting what you want. The ends justify the means and all that. At sixteen, God only knows what kind of path that mindset would have taken me down. I'd certainly never have felt compelled to make amends, never volunteered at the nursing home, never written that admissions essay about it, never met James or had you...

We almost never know what our key choices will be in life, the ones that change the trajectory of our lives for good or ill. You're at a time in life when you'll face many choices, big and small, and in some cases, you will choose badly, like I did. And if you get caught, like I did, I hope you learn from the consequences, that as far as it is in your power, you make a choice to make things right. And know that no matter what you do, I love you anyway, just like my mother still loved me.

I hope you will take up my pledge to use this guitar to do good in the world. Even if you never join a band or ever play in public, play it for your sister and brother and father. The four of you with the notes of this guitar filling the room...well, maybe that's as close as we can get to being all together again.

My baby boy, every morning since you were born, I have woken up thanking God for the gift of your life in mine. You are intelligent, caring, affectionate, curious, full of life and energy, fierce and determined to meet every goal, and devoted to those you love. It has brought me indescribable joy to watch you grow. And if when I am gone, you find yourself at the end of your own strength, at rock bottom, remember--He who began a good work in you will be faithful to complete it.

My Love, Forever and Always,
Mom

The handwriting, the writing style… *This is Mom. This is real*, I have to assure myself as tears stream down my chin even as an incredible lightness fills my chest, spreading outward to my limbs. Reading what she wrote to me, it's like I can hear her voice again. Saying *new* words I've never heard before, words just for me. A story that shows that my mom was a complicated, flawed human being like the rest of us. Like me.

And this isn't the only story she left for me to find. A warm thrill of sudden remembrance spreads over my scalp, and I tip my head back to stare at the ceiling. What was it Aunt Kari had said? Eight full bins up in the attic. Years and years of Mom's life, her thoughts and hopes and fears...all waiting mere feet above my head. The prospect of what I might find there had scared me then, but not anymore. Because nothing in them could change my love for her..

After wiping my tears away with my arm, I neatly refold Mom's letter along the seams she made and slip the pages back into the envelope. I may not know what I'm going to do next week or next year or in ten years, but tonight, I have a letter of my own to write.

Author's Note:

For decades, YA literature has explored the many, multifaceted experiences of sexual violence survivors. As a teen reader myself, Laurie Halse Anderson's *Speak* was my first window into a survivor's experience. When I was sexually assaulted not long after, it became my mirror. *Speak* and the many powerful books that followed helped me to cope and heal in a way that non-fiction guides on the topic did not. As a secondary school librarian I have read, purchased, displayed, and recommended dozens of these books, and I believe it is absolutely correct that the survivor experience and viewpoint take precedence. But YA fiction offerings exploring the perpetrator's perspective are so limited as to be almost non-existent. And that means a part of the story remained incomplete within the realm of YA literature.

I wrote *Open at Rock Bottom* because I believe no human perspective should go unexplored, even when the human in question has done terrible things. Understanding how someone who is not sociopathic or morally bankrupt could inflict incredible pain and damage on another person, often someone they claim to love or care for, is a key piece in preventing these harmful choices in the future. And, for those who are willing to admit guilt for their crimes, I think it's important to explore viable paths to atonement and even reconciliation.

Good literature has the power to make you think and feel, to give you comfort, to make you uncomfortable, to change your perspective, to make you a better person, and to make the world a better place. As a fiction writer, I wanted to use my craft to explore the messy conglomerate of gendered/classist beliefs, psychological characteristics, cultural values, social structures, and personal circumstances that can increase the likelihood that people—particularly young men like those I teach—might commit this kind of crime.

It is reductive to simply perpetuate the idea that only terrible people can do terrible things and that a "good"/likable person would never commit rape or sexual assault. That simply isn't true. If only sadists and sociopaths committed rape, there would be far fewer of them. The messy, frustrating, tragic truth is that people who are commendable in many ways can still make destructive, predatory choices. One does not preclude the other, nor does one excuse the other. And exploring the complexity of human motivation and the sometimes challenging and painful experiences in someone's background should not be mistaken for an attempt at justification. It is the reality of human experience.

It is a sad, statistical inevitability that everyone will know someone who was raped or assaulted during their teenage or young adult years. It is also, conversely, inevitable that (whether we're aware of it or not) we'll all know someone who committed these crimes. Because vanishingly few rapists will ever be charged and even fewer will face legal consequences, the perpetrators remain among us. Without being forced to reckon with an accusation, the default for perpetrators is silence.

Plenty of those who perpetrate sexual violence have been and will be perfectly content to get away with their crimes. They may never acknowledge or care to understand the harm they have done, let alone face any consequences of that action. But others might.

If we as a society, as individuals, as survivors, want perpetrators of sexual violence to reject the status quo of denial and secrecy, we need to encourage another path--one that carries a cost to them, but also offers the hope of healing for all involved. Culturally influential media, including YA literature, is an important conduit for promoting action and change, so I wrote this book in the hope that more perpetrators will, like EJ/Eric, choose to hold themselves accountable even when the justice system does not.